MURDER OFF THE PAGE

ALSO BY CON LEHANE

MURDER OFF THE PAGE

A 42ND STREET LIBRARY MYSTERY

CON LEHANE

MINOTAUR BOOKS
NEW YORK

MURDER OFF THE PAGE. Copyright © 2019 by Con Lehane. All rights reserved. Printed in the United States of America. For information, address St. Martin's Press Publishing Group, 120 Broadway, New York, N.Y. 10271.

www.minotaurbooks.com

Designed by Omar Chapa

Library of Congress Cataloging-in-Publication Data

Names: Lehane, Cornelius, author.
Title: Murder off the page : a 42nd Street library mystery / Con Lehane.
Description: First edition. | New York : Minotaur Books, 2019. | Series:
    Identifiers: LCCN 2019029067 | ISBN 9781250317926 (hardcover) |
    ISBN 9781250317933 (ebook)
Subjects: GSAFD: Mystery fiction.
Classification: LCC PS3612.E354 M89 2019 | DDC 813/.6—dc23
LC record available at https://lccn.loc.gov/2019029067

Our books may be purchased in bulk for promotional, educational, or business use. Please contact your local bookseller or the Macmillan Corporate and Premium Sales Department at 1-800-221-7945, extension 5442, or by email at MacmillanSpecialMarkets@macmillan.com.

First Edition: November 2019

10 9 8 7 6 5 4 3 2 1

To Mary and Jerry Brennan

Acknowledgments

Many thanks to my editor, Nettie Finn, for shepherding this book from its clumsy beginnings to the shape it's in now and to everyone else at Minotaur—cover designers, copyeditors, marketers, publicists, sales folks, and everyone else on the publishing team who bring a book to life. As usual, a special thanks to Talia Sherer and the Macmillan Library Marketing crew who've been especially supportive of my fictional librarians.

Thanks also to Roan Chapin, a friend and early editor, who showed me the error of my ways in a number of places and helped Raymond Ambler see that things are not always as they seem to him. My thanks to Alice Martell, my literary agent, for her enduring and unfailing support especially when the way ahead is uncertain. I owe a debt of gratitude to Marcia Markland, the editor of the first two books in the 42nd Street Library Mystery series, for pointing me toward the 42nd Street Library in the first place.

Of course, thanks to the nation's librarians—and especially those at the New York Public Library, including Thomas

Lannon of the Manuscript and Archives Division who has for years now been helping me understand the 42nd Street Library and the work life of a curator. The importance of libraries and librarians—as founts of knowledge and protectors of liberty—to our nation's well-being is beyond measure. Thanks also to bookstores, book reviewers, bloggers, and others who keep the world of books vibrant.

Finally, my thanks to Ragdale, an artists' community in Lake Forest, Illinois, where I was fortunate to spend a month of uninterrupted time finishing a revision of *Murder Off the Page*.

Data! Data! Data!
I can't make bricks
without clay.

—SHERLOCK HOLMES

MURDER OFF THE PAGE

Chapter 1

That woman was back again. Raymond Ambler delivered the file boxes to her as she sat waiting at the library table in the crime fiction reading room of the 42nd Street Library. She stood out for him for a couple of reasons, one of them because she'd broken his glasses a few nights earlier in the Library Tavern under somewhat peculiar circumstances. He took a moment to take off the glasses and look at them. They were reading glasses, prescribed for him for the first time the day before she broke them, the circular lenses in dark red frames, the two broken halves fused together now with black electrician's tape.

Ambler had stopped at the Library Tavern—the after-work watering hole for the staff at the 42nd Street Library presided over by everyone's favorite bartender Brian McNulty—as he often did, although a bit later than usual on this Wednesday evening, and found his friend Adele Morgan sitting at the bar sipping a beer and watching intently a small drama unfold a few barstools away.

A woman who looked to be of Adele's age—a late

thirtysomething—was surrounded by a half-dozen men, resembling nothing so much as a pack of wolves circling in on
its prey. The woman apparently had a good deal to drink, as
she spoke too loudly and appeared to be losing ground in an
argument with the man sitting beside her. The men standing
around them appeared to wait impatiently their turn to ha-
rangue her. Ambler settled onto his barstool and took out his
new glasses to show Adele.

At that moment, a voice rang out loud enough to be heard
across the bar, "That's an absurd thing to say."

"That poor woman," Adele said to Ambler. "Look at how
they're treating her."

Ambler glanced over to see that the woman in question
was besieged, the half-dozen men sniping at her at once. She
sat back, a look of confusion bordering on panic replacing the
intent expression she'd worn a minute before.

Adele grasped Ambler's arm. Her touch surprised him; it
had been such a long time. He turned to her questioningly and
saw such emotion in her face, as if she herself was besieged by
those men, that he reached toward her with his free hand. "She
was in the library today," Adele said. The expression in her eyes
said something else. She was afraid for the woman under attack, and she wanted Ambler to help her.

Ambler stood. As he prepared to walk over to the woman
hoping to rescue her, he caught McNulty's eye to tip off the
bartender, who missed nothing that happened in his bar, as to
what he intended to do. McNulty made a small gesture with his
head—a nod by McNulty worth a thousand words—that told
Ambler to not worry; McNulty would handle the situation.

Ambler sat back down and watched McNulty saunter over
to that section of the bar. The bartender leaned toward the
woman and said something. As soon as he did, she turned her
full attention on him, and the men around her quieted. A moment later, when Ambler saw McNulty pick up the woman's

drink and nod toward him and Adele, he moved over, leaving an empty seat between him and Adele. The woman, a bit tipsy, tottered toward them, squinting slightly, wearing a crooked smile.

She remembered Adele from the library and was inordinately happy to see her. Speaking to Adele, and glancing disdainfully toward the group of men behind her, she put one hand onto the bar to hoist herself onto the barstool. As she made her little jump onto the stool, Ambler heard an unmistakable crackling and saw his glasses flatten beneath her hand.

Perched on the barstool after all that, she watched the broken glasses curiously.

"Where did those come from?" Adele asked no one in particular.

Ambler picked up the glasses, now split into two sections at the nose bridge. "They're mine." He made a dismissive gesture with his hand to stop any further questions.

McNulty, who'd caught the mishap, handed Ambler a roll of electrician's tape from a drawer behind the bar, so Ambler taped his reading glasses back together. As this took place, the woman who introduced herself as Shannon Darling, talked animatedly with Adele, not ignoring Ambler so much as being so pleased to see Adele that she wasn't aware he was there.

This state of things changed slightly when Adele told Shannon who Ambler was, and told Ambler that Shannon would be the latest reader to make use of the crime fiction collection. Adele had done the screening interview that afternoon while Ambler was away from the library.

A few minutes later, Adele and Shannon headed to the ladies' room—something women did in pairs quite often. Ambler didn't recall ever asking another man to accompany him to the men's room. He was about to ask McNulty, who was now standing in front of him on the other side of the bar, about

this phenomenon, when McNulty's expression as he watched
Shannon Darling walk away stopped him. For a moment un-
guarded, it was almost reverent.

"I'd like another drink," Shannon said to McNulty when
she and Adele returned.

"You have one on the bar," McNulty said. Their eyes met
and held for a moment. "You probably don't want any more
after this one."

"I can go somewhere else." Her tone was petulant.

"You could." McNulty spoke softly. "You asked me to tell
you."

"I'm not arguing anymore. Those guys are jerks. One of
them propositioned me."

"You say things . . ." He shook his head.

She turned from McNulty to look Ambler in the eye.
"My husband doesn't have sex with me. I think it's been—"
She paused, perhaps counting off some period of time—weeks,
months, years? Was she asking him for an explanation? In a few
minutes again, she'd forgotten about Ambler and Adele and
was whispering with McNulty. But she was fading. When she
wasn't speaking, she bowed, her chin drifting toward the bar
like a junkie nod.

McNulty called to one of the servers. When the server
came behind the bar, he told Ambler, "Gail here will watch the
bar. I'm taking Shannon to her hotel. I won't be long." He left,
walking beside Shannon, his arm under her elbow. She leaned
against him, talking. Ambler imagined that the three or four
men from the earlier group who remained at the bar watching
the bartender and the tipsy woman leave didn't expect to see
the bartender back for a good while.

Less than twenty minutes later, McNulty was back, contemptuous of the smirks and knowing glances of the men
who'd watched him leave, coming behind the bar to stand in
front of Ambler and Adele. "This one may do me in," he said.

"I told her she had to save me from myself . . . to stay the fuck out of here."

Ambler had paid particular attention to Shannon Darling for a couple of days now since that evening. She'd told Adele in the Special Collections screening interview that she was writing a book on women mystery writers and would be in the city for a few days. Adele had approved her application but had misgivings about her because a few of the things she said in the interview seemed odd. "It was as if she made up her answers on the spot. When I asked about her academic affiliation, she didn't know what I meant. I asked if she was a freelance writer. She didn't know. I said independent scholar, and she jumped at the answer like she wished she'd thought of it."

Her appearance was curious also, Adele said. "She doesn't dress like a researcher. The suit she wore was straight out of Neiman Marcus or Saks Fifth Avenue. Not what most readers wear to the library."

After observing her, Ambler saw that Shannon Darling was indeed amateurish, not aware of the protocols of research, not knowing for instance the procedure for calling up research materials. You'd think this was her first time using a library special collection. Still, she had an appealing way about her. On the young side of middle age, with blonde hair, large brown eyes, little makeup, and a pretty mouth, she was attractive and pleasant to be around. Her direct gaze and an air of expectancy in the way she looked at him when he spoke to her surprised him. He found it difficult to look away from her. That openness lasted only a moment each time, until she registered that he had nothing interesting to tell her so turned back to her work.

The file boxes he'd delivered on this morning were from the collection of Jayne Galloway, a mystery writer who'd recently donated her papers to the 42nd Street Library's crime fiction collection. Ambler stood for a moment more or less looking over the woman's shoulder as she opened the file box. "She's a much underappreciated writer," he said.

The reader glanced up at him with that air of expectation and then quickly back to her work as if she realized he might not be talking to her.

He'd tried before to engage Ms. Darling and gotten the same result. He thought of his comment as exchanging pleasantries, or would have except for the lack of pleasantries in return. Ambler had liked Jayne Galloway's mysteries and was pleased to have acquired the collection and now to see a reader interested in her work. Shannon Darling's brusque manner wasn't unusual; readers were often so engrossed in their work they weren't much for small talk.

Yet she intrigued him, so when she took a break to check her cell phone, he spoke to her again. "As you can see, I'm not busy," he said, getting up from his desk and walking over to where she sat at the long library table in the center of the room. "If you'd like, you can fill out the call slip for your next series of file boxes. I'll call them up, so you won't have to wait when you're ready to use them."

Her expression was startled, as if she didn't understand what he meant. She held his gaze and didn't say anything. He didn't say anything either. They looked at each other without speaking for longer than seemed normal, yet she didn't show any sign she was bothered by the silence or by the intensity of the exchange of glances.

"That would be nice," she said simply enough without looking away this time. "I'm not used to how things are done here."

He nodded. "I see. Is this your first book?"

She eyed him curiously, and again there was a long and what might be uncomfortable silence but wasn't. "Yes, my first book." Her expression softened, and he saw something gentle in her eyes, an unusual sensitivity. "I'm new at this. I guess you can see that."

"I'm glad you're interested in Jayne Galloway. You're the first person to use her collection. It's new to the library." He sounded to himself like a kid proud of a new toy.

Shannon shifted her gaze to the file in front of her, dismissive, not bothering to answer his question if she even heard it. Her action was abrupt if not rude, yet nothing suggested she was aware of that. One thing finished, she moved on to the next.

"Poor McNulty," Ambler said to Adele, a couple of mornings after their adventure in the Library Tavern. "He was smitten with Shannon Darling. She's such a different person when she's in the library, efficient, almost too business-like. I wonder if she even remembers him." They drank coffee while sitting on the terrace overlooking Bryant Park behind the library.

"He might be better off if she didn't," Adele said.

Ambler understood McNulty's plight, having himself been smitten, in his case by Adele some time back. Bewitched might be a better description. Yet because Adele was so much younger than he was, he felt too awkward to follow his romantic inclination, despite suspecting at times she might want him to. He watched her now as she daintily nibbled on a croissant and balanced a container of cappuccino on her pretty knee.

There was enough of a breeze to flutter her hair, which was blonde and light and feathery. She sat erectly with her face tilted slightly forward taking in the morning air as if she were on the prow of a ship instead of a terrace overlooking Bryant Park. The way she embraced life like that was one of the things that had gotten him smitten in the first place. She had her dark moments but mostly she had a brightness about her, an embrace of life that made him happy to be with her or even to watch her from across a room, or across a rickety wrought-iron bistro table as he did now.

She and Ambler had worked together in Special Collections, where Ambler was the curator of the crime fiction collection, for a couple of years now. In recent years, they'd become close, even closer since he'd taken over raising his grandson Johnny. She'd become a special person in his life and in his grandson's life, as unclear as he was as to what that specialness entailed.

"Something about Shannon disturbs me," Adele said. "It's the way she is with men when she's drinking. She has no defenses. Men see that and see her as someone to take advantage of. The other night in the bar, she was arguing one minute, crying the next, talking recklessly about anything that came into her head. She confided in total strangers, saying things about herself that you'd think she'd be embarrassed to say.

"To one man who wore a wedding ring, who I guess hit on her, she said, 'You're married. I'm not going to go to bed with you.'" Adele turned to watch one of their fellow New Yorkers crossing the terrace, coffee container in one hand, large red leather bag over one shoulder, smaller straw bag in her other hand.

Ambler followed Adele's gaze. "Why do women carry so much more than men?"

Adele ignored him. "I'm embarrassed to repeat some of the things she said."

"I didn't know you'd seen her in the bar again." Ambler continued watching the young woman who crossed in front of them. Dressed in business attire, except for running shoes, she walked quickly, though she didn't seem harried or even in a hurry, more like determined, a no-nonsense, get-things-done pace—the attitude you saw in the city nowadays more often than not. New York had always moved faster than a small town in Kansas. This ruthless, go-get-'em, don't-stand-in-my-way attitude was different; it slipped into the city in the eighties with the hedge funds, corporate real estate developers, and foreign investors and had spread like the flu since then.

"God, Raymond! You're off in your own head again." Adele glared at him. "You're not listening." She made a face. "Out of nowhere, Shannon—I'd bet Shannon Darling is a made-up name; it's like a stage name for a stripper. Out of nowhere, she said to the man next to her, 'I don't have sex anymore.'"

"She said something like that to me."

Adele's eyebrows spiked. "Oh? Did you help her out?"

Ambler blinked a couple of times. Adele moved on.

"When the man she was talking to left . . ." Adele lowered her voice. "At one point, I thought she would go with him. Anyway, when he left, she latched onto McNulty."

"As I said, he seems quite taken with her."

"She's pretty and charming and beguiling with that faint southern accent, little-girl, eyelash-batting appeal. What do you expect?"

He didn't have an answer.

Adele observed this, pursed her lips, and nodded. "Men."

That evening, for the first time in a long while, Ambler and Adele stopped off at the Library Tavern together. She'd come and gotten him when the library was closing, so while Ambler was cautiously excited, he didn't know what it meant. He sometimes unwittingly offended Adele. And he had done it again not so long ago. When she was hurt, she went into a shell; she didn't fight back. When she was in her shell, as much as he cared about her, he couldn't reach her. A wall of formality went up between them. Thankfully, her coldness toward Ambler didn't apply to Johnny.

By the time they got to the Library Tavern, McNulty had subdued the cocktail hour crowd buzzing around the bar, so he had time to stop and chat. McNulty did pretty much as he pleased behind the bar. The tavern owners long before had given up trying to rein him in, since, as curmudgeonly as he was, almost all of the bar patrons, including Ambler and Adele, came to the Library Tavern specifically because he was behind the bar. He earned the loyalty of the after-work imbibers by his craftsmanship and by his sincere interest in those things folks who frequented the bar wanted to tell him.

"What's up with your grandson?" McNulty asked. "I haven't seen him since I took him to the track. That must be a month ago."

"Johnny's fine," Ambler said. "School is busier now. He has more homework." Ambler's grandson, whom he cared for because the boy's mother was dead and his father in prison, was devoted to McNulty, as he was devoted to Adele who—despite her awkward relationship with Ambler—was like a mother to him. "He keeps asking when you'll take him to the track again," Ambler said. "I don't understand how he wins every time he goes with you."

McNulty took a reconnaissance glance around the bar before sticking his coffee cup under the tap and drawing himself a beer. "What he does is he has me bet for him on a horse I'm not betting on."

Adele's expression was playful as she leaned toward the bartender. "Where's your new friend tonight?"

Ambler cringed. He should have known Adele was gearing up for the question since she suggested having a beer.

McNulty stepped back from her. "I don't know who you're talking about."

"Yes you do." Adele's smile was impish. "Shannon, the pretty blonde with the big brown eyes."

"She's not a new friend." McNulty's tone was chilly. "I don't keep track of her, so I don't know where she is."

"She seemed fond of you." Adele's tone was sympathetic because she realized McNulty was offended.

"I don't do any better with women than I do with horses."

McNulty made his point and walked to the other end of the bar to make drinks for one of the servers who was icing glasses and placing them on the service bar.

"I hurt his feelings." Adele turned to Ambler looking for help. "I didn't mean to."

Ambler might have told her she was making a mistake. McNulty was the kind of bartender you found yourself confiding in. It didn't work the other way. Ambler had known McNulty for a few years but knew little about his life beyond the bar. He had a son whom he loved and an ex-wife, whom he didn't so much dislike as was disliked by. Ambler knew also that most of McNulty's pay went to support his son who was now in college.

Beyond that, most of what Ambler knew of McNulty, he knew from stories the bartender told. It would be, "I knew this girl once, a dancer with the Rockettes . . ." or "You know that guy who got shot in the East Village last night, he used to come into my bar when I worked . . ." "My ex-wife's newest boyfriend is a cop so she says she's gonna have me arrested if I'm late on my child support . . ." and so on. McNulty didn't tell you if he was lonely or his heart had been broken or he worried he drank too much or he hadn't been sleeping well or feared he would die alone. He kept that sort of thing to himself.

"I'd let it go for now." Ambler watched the bartender pour or stir or shake drinks for the servers, how deftly his hands moved, how quickly he did things, no wasted effort, pouring with both hands; for one drink, pouring from two bottles in one hand, one bottle in the other at the same time. "McNulty doesn't admit to feelings."

When Ambler and Adele left the bar, they stood together for a moment. A chill rode on the breeze but it was a pleasant early autumn evening, autumn the best time of year in the city. By the first of September in most years, the summer heat was gone taking along with it the stench from the black and green plastic garbage bags piled up by the curbs in front of the city's restaurants and apartment buildings. This evening as he stood with Adele for a moment in front of the Library Tavern before they went their separate ways, Ambler felt a strange longing for something he couldn't place and for that reason didn't want to part with her just yet.

"Did you apply for the assistant director position in Special Collections?" he asked. Adele was both a curator and a librarian with an MLS degree, all of the credentials she needed to apply for the job, but she was reluctant to apply for reasons he didn't understand. "You'd be Harry's assistant."

Harry Larkin, the director of Special Collections, was both their boss and a friend. A medieval historian, a former Jesuit, and the library's version of an absentminded professor, he'd retained enough of his priestliness to watch over his staff like a shepherd his flock, protecting Ambler in particular—a some-what notorious amateur detective—from the wrath of the powers-that-be in the library's upper echelons.

"The only reason I'd want the job is so I could boss you around." Adele smiled. Sometimes her smile was perfunctory. Other times, like this, it melted his heart.

"You already do," he said.

"Seriously, I like my job as it is. Harry lets me do pretty much what I want. I don't like being told what to do, and I don't want to have to tell anyone else what to do."

"What if Harry hires a micromanager who does tell us what to do? You could protect us from that by taking the assistant job. The library needs you."

Adele put her hand on her hip and assumed her school-marm pose. "Do I detect an ulterior motive?"

Ambler began his denial but they both knew what Adele was getting at. The 42nd Street Library housed the New York Public Library's humanities and social sciences collections. A number of the collections, including the Manuscript and Archives

Division, the Carl H. Pforzheimer Collection of Shelley and His Circle, the Berg Collection of English and American Literature, the Arents Tobacco Collection, and others, were world-renowned collections.

Ambler's crime fiction collection with its own reading room on the second floor, while not world-renowned, was one of a very few collections of its kind in the nation. Nonetheless, Ambler worried about its survival. The library continually dealt with financial pressure and in the not-too-distant past had closed reading rooms, such as the Slavic and Baltic division reading room, that to the library Board of Trustees' way of thinking, were underutilized. The axe could fall on the crime fiction reading room at any moment.

"Well, I'd trust you more than anyone to protect the crime fiction reading room—"

"Aren't you the flatterer?" Adele laughed. "Don't look so hurt. I'm teasing. You need all the help you can get with Mrs. Young out for your scalp."

Lisa Young, New York City society matron and member of the library's Board of Trustees, was Johnny's grandmother on his mother's side. Adele knew about the custody battles Mrs. Young and Ambler had had already. Despite Adele's teasing, she would protect him; he'd already seen how ferociously she'd fight for him and especially for Johnny.

He watched her face now and saw beyond the cheerfulness something else in her expression that reminded him of the longing he'd felt earlier that he didn't understand. "You'd be better at the job than anyone else. That's all I mean. You don't appreciate how wonderful you are." Something changed in her expression, surprise, confusion. "I mean at work," he said, correcting himself because he'd said more than he meant to . . . let on more than he'd meant to.

"You're quite persuasive." Adele had been watching the traffic that like a herd of cattle jostled its way uptown. "We're

lucky, aren't we, to work with books that we love? And we have
Johnny in our lives . . ." She looked into Ambler's eyes, the expression in hers sad, belying her words. She blinked rapidly a
few times, searched for something in his gaze and turned back
to the traffic. "And yet . . ." she glanced back at him quickly,
possibly angrily. "I'm just foolish . . . a foolish woman." She
sounded angry. "Don't pay any attention to me. I don't want
to be a supervisor." She glared at him. "I want to be left alone."
Turning from him, she started walking, if not stomping, up
Madison Avenue.

Ambler stood in front of the Library Tavern watching her
walk away. Once more, he didn't understand. Despite her anger, she moved gracefully as she always did, her hips swaying
gently as she walked. He watched her until she blended into the
other walkers on the sidewalk and the gathering darkness.

Chapter 2

The next afternoon as Adele was cutting through Bryant Park on her way back to the library from lunch, she saw Shannon Darling sitting in one of the park's bistro chairs next to the steps to the terrace at the back of the library. She was smoking a cigarette, so Adele walked over to her.

"Hi," Adele said. "Do you remember me?"

"I remember you." Shannon looked up at her, reminding her of how she'd described Shannon's eyes to McNulty. They were big and brown with something gentle and appealing, yet intense, in them.

Adele smiled. "I don't want to sound like the park police. It's against the law to smoke in the park. I don't want you to get a fine."

"Oh my goodness," Shannon quickly stubbed out her cigarette on the gravel in front of her. "I didn't know."

"It's not something you'd expect." Adele gestured at the park surrounding them. "First, you couldn't smoke inside. Now, you can't smoke outside. I don't know where you're supposed to go. I guess stand on the street corner."

Shannon continued to look at her intently, the scrutiny strangely not uncomfortable. "It's nice that you're not judgmental." Shannon said.

They talked easily, surprising Adele. Shannon said she started smoking when she was a teen to be cool and now it was difficult to stop because she'd been doing it so long. When Adele told her about the Arents Tobacco Collection in the library, Shannon was intrigued, so Adele took her in and showed her some of the collection. Afterward, Shannon wanted to buy Adele a cup of coffee, so they sat for a few more minutes in the small coffee area on the main floor across from the Library Shop.

"I know you saw me in that cocktail lounge the other night. I almost said hello, but I got distracted, talking with that man. I want you to know that wasn't me that night. When I drink I lose my internal filters and . . . say things." She looked away and then back at Adele who saw a great deal of sadness in her eyes. "Sometimes I freak people out. I say things." Shannon bowed her head before meeting Adele's gaze again. Her expression was that of a child who'd been hurt by someone whom she didn't expect to hurt her, so part of the hurt was bewilderment and disappointment. "I'm not used to socializing. I suppose I shouldn't do it. . . . I've been taken advantage of."

Late that afternoon, when Adele saw Shannon leave the crime fiction reading room for the evening, she popped in to tell Raymond what she'd discovered about Shannon. "She was entirely different than I thought of her, charming, intelligent, engaging, so different from the woman she was in the bar, a real Dr. Jekyll and Mr. Hyde."

"She's a bit of an enchantress," Raymond said.

Adele began to tell him more about her talk with Shannon that afternoon but changed her mind. The conversation was a woman-to-woman thing, a sharing of confidence. Raymond might understand, but he might understand what Shannon said in a man-way. What Adele realized was that Shannon was honest about herself in a way most people weren't and because of that was vulnerable in a way most people weren't. Adele understood without Shannon coming right out and saying it that men sensed her vulnerability, her openness, and maybe neediness, and took advantage of her because of it.

"She's very intense, Raymond, and not always aware of how she appears to people, so she can seem rude. And maybe she's embarrassed because you saw her in the bar with McNulty and those men." Adele paused. "Still, there's something mysterious about her. When I asked where she lived, she changed the subject to ask where I lived and where I grew up. She didn't want to tell me about her life." Adele took a deep breath and narrowed her eyes to engage Raymond's gaze. "She's hiding something."

Chapter 3

Two days later, a week to the day after Ambler first met Shannon Darling in the Library Tavern, Adele interrupted him at work in the crime fiction reading room. Her expression as she banged through the reading room door was a cry of alarm, so he sprang from his chair ready to throw himself into action with no idea what that action would be.

"McNulty's missing."

"What?" Ambler collapsed back into his chair.

"He didn't show up for work. He was supposed to work lunch today and didn't show up. The manager had to work the bar and was furious . . . as well as clumsy and slow."

"Well, that—"

"McNulty called while I was there and told the manager he wouldn't be back."

Ambler's mind raced, thoughts tumbling over one another. McNulty was a steady presence in his life, as solidly dependable behind the bar of the Library Tavern as the marble lions standing guard in front of the library. "Maybe he got a better job. He's been waiting for years for one of the bartenders at the Algonquin to die. If that job opened—"

Adele peered at him like a physician who discovered a worrisome symptom. "The manager said he'd make sure no bar in New York would hire him."

Ambler was about to say people didn't just drop everything and disappear. But sometimes people did disappear, up and leave like Flitcraft. "Maybe a beam fell," he said.

"A beam fell? What are you talking about? Did a beam fall on your head?"

He didn't want to bring up Flitcraft. "McNulty has not disappeared. He has responsibilities, his son, his dad. He wouldn't do that."

"I bet it has to do with that woman."

"Who?"

"Shannon."

Ambler's faith in McNulty was not rewarded. When he got home, his grandson Johnny handed him an envelope. "I found this under the door. It's from Uncle McNulty."

The note was succinct. "I need to disappear for a while. I gave Pop and Kevin your phone number and email. Theirs are below. I told them they can count on you if something comes up. I got a cat needs feeding, too. I don't know what you're going to do about that, probably Pop." In the envelope with the note was the key to McNulty's apartment.

"What's going on?"

Ambler looked up from the note to Johnny's troubled expression. The boy unfailingly knew when something happened or was about to happen that Ambler wanted to keep from him. "Nothing much." He tried to sound offhand.

"Can I read the note?"

"No." Ambler folded the piece of paper and put it in his pocket.

"What's wrong that you won't tell me?"

"McNulty asked me for a favor. You don't have to know everything."

Johnny was quiet for a moment. "You only get like this when something bad happens. You think I don't know when you worry; you think you can worry by yourself, and I don't know." He turned his cobalt blue, searing eyes on Ambler. "Well, I know when something's wrong and I worry anyway. I just don't know what I'm worried about."

The phone rang, so Johnny went back to his homework.

"Ray? Mike Cosgrove."

Ambler sighed. "One woe doth tread upon another's heel."

His friend Mike Cosgrove was a homicide detective with the NYPD. "I'm not sure what that means, but I have a feeling you're right."

"I'm afraid to ask what you want."

"You don't have to ask. I'm going to tell you . . ."

Ambler waited.

"I'm looking for your friend, the elusive bartender."

"McNulty? Why?"

"I get paid to ask questions not answer them. When'd you see him last?" Cosgrove's tone grew more cynical, if that were possible. "Take your time answering. You don't have a spotless record letting go of what you know about folks who've gone missing."

"You're not so forthcoming yourself. I don't know where he is. I'm told his employer said he's missing."

"Have you heard from him?"

Ambler hesitated. Cosgrove wouldn't be looking for McNulty when he was on the clock unless McNulty had some knowledge about a homicide. Such a thing wasn't out of the question given the bartender's lifestyle and some of his acquaintances. Ambler didn't see how telling Mike what he knew would hurt McNulty. It wouldn't much help Cosgrove either.

"He left me a note asking me to look in on his elderly father and his son . . . and his cat."

"Why?"

"He didn't say."

"Do you know where I can find his father and son?"

He gave Cosgrove McNulty's father's phone number.

Cosgrove, expecting less cooperation, was gruffly appreciative.

"I can give you the address for the cat." Ambler glanced at the floppy eared mutt in the corner who was beginning to grow into his galoshes-sized feet. "We have a dog here. I don't think a cat would fit in."

"Cat? . . . Oh, yeah. . . . No." Mike forced a laugh. "The bartender's name came up. I remembered he was a friend of yours. I wanted to ask him a few questions; I didn't expect he'd disappear." Cosgrove cleared his throat.

"Do you want to tell me what it's about?"

"I don't. But I will. As you might expect given what I do for a living—though God knows why I do it—there's been a murder. This one took place last night in a five-star hotel not far from your library. It being a five-star hotel there's more than the usual interest from One Police Plaza. The victim's body was found in a female guest's room. He was shot. She's gone. We don't know much more than that. What we do know, from a bartender in the hotel's lobby bar, is that at one point in the evening she had a drink with a well-known bartender-about-town named Brian McNulty."

"He's a witness?"

"I don't know."

"Any other witnesses?"

"Not so far. This is New York City, where someone can put a bullet in someone else in a hotel room and no one sees anything."

"They must have heard the shot."

"That's not the same as seeing the shooter."

"Was it her?"

"I don't know."

"Was McNulty in the hotel room? Is he a suspect?"

"I told you what I'm going to tell you, Ray. I want to talk to him."

"Oh my God, Raymond! I'm sure the woman was Shannon," Adele said when he called to tell her about his call from Cosgrove. "Did he describe the woman?"

"I was afraid to ask."

"So you think it's Shannon, too."

Ambler didn't answer.

"Are you going to try to find McNulty?"

"If he wants to see me, he'll let me know."

"And Shannon?"

"We don't know who the woman in the hotel is."

"You think it's Shannon and you think she's with McNulty." It wasn't a question. "I'm worried, Raymond." She didn't have to tell him; the worry was in her voice. "Shannon scared me. . . . Not that I was afraid of her; I was afraid for her. I felt like she was doomed, that something terrible might happen to her, like you feel when someone is ill and you're afraid they'll die."

Chapter 4

The next afternoon, Mike Cosgrove showed up at Ambler's crime fiction reading room with a still photo of the woman who'd been with the murder victim. The photo was copied from the hotel security video so it was blurry.

"What happened to your hand?" Mike nodded toward the raw, angry scratches on the top of Ambler's left hand.

"McNulty's cat. I had a rough time rounding him up this morning to take to him to McNulty's father's apartment. He's an alley cat who crashes at McNulty's place. The cat comes in and out the window whenever he wants, so I had to wait for him to get home, and then it was hell to catch him, and worse when I did and tried to get him into the carrier."

Mike nodded somewhat uncertainly. "Sounds like quite a cat."

Ambler looked at the photo the detective handed to him. Despite it being grainy and blurred, it was clear enough. "It's Shannon," he said.

Mike waited.

"How'd you know to ask me?"

"You know the bartender she was with."

"She was doing research in the crime fiction reading room."

Mike's jaw dropped. "Again? . . . That's it. One more murder connected to your crime fiction collection, I'm going to
have the city close it down as a public nuisance."

Ambler hesitated; Mike might be serious. "She'd only been
in the library a couple of times."

"I wouldn't think she'd be back anytime soon." Mike followed his own line of thinking. "Did she sign any forms? She
might have used her real name." He looked into Ambler's questioning expression and caught himself. "You're not going to tell
me, right? . . . Privacy. Confidentiality. I'll need a warrant to
find out what she was doing?"

"I'm afraid so, Mike." Ambler and the library took privacy
rights and confidentiality seriously. This created a conflict with
Mike who didn't want anything obstructing him when he was
on the trail of a murderer. If you murdered someone, to Mike's
way of thinking, you gave up your rights. He and Mike didn't
always agree, yet they got along because they argued without
rancor. Mike talked tough—he was tough—but he treated people,
including criminals he hounded and brought in, with respect.

"She's been in the Library Tavern a couple of times," Ambler
said, hoping to send Mike off on another scent.

"A couple of times?"

"Maybe a few times. I'm not sure." He watched Mike put
the photo back in an envelope and the envelope in his inside
jacket pocket. "Do you have an extra copy of the photo?"

Mike opened his eyes wider, silently asking why Ambler
wanted the photo. Ambler ignored him. Mike let it go and
handed him the envelope he'd put in his pocket. "She there to
see the bartender?"

"They talked to each other. I don't know that she came to
see him." He remembered the expression on McNulty's face
when he looked at her and wasn't so sure.

"Did she leave the bar with him?"

"He took her to her hotel in a cab one night when she'd had a lot to drink but he was back a few minutes later. McNulty does things like that. He's a tarnished knight." Ambler hesitated. "She mentioned a husband, if that helps."

"Not unless he comes looking for her."

"What do you know about the victim?"

"He wasn't registered in the hotel. His name was Ted Doyle; he worked for a security agency in Long Island. He'd been married forty years. His widow, not surprising, was shocked he was murdered and shocked he'd been with another woman. She said he wasn't that kind of guy." Mike raised his eyebrows. "Nothing like this happened before. She meant the other woman thing."

"Could someone have followed him? Someone from a case he was working on? Something that had nothing to do with Shannon or McNulty?"

"Lots of things are possible. Nothing points to that. His agency said he didn't have a case that would bring him to the city. You'd have to wonder why someone from a case he's working on kills him in this woman's hotel room."

"Fingerprints?"

"They got some. Too soon to tell whose they are."

"You've had Jane Does before."

Mike squared his shoulders. "Some of them we still don't know who they are years later."

"Nothing on the surveillance camera in the lobby?"

"That's where the photo I gave you comes from. The victim got on the elevator around ten by himself."

"Someone might have followed him."

Cosgrove shrugged. "No forced entry into her hotel room. But she might have let someone in to help her."

"Help her do what?"

"Kill him."

"Not McNulty."

Cosgrove didn't say anything.

Ambler sat for some time after Mike left, disturbed more than he'd let on by Mike's suggestion that the 42nd Street Library's crime fiction collection somehow begat murders, not only on the pages of its mystery novels but off the page as well. Ambler's sensibility was such that he wanted murder confined to the realm of entertainment, more so since the arrival of his grandson in his life.

Ambler became a sleuth, a solver of crimes, a pursuer of killers, almost on a whim years before when he'd discovered an incongruity between a news story about an apparent accidental death, an accompanying news photo, and the existence of a double-indemnity life insurance policy. He'd met homicide detective Mike Cosgrove during this time; they were both intrigued by inferences they drew from what they saw that no one else drew. Since then, they'd been friends despite the differences in the worlds they worked in and their consequent worldviews.

Ambler had since made use of his talent for observation and deduction because he realized he had such talent and in using it might prevent a murder, keep someone alive who might otherwise be dead. In more than one of those cases, as Mike had just pointed out, there had been a connection to his crime fiction collection.

A good deal of time had passed since he'd allowed himself to think his crime fiction collection might have anything to do with a murder. A year ago, two years, perhaps longer ago now, someone was murdered in the library. Ambler joined that investigation because he saw connections that no one else saw or made. Hundreds of poor souls had died at the hands of others in the city since then, none of them connected to the 42nd Street Library or its crime fiction collection, none of the murders such that he felt he could help solve the crime. At the moment, he was troubled that this state of affairs might have changed.

He didn't buy the idea that Shannon and McNulty killed the man in Shannon's hotel room, although he did suspect McNulty was with Shannon and they were in hiding, possibly hiding from the killer. For one of the few times he could remember, Ambler didn't know what to do next. He wasn't sure he should do anything. McNulty had asked him to take care of the cat; he hadn't asked for help beyond that. Why not wait until McNulty asked him to do something else?

Of course Ambler wouldn't do that. McNulty was in trouble; he needed help so Ambler wasn't going to let it go. Yet McNulty had called in to work, had left a note for Ambler, so most likely he did what he did of his own volition. This might be okay if the bartender hadn't dropped everything and disappeared with this woman he was smitten by on the heels of a murder.

The more Ambler thought about it, the more skeptical he became that Shannon Darling was a scholar writing on women mystery writers or that Shannon Darling was her real name. Yet why would she pretend to be someone she wasn't in order to do research on an obscure mystery writer? Too many questions hung in the air that he didn't have answers for. At least with this one, he knew where to start looking for an answer.

He checked the form Shannon had filled out for access to the collection. She'd used the name Shannon Darling and an address in Somerset, New Jersey, the same address she gave at the hotel, that Mike told him didn't exist. The file boxes she used were on the shelf behind his desk. When there were only two or three readers, Ambler often stored their materials in the reading room overnight so they didn't have to wait to call up the files when they arrived each morning.

Shannon had separated a stash of letters a man named Dillard Wainwright had written to Jayne Galloway. Wainwright, he learned from the letters, was a scholar, as well as a "literary" writer, Wainwright's term for himself, published by a small "literary" press, The Black and White Wheelbarrow. Ambler had to look it up, but sure enough it existed, based at a small liberal arts college in New England. Ambler had never heard of the press, and couldn't remember ever seeing a black and white wheelbarrow either.

There were maybe a dozen letters from Wainwright, mostly a correspondence about books and literature and the failings of contemporary American writers and critics, the latter who, Ambler gathered, didn't think much of Wainwright's writing. There was a subtext to the letters, too, hints they were faintly disguised love letters. Jayne Galloway was locked into an unsatisfying marriage. Wainwright was separated from his wife, aloof, and despairing of finding happiness in love or in life, a tragic Romantic hero. Appropriate enough because Wainwright's field of study was early American dark romanticism, a school of literature Ambler knew something about because of his own interest in Edgar Allan Poe. Poe, besides being one of the progenitors of crime fiction, was the darkest of the dark romantics.

Shannon had pulled letters from various files and stacked them separately, though she left markers in the files she'd taken the letters from. You could guess she was trying to follow a story told through the letters. There were gaps, some letters undoubtedly had been lost or damaged or even purged from the files by Galloway. Shannon's frustration with this was clear from her notes.

It struck Ambler as peculiar that the correspondence she concentrated on wasn't about Jayne Galloway's work. If he were to describe Shannon's research interest based on what he'd seen so far, he'd say she was researching the relationship between Jayne Galloway and Dillard Wainwright, whom—according to the letters—Galloway later left her husband for. What ultimately piqued Ambler's interest was an address Shannon had written and underlined—an address for Jayne Galloway in Great Neck, New York. After some thought and a brief conversation with Adele, he decided he'd rent a car and take a quick trip to Great Neck the following day.

Chapter 5

Ambler arrived at the small house on the edge of Long Island Sound in the waning afternoon of a crisp autumn day. He'd driven across a narrow stone bridge onto a lightly traveled road that cut between marsh grass and a lagoon on one side and stately weathered, wood-framed houses set back from the road on the other side. The sky was blue and practically cloudless, the sun low in the sky behind the houses, which appeared to have been in place a good long time and to plan to stay a good while longer no matter what the elements pitted against them.

He'd decided to visit Jayne Galloway because Shannon's interest in her was so intense and personal he thought it likely they knew one another, and if so Ms. Galloway might tell him something about the mysterious Shannon Darling. He'd told Mrs. Galloway on the phone that he had questions about correspondence between her and a British literary organization about a prize he couldn't find any record of in her papers, which he hoped would give him an official reason for the visit.

He'd missed the house the first time he went by; it sat back from the road with a large front yard and a large maple tree in full autumn splendor, with no house number. When he did pull in the driveway, he was struck by the number and size of the windows in the front of the house facing the lagoon, more of them than you'd expect and larger than the house's original windows would have been. He climbed worn wooden steps to a weathered porch and pushed the doorbell, which chimed gently into the peacefulness of the afternoon.

Peace was short lived, interrupted when the woman opened the door and a screeching squawk pierced the air, like the grating of metal-on-metal of freight cars at an earsplitting level. Trying to talk above the incessant squawking was like talking over a blaring horn.

"That's Buster," the smiling woman who stood back from the doorway said. "He'll quiet down in a moment."

"Is he being tortured?"

She threw back her head and laughed heartily. "He's a parrot." Her voice had a pleasant Midwest twang. "He doesn't like company." Her smile faded and she coughed quietly, covering her mouth with her arm. When the coughing stopped, the screeching did, too. The woman held out her hand. Her blue eyes sparkled, her face had a kind of friendly beaming you might expect on your favorite kindergarten teacher's face. "I'm glad you came, Mr. Ambler. I was afraid because I didn't understand your phone message you'd think I was a crazy old lady."

Ambler hesitated. When they spoke on the phone, she'd had trouble grasping why he wanted to come to Long Island to speak with her. This was more because he didn't tell her the real reason, telling her instead about a literary prize she didn't remember. She wasn't an old lady and she wasn't crazy. She was about his age. "Ray," said Ambler. "Call me Ray. I've been a fan of yours for years."

"I bet that's what you say to all the authors." She chuckled when he blushed, an easy comfortable sound. "Would you like some tea?"

He followed her to the kitchen, a mostly wooden and brown place, plain, almost austere but pleasantly so; the cabinets and the appliances were new, the room, like the front of the house, recently remodeled. She turned on a kettle and pulled a teapot and cups from the cupboard. Doing this, she moved gracefully, while a knee-length sweater she wore over a flowered blouse and a pair of jeans flowed with her as she moved. She stopped for a moment, leaning on her hand against the large dark wood table, and coughed quietly.

"I've been ill," she said.

He nodded.

She placed the teapot, cups, and a package of what she called biscuits on a tray. He offered to carry it. She hesitated and then nodded before leading him to a table at the front of the house that sat against the wall under a window that looked out over the lagoon. They sat at opposite ends of the table and gazed out the window.

"It's a beautiful view," Ambler said, "a nice place to sit."

She told him she'd had the house renovated when she bought it after her divorce some years before. "I spent more on the renovation than I meant to. The architect, a young woman, was enthusiastic about the possibilities. I caught her enthusiasm. My desk is in front of a window like this one upstairs. I thought the house, with the view, was going to be a wonderful place to live and write." She turned from the window and he saw in her face a kind of wistful beauty. "It turns out to be a beautiful place to . . ." she turned to gaze out the window again, ". . . to be ill."

They drank tea while she told him how much she liked her neighbors. "I can't walk down the street without stopping every few steps to talk to someone in their yard or someone driving by who stops to chat." She paused. "I don't walk much anymore, so now folks stop by here with flowers or a cake." She spoke with energy and enthusiasm, but the energy faded as they continued to talk, and her spells of coughing became more frequent. Visibly tiring, she reminded him of a child past her bedtime.

"I tire easily." Her gaze was clear and steady. "We'd better get to your questions while I'm coherent."

Ambler told her about Shannon Darling and her research, her most likely fake name, and the murder in her hotel room. "She had your address in her notes. I wondered if she might have come to talk to you or corresponded with you."

Jayne Galloway leaned back for a moment as if to gather herself. Some change in her bearing or her expression told him he'd hit a nerve. "I'm flattered a young scholar is interested in my work and horrified she might have been witness to a murder. This is the first I've heard of the project, and I've never heard of or from Shannon Darling."

For the first time, she didn't look at him as she spoke. An ominous feeling drifted over them like a shroud. Her uneasiness made him uncomfortable. Despite the plausibility of what she said, he suspected she wasn't telling the truth, or not the whole truth. More unsettling was the sense he got from her reaction that she knew she hadn't gotten away with her evasion.

"I'm not sure I understand," he said to cover the awkward silence. She wasn't accustomed to lying. He didn't want to embarrass her further by acknowledging what they both knew.

She recovered. "I was pleased that the library accepted my papers. Actually, I was intrigued by you, Mr. Ambler." She paused, waiting for him say something.

He didn't.

"I've learned you solve mysteries, an amateur detective; what I write about in books." She laughed gently, which caused a spasm of coughing. "I have my own mysteries, I guess, a mysterious mystery writer." She colored the words with bitterness.

He didn't know where this was going. Yet he felt an opening to give her a chance to rethink her first response. "When I mentioned Shannon Darling, I thought her name might have reminded you of someone. You might have met her in the past—"

The cough again. She slumped in her stiff wooden straight-backed chair. "Can we move to the couch?"

The front of the house was a large open space, living room and dining room, armchairs in the corners of the living room behind her, bookcases against two walls. Two couches faced each other in the middle of the room. "Would you help me, please? To the couch. Hold my arm. I don't want to fall."

He placed his hand under her elbow and she leaned into him as he led her to the couch. Her body was light, insubstantial like a bird's, yet something feminine about her, a warm scent, a softness, a kind of seductive ardor that enveloped her, made her attractive. When she was seated, he went to sit on the couch across from her but changed his mind and sat on the couch beside her.

"The woman I asked you about was interested in letters written to you by a man named Dillard Wainwright."

She winced as if she'd been slapped. "Oh yes, Dillard. I considered burning those letters. Obviously, I didn't. They portray the truth at a certain time. We write to try to get to some kind of truth, don't we? One day, someone might find some kind of truth using my books, my journals, my letters. That's why I donated everything to the library, why I didn't burn the letters."

Over the next half hour, speaking into the fading light of the autumn afternoon, she told him about her life, which was immeasurably sad. Her first husband, with whom she had a child, ridiculed and demeaned her. "There's a kind of cruelty between a man and a woman that doesn't involve assault or physical violence, yet is equally destructive to the woman it is aimed at. I won't tell you more than that. I was a fool to allow it, yet I did. And to my regret, I allowed it to happen to my child by leaving her with him. The sins of the mother are revisited upon the daughter." She met his gaze as if to sear her meaning into his brain.

Jayne Galloway's first husband didn't take her mystery writing seriously. He called it her hobby. After the publication of one of her books, she received a letter from Dillard Wainwright, out of the blue, praising the book. She read some of his as yet unpublished writings and found his writing appealing. "We began an affair of letters. We fell in love through books. Or that was what I thought. Writers are a fragile lot, at least I was. None of us—at least none of the writers I know—think we're any good. We suspect we're frauds about to be found out as soon as our next book comes out. Dillard was a scholar; his praise was important to me.

"As it turned out, in his own way, Dillard was as much of an asshole as my first husband, if not as cruel. He was manipulative. He wanted an introduction to the world of publishing. I was fairly successful at the time, despite my doubts. The publisher would invite me to New York and throw a little party for the launch of my books. That's what the love of my life, Dillard, the man for whom I'd forsaken all others including my daughter, wanted: an introduction to that world.

"It took a long time for me to realize I'd been had like a local yokel in the spell of a sideshow barker." She glared into the space in front of her and caught up with herself. "I'm not sure I wanted to tell you all of that or why I did. You came to ask me about the collection, about my books I hope, not my personal life." She coughed quietly into a tissue she held in her hand.

"The woman I'm asking you about was most interested in those letters. They didn't bear much on your writing. I was puzzled she'd have such a narrow interest."

He wasn't close enough to Jayne Galloway on the couch that either could reach out and touch the other, yet she seemed to want to try to do it, to reach for him. "Well, now you know what they have to do with. Perhaps this woman wanted to write about that part of my life. People like sordidness. You don't know what it is to have deserted your child."

Ambler thought about his son. He understood more than she knew about neglecting a child. He tried again. "Because her research interest was so personal, as I said, I thought you might know her. She registered in the library and the hotel under an assumed name."

Jayne Galloway waited a moment before shaking her head. "I understand your interest, especially since there's a murder involved. This woman couldn't possibly be my daughter. . . ." For a second she froze. She'd said something she hadn't meant to, ". . . if that's what you're thinking."

"I didn't know you had a daughter until you told me just now. But it does seem possible. She might—"

Jayne Galloway suffered another bout of coughing. Each time she coughed quietly as if clearing a tickle in her throat. Yet she'd grown pale and frailer than he'd first thought. The coughing fit brought tears to her eyes. "My daughter has no interest in me. I'm not hiding. She could find me if she wanted to. She doesn't want to find me."

"I'm sorry. . . . I'm sorry to bring up such a painful subject."

"My first husband was an alcoholic and no more interested in her than he was in me, uninvolved in her care, handing her off to nannies. I should never have left her with him. He committed suicide while she was in college. She blamed me for that also. . . . And why shouldn't she?

"She put herself through college with a small inheritance from her grandmother and attended medical school on a fellowship. She's married with a child of her own." Jayne Galloway had hired a private detective who'd found her daughter. They'd had a reunion of sorts. "I tried to make amends. She wasn't interested. Why should she be?"

Ambler didn't like browbeating a dying woman, raising painful memories, yet he couldn't ignore the possibility that Shannon Darling was Jayne Galloway's daughter, and he needed to understand why Jayne Galloway insisted she couldn't be. "Do you know what your daughter's married name is?"

Her tone of voice took on an edge now, anger boiling up, edging toward him. "I found her. I visited her. Her husband didn't like me. He doesn't want her to have anything to do with me. That wasn't right either, a husband keeping his wife from her mother. She was too much under his influence, as I was with her father. I never heard from her again after that. She wrote me out of her life. I don't know her name." She sounded irritated. "You had questions about my papers?"

He told her about the literary prize he couldn't track down but said it wasn't important. He could get back to her. The sun had gone down. Shadows seeped into the room. Jayne Galloway turned to watch the darkening windows behind him. "Do you by any chance know where I can find Dillard Wainwright?"

A strange look came over her face, as if she'd drifted away from him to some time and place of her own. Her answer was dismissive. "He's at a college in Massachusetts. I forget the name."

"One last thing," Ambler pulled the grainy photo from the hotel video Mike Cosgrove had given him and handed it to her. "On the chance you might have seen her without knowing who she was."

She looked at the photo and there it was again, that shock of recognition. This time she was ready for it. She held the photo a moment longer before handing it back to him and shaking her head. "I'm sorry. I don't."

Chapter 6

"I almost wish I hadn't gone to see her," Ambler told Adele the evening he returned from Long Island. Johnny was spending the night at his grandmother's, so they had a dinner at a wine and tapas bar off Tenth Avenue near Adele's apartment. The restaurant was small and cramped, but quiet. He told her about his afternoon on Long Island.

Adele ate small bites of the tiny appetizers and sipped from her glass of white wine, watching Ambler as she listened. "I shouldn't judge," she said when he'd finished. "But deserting her husband and young daughter to run off with someone who pulled the wool over her eyes . . . it's difficult to feel a lot of sympathy."

"She paid a heavy price."

Adele looked at him quizzically. Of course, she wouldn't understand the sympathy he felt for Jayne Galloway. Adele hadn't spent part of an afternoon with the dying woman, didn't see how pain and regret and loss create a presence that requires you to recognize its humanity. Galloway's story wasn't a noble one, and she was lying about at least part of it. Still, she'd suffered and something about her suggested she'd learned kindness through her suffering, so he'd forgive her if she had something to hide. People lied for a lot of reasons, not all of them self-serving or evil. He remembered now that Jayne Galloway's books were dark, with cruel and domineering men, a great deal of retribution. He could see now where that came from.

Adele tried to meet his gaze. "I'm not saying you can't feel sorry for her. Go ahead. Why did you go out there anyway? You thought Shannon was her daughter?"

"I thought she might know something about Shannon. I didn't know she had a daughter until she told me."

"She recognized Shannon when she saw the photo and didn't want to tell you? You think this means Shannon is her daughter?"

"Her daughter's name is—or was until she got married—Sandra Galloway."

"You could tell Mike Cosgrove what you found and let him sort it out."

"I could. . . ."

Adele smiled fetchingly and then winked. "We want to get McNulty out of harm's way first, right?"

She said she'd do a genealogical search on Sandra Galloway. She might find a marriage license or a medical license. Meanwhile, Ambler wanted to track down Dillard Wainwright. No reason for Wainwright not to be forthcoming if he'd sent someone to do research on Jayne Galloway. It was unlikely he'd know about the murder, and Ambler checking on a researcher's bonafides wouldn't be out of the ordinary for a Special Collections librarian.

That night when he got home, he began his search of the faculties of New England colleges for Wainwright. He was sifting through faculty biographies on the Tufts University website when Adele called.

"I think I'm getting somewhere," she said.

"I'm surprised you're calling so late."

"Because I think I'm getting somewhere and wanted to tell you and knew you'd be up trying to find that man . . . Wellington?"

"Wainwright. . . . It's nice to hear your voice at night. You sound dreamy."

"You sound grumpy . . . or you did. Now you sound nice."

Her voice had a soft murmur in it. Ambler felt a stirring of desire he often felt for her, sometimes from a whiff of her hair, sometimes a tremor in her voice; other times it was a memory of touching her, the softness of her mouth when he'd kissed her what felt like ages ago. At the same time, he felt the emptiness of his apartment. Johnny was at his grandmother's. The dog slept next to the door waiting for his nightly walk.

That murmur in Adele's voice was, perhaps unintentionally, an invitation for him to flirt with her. He didn't. When she wanted to be, she was a tantalizing flirt. Her sigh was a surrender of some sort and her tone became matter-of-fact, the tone she used to answer a question from a reader in the library, except for an underlying hum of excitement. She'd found Sandra Galloway.

"I'll look up marriage licenses tomorrow. She went to medical school in New York and did her residency at NYU and Bellevue. I'm hoping she got married here. It would make sense."

Ambler returned to his search. Around midnight, he realized he should look up one of Wainwright's books. The author biography should include his academic affiliation. And there he was, professor of English at Pine Grove College. He'd call him in the morning.

Something Ambler learned in his time looking into murders and calling people to ask questions was not to leave a message asking for the person he was looking for to call back. If he did that he'd have to wait until they got around to it, if they ever did. His call wasn't an important matter to them. It was important to him. So when he called Wainwright's number at Pine Grove College in the morning, he didn't leave a message. He'd keep calling until he reached him.

Adele traced Sandra Galloway to Greenwich, Connecticut, where she was a practicing dermatologist and married. Her married name was Dean. Her husband's name was Simon. "That wasn't so hard," she said. "But you probably could have asked her mother."

"I did. She didn't know her daughter's married name or wouldn't tell me."

"Is Shannon Darling and Dr. Sandra Dean one and the same? Should I call her?"

"If you have her home address, I think I'll go and see. You might not get an answer over the phone. If she is Shannon, she's hiding. If she isn't, she'll think you're nuts."

That afternoon, Ambler left work early. Johnny's after-school nanny, Denise Cosgrove, Mike's daughter, would deliver him to Adele's apartment after school. Ambler would be back for him that evening. Greenwich was an easy commute. He caught a Metro-North train at Grand Central with the early homebound commuters, arriving in Greenwich in less than an hour. He found a taxi in front of the station. The cab followed narrow winding roads past long driveways that led to mansions deep within the trees and shrubs and deposited him at the midpoint of a circular bluestone gravel driveway under a portico in front of a large stone mansion that was closer to the road than most of the other homes in the area. He stood for a moment taking in the sculpted gardens, lawns, shrubs, and hedges before he rang a doorbell and waited for what he expected might be a butler to open the front door.

Instead, a bright-eyed, pink-cheeked, blonde-haired girl about Johnny's age came from the side of the house before he could ring the bell. She wore jeans, her hair was in a ponytail, and she carried a size-appropriate baseball bat.

"I hope that's not for me," Ambler said.

"T-ball." She appraised him for a few seconds. "I suppose you're looking for my dad. Whom should I say you are?"

Ambler smiled. Part refined young woman, part-tomboy, the little girl was as cute as a button. "What about your mom?"

A troubled look came over the child's face. The light in her blue eyes dimmed. "She's not here." He sensed she wanted to say more.

"I was really looking for her. Do you know when she'll be back?"

Anger smoldered under her troubled expression. "I don't know when she'll be back. She won't—" She caught herself. "You better talk to my dad." She turned and walked up the steps to the front door but turned back. "Do you know my mom?"

He was stuck. The frankness of the little girl appealed to him. "To tell you truth, I don't know if I know her or not. That's why I'm here."

The girl looked puzzled but not disbelieving. "That's a funny thing to say. You're not a patient are you?" She answered the question without his help and went on. "Are you a doctor?"

"No." He held out his hand. "I'm Ray Ambler. I'm a librarian."

She held out her hand. "Carolyn Dean. I go to the library sometimes after school."

"Actually, I work at the big library on Fifth Avenue in New York. Have you ever been there?"

"Mom used to—" She paused. After a moment, she went on. "We go to the city at Christmas to look in the store windows and to shop and we always go to the library." She paused, this time for emphasis. "The lions have wreaths with big red ribbons around their necks."

"Yep. They do. Every year. Is your mom traveling?" He felt dishonest slipping in the question. He didn't like the possibility the little girl had anything to do with the woman he knew as Shannon, that she had even the remotest connection to a murder.

But children too often are acquainted with evil. More ominous, he saw Shannon in the quick flash of her smile, the squint when she stopped to think for a moment. He didn't know what was in store for Carolyn but feared for her happy days of childhood.

"My mom travels sometimes." She looked over her shoulder and rolled her eyes at the same time. "You'll have to ask my dad. It's weird what you said. How come you don't know if you know my mother?"

"It's hard to explain. I think I need to talk to your dad."

Worry narrowed her eyes. "Is my mom in trouble?"

He fought back the urge to ask why she thought that. He didn't want to use trickery to get her to answer a question when she didn't know what her answer was contributing to. He'd done it many times to witnesses or suspects in the past but he didn't want to do it to her. He couldn't bring himself to reassure her with a lie either. "I have a grandson about your age," he said instead. "He lives with me."

Something sparked in her eyes. "Why doesn't he live with his mom and dad?"

He was sorry he brought it up. What could he say? Because his dad is in prison and his mother was murdered? "He can't. His mother died."

"Oh." She bowed with such solemnity that it carried unexpected sincerity. "I'll get my dad."

Ambler waited in the doorway. He wasn't concerned about using a bit of subterfuge on Simon Dean. If his wife Dr. Sandra Dean was also Shannon Darling, there was a good chance the man didn't know his wife had a second identity. Ambler didn't know this for sure himself. He planned to tell Mr. Dean that while he was cataloging Jayne Galloway's papers he came across some questions he hoped Dean's wife could answer about her mother. Dean wouldn't, Ambler hoped, ask how he tracked down Jayne Galloway's estranged daughter.

He had no idea how Dean would react to his questions. If Ambler simply confirmed Sandra Dean was Sandra Galloway, this would be something but not much. If Sandra Dean was missing, this would add something else. If Mr. Dean knew his wife had gone to the city to do research on her mother at the library, this would be something indeed.

When Simon Dean appeared a moment later, walking behind his daughter with his hand on her shoulder, he wore the startled expression of someone interrupted from deep thought and met Ambler's gaze with one that was not unfriendly but cautious.

Not a big man, he was fit, athletic, and handsome, with a kind of easy assuredness that showed his awareness of being all of those things; he was in his forties, maybe a little older, maybe a littler younger. Ambler wasn't good at guessing ages. Dean dressed neatly in what Ambler thought of as a kind of uniform of the affluent suburbs: khaki pants, button-down Oxford shirt, hair short and neatly trimmed. He didn't show much interest in Ambler, willing to wait for the conversation to come to him.

"I was hoping to speak with your wife, actually" Ambler said. "I'm the curator of Jayne Galloway's papers at the Forty-second Street Library. I came across some things in Mrs. Galloway's journal and wanted to meet Dr. Dean and ask her some questions about her mother. An informal meeting often works well for that. I took a chance coming here. I should have called."

"We can go into my office," Simon Dean said. "Carolyn, go do your homework."

"I was practicing hitting."

"You answered the door? I didn't hear the doorbell."

"I was practicing hitting. I was outside." By a quick change of expression, a frown, she let her father know she'd already said that.

"You're not allowed to answer the door by yourself."

"I didn't answer the door." She shook herself with indignation, glancing at Ambler, rolling her eyes, before picking up her bat and heading out the door.

Simon Dean's office was high-ceilinged with large windows; a drafting table sat prominently in the middle of the room; another leaned against a wall; there was a desk against one of the windows. On all of the surfaces, drafting paper, blueprints, and plans were rolled out, some with lamps or a tape dispenser holding down the corners. Other blueprints and plans were rolled up and leaning against the wall.

"You're an architect?"

"At the moment, I'm doing costs and estimates. Have you ever seen a $30 million house renovation?" He grabbed one of the rolled up plans or blueprints and laid it out across a drawing table. Pointing to different sections of the plan, he showed Ambler a giant master suite with a marble bathroom, what he called a madam's suite with its own marble bathroom and a dressing room stretching the length of a hallway. Ambler couldn't really understand the plans, so he just looked at them. "They're adding a third floor with a weight room and an indoor tennis court." He met Ambler's gaze triumphantly.

Ambler wasn't sure if the look of triumph was because Dean was impressed by the accomplishments of wealth or shared Ambler's astonishment that such a house existed. "My goodness," Ambler said, hoping to sound agreeable to whatever Simon Dean thought about his work.

Dean rolled up his plans and returned to Ambler's question. "My wife and her mother have been estranged since Sandra was a child. I doubt Sandra would be interested in talking with you about her."

"Her mother said they'd had a reunion of sorts not long ago."

Dean glanced at him sharply. "Hardly a reunion, it was a brief and awkward encounter that accomplished nothing. My God, the woman deserted her daughter, a child." His icy glare suggested Ambler was an accomplice.

Jayne Galloway said her son-in-law didn't like her, Ambler recalled. Dean's reaction certainly reinforced that. "I see. Did your wife mention an interest in her mother's papers after that?"

Dean narrowed his eyes, something like his daughter did. "Papers?"

"Her mother's papers, the collection in the library."

"No. Sandra wouldn't be interested." Dean was deliberate in what he said. It could be he was a cautious person by nature. It could be something else. "Why do you ask?"

"Do you know anyone who'd have an interest in Jayne Galloway's papers?"

"I don't know or care anything about Sandra's mother. Neither does Sandra. No one we know would be interested in her papers."

"Does your wife work in the area?"

He seemed to relax. "She's part of a plastic surgery practice in Greenwich. Her patients are the women who live in multimillion-dollar houses. They require a lot of upkeep."

Ambler began to like the man he was talking to. More to the point, he liked his daughter and felt protective of her; his wish was for Simon Dean to be honest and forthcoming, to have nothing to hide, for her sake. His more fervent wish was that Dr. Sandra Dean be easily accounted for and have no connection to Shannon Darling whatsoever. This was one of the times he hoped he wouldn't discover what he was afraid he would discover. "Is Dr. Dean at work now?"

Dean's discomfort returned, apparent in the stiffening of his stance, the tightening of the muscles of his face. "She's traveling." His glance evaded Ambler's.

Ambler waited. When someone expects a question they don't want to answer, Mike had told him years ago, they sometimes answer the question even if you weren't going to ask it, even if you didn't know to ask it.

"We're busy people. Our work lives are separate. I don't

know where she is. A conference. She's usually gone two or three days."

"She's not in New York, by any chance?"

Hesitation, more deliberation, weighing possibilities before he answered. "Not as far as I know. She hasn't called."

"When did she leave?"

He thought this over, too. "The day before yesterday? I don't remember."

Dean didn't object to the questions or ask why Ambler was asking about his wife's whereabouts. Did he anticipate an interrogation? For the second time in as many days, Ambler felt the person he was speaking with knew something they wouldn't divulge.

The logical thing to do next was to show Dean the photo he had in his breast pocket. Yet Ambler held back. Suppose he showed him the photo of Shannon, and Dean recognized his wife. Then what? Ambler would explain what happened—a man was killed in this woman's hotel room; and, from the look of things, she'd gone missing, taking another man with her. You had to think from how he acted Dean anticipated Ambler might tell him something about his wife he didn't want to hear. But why? What might he suspect?

Dean took the opportunity presented by Ambler's hesitation to change the subject. "The library you work at, the one on Fifth Avenue? It's a Carrére and Hastings Beaux-Arts building. New York has more Beaux-Arts than any city other than Paris; the library and Grand Central Terminal are two of the best. It's functional, isn't it, the library building? Majestic, and it gets the job done."

If Dean's aim was to throw Ambler off-track, it worked. They began talking about an effort by the library's Board of Trustees not long ago to dismantle the interior of the 42nd Street Library building, take out the seven floors of shelving beneath the reading room, and reshape the space into something like a mall. As they talked it was apparent that Dean had followed the battle between the developers and the scholars and preservationists over the redesign of the library and was passionate about the library's preservation. Ambler liked that.

Dean stood abruptly. "It's past five o'clock. I've done enough for today. How about a drink?"

Surprised, Ambler took a moment before he said yes.

"Scotch okay?" He led Ambler to the living room, went to the kitchen for a bucket of ice cubes, and made the drinks, scotch on the rocks, atop a portable bar. Handing one to Ambler, he sat down across from him. "Are you married?" He took a sip of his drink.

"I was." Ambler sipped his drink. "Divorced."

Dean was more relaxed. Maybe it was the scotch. "What did Mrs. Galloway say about Sandra that you want to ask Sandra about?"

"In general, I want to ask her what she thought about her mother."

Dean took a long drink of his scotch before he said, "Sandra's mother deserted her. Her father ignored her. She had an unhappy childhood. You may know that, or have guessed it, if you've met Sandra's mother." He looked at Ambler significantly. When Ambler didn't respond, he went on. "My wife didn't want to have children. After the childhood she had, she wouldn't consider it, wouldn't talk about it for the first years of our marriage."

Dean went to the portable bar and poured himself another drink, gesturing with the bottle to Ambler who shook his head. "Her residency was grueling, long hours at the hospital, more hours reading and studying at home. Little time for anything else. She still works hard, long hours. She's a good doctor. Her patients admire her." He paused again to savor his scotch. "Yet there's a side her patients don't see. Sandra suffers deep depressions. She has a great deal of repressed anger." He regarded his glass of scotch before taking another sip and spoke without looking at Ambler. "No one really knows what anyone else's marriage requires."

Ambler sat back to try to catch up with what was happening. For all the connection Ambler had to him, Dean might be talking to himself. He hardly looked at Ambler. A couple of minutes ago, Dean had been engaging, enthusiastic about his work, about architecture, about preserving the 42nd Street Library. He'd also, without saying so, let on that he worried about his wife and was perhaps embarrassed that he didn't know where she was, not so much covering for her as pretending to Ambler, and perhaps to himself, too, that everything was normal, life was as it should be. Now, his manner showed worry and concern, such that Ambler sympathized, felt embarrassed for him.

After a pause, Dean leaned toward Ambler. "What did you come here to tell me about my wife?"

So Dean did expect to be told something about his wife. Ambler was about to take the photo of the woman he knew as Shannon from his pocket when out of the corner of his eye he detected movement at the back of the staircase behind Dean. He paused. Almost as soon as he did, Dean noticed, following his gaze and springing out of his chair.

"Carolyn!" he shouted.

The movement near the stairs quickened, a flash of blonde hair, and the blue of blue jeans exploded into view, like a partridge being flushed out of the bushes. Ambler heard the front door slam.

Dean turned back to Ambler. "She's a strong-willed child. Too strong-willed. She's not at the problem age yet, but I see it coming. Her mother doesn't stand up to her."

Ambler took the photo from his pocket and handed it to Dean, who stared at it for what seemed like a long time.

"Who is this?" He held the photo toward Ambler.

"Is that your wife?"

Dean pulled the photo back and stared at it again before looking up, his face wracked with anguish. "My wife? It couldn't be. There's a resemblance perhaps." He turned the photo to look at it at different angles. "Sandra doesn't dress like that. Where's this from? It's grainy and blurry. You couldn't say for sure who it is."

"It's from a hotel surveillance camera. The woman in the photo was with a man who was later found murdered in her hotel room."

His expression was incredulous. "And you think this is Sandra? That's absurd. Why would she—is there a medical conference at this hotel? Medical equipment? Why would she be there?" He paused, gathering fury. "Who the hell are you? What are you talking about? Why are you talking about Jayne Galloway . . . and now this?"

Ambler kept his voice calm. "The woman in the photo was doing research in the Jayne Galloway collection in the library."

"This woman?" Dean's voice rose in indictment. "You can't be sure with the quality of this photo who this woman is. You came here to make some crazy accusation? Some half-baked idea that this is my wife?" He stood, his hand clenched into a fist around the glass of scotch he was holding. "Get out!"

"There's more." Ambler's tone was firm but sympathetic.

The expression on Dean's face, frozen into a snarl, crumpled, as if he knew there would be more, knew his indignation was misplaced; he collapsed into the chair he'd been sitting in.

Ambler told him about McNulty's connection to the woman in the photo, downplaying her curious behavior with men in bars, but not her drinking.

As if talking to himself, Dean said, "She shouldn't drink. She becomes a different person when she drinks. Is she having an affair with the bartender? Who is he?"

"His name is Brian McNulty. He works at a bar a lot of us

from the library go to after work. He's been there for years . . .
or was. I don't know that he's with her. They disappeared at the
same time."

"You don't know this person is Sandra." Dean tried once
more but without the indignation, his tone regretful. "There's
a resemblance. This woman was doing research on Sandra's
mother? I told you Sandra didn't care anything about her mother.
It's more likely a stranger would be interested in Sandra's
mother for some reason. Not Sandra. That's all."

"Is your wife missing?"

Simon Dean buried his face in his hands. He spoke without
looking up. "I don't know what to think. Sometimes, you suspect things; they're like noises that wake you in the night you
pretend to yourself you didn't hear; you don't want them to exist so you pretend they don't."

When he looked up at Ambler, his eyes were bloodshot.
"Sandra has a behavior disorder. Sometimes, she'll leave like
this. She'll come back and she'll be contrite. She's been at a conference or needed time to herself, shopping in the city, or at a
spa. I've learned to accept her. Despite those excursions, she's
devoted to me. I might have told her to go years ago, thrown
her out. I can't do it. She needs me too much, so I forgive her."

"This might be your wife?"

Suspicion clouded Dean's eyes. "If there's reason to think
this woman is my wife and was witness to a murder, why
haven't the police come looking for her?"

"The police haven't identified the woman in this photo.
The connection to you, to your wife, is what I found in Jayne
Galloway's papers. I went to see Jayne Galloway. She told me
enough for me to find my way here."

"I don't know what you are or why you're doing this. You
said you were a librarian."

"I am a librarian. For one thing, the bartender I mentioned
is a friend of mine. For another, your wife, if this is your wife,

was using the collection I'm responsible for. It's possible the bartender and your wife are in danger from the killer of the man in
the hotel. I guess I'm looking for an explanation that will bring
my world back to some sort of normalcy."

Simon Dean's expression was sad. "Are you going to tell the
police about Sandra, about me?"

Ambler didn't answer. Soon he'd have to tell the police.
Until now, he hadn't known anything to conceal. Now, he had
something he should tell Mike. He understood Dean's desire to
shield his wife. Wasn't Ambler doing the same thing to protect
McNulty?

Later, as he waited in front of the house for the cab to take
him back to the train station, Carolyn came up to him. He'd
heard her thwacking the t-ball as he walked out and watched her
take a couple of swings. She noticed him watching and took a
hefty swing. Now she'd walked over to where he was standing.

"You're a t-ball player, I see."

She shook her head, her ponytail swaying from side to side.
"Not t-ball. That's for younger kids. I play softball. The tee is for
practice. I want to play baseball." She hefted the bat. "Do you
like baseball?"

"I do, since I was your age."

"I want to be a major leaguer." She watched the cab pull up.
"Or maybe a doctor."

"Maybe both," Ambler said.

She nodded vigorously. "That's what my mom said." Ambler watched Carolyn gather herself together for her next question. "Did you find out if you know my mom?"

Once more, answering would be difficult. He hesitated.

She went on without him. "You'd know if you knew her.
She's quite special. And she's really smart. And beautiful." Her
attempt to muffle her enthusiasm with a matter-of-fact tone
was charming. "And she's very nice." Carolyn beamed.

"I think I do know her." Ambler said. What else could he say? "And she is all those things. I hope she gets home soon."

"Me, too." Carolyn's blue eyes, almost as blue as Johnny's, opened wider, filled with hope.

Ambler tried for some hope himself. "Your dad's nice, too. I just spoke with him."

Carolyn nodded. "He's okay. Mom says he's old fashioned." She walked to the end of the driveway with him and watched the cab drive away from there. Ambler turned and watched her, too, until she was out of sight

Chapter 7

The day after Ambler's visit to Simon Dean, Adele called him after work. He'd been home only a few minutes and had seen her less than an hour before at the library and told her about his visit to Simon Dean.

Johnny's after-school companion, Denise Cosgrove, was getting ready to leave when the phone rang. Adele asked Ambler to have Denise stay with Johnny a little longer. She needed to see him right away. She was fine, she said, but could he please not ask stupid questions and meet her at a pub called The River Lee on Third Avenue right away.

When he got to the bar, about four blocks from his apartment, Adele was sitting in a booth across from the bar talking to a man who sat across from her, his back to the door. She was talking as she saw him. Her expression didn't change and she didn't stop talking. When Ambler got closer, he realized the man she was talking to was McNulty. There was no reason Ambler should know this, not from the slope of the man's shoulders, the blue jacket stretched across his back, or the backward Yankee cap on his head. Yet he knew it was McNulty.

He slid in alongside Adele. Greetings didn't seem to be in order.

"I don't have much time," McNulty said. "In this being-on-the-lam business, you don't stay in one place too long, especially a public place."

"Will you stay long enough to tell us what's going on?" Ambler said.

"Not to answer questions. I've got a journal that belongs to Shannon. I've copied some pages that are about men she's encountered. My belief is one of the names is that of the killer of the man who was with Shannon the other night." He sipped from his beer. "She doesn't know I have her journal or that I've made these copies I'm giving to you." He stopped again as if he'd lost his train of thought or gone off on another train. "She's a complicated woman. I won't try to explain her to you, nor why I know she isn't the killer, nor why she was with that man who was killed, nor what her relationship is or was to the men listed in her journal. The journal will tell you some of that."

"What do you know about Shannon, Brian?" Adele asked. "Do you know we think that's not her real name?"

He held up his hand, cutting her off. "I know who she is." Something had changed in McNulty. Never jovial, often dour, he'd never been hail-fellow-well-met, yet there'd been something about him, a chuckle behind the grumble, a twinkle behind the jaded glance. Not now. He'd developed the calculating manner of the insecure, the hesitant movement of the hunted, ready to run or duck for cover at any moment. "In some ways, I misunderstood. Maybe I was misled."

To Ambler, McNulty was answering another question entirely from the one Adele asked him.

"I might do it differently if I had it to do over. I thought she wanted something different than she wanted. She let me think that. You'd have to see that as deceit. She let me think . . . well, she let me because she needed something from me. She may not have meant to mislead me. She was desperate. Probably she'd gotten used to being that way so it came naturally. She wouldn't realize that's what she was doing. I thought one thing, realized it wasn't what she thought at all. By then, I was caught up in it, caught up in her. Now who knows what will happen?"

In the silence, McNulty stewed in his thoughts. Ambler let him stew. After a moment, McNulty shook his head. "She makes things up. I don't know if she's brilliant or crazy. She didn't kill the man in her hotel room. She knows who did."

"She's protecting the murderer. You're protecting her. Why?" Amber didn't like McNulty's thinking.

McNulty looked at him steadily. "I'm asking you to find the killer."

"If she's who I think she is, she's married." Ambler told McNulty he'd found Simon Dean.

McNulty wasn't surprised. He knew. "Did you tell the police?"

"Not yet. She has a little girl, a daughter." Ambler didn't intend what he said as an accusation. The words had a power of their own.

"She's not going to leave the kid."

Ambler's impatience got the best of him. What in hell was McNulty doing? This woman he was with was a menace.

"Brian," Adele spoke for him, "you're not making sense. Have you thought ahead? Where do you go with Shannon or whoever she is? Even if everything works out. Someone is arrested for the murder—and it isn't her—where do you go? Do you want to take her away from her husband, from her little girl?"

Ambler hoped for a response he knew wasn't coming. Sheepish and apologetic weren't qualities you found in McNulty. This was a guy who took care of problems himself without asking for help. He might do favors. He might accept a favor. He didn't ask for one. It didn't take much to get his back up. "I thought you'd look into this," he said to Ambler. "You don't want to do that, give me back those copies."

Ambler turned to Adele for help.

"We do want to help—you," she said. "She's using you. She might be tricking you."

McNulty's eyes closed for a moment. When he opened them, some part of his old self was back. "I don't know from one minute to the next what's going to happen. I may not be alive five minutes after I walk out that door." The twinkle was back. He pursed his lip. "I won't put you on the spot, Ray." He reached for the pages he'd given to Ambler. "I'll look into some of this myself. I should've done that in the first place. It's not right to get you tangled up in it."

Ambler released the small stack of papers. McNulty wouldn't ask any more of him. You could see his embarrassment. For a few more seconds, they sat not talking. As McNulty stood to leave, Ambler fought back the urge to ask him to wait, to try to find another way to look at things. McNulty might have wanted to say something also, as did Adele. In the end, no one said anything, and he was gone.

Ambler and Adele sat together in silence for a while longer. Ambler got them both another beer, and the mugs sat in front of them untouched.

"He looked so alone," Adele said, watching the space in the doorway where they'd last seen McNulty.

Already, Ambler regretted turning McNulty down. So what if he checked up on a few men McNulty told him about who for whatever reason were listed in Shannon's journal?

"Are you going to tell Mike Cosgrove what you found out about Shannon? About her husband?" Adele's tone was somber.

"I want to think about all of this before I do. There's no hurry. Her husband doesn't know where she is."

Ambler and Johnny had dinner that night at Adele's apartment. Johnny watched TV while Ambler and Adele talked.

"You're moping because you didn't help McNulty look for those men, aren't you?" Adele didn't wait for an answer. "He shouldn't be doing what he's doing. Even he knows that. So he shouldn't ask us—well, shouldn't ask you—to help."

She was trying to make him feel better. She'd thought they should help McNulty and she knew Ambler was wrong to turn him down. He saw it in her face at the time, yet she didn't disagree when he said no. She didn't criticize him. She'd let him figure out he'd been wrong, and she wouldn't tell him then she knew all along he was wrong. "McNulty needed help. I let him down. He wouldn't have let me down. He wouldn't let you down."

Adele nodded, sadness in her dark eyes. "Everything is terrible, isn't it?"

They ate pasta and talked with Johnny about school and— of more interest to him—his training sessions with Lola, his finally named dog who at the moment was gnawing on one of Adele's chair legs.

"Could you get her to stop doing that?" Ambler said.

"Doing what?"

"Chewing on the chair."

"Watch," Johnny leaned over toward the dog. "Lola! Place. Go to your place."

The dog, responding to the tone of his voice, tilted her head to look at him.

"Go to your place!" Johnny said louder.

The dog continued to watch him, tilting her head.

"Lola!" he shouted, rising from his chair.

Adele said softly, "She doesn't know where her place is in my apartment."

"Right," said Johnny, bending down to pat Lola on her head.

Adele appraised the dog. "Do you think she's going to stop growing soon?"

Ambler smiled weakly. "She'll have to or we'll need to rent a stall for her somewhere."

Late that night, after Johnny had gone to sleep, Ambler's cell phone rang. In the stillness of the night, the ring sounded ominous.

He grabbed the phone. "Yes?"

"Ray?"

"Mike?"

"I got bad news." Mike wasn't one to hem and haw, yet he did this time. "Your friend, the bartender . . . There's been a murder. He's a suspect."

Ambler took a moment to absorb what he heard. "I know about the murder. I didn't know he'd become a suspect. Why McNulty?"

"That's not it. . . . The victim is a woman. At a hotel in Stamford, Connecticut, around midnight tonight. I got a call because I'd put out a BOLO on the bartender. He was registered under his own name, with a Mrs. McNulty."

"You think it's Shannon. You think McNulty killed her?"

"Is he married?"

"He has an ex-wife and a son."

"I'm driving up to Connecticut in the morning. I won't bring you into it unless I have to. I trust you don't know anything you haven't told me." Accusation hung in the silence.

After talking to Mike, Ambler was numb. He didn't tell Mike he'd spoken to McNulty a few hours before. He didn't tell Mike about his talk with Simon Dean either. Nor did he tell Mike about a list of names McNulty tried to give him. Tomorrow morning, tomorrow afternoon, he'd tell Mike what he knew. There was no reason not to. Mike might have some information for him, too. Nothing the police kept under wraps. Mike wouldn't invite Ambler or anyone else into police business—as he hadn't told Ambler about the BOLO, that he had a Be On (the) Lookout bulletin for McNulty. Still, he might let on how the Connecticut police saw the case.

Ambler had been in situations similar to the one he was

in now where you don't know enough to do anything. If you started off to do something, one direction was as good as another and you were more likely to start off on the wrong track than the right one. In such situations you needed to let the world take a couple of turns and then take another look to see what you knew, if you knew anything.

Sometime later—Ambler didn't know how long—he was still staring at his computer when the phone rang. This time, he didn't need an ominous ring tone to tell him it was trouble. As he suspected, it was McNulty.

"Something's come up. You'll know soon enough. I don't have time to—"

"I already know most of it. Shannon's real name is Sandra Dean. And she's dead."

"Whatever you wanna ask, I don't have an answer. Yes. Sandra Dean is dead, murdered. This is a world with no justice and no mercy, not for her." McNulty's breathing was labored. "I'm not sure I care about who killed her . . . or anything else. It's such a goddamn shame. She was about to . . ." His voice cracked and he stopped. Ambler stayed quiet, listening to McNulty's choked breathing. After a moment, McNulty cleared his throat, a sound resembling a growl. "I should have been with her. I should have known. . . ."

"Where were you? What should you have known?" Ambler knew McNulty wouldn't answer.

McNulty spoke softly. Ambler could barely hear him. "The pages I copied from the journal? Someone's gonna drop them off for you. It's all I got. Give it to the cops if you want. I'm gonna get lost again. I'll keep tabs on you." He disconnected.

Ambler called Adele as soon as he finished the call with McNulty. She sobbed into the phone when he told her the woman she knew as Shannon Darling was dead and McNulty was suspected of killing her. Ambler didn't know if she cried for Shannon or McNulty. Maybe for both of them. It didn't matter. Tears formed behind his eyes, too.

"McNulty didn't kill her. What are we going to do?" Adele spoke haltingly between sobs. "Wait." The crying stopped. Her voice cleared. "He couldn't have done it. He was with us. We can vouch for him."

Ambler had thought of that. He didn't like disappointing Adele, yet false hope wasn't useful either. "He was with us around six thirty. She was killed around midnight. Stamford's an hour away on the train. He could have been back in Stamford by nine or ten easily."

"Oh." He could hear her disappointment. "Are you sure it was Shannon?"

An immense weight pressed on him. "I wish it wasn't. Shannon is—or was—Sandra Dean and she's dead, leaving a husband and a little girl behind."

"Poor Shannon. . . . Sandra. I guess we should at least use her real name."

It was long after the phone calls that Ambler fell asleep. He couldn't stop thinking about Sandra Dean. His taped-together eyeglasses were on the side table next to his chair. He picked them up and pictured Shannon, first at the Library Tavern, later as she examined his crushed glasses with a slightly bewildered expression, and later still at the library table in the crime fiction reading room surrounded by file folders, when her expression as she concentrated resembled worry as much as intensity. He remembered Adele's foreboding that Shannon was doomed. He'd been afraid for Shannon, too, that she would be too easily harmed.

Immensely sadder was to picture Carolyn, her ladylike manners in introducing herself, the excitement when she talked about her mother, the determination in her blue eyes under her baseball cap as she talked about her hitting. He couldn't imagine the grief the child would now endure.

So many things didn't make sense. His head buzzed with questions he couldn't answer. Why did Sandra Dean use an assumed name? What was she trying to find in her mother's papers in the library? Why was Ted Doyle murdered in her hotel room and who killed him? Who were the men in her journal and why did she write about them? Why did Sandra Dean's mother and husband both deny recognizing a photo of Shannon Darling?

Chapter 8

Mike Cosgrove drove his own car to Connecticut the morning after the murder of Sandra Dean, leaving from his apartment in Queens, making it over the Throgs Neck Bridge into the Bronx before the morning rush hour traffic picked up. He wanted to meet the Stamford homicide detectives—who worked out of the Stamford Criminal Investigations Bureau—in person. He hoped to talk to the cops who were first on the murder scene and read their notes on the case. With luck he might get to do an interview with the victim's husband, who might be able to tell him something about the man murdered in his wife's hotel room a few days before her murder. The Stamford cops would interview the husband because when a wife gets murdered, especially a wayward wife, you want to rule out the husband early on—or not.

The two cops from the Stamford Criminal Investigations Bureau he met with were standoffish, not so willing to share information. Cops in smaller jurisdictions sometimes got like that when you met with them; they had to prove to the big-city cop they knew what they were doing and didn't need any help from him. They knew the city had more killings most week-ends than they did in a year. Did they think this was something a big-city cop was happy about?

They loosened up when he told them he was looking for help with his unsolved murder. Their suspect, Brian McNulty, he told them, linked the two murders, and Dr. Sandra Dean, most likely, was the woman in whose hotel room the murder he was investigating took place. So they said they'd put their evidence technician in touch with the NYPD Crime Scene Unit and pass along whatever forensic stuff they had—blood, prints, DNA.

They weren't sure about him interviewing Simon Dean, with whom they'd had an initial interview and were about to interview again. After a muffled conversation, during which they took turns looking over their shoulders at him, the two detectives trudged off to get a decision from the captain, who said Cosgrove could go along.

The guy he went with, whose name was Green, asked the right questions, so Cosgrove kept quiet and listened. Sometimes, listening was more productive than doing the questioning.

Simon Dean's answers were short and to the point. He didn't embellish. He didn't volunteer. He didn't stumble. He didn't exhibit any of the known characteristics of a liar. He answered he didn't know to a lot of questions. From those, you got the feeling he didn't know what his wife had been up to. Green asked him where he was on the night of his wife's murder. Dean didn't take offense at the question. He said he was home. His daughter was at his sister's for the night, so he was alone. He couldn't think of any way to verify what he said. Not much of an alibi. But he didn't really need one. A lot of folks sit at home alone at night.

Dean's answers to the couple of questions Cosgrove asked him were about what the detective expected. He had no idea his wife was in New York City on September 7, the day Ted

Doyle was murdered. He had no idea why she'd be staying at the Commodore Hotel under a fake name, and had never heard of the murder victim.

"Do you know the name Brian McNulty?"

Dean, who sat uncomfortably in an armchair in his living room for the interview, had been looking down at his hands that were folded in his lap. He looked up now, meeting Cosgrove's gaze with red-rimmed sad eyes. "He's the man who was with my wife. He killed her."

"He's a suspect, yes. Do you know how your wife knows him, why she was with him?"

Dean shook his head and looked down at his hands again.

"When you feel up to it, we'd like you to make a list of your wife's close friends."

For whatever reason, Dean didn't like the question. "Why? She doesn't have a lot of close friends; my sister is her closest friend."

"Friends," Cosgrove said. "They don't have to be close. She might have told a friend things she didn't tell you. Did your wife have any enemies, disputes with anyone?"

Dean raised his head again, fixing his gaze first on Cosgrove and then on the other detective. "You don't believe the man she was with killed her?"

"We're looking for him. He's a suspect," Green, the Stamford cop, said.

Cosgrove said, "We're sorry to put you through this, Mr. Dean." He meant what he said, sure that Dean saw him as a cold-hearted bastard. "We have to do a thorough investigation, even if what happened seems obvious to you. It's better for everyone in the long run if we touch all the bases."

"It doesn't help my wife." Dean spoke dully, again looking at his hands.

"I'm sorry for your loss, sir," Cosgrove said.

Dean nodded.

Green said they'd be in touch and they'd keep him informed as the case proceeded.

"I'd appreciate that." Dean stood to walk them to the door.

"We're hoping it won't take long," Green said. "Contact us anytime for anything at all."

Cosgrove handed Dean his card. "You probably don't want this. If you think of anything you forgot to tell me—"

"About what?" Dean locked his gaze on Cosgrove.

"Anything that might help us."

Dean put Cosgrove's card in his pocket.

"What did you think of him?" Green asked as he drove Cosgrove back to the Stamford police station.

"His wife's been murdered. That's bad enough. If we believe him, he had no idea what she'd been up to, why she was in New York using a fake name, why a man was murdered in her hotel room, why she was with this bartender. You figure having to swallow all that he ought to be a basket case."

Green was a gregarious guy and must have felt he should entertain his visitor despite the grizzly nature of the visit. "This is the Post Road; we used to call it the Boston Post Road." Green kept his eyes on the road. "U.S. 1, from Maine to Key West, Florida. It takes a little longer but I like to take it over the Thruway sometimes. It brings me back to when I was a kid." He glanced at Cosgrove. "You suspect him? Do you know something I don't know?"

Cosgrove adjusted himself in his seat. He watched the road also, somewhat nervously; he wasn't used to not being the driver. "I'm afraid I've gotten to where I suspect everyone until something proves otherwise. Most likely, there's a simple explanation for why this woman was murdered. Most cases look simple after you figure them out." He chuckled drily. "We got your murder and we got my murder. You figure yours out; you might figure mine out."

"But maybe not?"

"Maybe not. I'm not going to tell you how to investigate your case."

They rode in silence until Green said, "You'd want to know about the marriage, right?"

Cosgrove liked that Green, as laid back as he was, thought about the case, considering the angles, not satisfied with the most obvious answer . . . yet. "Yep. I'd want to get to know this woman whom, my guess is, her husband didn't know very well."

On the drive back to the city, Cosgrove considered that he'd have to leave the investigation of Sandra Dean's murder to the Stamford police. He didn't have a choice. They'd concentrate on the missing bartender, which was what they should do. Interviewing the hotel guests at the crime scene would keep them busy for now, too. Green had asked Cosgrove for a photo of the bartender. Usually, the hotel made a copy of a guest's driver's license. McNulty didn't have one. He didn't drive. Cosgrove asked how he got away from the hotel after the murder. They were looking into that, too.

Green was a competent investigator; you'd expect him to find out what he could about Sandra Dean, her husband, and their relationship. Most women, women doctors to boot, didn't spend their time in hotel rooms under assumed names and didn't go on the lam with a ne'er-do-well bartender. They didn't wind up murdered either. He'd like to do the investigative work he suggested Green do, not so much because he suspected Simon Dean of anything but because he wanted to know more about Sandra Dean and what she was up to. Her murder wasn't his case, so for now he'd rely on Green.

For Cosgrove, in most homicide cases he wanted to know why. The killer might not know himself why he killed, but Cosgrove would know before he was finished. Motive was the first thing he looked for. In some cases, more than one person had motive, like when a boss who mistreated his workers gets whacked, you've got a whole shop full of suspects. So motive was important but you looked for a special kind of motive. You needed more than being angry or being mistreated to murder someone—at least most people did. It took something to do with the murderer himself or herself, a different kind of anger or hatred; not even of degree, it was more like another species of motive—something different about the murderer, something different about the victim, too, and whatever it was that went on between them. At the moment, he didn't have a motive for either Sandra Dean's killing or the first murder, Ted Doyle.

Who knew what grudges the bartender might hold? When a woman was murdered, it wasn't always the victim who brought out the murderous impulse. Often, she was on the receiving end of hatred the killer had developed for girls in middle school who mocked him or a mother who neglected him or didn't protect him from an abusive father. He nurtured this hate until this woman comes along years later and treats this guy with the grudge the wrong way, and wham, something goes off in his head and he stabs her thirty times.

Cosgrove's thoughts drifted on the drive back to the city. The parkway he drove along, a dark ribbon cutting through the countryside that would eventually become the Henry Hudson Parkway and then the West Side Highway, brought weird things to mind. It was the time of year when you notice that the days had gotten shorter, there was a chill in the air, and leaves on the trees along the Parkway had had turned yellow or bronze or red, a form of dying itself.

For whatever reason—the time of year, the dying leaves— he thought about the sick and cruel things people do that you think you can't possibly understand. But then you do understand those people. Because weird and sick things have a cause, too; you find reasons why someone might do such a terrible thing when you look long enough, and the reasons too often had to do with the sick and weird things done to them, almost always in childhood, when they were young and innocent, too. Those killers so monstrous we don't even want to try to understand them almost always have their roots in innocence.

Chapter 9

At some point Ambler must have gone to sleep because he woke up what seemed like minutes later to get Johnny to school and to go to work. It took him a moment to get his bearings and remember Mike's phone call and that Sandra Dean was murdered last night and why he was so confused. Most mornings, he took Johnny to his school on the subway. This morning, he called a car service, calling the driver he often used, an Irish guy he'd known for years through McNulty. The guy whose name was Finnegan said he was in the neighborhood and would be by in ten minutes.

When Ambler went downstairs for the cab, a large manila envelope was leaning against the wall beneath the mailboxes waiting for him. He thought of asking the cab driver about it but decided not to. Finnegan—if he had a first name, Ambler had never heard it—was unusually reticent himself; for the first time in memory, he didn't talk about his pal McNulty and the glories of the old days.

Ambler's day at work was a string of meetings. When he

wasn't at a meeting he was orienting readers to the Manuscript and Archives collection as well as two new readers to the crime fiction collection. When he finally got home, he tucked the envelope McNulty sent him in the back of his desk before he took Lola for her walk. Most of the time, he and Johnny walked the dog together when Johnny got home from school but walking her alone gave him time to think. For this outing, he needed to figure out whether or not to tell Johnny his Uncle McNulty was a suspect in a murder.

Violence had played too large a role in the kid's life already. Johnny should be living in a house in the suburbs where he could take the school bus, ride his bike, and play soccer with his friends. Too much happened too fast in the city. This evening, Ambler walked Lola along Third Avenue among a parade of baby buggies and strollers amid homebound office workers. Lola liked the tykes, especially when they held some food she could lick out of their hands. She'd made friends among the mothers and the nannies, too, so she'd stop every couple of blocks for a mother or a nanny to pat her head. This afternoon, even after a couple of extra blocks, Ambler hadn't come up with a way to tell Johnny his honorary uncle was a murder suspect.

When Johnny got home, he was excited about an after-school soccer program he wanted to join. Ambler said he'd look into it, which meant a conversation with Johnny's grandmother. Not something he looked forward to. He hung around Johnny as he did his homework in the bedroom they shared, hoping for inspiration. Johnny knew something was up. After fifteen minutes of Ambler looking around nervously—first over Johnny's shoulder, then toward the bookcase, and then out the bedroom window at the brick wall of the building next door—Johnny stopped what he was doing to watch him and wait.

"McNulty is in trouble," Ambler said. "It's worse than

before." Johnny listened somberly as Ambler told him pretty much everything he knew.

"He's in a lot of trouble." Johnny spoke in a hushed tone. "Will he get arrested?"

"They have to find him. If they do, they'll arrest him."

"What are you going to do?"

"I don't know yet. I hope we can find something that shows he didn't kill anyone."

"Are you helping him hide out?"

Ambler said no.

"We'll help him get away if we need to, right?"

"I hope it doesn't come to that." What did the parenting manual say on this one?

"I'll help him."

"We'll all help. We'll do everything we can to get him out of this mess."

Johnny stopped asking questions. Ambler would have liked to know what the boy was thinking, but didn't want to ask because he half hoped his grandson would put this in the back of his mind and think about something normal instead.

"Looks like you've got a lot of homework," Ambler said, attempting to change the subject.

"Yeah." Johnny's eyes were big and wide. "Can we get a message to McNulty?"

"No."

"He knows we're on his side, right? Maybe you could send him an email or post something on Facebook, so he knows he can count on us."

"He knows."

When Johnny went to bed, Ambler took out the packet McNulty had sent him that held the pages photocopied from Sandra Dean's journal. Her handwriting was neat, easily readable, pretty to look at, script or cursive, he forgot which was which.

Since the journal wasn't meant to be read by anyone else, she wrote in a kind of shorthand, despite the careful penmanship.

It wasn't as if there were hundreds of entries either. Maybe only a half dozen. On a first reading it wasn't clear what her intention in keeping a journal was. What was clear was that she was writing about assignations with men, strangers she'd met in hotel cocktail lounges. No lurid details, no hint of titillation, most of the late-night liaisons she described were consequences of drinking too much; she regretted them by the time she made her journal entry.

She wrote her recollection of what happened soon after it happened. She didn't always remember everything—there were sometimes blank spots in the evening. In one instance, she was scared when a man wouldn't leave her hotel room when she wanted him to go. He was too drunk. So she left, walking the streets until she felt it was safe to go back and not find him in her room.

It appeared the men she picked up had in common that they were married and older than her. Ambler didn't understand why she did what she did. Neither did she. She was depressed. She wondered if she might be insane. It would be clear to anyone who read her journal entries that she often misjudged the intentions of the men she encountered and put herself in dangerous situations. Yet it was clear also that she either didn't know or didn't care about the danger she described.

She referred to the men by initials, but a note at the end of the entries matched the initials with names. Ambler was sleepy, so it took a moment for him to realize when he came across it that one of the names was Dillard Wainwright. When he did recognize the name, he went back through the pages to see what she'd written about DW and didn't find anything. Had she removed those pages or decided not to write about him after all? It could be she wrote about him elsewhere in the journal, in a section Ambler didn't have. She'd written nothing about her husband either. But McNulty had given him only a few pages of the journal.

The following morning, Ambler made another copy of the journal entries. He called Mike and told him what he had and asked him to meet him at a coffee shop near Johnny's school. When Ambler got there, Mike was in a booth on his second cup of coffee. Ambler handed him the journal pages and told him how he got them. Mike looked over the pages while Ambler got his coffee from the counter.

"There's something to look into here," Mike said when Ambler sat down across from him. "Where's the rest of the journal?"

Ambler said he didn't know.

"You want me to pass this along to the Criminal Investigation guys in Connecticut? They've got a warrant for the bartender."

"I was hoping you'd take it on."

Mike shifted in his seat and took an interest in his coffee cup for a long moment before engaging Ambler again. "McNulty gives you this and disappears again. There was a lot of confusion in that hotel in Connecticut after the shooting. When the cops got there, one of the guests and the hotel security guard had a guy pinned on the floor—a software developer from Minneapolis.

"Lots of people milled around the hallways after the shots were fired. Since McNulty was registered in the room, the investigators concluded he'd left while everyone milled around in the hallway. This makes McNulty a suspect—*the* suspect. A falling out among thieves isn't an unusual thing."

Ambler knew what Mike was getting at. "You think McNulty and the murdered woman were running a scam. She'd take the guy to a hotel room. McNulty would show up when she had him in a compromised position and they'd shake him down. That's what you think happened in the hotel in New York?"

"It's been done."

"Not something McNulty would do. And if the victim is who I think she is, she'd have no reason to try that kind of hustle."

Cosgrove took a sip of coffee and put the cup down. "You know something you've forgotten to tell me?"

Ambler told him about Simon Dean. "His wife is missing and I'm virtually sure she's Shannon Darling. He wouldn't admit it. There are other things that connect her."

Mike held his gaze a long time. "It's nice you've gotten around to telling me. I talked to Mr. Dean yesterday about his wife's murder. How long have you known?"

Ambler started to say something. Mike stopped him. "I know. You needed to check on a couple of things before you passed the information along." Mike sat back in his chair. He had a way of spreading out and taking up more room, becoming more of a presence, when he wanted your attention. "You've given me a half-dozen suspects to keep busy with." He paused significantly. "Did McNulty tell you where he was going?"

"No. You're making this sound like—"

Mike held up his hand. "Like the bartender gave you what you need to set up an alternate version of what happened?"

Ambler felt he'd been tricked. Mike turned what made sense into something that appeared fabricated. Anything Ambler said would make it worse, so he kept quiet.

"It doesn't look good for your pal, Ray. If I had a hypothesis, it would be close to what I said. Maybe not the shakedown, but something like it with the same result. I have to think McNulty or the Dean woman killed Doyle in her hotel room for whatever reason; they then had a falling out and he killed her."

"McNulty says otherwise."

"I imagine he would." Cosgrove rubbed his eyes, a habitual gesture as if to rub the pain of a headache away. "This victim, she's a doctor with a family in the suburbs. Those journal notes say she went for a walk on the wild side and paid the price. Usually it's a man, wife and family in the suburbs, turns up dead in the backroom of a strip club. No reason it can't be a woman who has her dark side, too.

"Let's say the bartender got too attached to her; she did him wrong, stepped out on him, as I gather from what I just read was her wont; he snapped and killed her." Mike held up his hand. "I know you don't like it. For the sake of argument, let's say it's possible. She did her husband wrong, why wouldn't she stray on McNulty?" He held up his hand again to stop whatever Ambler was about to say. "The question I don't have an answer for is why did he or she—or they—kill the man in her hotel room."

Ambler spoke too loudly, letting go his pent-up eagerness to speak, to get things straight. "You could make the argument you just made for McNulty for all of the men in the journal he gave me. You could make an argument for her husband, since he's the man most wronged."

Cosgrove raised his eyebrows. "Oh, was the husband there with them?" He held out his hands palms up in a pacifying gesture. "I'm not ready to take my argument to the bank. I'll do the interviews." He picked up the pages of journal entries. "It won't be pretty. I doubt any of these guys will want to talk about their night in a hotel room with a woman not their wife who's now a murder victim. Lots of 'I'll have to call my lawyer,' or 'Can we talk about this privately, not at my office and not at my home?'" He met Ambler's gaze and held it. "While I'm doing that, suppose you find McNulty for me. Ask him if we can have a chat."

Chapter 10

After his talk with Mike, Ambler dragged himself to work with a lot on his mind. Mike would follow up the list of names he gave him because he said he would. He might think McNulty was guilty. He certainly considered him a suspect. But Ambler knew Mike well enough to know he'd keep an open mind. He'd take seriously any ideas Ambler presented to him. The problem was Ambler didn't have a lot to give him. The list of names. A shot in the dark.

Ambler usually kept an open mind himself, something harder to do this time because McNulty was involved. He'd believe the bartender innocent, even though he didn't have anything concrete to prove he was. The good thing so far was nothing had proved him guilty.

"Well, what's going on?" Adele had stopped by the crime fiction reading room to find Ambler staring at a Swann auction catalog; he'd been on the same page for ten minutes. They hadn't spoken since he'd called her two nights before to tell her of the murder. Yesterday had been hectic at work and he hadn't

seen her. She'd called last night. It was late and he didn't have
the energy to call her back.

She watched him for a moment. "You didn't call me back
last night."

He almost always returned Adele's calls and wasn't sure
why he hadn't this time. "Too much is happening too fast. And
in another way, nothing's changed at all. I have the photocopy
of part of the journal McNulty tried to give me the other day."

Adele looked confused. "How?"

"It was in the lobby of my building the morning after Sandra Dean's murder."

"How could that be?"

"My guess is a cab driver named Finnegan dropped it off.
How that worked, how McNulty got the envelope to him, I
have no idea. Finnegan's an old IRA guy. He wouldn't tell me
he saw McNulty if I tortured him. I gave a copy to Mike."

Adele spoke sharply, surprising him. "Why would you do
that? McNulty wanted you to find those men."

"Mike can do a better job. He may not be as sure as we
are that McNulty's innocent, but he's not convinced the other
way yet."

Adele looked at him curiously. "Are you sure you're convinced McNulty is innocent?" Her tone wasn't critical. But Ambler felt criticized anyway.

She was right to question him, Convinced wasn't the right
word. He believed in McNulty. That was different. He couldn't
say for sure circumstances might not arise that could drive anyone to murder. He wanted to say he knew no such circumstances
existed for McNulty. If he tried to, Adele would see through
him to the truth, so he met her accusing gaze and didn't answer
her question. Instead, he told her Simon Dean had positively
identified his wife's body the morning after the murder.

He handed Adele the journal pages rather than tell her
what was in them. After she skimmed through them for a few

minutes, she said, "That poor woman. Imagine how it must feel when you realize you've gotten involved in something you didn't mean to get involved in and don't know how to get out of. And those men . . . they didn't care about her. I bet they only pretended they did."

"I don't think I understand. She sought out—"

"That's right! You don't understand." Adele's outburst was like a sob. She buried her face in her hands. When she raised her head, her eyes had reddened. "It's so hard to explain and so hard for you to understand, it might not be worth the effort." Her tone softened. "Women—at least most women, most of the time—want something different from an encounter than most men, most of the time, want. Shannon needed something, comfort, understanding, caring; I don't know exactly what. She was vulnerable and trusting. But she was pretty, too, alluring. Vulnerability in a woman is erotic, seductive. . . ." Adele shook her head and lowered her eyes. "I don't want to try to explain anymore. It's too difficult."

Ambler had missed something; he hadn't gotten out of those journal entries what he should have; he didn't understand Shannon after all. But he didn't know what he missed. And he didn't understand what Adele was getting at either. "Shannon was attractive. It was easy for her to pick up men. Some women like to have sexual adventures. Yet Shannon was angry at herself for her adventures. So why did she have them?"

There was an edge to Adele's tone. "I'm sure you don't mean what you say the way it sounds. You're blaming her again."

"I am?"

"Men believe they're superior to women. Some men cover it better than others. But it's built into our culture." Adele's eyebrows went up, just the tiniest flicker. Did she mean him? "It's built into women, too, so we can get taken advantage of. It might be Shannon was easily taken advantage of."

Ambler didn't follow Adele's thinking but decided not to

tell her. He'd believed pretty women had an advantage with men because they had so many men desiring them; they could take their pick. Now Adele was saying something different, so he'd need to think about that. Part of figuring out who killed Shannon—or Sandra Dean—was determining what there was about the connection between her and her killer that led to her murder. This meant finding out as much as you could about her, as well as finding out about the people in her life—a lot of men, including McNulty.

Adele had meanwhile moved on. She stood and waved the pages of Sandra Dean's journal at him. "You can't for a moment think McNulty murdered her. But you do, don't you? You think it's possible."

Ambler took refuge in one of his Sherlock Holmes maxims. "What I think doesn't change anything. 'Data! Data! Data! I can't make bricks without clay.'"

Adele paced the marble floor of the crime fiction reading room waving the journal pages. "The men in this journal, one of them killed her. That's why McNulty gave the list to you, right?" There wasn't much floor space in the small reading room, so Adele would walk five or six steps one way toward a wall of books and then five or six steps back the other way to another wall of books on the other side of the room. She wore a dark blue dress that hugged her body and brown boots that reached almost to her knees.

Ambler watched the hem of her skirt play against the white skin of her knees above the boots for a moment before he said, "One man listed in Shannon's—we should call her Sandra—journal is Dillard Wainwright. He's the man Sandra's mother abandoned Sandra for. It's surprising her mother's ex-husband would be among the men she wrote about in the journal. Beyond that, there are notes on all of the men in her journal except him. I wish McNulty had given me the whole journal."

Ambler's desk phone rang. He answered, said yes, and after

a moment's hesitation turned to Adele. "Simon Dean is on his way up."

"Oh my God!" Adele began brushing at her dress with her hands and then brushing back her hair. She walked back and forth faster, shooting glances at Ambler that implied he'd done something unforgivable. "Why on earth is he here?"

Dean appeared in the doorway, standing for a moment looking dazed; his face was deadly white except for his bloodshot eyes.

"Come in," Ambler said. "Sit down, please. I'm so sorry about the loss of your wife." His words sounded empty and he felt extremely uncomfortable.

"I'm so sorry," Adele said, holding out her hand. "I knew your wife only slightly. She—"

Dean ignored Adele's hand. Ambler didn't know if, still in shock, he didn't notice her gesture or it was meant as a slight. She pulled back her hand.

"You." He trained his glittering eyes on Ambler. "Have you told the police what you told me about the man, the bartender, who was with her? Did you tell them she'd been abducted?"

Ambler came around the library table and pulled out a chair. "Please sit down."

Dean sat as if compelled, like a man in custody might follow an order from the cop who'd arrested him. Dean looked at Adele as if he saw her for the first time but spoke to Ambler. "Sandra was as sensitive as a child. Why was she with a man like that?" His tone grew harsh. "She wouldn't be. He abducted her. And killed her."

"I'm sorry," Ambler said. "I can't imagine the depth of your loss. I wish—"

The expression in Dean's eyes was ghastly, burning out of his face, filled with rage and pain. "You know the man who killed her. I didn't think to tell the police about you. I was in shock. I couldn't believe Sandra was dead. Dead in a seedy hotel room." He turned to Adele. "There'd been another murder at another hotel a few days ago. She'd been—" He turned back to Ambler. "You've got to go to the police."

Ambler spoke softly. "I've told the police everything I know."

"That bartender. Your friend. You told me he was with Sandra. You knew."

"The police know he was with her." Ambler didn't want to argue with a distraught man.

Dean glared at Ambler and then at Adele, daring a response. "I'm not stupid." Spittle flew from his mouth as he talked. "Do the police know you were trying to find that bartender and my wife?" He laughed, a mocking, choked sound. "You didn't tell them, did you? You tried to find the bartender because you knew something dreadful would happen if you didn't. You wanted to find him before it was too late. You knew he'd kill her if you didn't find them." Dean's body went rigid, his eyes for the moment clear, pain and bewilderment replaced by accusation. "Why didn't you tell me she was in danger? Why didn't you tell me the truth?"

Adele approached the man. "You're under terrible pressure." Her tone was gentle. "After such a loss, it's—"

He turned on her and snarled. "I don't want your sympathy. I want my wife's murderer. No excuses. No apologies."

Ambler moved carefully. He'd let the man berate him. He'd do that until—Ambler's cell phone rang. He answered hoping the interruption might slow things down, give Dean time to collect himself. The voice at the other end startled him. For a second, he couldn't place it, before he realized it was Jayne Galloway.

"I need to talk to you," she said. "Can you come here to Long Island now?"

"I'm so sorry for your loss," he said. She had to have learned of her daughter's death and he was sure this was the reason for the call. Yet speaking with her was awkward. The last time he'd spoken to her she'd denied recognizing a photo of her daughter. He didn't want to go into that with Simon listening, so he said, "I'm here with her husband at the moment. I'm—"

A gasp. "Oh. . . . I don't want to intrude. I'm sorry. I'll call back."

Dean's expression was one of disgust. "Her mother? Why would she call you?"

"I don't know. She didn't want to interrupt us. I told you I'd spoken with her before I spoke with you a few days ago."

In a moment, the rigidness left Dean's body; he moved backward a couple of steps to sit down in the chair he'd been sitting in a few minutes before and pressed his hand against his forehead. "What can I tell Carolyn? She's with my sister. I can't bring myself to go get her."

Ambler thought to put his hand on Dean's shoulder. It seemed like what you'd do, the physical human contact a grieving person needs. Yet, something forbidding, some coldness, stopped him as he moved toward the man. He felt Dean didn't like him, didn't want him to come near, so he stopped midstride. "You'll find a way," he said.

Agony distorted Dean's face; no longer anger in his expression but fear.

"You might wait a day or so," Adele said softly. "See a doctor now, get a sedative. You've endured more than anyone should have to."

Dean sat in silence for a few moments. "I keep thinking that person couldn't be my wife. The woman the police told me about can't be Sandra. There's a mistake." He glared at Ambler. "I don't know what I'm going to do." He stood uncertainly. "A doctor is right. I'll call the doctor. I'll go home." He shuffled toward the door and stopped in the threshold. "Strange isn't it? I'll call a doctor. Sandra was a doctor. . . . And something else, a slut . . . a whore." His face took on a grotesque expression.

When he was gone, Adele collapsed into the chair in front

of her; Ambler sat down in his own chair. Each watched the space Simon Dean had vacated.

Adele broke the silence. "That was awful. I don't think I could stand being him."

Ambler felt a wave of weariness, despair. "Mr. Dean is convinced McNulty killed his wife and that arresting McNulty and punishing him or better yet the police shooting the poor bastard will make everything better. It won't."

"Of course, he thinks McNulty killed her. He's overcome with grief, so he's not thinking straight." Adele stood and glared at Ambler. "What's your excuse?" She stomped out.

Chapter 11

After Mike Cosgrove read over the pages from the murdered woman's journal a couple of times, he talked to the captain about his case. He'd sent the pages to the Stamford detectives and kept a copy for himself. He hoped they might have picked up the journal itself in the victim's hotel room. But they didn't have it.

The captain's thinking was for Mike to give what evidence he had to the detectives in Stamford who were investigating Sandra Dean's murder. If they brought in their suspect, the bartender, and that solved the Stamford case, it would likely solve Cosgrove's case as well.

With some effort, Cosgrove persuaded the captain it was worth the time to interview the men named in the murdered woman's journal, arguing that despite everything pointing to McNulty as the killer, the evidence wasn't conclusive. The captain was skeptical, as brass in the NYPD tended to be, but he trusted Cosgrove's hunches, so he said okay.

Cosgrove started his rounds with the first name that came up in the journal. Arthur Manning, referred to in the journal by his initials A. M., was an executive at one of city's few remaining publishing companies. The company headquarters was on Sixth Avenue in one of the Rockefeller Center Buildings. A. M. didn't keep Cosgrove waiting, having him ushered into his corner office on the building's top floor as soon as he arrived. The man, polite, cautious, and nervous, waited for Cosgrove to begin the conversation. What Cosgrove knew about the man was he'd been divorced twice and had no police record.

"I'm going to ask you some questions about something you'd probably rather not talk about," Cosgrove said as he settled into a leather chair with his back to a window; another window was behind Manning.

"Do I need a lawyer?"

"You'd know better than I would," Cosgrove said. "I don't know what you've been up to." It was a joke, but also not. He didn't know what the guy had been up to. You never knew what you might stumble across.

"What are you going to ask me about?"

"Your name came up in the journal of a woman who was murdered."

The man froze. No part of his body moved, not even his eyes, and the expression in them went vacant. He sat like that for a moment and then began to move—or appeared to move though he didn't go anywhere. It was like watching his brain work through his eyes. "Go on."

"You'd have known her by the name Shannon Darling."

"I don't recognize the name."

"The woman's journal didn't have dates, so I don't know how long ago it was." Cosgrove believed the man did remember her name; he denied knowing it hoping to find out what Cosgrove knew, hoping to not admit to anything unnecessarily. Reasonable enough. "You met her in a hotel bar . . . and went to her room with her."

The man shifted in his chair uncomfortably, his gaze traveling around the office as if he were a stranger in the place until it rested on Cosgrove where it seemed to ask for sympathy.

"What happened in the hotel room is now known only to you. In her journal, this woman described a conversation you had. Her thoughts and feelings were regret for what happened and anger at herself. She didn't blame you." Cosgrove tried to reflect sympathy when he met A. M.'s gaze. It probably didn't work because he didn't feel any sympathy.

"Nothing happened in the hotel room."

Cosgrove nodded. "So you do remember being there."

A look of crushing disappointment crossed the man's face.

Cosgrove nodded a couple of times more and waited longer than usual before he spoke. "I'd like you to tell me what went on between you and her—conversationally, I don't care about the gymnastics. There's no evidence you murdered her. If you did kill her, you should call your lawyer."

Manning spoke so softly Cosgrove could barely hear him. "This encounter happened a year or so ago, maybe longer. I never saw her again. When it was over . . . when I was leaving, I actually thought *she* might kill *me*."

"Did she threaten to kill you?"

The question slowed him down. He answered carefully. "No. She acted strangely. She was angry. I didn't know what she'd say or do next." He took a moment, looking past Cosgrove to the window behind him. "I'd had dinner with an author staying at the hotel. After he went to his room, I had a drink at the bar before I left for home." He leaned back in his chair more relaxed now that he'd decided to talk openly.

Cosgrove relaxed back into his chair himself. Truth, so much harder to come by, was easier once you got to it.

"She was charming, refreshing in a way, different than the sophisticated, worldly women I'm used to meeting. She was an innocent. She told me she was afraid of the city and didn't usually come here by herself. She drank scotch on the rocks but said she didn't usually drink. Earlier in the evening, she said, she'd been propositioned by two men. She was shocked that this could happen in a fashionable hotel.

"I spoke with her without expectation. She was charming, pretty. I liked the sound of her voice. In a way—as I said, she seemed innocent—in a way, she was girlish. She said something. I wasn't quite sure what she'd said, so I asked her if she was married. She said she was but she thought her husband was gay.

"This was part of her charm. She blurted things out. And I found that intriguing, the way she told me intimate things about herself. I was attracted to the sound of her voice. She brought up sex a couple of times. I thought this meant she wanted to have sex with me. It was around one. The bar was closing. She asked if I wanted to come to her room for a drink.

"Here she was inviting me to her room like there was nothing to it, like she was inviting me for a cup of tea.

"It's not unusual for women to flirt with me." He waved an arm about. "I'm in publishing. Some women with books they want to get published, they're flirtatious, seductive. But they require courting. It's a ritual. They don't want to appear easy. They don't jump off a barstool after sharing a drink and invite me to their room.

"Yet she was demure, ladylike, not vampish at all. As I said, I thought her innocent. I felt she really liked me, trusted me. I felt a special connection to her." He met Cosgrove's gaze. "We talked easily. She was smart and unusually honest. She read. She knew books. I thought she might be a writer. She told me her mother was a writer, but wouldn't tell me her mother's name.

"When we got to her room, she cried. For what seemed like hours, I held her and she cried and talked, mostly about what was wrong with her, things that happened when she was young. She didn't tell me the particulars. I got the idea that she'd been raped when she was quite young—and almost murdered—in a situation similar to the situation she was in with me, except there were two men.

"I put my arms around her, at first to hold her when she cried. I thought the embrace would turn into something more passionate. When I kissed her, it was gentle. I thought her so vulnerable. She pulled away and began talking again. She was like what we used to call a speed freak. I tried to coax her into bed. She'd lost interest in sex, if this had ever been her interest. All she wanted to do was talk about her mother and her husband. There was a couch in her room and we sat on it talking . . . or her talking, me listening. We stood. I put my arms around her and tried to kiss her again, tried to move her toward the bed.

"When I did this, she stiffened. She became formal, businesslike, as if we'd had a business meeting and it was time to shake hands and say good evening, as if there'd never been anything sexual or romantic between us at all. She said goodnight, pushed me toward the door, wished me well. I felt like a fool. I reminded her she'd brought me to her room to be romantic. I thought I was being reasonable, but she got scared. I mean really scared. I thought she was becoming hysterical, that she'd run down the hall screaming or pull out a knife and stab me. I didn't know what she'd do, so I left—quickly."

It wasn't often that when someone finished telling him his story Cosgrove didn't have questions. He might want to follow up on discrepancies he caught, or poke around the edges of a description that seemed too pat. Or try to get the guy to repeat parts of the story to see if he might tell it differently the second time. This time, he didn't have questions. At a certain point, Cosgrove reminded himself, you're told more than you can absorb.

"She turned you down. Built you up and didn't come through. Prick teaser we used to call them. It would piss most men off. Some men wouldn't take it."

Manning caught his drift. "I was angry. I felt foolish. It was late, probably three or four in the morning. All I wanted to do by then was go to sleep. I grabbed a cab and went to my apartment."

"You didn't think about her after that, want to find her again, finish what you started, make her follow through on what she promised?"

"I'm not like that." He glared at Cosgrove for a moment and then turned to look out the window behind him. "I'm sorry she's dead, that she was murdered. How did it happen?"

"She died in a hotel room."

He nodded. "In circumstances like those I described?"

"Something like that."

"Strange. I thought with me it might have been a one-time thing for her, that inviting me to her hotel room was an aberration. It was foolish to think so. I wanted our coming together to have been something unique."

"Then you did think about her."

"I might have. I'm thinking about her now, remembering her."

Cosgrove stood. "You didn't see her again, try to find her?"

Manning stood also but didn't come from behind his desk. "I didn't know how to find her. I gave her my card before I left. I guess I did want to see her again. She was a remarkable woman. It might be she revealed too much of herself, so she was more vulnerable than it was safe for a person to be. Still, because of that she had a kind of beauty that tugged at your heart. I'm sad thinking about her."

Chapter 12

Ambler wasn't pleased with the questions from the clean-shaven, crew-cut, jock-like detective from the Stamford Police Department Bureau of Criminal Investigations who was questioning him in the crime fiction reading room. Men who looked and carried themselves like his interrogator had rubbed him the wrong way since he was in college. He preferred guys with unruly hair and dumpy physiques who muddled through life to the muscular, smooth-shaven, decisive men who greeted each new day as a challenge and believed they always gave 110 percent.

"He's a friend of yours, right? Did you ever travel together? Go fishing? Hunting? Skiing?"

"I don't do any of those things. Neither does McNulty. He goes to baseball games and the track."

The detective frowned. "Mutual friends? People you know he might contact?"

"No. There are many facets of his life I know nothing about."

"Are you aware of problems he had with women . . . assaults, complaints against him?"

"None that I know of. Women seem to like him."

"He was divorced."

"There's that. Maybe you should talk to his ex-wife."

The detective's mouth went square. "I know who I should talk to. Right now, I'm talking to you."

"I've answered your questions," Ambler said mildly.

"Holding back information in a homicide case is serious. I've heard some questionable things about you." This cop, whose name was Bill Smith, was as bland as his name. Nothing about him hinted he would ever be unpredictable. An impression he fortified by saying, "I don't know what you're used to in dealing with the police. In our department we go by the book. And the book doesn't like fraternizing—or information sharing—with private citizens. If you think you know better how this case should go, you better think again."

Ambler caught the guy's drift. "McNulty was with the woman who was murdered. He's missing. That makes him a person of interest. Do you have forensic evidence that makes him more than that?"

"That's the kind of information we don't share with private citizens."

"Right," said Ambler, smiling. "You said that."

Detective Smith looked puzzled.

"Anything else?"

Smith's expression hardened. "A woman is dead. We don't need smart-assed comments about a murder. We're going to bring in her killer. Make fun of me if you want, but don't get in my way." He held Ambler in a hard stare until Ambler had enough. He purposefully broke eye contact and turned to his computer.

Smith stood and gestured at the book-lined walls around him. "All these books, they're detective novels?" He seemed partly in awe and partly angry at them. "You read all these books . . . these writers? You think they know what it's like being a cop, investigating a homicide?" He looked at Ambler with something like sincerity. "They don't know."

"Have you read any of them?"

Detective Smith looked puzzled again. "I seen the TV shows. They get it wrong."

"A lot of the books are better."

This struck a chord. "Which ones?"

"You might try *The Onion Field*. A cop wrote it."

When the detective left, Ambler realized their parting conversation was similar to one he'd had years before with Mike Cosgrove after they'd butted heads over one of Mike's investigations. Things probably wouldn't turn out as well with Detective Smith. For now, Ambler was mad at himself for looking away from the cop's stare. It's what you do when you're not confident of the stance you're taking.

That evening after work, he took Adele to dinner to make up for making her mad the day before. They shared a bottle of wine and a plate of charcuterie at a wine bar on Ninth Avenue in her neighborhood. Without talking about it, they'd avoided the Library Tavern since McNulty's departure. Adele seemed to have forgiven him, though the formality was still there.

"I've been advised to stay away from the search for Sandra Dean's killer. As if I knew how to go about it anyway." Ambler told her about his visit from the Stamford investigator, Bill Smith.

"Well, too bad. I'm on the list of people advising you to clear McNulty." She picked up steam. "How could you not help him after all he's done for you? I can't believe you, Raymond. What's wrong with you?"

He couldn't help smiling, even though he knew it would make her angrier. "Hold it." He held up both hands as a shield. "I didn't say I wouldn't. I don't know where to start."

Adele sipped her wine. She wore a brown leather jacket over a white blouse that was open an extra button at the top, so he watched the graceful slope of her neck and the place where the blouse gaped against her chest at the curve of her breast. "You look pretty," he said.

Her eyelashes fluttered and her cheeks turned pink. She reached for the neck of her blouse and pulled the two parts together. The blouse gaped open again as soon as she let go. After a little embarrassed laugh, she said, "You always—" She didn't finish. He thought her even more fetching when she blushed.

After a moment, she asked, "Do you think we could find McNulty? Maybe you could call him."

"He most likely got rid of his cell phone because the police could trace him through it."

"If they knew the number."

"They'd get the number."

"I guess." Adele pouted for a moment.

"His dad might know. But Kevin McNulty wouldn't tell where his son was if they hung him by his thumbs."

Adele often locked her eyes on his when they talked; she did now and practically hypnotized him. "Wouldn't he tell you?"

Ambler had come to believe McNulty didn't have anything to tell him. He'd have to figure things out for himself and he wasn't doing a very good job at it. "There's something fundamental I've overlooked in why Sandra Dean was murdered."

"You sound like she got herself murdered on purpose."

Ambler shook his head. "People are murdered for a reason. Someone benefits from her death. Did her husband take out a life insurance policy on her? Might she have discovered something so devastating about someone that someone needed to kill her to keep her from revealing it? Did she do something in the past that caused someone to hate her enough to kill her?"

Adele sat bolt upright. "One of the women whose husband

Shannon—I mean Sandra—was with might have hated her. The woman would hate her husband, too." Adele's eyes widened. "She followed them that night to the hotel in New York. She found them together in Shannon's hotel room and shot him. Sandra Dean hid or got away somehow. Maybe the wife just let her go and then panicked and ran away. The killer stewed over the whole episode. Maybe she felt remorse. She blamed Shannon, I mean Sandra. She got angry and tracked Sandra down and shot her."

Ambler listened with mild interest. "And McNulty?"

"Why would she shoot McNulty?"

"He was a witness."

Adele took a moment to consider this. "The wife didn't care if he was a witness. She's not evil. She wouldn't kill an innocent man. She only killed those who wronged her."

"So why did McNulty disappear?"

Adele thought about that. "He understood why this woman did what she did, so he couldn't turn her in. You know how he is. He won't turn someone over to the police. He disappeared so he wouldn't have to rat on the killer wife."

Ambler's eyebrows shot up. "Rat on her?"

"That's what he would say. That's what McNulty would say."

"That is what McNulty would say." Ambler looked at the empty wine bottle, a generic Burgundy that had tasted pretty good, and thought about ordering another bottle. Adele's eyes sparkled after the two glasses she'd drunk. With two more, who knows what might happen? They might walk to her apartment holding hands; they might kiss in her doorway . . . and then kiss again. She might invite him in.

"Raymond! What's that stupid grin about? . . . Were you listening to what I just said?"

Ambler caught himself. No more wine. "It's also possible the man murdered in Dr. Dean's hotel room had the double-indemnity insurance policy, his widow the beneficiary. Mike talked with the widow. If there was something there, he would have caught it. Still, if McNulty wasn't such an easy fall guy, you could wonder if the widow hired a killer."

"But why in Shannon's—I keep thinking of her as Shannon. Sandra Dean is a different person that Shannon became when she was murdered." Adele's expression changed; the glow— her rosy cheeks, sparkling eyes—gone, sadness in its place. "I should use her real name."

Ambler's mood changed, too. His daydream burst. "Up until now, we've thought of Ted Doyle's death in relation to Sandra Dean. His murder might have had nothing to do with her. The man might have been murdered for reasons all his own. Later, Sandra was killed because *she* was a witness."

Adele frowned. "You're right that speculation doesn't get you very far. We need data, information . . . whatever it is Sherlock Holmes wanted to make bricks out of."

"Clay. Holmes said, 'I can't make bricks without clay.'"

Adele put on her coat and wrapped her scarf around her neck with a kind of flourish. "Why did Jayne Galloway call you yesterday?"

Ambler watched her intently. Even putting on her coat and scarf, she was entertaining. "I don't know. I haven't been able to reach her. I can't reach Dillard Wainwright either. They don't call me back."

"Maybe they've made up and run off together again," Adele said. "Maybe they got together and killed Sandra Dean. Maybe Sandra Dean's husband killed her and was faking all that grief. Maybe . . ." Adele's voice cracked.

Ambler tried to sound upbeat, as cheery as he could get. "Do you want me to walk you home?"

Adele frowned. "Why would you do that?"

Ambler felt his cheeks redden. "No reason."

"Is Johnny at his grandmother's?"

Ambler nodded.

"Poor Raymond." She patted his shoulder as she squeezed by. "All alone."

"I've got the dog."

She laughed and then lowered her head to make his gaze meet hers. "Am I missing something? Are you okay? Is there something—"

He shook his head.

Chapter 13

Later that evening, Adele was mindlessly watching the TV news, which she did rarely, thinking about Raymond and why she didn't let him walk her home, knowing she embarrassed him by turning down his offer. She was angry at him in some vague way that came from her sadness over Sandra Dean's death. Restless and at odds with herself, she was too tired to do anything and too jittery to go to bed when her phone rang. She didn't recognize the number or the 203 area code and considered letting the call go to voice mail but changed her mind before the phone stopped ringing. She answered without speaking, expecting a tape recording offering her a free resort stay. Instead she heard a familiar voice, gasped, and almost dropped the phone. "Brian, is that you? Where are you?"

"I'm using a cell phone I borrowed from a stranger. Hang onto the number. I owe him and will pay him back someday . . . if I can. I can't talk for more than a few seconds. I need a gigantic favor. Someday, I'll have to pay you back, too, once more assuming I'll be in a position to do so."

"You know I'll help."

"You'd think by my age I'd have more than one friend I can trust. But there you go." McNulty told her what he wanted her to do, which under normal circumstances would be a lot to ask. Under current conditions—the possibility of arrest for harboring a fugitive, for example—no one in their right mind would agree to what he asked. Except because it was McNulty—who'd once harbored her when she was something of a fugitive herself—of course she'd do it.

The first part of the plan went more smoothly than she had a right to hope for. She waited until after 11:00 when the night doorman at McNulty's building, a longtime pal of McNulty's, would come on duty. McNulty had already called him to tell him his part in the plan, so the doorman buzzed her in when she rang the bell in the outer lobby, showed her to McNulty's apartment, which was on the first floor, and unlocked the door for her.

McNulty had told her there would be a stack of clean laundry and dry cleaning in the hallway. The day doorman put it there each week when it was delivered. And there it was. McNulty told her there would be two suitcases in the hall closet, which there were. And he told her she'd find a couple of envelopes taped to the wall behind the books on the top shelf of his bookcase in the living room–dining room. And there they were.

The envelopes contained what looked like a great deal of cash, mostly in twenty dollar bills. She put the cash and the clothes in the suitcase and carried it to her apartment. The next morning, carrying the suitcase, she took a train to New Haven, Connecticut. She thought she should call Raymond but McNulty had told her not to, so she didn't.

The waiting room in the New Haven railroad station, a Beaux-Arts building like the 42nd Street Library, was a relic of the golden age of railroads—cavernous, ornate, tile floors, limestone walls, chandeliers, and rounded, curved, dark wooden benches like the ones in the Grand Central Terminal waiting room when she was a kid.

She assumed—correctly, it turned out—that McNulty would find her when the time was right, so she took a seat on one of the benches where she could watch the hustle and bustle of folks coming and going from the trains. She worried again about not calling Raymond—she hadn't told him about the call from McNulty or the adventure she was undertaking because McNulty told her Raymond's phone was probably tapped. This was why McNulty called her instead of Raymond.

She didn't pay any attention to the woman who sat down beside her, except to note her resemblance to Mrs. Doubtfire. After a moment, the woman spoke to her. "We're going to sit here for quite a while," the woman said, and Adele realized it was McNulty. "In about an hour—moments before my train is to leave— I'll pick up the suitcases. Everything's in the suitcases, right?"

"Yes." She turned to face him, barely able to contain herself. "Are you—"

"You have to stay calm. You're playing a part. I realize you lack training as an actor, but give it a try." He spoke quietly and was as calm as he usually was. "For a moment, sit quietly and remember the last conversation you had with a stranger, on a plane, in an airport, something like that. Put yourself in that memory. Recall the situation with your senses. You don't have to remember the exact words you used, but the tone, how often you looked at each other, silences, topics you touched on: her grandchildren? where you call home?"

"What is all this?"

"It's an acting lesson."

"Jesus, McNulty . . ."

"It's ma'am. Get with the program."

Adele did what she was told. She hadn't traveled often. When she did, she liked to find out about people. Sometimes they turned out to be boring but often she'd been surprised by how much people told you about themselves and how interesting they were.

"You're going to New York for the weekend?" McNulty asked amiably. "Are you married, dear?"

"No . . ." Adele stammered. She didn't have to act taken aback by the question.

"Such a lovely girl, too. . . ."

They talked like that with Adele imagining herself in an airplane seat talking with a stranger. After a few minutes, she felt comfortable with it, as if this were actually happening, the person next to her was a woman she'd never seen before who happened to sit down next to her. As time passed, she worried she might end up spending all this time talking like this and not find out anything she could report back.

"What should I tell Raymond?" she whispered.

"Is that your young man?" McNulty stayed in character.

"He's not so young." Adele didn't know if she was in character or not.

"Well, dear, ask him what his intentions are. How serious is he? Marriage or not?" When her matronly partner turned to her, she saw the old McNulty twinkle in his eyes. "You're not getting any younger, you know."

Adele blushed and opened her mouth to complain.

McNulty shook his head. "I'm going to stand up in a minute. When I do, you stand up, too. We're no longer strangers. Everyone who first saw me sit down next to you is gone by now. I'm your sainted aunt about to leave. You were waiting with me. You'll hug me good-bye. If you could get some tears in your eyes as I walk away, that would be good—but probably too much to expect from an amateur. You have time for one or two quick questions."

"Is there a way Raymond can get in touch with you?"

"I'll get in touch with him. In a dire emergency, Pop. I know it's a lot to ask of Ray, looking into this. It's my problem. He doesn't have—"

Adele was disappointed McNulty thought only Raymond

was helping him but kept this to herself. "We're going to find out what happened. We know you couldn't have . . ." her voice trailed off. "Do you know anything that could help us—him—find Sandra Dean's killer? You know Shannon is Sandra Dean, right?"

McNulty nodded. "I know she's Sandra Dean. I don't know who killed her. I'd like to say I do. But I might be wrong and can't risk that now." He met her gaze. "The first time, Sandi knew who the guy was who was killed. She also knew the killer." He bent for the suitcases; when he looked up at Adele the pain in his eyes, those deep pools of sadness, brought tears to her eyes. "She said it wasn't what I thought it was, wasn't what it looked like, with the guy who was killed."

"Why did she talk in riddles? Why didn't she tell you what she was doing, what was going on? You went away with her; you took care of her. Why wouldn't she tell you? A man was murdered, for God's sake."

"She was scrambling. She had to figure out how to go home to her daughter and her husband. If I knew, I might screw it up. She couldn't risk that. Sandi was complicated. She had more going on than she could handle and foolishly thought she had to handle it herself. I think she did love me. That was complicated, too. She loved her daughter and her daughter was with her husband."

"You called her Sandi. Did you know her real name all along? Are you telling me everything?"

McNulty's expression was otherworldly. "The last thing I said to her, the last thing, 'It would be better if you told me everything.' She almost did."

Chapter 14

Ambler listened with interest late that afternoon as Adele told him about her visit with McNulty. "He thought your phone would be tapped and you'd be followed, that's why he called me."

"You have quite a talent for espionage."

"It wasn't hard. McNulty arranged everything. He even had his laundry washed, folded, and delivered. Who does that? And he had all that money hidden in his apartment in cash."

When Adele went back to her desk for what was left of the day, Ambler thought over what she'd told him and kept coming back to the same thought. Sandra knew the man murdered in her hotel room and she knew the murderer. She was up to her neck in something and wouldn't tell McNulty what it was. And she planned to return to her husband. It all meant something. But what? He should tell Mike what Adele told him but if he did, Mike would know she'd been in touch with McNulty, so he couldn't.

Ambler had been trying to reach Dillard Wainwright for a couple of days now with no luck, and he hadn't reached Jayne

Galloway either after her strange call the day Simon Dean came to the library, the day after her daughter was murdered. He'd already taken tomorrow off for Sandra Dean's funeral and thought he might drive out to Long Island afterward to talk to Jayne Galloway.

Near the end of the day, after another failed attempt to reach Wainwright, he called the English department office at Pine Grove College. The administrative person who answered the phone gasped when he told her he was trying to reach Dillard Wainwright. After a stunned silence, she asked him to hold on. In a few minutes, a cultivated woman's voice with a faint British accent asked to whom she was speaking. He told her.

"Amelia Hamilton here. I'm the chair of the English department." She paused for longer than seemed ordinary. "Might I ask why you are inquiring about Professor Wainwright?"

"That's not so easy to answer," Ambler said. "I'd rather tell him."

"This is awkward." Professor Hamilton's voice wavered. "I'm not sure what to say. That is . . . I'm not sure what I can say."

"If you don't want to tell me how to contact him, I'll give you my number. You can ask him—"

"That's not it, not it at all. I can't put you in contact with him. . . . I can't give him your number. Or I could but I can't. . . . Oh dear . . . I'm afraid we don't know where he is."

"I see," said Ambler. "He's no longer with the college—"

"I'm afraid it's not that either. . . . I think I must put you in touch with the police. You see, he's gone missing."

Ambler called the number she gave him and spoke with a captain, the head of the detective bureau, who told him he'd passed the case along to the state police missing persons bureau. Ambler asked if he could tell him anything about the disappearance.

"Not really," the captain said. "We talked to his neighbors and a bunch of professors at the college. No one knew anything about him. Some of the professors didn't know he was gone."

Wainwright was reported missing by some students when he didn't show up for his classes for a week straight, one of the classes, oddly enough, a seminar on Edgar Allan Poe and dark romanticism. After another week went by, Professor Hamilton went to Wainwright's small house within walking distance of the college and found mail and newspapers piled up on the porch around his front door. She talked things over with the dean and the college vice president, and was told to contact the police.

Ambler doubted he'd find out much more from the state police, and he was right. He was referred to the public information office, which gave him the information he might have read in a newspaper if there'd been anything in the newspapers about Wainwright's disappearance.

"He might as well have disappeared into thin air for all I found out," Ambler told Adele after work when they had dinner at Szechuan Gourmet near the library. Her visit with McNulty, despite not providing any helpful information, had cheered her up.

"This Wainwright person upped and disappeared?" Adele deftly pushed rice from a small bowl into her mouth with her chopsticks.

"People disappear. But not from a tenured teaching position."

They ate in silence until she asked, "Why do we care about him? I don't get what he has to do with Sandra's murder."

"Maybe nothing. Maybe he killed her."

Adele stopped eating and stared at him. "Why would he?"

"No reason I know of. Sandra Dean was reading the letters he wrote to her mother when she was in the library. I wanted to ask him if he knew why. Now, I want to know why he's disappeared.

"There's an outside chance he'd be at Sandra Dean's wake. I'm also hoping to see Jayne Galloway there. If I don't, I'm going

to her home in Long Island. I expect she'll tell me more this
time than last time. Perhaps she knows why her daughter was
so interested in those letters, after all."

"Are you sure you want to go to that viewing? I'd think
you wouldn't want to run across Simon Dean again. He thinks
you're McNulty's accomplice."

"He was upset."

Adele waved her chopsticks like a sword. "He was enraged."

"We'll see."

"I should go with you."

"What would that do?"

"I'd protect you."

"I'm also going to drive out to Long Island and talk with
Jayne Galloway if she's not at the wake."

"I should go with you there, too."

"To protect me from her?"

"She might talk more easily to me. Women are like that
about some things."

The next morning, after arranging for Denise to pick
Johnny up after school and take him to his grandmother's, Ambler rented a car and picked Adele up at her apartment.

The funeral home in Greenwich was on the town's main
street, situated among a row of expensive looking boutique-
type stores, a kind of old-fashioned downtown of one and two
story storefront buildings on a sloping street with diagonal
parking. The facade of the funeral home had a churchlike appearance, gray stone with cathedral windows and heavy blond
wooden doors.

The sidewalk in front and the funeral home itself were
crowded; a line of mourners snaked from the doorway into
a hallway and then into an ornate room with rows of chairs,
all of them occupied. The line moved slowly between the wall
and the rows of chairs, past the casket and an array of floral

wreaths, up to Simon Dean who stood not far from the casket. His daughter, Carolyn, stood next to him and next to her, a woman in a black dress who bore a slight resemblance to both Simon and Carolyn.

Ambler didn't know what to expect from Simon Dean, so he steeled himself after he'd knelt down in front of the coffin. A pair of rosary beads was wrapped around Sandra's hands. He'd knelt because Adele did, stayed kneeling as long as she did, and stood when she stood. She held his hand as they approached Simon Dean, who met Ambler's gaze and held out his hand, his face drawn and his expression blank. Ambler grasped his hand and said, "I'm sorry."

Dean nodded. "Thank you for coming." Ambler wasn't sure the man even recognized him.

Adele shook Simon's hand also. They moved on, shaking hands with Carolyn who smiled slightly at Ambler and the woman next to Carolyn who whispered she was Simon's sister. Adele whispered that she and Ambler were friends of Dr. Dean's from the city. She'd started to say Shannon but caught herself. There were no empty seats in the viewing room and not much space to stand near the walls or in the vestibule, so Ambler and Adele went outside.

"What do we do now?" Ambler asked, relying on Adele because she'd been raised a Catholic and knew the religious trappings of a Catholic wake.

"If we want to be proper, we wait. A priest will come by and say some prayers. After that, we pay our respects once more, and then we can leave."

Ambler told Adele he'd meet her in a half hour. He asked directions at the drugstore across the street and found his way to the public library. It was a large modern, open, and airy building with a high glass ceiling, a kind of atrium. He sat down at a computer and looked up Dillard Wainwright, discovering two of his books in the library's collection, one of which he found in the open stacks. He sat down in a comfortable stuffed armchair near a window and began to read.

The Wainwright book was a collection of short stories from more than a decade earlier, the kind of stories with lyrical descriptions in which not much happens. The story he read was about a man in middle age, a college professor, who hasn't been afforded the recognition he deserved, and his conflicts with two women he's romantically involved with. The point of the story, Ambler gathered, was that the man's life was tragic, despite nothing especially bad happening to him. More useful to Ambler was a photo of Wainwright on the inside flap of the book jacket.

When he returned to the funeral home, Adele was chatting with Simon's sister and Carolyn on the sidewalk in front. He stood next to Adele and listened to the sister, whose name was Andrea, talk about how well-loved and admired the woman she called Sandi was. Carolyn huddled against her aunt. She looked up at Ambler a couple of times, her eyes open very wide. She didn't smile. He did and hoped she remembered him. He thought he should say something to her, yet he couldn't come up with any words that could say how sad he felt for her.

When the priest arrived, Ambler took up a position in the vestibule where he could scan the room and get a good look at everyone who'd come to pay their respects. After that, he and Adele stood near the door because of the crowd and listened to the priest drone on.

"I think we should leave. We don't need to say good-bye." Ambler said.

Adele agreed.

As they walked to the car, Adele said, "Did you hear Andrea call Sandra Sandi? McNulty called her Sandi."

"It's a diminutive of Sandra, right?"

"Yes, that someone close to her would use." Adele was lost

in thought for a moment. "Or who'd known Sandra a long time."

"So you think Simon's sister was a close friend of Sandra's?"

"Yes and I could tell she really loves Carolyn. They had a connection almost like a mother and child."

"If she was a good friend of Sandra's, it would be good to talk to her," Ambler said when they were back in the car. "Maybe you could do that."

Adele eyed him dangerously. "Women's work, eh?"

Again, Ambler had done something wrong, and once again didn't quite understand what it was. After a long silence during which he thought of and dismissed a half-dozen answers to Adele's question about women's work, she broke the silence.

"What were you looking for when you were standing in the doorway surveying the funeral home?"

He told her he'd found a photo of Dillard Wainwright. "It was from a long time ago but still."

"You thought he might be at the funeral? That was a wild-goose chase. Jayne Galloway wasn't there either."

Ambler shrugged. "I'm not sorry I went. Maybe Carolyn will remember the respect shown to her mother."

"The poor kid." Adele sniffled. "It makes me think of Johnny when his mother . . ."

Ambler cleared his throat. "I thought about Johnny, too." Johnny lost his mother some time back. However much Ambler and Adele loved the boy, something would always be missing, a hole in his heart that would never be filled, as it would never be filled for Carolyn. At least, Carolyn had her father. Johnny with his father in prison was in a way an orphan, his father in prison as hard to understand for a child as the death of his mother.

He and Adele were quiet for most of the drive. His thoughts were somber. Adele appeared melancholy also. She wore a black dress that looked pretty on her, prettier as the drive went

on. Ambler wondered for a moment if they might stay overnight on Long Island. Despite the gloom around them, being
together in the car away from the city, away from their regular
lives, felt pleasant and intimate.

He'd thought in the past about inviting Adele to go away
for a weekend. They'd been on the verge of romance in the
past, very close, but something got in the way. They'd kissed
passionately one night but then didn't kiss again, so he no longer knew what there was between them. And now? Was she
coming with him to see Jayne Galloway because she wanted to
be alone with him? Was she thinking, too, they might find a romantic inn out on the island and spend the night? Should he ask
if they should look for a hotel? He wondered what she'd wear,
how she'd look.

"Raymond, are you there?" Adele's voice held a kind of tenderness. "I swear you drift away like a daydreaming child."

Her voice shook him out of his reverie. He considered how
he might say something suggestive, about how she looked, how
he felt about her, about spending the night together. But he
couldn't think of the right words, so he kept quiet.

The traffic and super aggressive drivers on the Long Island
Expressway required careful attention since he wasn't an experienced driver. Whatever thoughts he had about a romantic
journey disappeared, as Adele had become tense and irritated
for some reason. Her moods were beyond him.

Once they left the expressway, they hit upon blacktopped
state roads that wound through more rustic areas. The North
Shore had a kind of verdant, idyllic feel to it, so that as they got
closer to Jayne Galloway's neighborhood, Ambler felt a kind of
peace and gentle pleasure. He turned to face Adele who stared
out the windshield in front of her. "I'm glad you came along."

His speaking out of the silence startled her. "Oh? I was
thinking I probably shouldn't have come. I'm afraid it's going to
be unpleasant." She faced him also. "I was thinking we're doing

this wrong. If McNulty didn't kill Shannon or the man in her hotel room—and unlike you, I'm sure he didn't kill anybody, that he wouldn't in a million years do that—if he didn't do it, let the police arrest him. They can't prove he did something he didn't do. That wacky lawyer friend of his, what's his name, should be able to get him off. The guy makes a living getting *guilty* people off."

"David Levinson. Even good lawyers need to know what happened. They need facts to make a case."

"Bricks." Adele said. "They need bricks to make a case."

"Clay. Clay to make bricks."

Ambler watched Adele who was gazing out the car window. Stately groves of trees and flowing fields of autumn grass drifted past the car. "It's so peaceful here," she said dreamily. "Imagine what it would be like living in a big house with all that land around you." She waved at a passing field and then bounced around to face him. "Did you ever think about living in a place like this? You and Johnny . . ." Her voice trailed away.

"And you?" The words popped out of his mouth.

"I wasn't thinking about me." She turned to look out the window again.

Ambler spent the rest of the ride wondering what she'd meant . . . and what he'd meant. Did she misunderstand him? Did she think he'd offered an invitation and turned it down? And did he mean an invitation or was it simply a question? How could he know what she meant if he didn't know what he meant?

The yard of Jayne Galloway's house looked untended, neglected. You'd think plants killed by the first hard frost might have been cut back or pulled out, that leaves from the massive maple trees near the road would have been raked and hauled away. The yard had a cluttered, abandoned feel.

"It looks like a haunted house," Adele said as Ambler pulled into the driveway. She was right. The last time he'd visited the sun was shining. A sunny day would have made the house look brighter. He couldn't remember what the yard had looked like that time. The large windows were still inviting but with the day overcast and gray, the house felt lifeless and brooding.

They went to the porch and rang the bell. Ambler remembered the parrot and waited for the screeching squawk. But none came. "Strange," he said.

"What's strange?"

"Nothing." He pushed the doorbell again. It echoed against the emptiness within.

"I guess you should have called." Adele moved her feet restlessly, a sign of her irritation.

"I did call, a bunch of times. She never answered. That's why I drove out here. I think she's inside. And I'm afraid something's wrong. The parrot—"

"Parrot?"

"She had a parrot in the basement; not always in the basement. She told me she lets it ride on her shoulder and hang out with her. It makes a horrible racket when someone comes to the door."

"And?"

"It didn't." Ambler walked toward a wooden bench with an ornate back that rested against the wall of the porch in front of a large window and began to slide the bench out of the way.

Adele watched him from where she stood by the door. "What are you doing?"

"Looking through the window. She's sick and frail. She might need help."

The dining room and the part of the living room he could see were empty and lifeless, as if he were looking into the front room of a summer cottage closed up for the winter.

Adele tried peering over his shoulder. "If she's sick or not feeling well, she'd be in her bedroom, which I imagine is upstairs. She might be too sick to get out of bed, even if she did hear the doorbell. We should call someone."

Ambler backed away from the window. He and Adele walked down the porch steps and stood on the walk. "Would you try to reach the local police? The name of the town is Glen Cove."

"Someone's home over there." Adele nodded toward the house next door. "A woman watched us from a window as we came in the driveway. She might know if Mrs. Galloway is home."

"Yes. Please." Ambler headed toward the back of the house, Adele to the house next door.

A few moments later, Adele came back from speaking to the neighbor. She met Ambler on the driveway, as he came around the corner of the house, moving faster than she'd ever seen him move. "Call the police," he said before he reached her. "She's lying on the floor in the kitchen. I think she's dead. I'm going to break in."

"No." Adele rushed toward him. "The neighbor gave me the key. She looks in on her sometimes. Mrs. Galloway was home the day before yesterday. The neighbor spoke with her. She hasn't seen her since then." Adele handed him the key. "It's to the back door. I'll call the police and an ambulance."

A few minutes later, she went around to the back door to join Ambler.

He stood on a small porch outside the back door. "She's dead."

"She wasn't murdered, was she?"

He shook his head. "I couldn't tell how she died. There's nothing—"

Adele interrupted him. "I'm sorry she's dead. She was dying. . . ." Adele clutched at him. "You told me that. She had cancer."

A few minutes later, a police car came across the bridge behind them and pulled up alongside the edge of the yard. Before the officer had gotten out of the car, an ambulance came

over the bridge, lights flashing but no siren. Not far behind the
ambulance came another police car. The police appeared to
let the paramedics from the ambulance handle the scene. One
of the cops took down contact information from Ambler and
Adele. The other cop watched the paramedics, more of a spec-
tator than participant.

"Do you think we should say something?" Adele whispered.

"I don't know. We could tell them they should treat this like
a crime scene. But what reason would I give them?" The police
didn't have any reason to think they were dealing with a crime.
They had a procedure for an unattended death, which they'd
follow, so that should be good enough. You'd think they'd ask
why he and Adele discovered the body, why they were at Jayne
Galloway's house. That would probably come later. Someone
else's job to investigate. Ambler approached one of the officers
and asked what would happen next.

"We wait for the medical examiner."

"Will there be an investigation?"

The officer's eyebrows went up. He scrutinized Ambler and
his manner changed in the way a cop sometimes goes from
calm to high alert because the person they're engaged with tips
them off that there's more to what was happening than they
thought. This cop walked over to the other one and they con-
ferred quietly, their backs to Ambler and Adele, taking turns
looking over their shoulders at them, while Adele and Ambler
fidgeted.

The officer who'd spoken with Ambler went and talked for
a moment to the EMTs and then came back to Ambler. "We're
going to leave everything as it is until the ME gets here. I'd appreciate it if you'd wait."

"Do we have to?" Adele asked.

The officer glanced at Ambler and back at Adele. "Let's not
go there."

They waited, Adele and Ambler leaning against the front

fender of the rental car they arrived in, the police in their cars, where they did something with computers on their dashboards.

When the doctor from the medical examiner's office arrived, she spoke to the police officers and they followed her into the house. Not long afterward, one of the officers came out and told Ambler and Adele they could leave. On the way back to the city, Adele drove and Ambler called Mike Cosgrove and told him the Nassau police should look for forensic evidence in Jayne Galloway's house, even if the medical examiner ruled her death to be from natural causes.

"So he's going to do it?" Adele asked when he finished talking to Mike.

"He has a friend—someone he used to work with—who's now on the Nassau County homicide squad. He said he'd talk to him."

"Will they look for a parrot buried in the yard?"

"I don't know. I should have looked around myself instead of standing there doing nothing."

"If someone murdered the poor woman, who do you think it was—certainly not McNulty?" Adele's irritation was back.

"They might find fingerprints. . . ."

"They won't be McNulty's."

Chapter 15

Mike Cosgrove didn't like gyms. In particular he didn't like the smell. He didn't like locker rooms; the one at the precinct was bad enough. At least there, guys were coming and going from work. They wouldn't be there if they didn't have to be. No one needed to be in health club locker rooms; too much exposed flesh and too many muscles; plus the smell. It was as bad as the morgue.

He was at the health club to interview one of the men listed in Sandra Dean's journal. The facility was on the Upper East Side in one of the new upscale high-rises that were changing the face of Lenox Hill and, for his money, ruining the neighborhood. The health club was on the first floor. Its glass doors opened into a reception area with wall-to-wall carpeting and spare modern furniture. A young blonde woman with very white teeth, a big smile, and a bubbly personality sat behind a desk facing the door. She was enormously glad to see him.

"I'm looking for Victor Morales. He's expecting me." Cosgrove returned her smile with some effort.

"I'll be right back." She sprang out of her chair and headed for the door behind her. "You sit right here and make yourself comfortable."

The bubbly young woman was back before he had a chance to sit down and gave him directions to an office down a hallway past the men's locker room on one side, the women's on the other side. He suspected the odor came from the men's side, but he wasn't sure. It could be both. Victor Morales looked up from where he sat behind his desk. The spare office had the same kind of tile walls as the hallway and, Cosgrove assumed, the locker rooms. The office door was open so he walked in. Morales, whose deeply tanned face was probably handsome, didn't say anything, but his tight-lipped expression made clear that he wasn't happy about the visit.

"You're not under arrest," Cosgrove began. "You aren't really under suspicion. Your name came up in a murder investigation, in a notebook kept by the victim. You spent some time drinking with her and went with her to her hotel room."

"Can I see the notebook?"

"No."

"How do I know there is a notebook?"

Cosgrove sighed. "Do you remember a woman named Shannon Darling?"

Morales gripped the arms of his chair tightly enough that his knuckles went white. Here was a man with secrets. Cosgrove took an immediate dislike to him. You had to admit he was robust, good color in his face, his arms and shoulders muscular, his neck sloped. Not a show-off but you'd believe he'd appeal to a lot of women. His eyes were small and shifty and didn't give away much. He might be a dumb jock or might have the intellect of a nuclear physicist.

Cosgrove knew he should make an effort to get the guy to relax; he'd do it but his heart wasn't in it. "Maybe you're married . . ." He held up his hand as Morales began his denial. "I don't care if you are. You might have known she was married.

She was forthcoming about things with men she met. You might not have." He appraised Morales. "You're a good-looking guy. I'm sure you meet a lot of women. Nothing we talk about here gets out to anyone else. I'm not the sex police. The woman was murdered. Sometimes, we find out something about the victim's past, it helps us find the killer. That's it. I have no reason to think you killed her, no reason to think you ever saw her again after that time. All I'm asking is for you to tell me about her."

"She gave me a blow job. That was it."

His answer and especially the way he said it made Cosgrove sad. The guy might have been saying he bummed a cigarette. Cosgrove didn't know Sandra Dean, yet she didn't deserve the callous way this guy thought of her. They'd had this intimate time together. The least he could do is appreciate it, appreciate her.

"You didn't talk? She didn't tell you anything about herself? You didn't tell her about yourself?"

"It was a physical attraction. We talked I guess. She talked a lot, about a lot of things. After a while, I lost track of what she was saying."

"You stopped paying attention?"

"Yeah, I guess. She wanted to talk. I wanted to get laid. I settled for a blow job."

After the interview, Cosgrove sat for a long while in his car. He was trying to understand Sandra Dean. Why wasn't a prosperous life in the suburbs, a professional career, a husband, and a daughter enough for her? What did she get out of her sexual escapades? . . . What she got, he answered himself, was murdered.

He'd seen it before, this courting danger. A lot of guys who become cops court danger—for the adrenaline rush, the type-A guys who want the action. What he was thinking was different—courting danger not for the excitement but for the risk: tempting fate, daring the danger, risking being hurt from some need to suffer, some sort of penance . . . for what?

He started his car. He was thinking too much. What was

that about him? Why not take the simple answer? The guy he just interviewed, Morales, didn't need to know about the woman he was with, didn't wonder what she was looking for, what kind of emptiness she was trying to fill. She could have been an inflatable doll so long as he got off. Cosgrove wasn't so attractive to women. He wondered what he'd be like if he were. He hoped not like Morales.

He'd told Ray he'd call his former partner Frank Zimmer in Nassau County about the woman who died on Long Island. It was a coincidence, a glaring one, that Ray would find the body of the mother of a murder victim a few days after the murder. But coincidences happen, people die on their own, especially if they're sick and already dying. He'd ask Frank but he didn't see an investigation going very far.

Frank had taken the leap to the suburbs years ago—higher pay, better working conditions, safer—why the hell was Cosgrove still in the city? When he called Frank, he didn't know what to expect. Sometimes, a detective gets leeway to follow hunches, use intuition, snoop around, follow a lead no one else thinks important. Other times you have a supervisor on your ass, second-guessing everything you did. Cosgrove was lucky to have a good boss. Turned out Frank was lucky, too.

"Sure. I can take a look," he said. "I'll send in the crime scene unit. Someone will ask me why somewhere along the line, but I don't need permission. The captain believes me when I tell him things might not be what they seem. What am I looking for?"

"A parrot."

There was a pause. "You're messing with me, right?"

Cosgrove went over the situation. "Her daughter was murdered. Now, she's found dead. It could be a coincidence. It most likely is."

Frank had been around long enough to understand the feeling you get, not being satisfied even though you have a suspect or what looks like an explanation, something about it not feeling right. Frank would catch the drift. What he wouldn't catch would be that the uneasy feeling belonged to Ray Ambler, a librarian, and not to Cosgrove. This wasn't something he would try to explain.

Frank said he'd have the place dusted and anything that might be evidence bagged. He wasn't sure how far he'd get with digging up the yard in the hope of finding a dead parrot.

"You could look in the trees," Cosgrove told him. "It might be alive."

Despite the workday being too long already, Cosgrove had scheduled another interview with a man from Sandra Dean's journal for that evening. Peter Esposito, the man he was about to interview, was cooperative when he reached him on the phone at his office in Denver. He said he'd be in New York later that week. Tonight was the evening he'd be free and they could meet at the bar of the Commodore Hotel where he was staying.

The lounge on the lobby level, an escalator ride above the street, was quiet, only one couple at the bar. Esposito sat by himself at a table against the picture window overlooking 42nd Street. Esposito's take on Sandra Dean, whom he knew as Shannon Darling, was the full opposite of that of Morales, the last guy Cosgrove spoke with, and in its own way just as mystifying.

"She was remarkable. Fascinating. I was bewitched by her. I think I fell in love with her." Esposito came across as sincere, a lost soul who'd been touched at some point with profound sadness. Since he was willing to talk, more than willing, Cosgrove let him.

"She'd had a lot to drink and what she drank went to her head. Still she was charming and articulate and smart. Brilliant. She had a direct way of engaging you, and was almost childlike in trusting that you were as guileless as she was. I don't remember everything we talked about. Her mother had deserted her when she was a child, she told me, and she was trying to understand who she was by learning about her mother and the man her mother deserted her for."

The server interrupted them and Esposito ordered another drink—scotch on the rocks—and tried to persuade Cosgrove to join him. It was tempting—and in another situation he might have a drink, but for this one he needed to pay close attention. Something was different here. Peter Esposito was obsessed with the murdered woman. Cosgrove ordered a scotch to maintain the spell they were under. But he didn't plan to drink it.

Esposito took a deep breath, shook the ice cubes in his glass and drained the last of his first drink, watching anxiously toward the service bar for the next one. "I felt a connection to her, as if I'd been looking for her or someone like her for years and finally found her." He paused. "I'm married. It's a difficult situation." He laughed, not bitterly. "That's the story a thousand guys tell in a thousand bars every night. You've heard it before, I'm sure: 'My wife doesn't understand me.' I don't need to justify myself. Nothing in my feelings for Shannon was sordid."

Cosgrove knew the "difficult situation" story from his own wrecked marriage. Good thing he wasn't drinking or he'd be here with Esposito for the rest of the night crying in their beer . . . or in this case scotch.

"She was in a loveless marriage like mine." Esposito took a peek at Cosgrove. "That's not right. Something was wrong with her husband and sex. She was sad, confused. She cried. So I thought she did love her husband and he didn't love her." The drinks arrived. Esposito took the glass from the server's hand before she had a chance to set it onto the table. He took a large gulp.

"I thought she was saying she loved her husband and wanted

to stay with him but wanted to have sex. I couldn't leave my marriage—I have kids; there are other complications, too—and I wanted to have sex, too, with someone I cared about. I thought we hit on something. There we were, two lonely people and we made a connection, a sincere connection."

He laughed. "I'm going to say 'It wasn't what you think' and know how foolish that sounds. But it wasn't what you'd expect of a man and woman coming together in a hotel bar, a one-night stand, something tawdry. She was beautiful and sensitive. I wanted to be with her. It didn't have to be sex that night. I wanted to know her better, to know her for a long time. We talked for a long time and then the bar was closing. I was afraid I'd never see her again.

"She didn't want to leave me either, I guess. She invited me to her room. The room had a couch and we sat together on it and talked more." Esposito took a long drink from his glass and began looking for the server again. "I wanted to stay with her, even if only to sleep beside her. She said no. I didn't argue. I said I wanted to see her again. She said she didn't know and then she said maybe. I believed she was attracted to me. I knew she felt what I did. She didn't know how to handle it, how to fit me into her life. Even though she wanted to, it was too much for her. But I knew we could do it. I was sure we could do it."

Esposito began to show signs of dissembling. Beads of sweat broke out on his forehead; he no longer met Cosgrove's gaze, fidgeting where he sat, crumpling up the bar napkins on the small table in front of him. He acted like suspects do when they're afraid you're going to ask a question they don't want to answer.

Cosgrove picked up his rocks glass, examined it, and placed it back on the table, watching Esposito squirm. "So how did that work out? Did you see her again?"

"No. Not really." Esposito's embarrassed smile begged for help, or mercy.

Cosgrove felt sorry for him like a hunter might feel sorry for a deer he was about to shoot. He liked the guy, a kind of innocent himself like the woman he'd described. "Not really?" Cosgrove raised his eyebrows.

Esposito fidgeted, casting his gaze first at the bar on one side of them; then, something outside the window below them on 42nd Street caught his interest. He snuck a couple of glances at Cosgrove. "I saw her again. It was by accident. When I'd phone her, she'd tell me she couldn't see me again. We were both married. She was too busy. It wouldn't be right. I shouldn't ask her."

Esposito's manner changed. When he first described the woman he knew as Shannon, his tone was lyrical, the words he used verging on poetic; now, his tone was bitter, scolding. He'd ordered another drink, not bothering this time to ask if Cosgrove wanted one, not noticing Cosgrove hadn't touched his. "I saw her right here in this hotel, in this bar, all wrapped up in conversation with another guy, talking to him, I'm sure, the way she'd talked to me."

Cosgrove wanted to keep Esposito talking without being so eager he scared him off. For the moment, Esposito's strong sense of grievance overpowered his judgment. He recounted things, including his rage, that when he woke tomorrow he'd wished he'd kept to himself. Scotch will do that to you after one drink too many, bring up from your memory to color your evening an array of slights and insults and injustices you've suffered. Esposito poured out his story. He'd confronted the woman of his obsession that night and she'd told him to go away, get lost. They'd argued. There was a scene that ended with Esposito, Shannon, and the man she was talking with being asked to leave the bar.

Cosgrove wanted to see just how angry Esposito had been. "Did she leave with the man she'd been talking with."

"Yes." The sneer on Esposito's face crumbled. Cosgrove

turned away and went to the men's room to let the guy compose himself. By the time he got back, Esposito had ordered
another drink and composed himself enough to realize he'd
talked too much. Cosgrove saw his resolve to be more circumspect as clearly as if he'd zippered his mouth shut.

Cosgrove wanted to keep him talking. "Could you tell me
about this man she was with?" After all these years, Cosgrove
still didn't understand why people with something to hide,
who'd made themselves obvious suspects, kept answering
questions when all they had to do to keep themselves from
getting in deeper was stop talking. Still, you had to ask. You
never knew where a question might lead. He might describe
Ted Doyle.

Esposito shook his head. "Nothing much about him. He
didn't like the commotion. With him it wasn't like when she
was with me. He didn't connect with her the way she and I connected. She could see that. I knew Sandra better than she knew
herself. I knew she'd be sorry she spent time with him."

Sandra? Cosgrove didn't comment, just made a note in his
head. "This other man, did you catch his name?"

Esposito wasn't ready with an answer, his hesitation longer
than it should be. "No. If I did, I don't remember."

"Can you describe him?"

"He was foreign. He had an accent. Dark hair, dark skin,
olive complexion, tall, well built. He didn't say much."

Neither did Esposito's description, nothing distinctive in it,
generic. It wasn't for sure he made it up, but more than possible.
"Does the name Ted Doyle mean anything to you?"

He didn't give his answer much thought. "No. Should it?"

Cosgrove didn't answer. If Esposito had followed the story
of Sandra Dean's murder in the news—and why wouldn't he,
as obsessed with her as he was?—he'd have come across the
name of the man murdered in her hotel room. Esposito was

glassy-eyed by now, so he wouldn't be good for many more questions.

"You said you saw Sandra Dean here in this hotel. Do you stay here whenever you're in the city?"

Esposito closed one eye, an attempt to be cagey that Cosgrove almost laughed at. Neither did he flinch at Cosgrove's use of the woman's true name. "I stay in different places."

"That's pretty easy to check."

The closed eye popped open; the caginess went south. "Most of the time, I stay here."

Cosgrove took out his notebook and paged through it. "Were you in the city, staying in this hotel, on September 7?" This was the day of Ted Doyle's murder.

"No. . . . I don't think so. . . . Why? Why that date?" His voice rose with alarm. Adrenaline must have surged through him because he sobered up. "What are you getting at?"

"Do you own a handgun, Mr. Esposito?"

"No." He stood, knocking back his chair, lunging into the table as he righted himself. "I do. . . . I have guns. They're legal. I've had enough of this. What are you trying to do?"

Cosgrove stood also. "I'll be in touch." He'd let Esposito pick up the tab for his drink. As he walked away, he watched Esposito reach across for the untouched scotch.

Leaving Peter Esposito to his scotch and his sorrows, Cosgrove headed home to Queens, his own sorrows, and a glass or two of wine to assuage them. Esposito had revealed too much for his own good. His unwillingness to let go of a woman who made clear that his interest in her wasn't returned made him a danger to her and a suspect in her murder.

She told him she didn't want to see him again. Still, he pursued her when he should have let her go. He also called the person he knew as Shannon by her actual name, Sandra. He'd tracked her down. He didn't account for his whereabouts on the night Ted

Doyle was murdered in her hotel room. Cosgrove hadn't gotten to the evening of her murder. In time, he would. He prowled the quiet streets of Queens until he found a parking space a couple of blocks from his apartment and sat in his car for a few more moments decompressing. He might have a new suspect. That would cheer Ray up. It might also be wishful thinking.

Chapter 16

Ambler was still shaken up by his discovery of Jayne Galloway's body when Mike Cosgrove called him the next day about the Nassau County investigation of her death. "The preliminary indications are that she died of natural causes. They'll do an autopsy because it's an unattended death, but those results we won't get for a couple of months. They did dust the place for fingerprints, some hers, some unidentified. One more thing . . ." he hesitated. "This gives your theory she was murdered a bit of a push but not in the direction you want it to go."

"What?"

"They found a car parked in the garage. It has Connecticut MD plates and is registered to Sandra Dean. I checked with Stamford. They have a car with New York tags registered to Jayne Galloway in the parking lot of the hotel where Dr. Dean was killed. It looks like when Sandra Dean and McNulty left the city after the Doyle murder, they went to her mother's house and exchanged the cars. Dr. Dean wasn't on good terms with her mother; I think you told me."

"Are you saying Sandra Dean and McNulty murdered her mother and stole her car?"

"You're the one who brought up murder. If it turns out that way, you came up with a new problem for your pal. On a more positive note: a parrot once lived at the Galloway residence but no sign of it." Mike cleared his throat. "One more thing. Don't get your hopes up on this. It may not mean anything." Mike told him about Peter Esposito. "I have some things to look into. I'll let you know how it goes."

"Would you mind if I spoke to him?"

"I'd rather you wait."

Ambler was okay with that. The only reason for Ambler to talk to Esposito was to get his own sense of the man, which would be important only if Mike got stuck or gave up on him without sufficient reason. Meanwhile, Ambler was more concerned about what it meant that Sandra Dean and McNulty had been at Jayne Galloway's house.

The likely sequence of events was that McNulty and Sandra Dean left the city knowing they were or would be under a cloud of suspicion and went to Sandra's mother to hide and to exchange cars in case the police discovered Sandra Dean's true identity. Other scenarios were possible but this was the most likely. The scenario meant that when Ambler first visited Jayne Galloway, Sandra Dean and McNulty had already been there. What Ambler didn't know and couldn't surmise was why Sandra and McNulty went to Sandra's mother for help, if this was why they went there. Nothing Ambler ran across so far suggested Sandra and her mother had reconciled. Simon Dean said the opposite as had Jayne Galloway. Of course, Galloway lied about many things and might have lied about that. Simon Dean might have lied, too, or he might not have known.

Ambler surely wished he knew what Jayne Galloway wanted to tell him. Sandra might have told her mother who murdered Ted Doyle. Jayne Galloway might have known who murdered her daughter. Now mother and daughter were both dead. No one was left to tell him what they knew.

Yet there was one possibility. Jayne Galloway was a diarist in addition to keeping a writing journal. Ambler had found dozens of diaries going back to when she was a girl in the collection she donated to the library. According to the deed of gift she'd signed, the library was to get any papers or manuscripts she had in her possession upon her death. This would include the diaries she was writing in up until the time of her death.

He called her literary agent who had negotiated the donation of her papers to the library. She told him Mrs. Galloway bequeathed all of her possessions to her daughter Sandra. They would now belong to her granddaughter Carolyn. It would be up to her and her guardian to fulfill the promises in the deed of gift.

"Her guardian. Her father?"

Adele was with him in the crime fiction reading room when he made the call. "You have to ask Sandra's husband? That's going to be a problem," she said when he'd hung up.

Ambler grumbled but recovered quickly. "I've got an idea."

"You're not going to send me." She folded her arms across her chest.

"Not you. Harry." He remembered the priest at the funeral home and all of the Catholic trappings. Perhaps priests—even ex-priests—had a kind of professional code, like lawyers, where they would talk with one another in ways they wouldn't talk with a lay person. Adele was skeptical.

Harry Larkin, the former Jesuit, despite having left the priesthood a couple of decades before, had held on to his priestly manner or more precisely his spirituality. He exuded kindness and forgiveness and practiced humility, seldom raised his voice, and was loath to discipline his staff.

Yet, in contrast to his mild manner in all things dealing with his staff, and the rest of the world for that matter, was his respect for authority, in his case the powers-that-be of the New York Public Library. Harry's tendency toward understanding and forgiveness most often came into conflict with his respect for the dictates of authority in situations involving Adele and especially Ambler, neither of whom had any inclination to accept the dictates of authority. This state of affairs kept poor Harry in an almost constant state of high anxiety.

Unfortunately for Harry, Ambler knew that when push came to shove the former priest would consider it his pastoral mission to protect one of his flock, again often Ambler, from the consequences of an ill-advised undertaking. With this in mind, Ambler prevailed upon his supervisor to travel with him to Greenwich, Connecticut.

"You're the director of the Manuscripts and Archives Division," Ambler said when they were seated in the bare-boned Metro North railway car on their way to Greenwich the next morning. "Jayne Galloway's diaries and other papers belong to the library."

"I know what I'm responsible for. I'm afraid that with you it's going to involve some kind of subterfuge."

"A priest is helping the family, the father and the little girl—"

"A priest? I knew it." Harry jerked himself up straight, darting glances around the car as if he might try to jump off the moving train. "That's why you enlisted me, to con a priest into something. You better tell me what you're up to, or I'm going to turn around as soon as we get there and take the next train back—after I tell the priest you're a fraud." Harry's voice rose as he spoke, so a number of heads snapped around.

Ambler calmed Harry down by promising he'd tell the truth and wouldn't bother Simon Dean if the priest thought he shouldn't.

The meeting with the priest, Fr. Jerome, which Ambler had set up the previous day over the phone, was at the rectory for St. Mary's church a few steps up Greenwich Avenue and across the street from the funeral home. The priest was friendly enough but unctuous. Harry's manner changed while they talked, so he, too, became excessively polite. They went back and forth in a way that for most people would be an argument but was for them more like a fencing match, where they gracefully bowed and scraped, each pretending to be more than accommodating to the other, while neither gave an inch. In the end, the priest said he would call Andrea Eagan, Simon's sister, who was handling the family affairs and watching over Carolyn during this difficult time.

Andrea Eagan remembered Ambler from the funeral home. She was sure Simon would be fine with her meeting him at Mrs. Galloway's house in Long Island to retrieve the documents he would take to the library. She thought it would be wise for her to be there and to take an inventory of what he took. Simon could look it over later to see if everything was okay.

Because the trip to Greenwich worked out successfully, Harry was closer to his good-natured and agreeable self on the train ride back to the city. Ambler told him about Jayne Galloway's phone call and about her death. Harry was already aware of the deaths of Ted Doyle and Sandra Dean and that she had been using the crime fiction collection at the library.

"All that is tragic and quite sad," Harry said. "Nonetheless, I hope your involvement in any investigation is limited this time around. The library is a place for scholarship and contemplation and perhaps relaxation, not adventure except on the pages of a book."

"The crime came to me. I didn't go looking for it. I told you McNulty is the main suspect. I have to do what I can to help get him out of trouble."

Harry sat back and folded his hands across his midsection. Ambler took this to be a priestly counseling posture. "I think you make a mistake if you set out to prove the man innocent rather than setting out to discover the truth. I came across a piece of advice in my reading—a detective story you'll be happy to know. 'Sometimes, you think you've found what you're looking for when it isn't there because in your eagerness to find it you don't ask yourself all the questions there are to be asked.'"

Ambler turned to Harry in disbelief. "What have you been reading?"

Harry's pious expression bordered on smug, unusual for him. "Actually, I've been reading stories featuring a priest, written by G. K. Chesterton. I don't suppose you're familiar with him."

Ambler laughed. "Of course, Father Brown. I hope they don't give you any ideas." He thought for a moment. "Actually, I hope they do."

Chapter 17

The following morning Ambler again rented a car and drove to Glen Cove, this time without Adele and on library business. A car was parked in the driveway when he arrived and Andrea Eagan got out of it when he pulled up on the roadway in front of the house. She greeted him and they shook hands. Slight and thin-faced with raven black hair, she was pretty in the same careless, winsome way Adele was.

"It's a beautiful house," she said when she'd opened the front door with a key and they stood a few steps into the open hallway. "I love the windows."

Jayne Galloway's study was on the second floor, a corner bedroom made into an office, with wall-to-ceiling bookshelves on two walls, a leather couch against a third wall with paintings on either side. A desk was against the fourth wall beneath two windows overlooking the roadway and the lagoon beyond. Ambler went to the bookshelves, while Andrea stood in front of the windows watching something in the lagoon.

"It must be difficult for your brother," Ambler said. "I can't imagine what he's going through."

Her pretty face contorted into a grimace. "Simon's taken to the role of a grieving widower, assuming the manner he believes is expected of him."

Ambler had been examining the spines of the writing journals that took up half of one of the bookshelves. The spines weren't dated and he didn't know if they were in any sort of order. He wasn't paying full attention while passing along his condolences, so he was taken aback. "I'm not sure I understand."

A veil fell over Andrea's eyes as she lowered her eyelashes. "Don't mind me. It's been a lot. . . . My heart is broken for Carolyn."

They talked, standing in the office of the recently dead Jayne Galloway. Andrea, outgoing, at ease, talked easily to a stranger. "I love books," she said. "I once thought I might own a bookstore . . . or be a librarian. I envy you."

She was an elementary school teacher in Stamford, one town north of Greenwich, the town where her friend whom she called Sandi, was murdered. "Sandi and I were close. We became fast friends even before she married my brother. Strangely, Sandi didn't have a lot of friends, despite her being the kindest and most sensitive person I've ever known."

While Andrea gazed out the window, Ambler skimmed the first few pages of a few of the journals looking for mention of Dillard Wainwright or mention of Sandra. He didn't come across anything, except to discover Galloway had been careless with dates in the diaries he glanced at.

"I have an idea," Andrea said. "Why don't you begin a list of what you're going to take, while I'll go down to the village and get us something to fix for lunch. I can check your list or copy it when I get back."

She was gone almost an hour and came back with the wherewithal to make chicken salad sandwiches, along with tea and some little cakes. While she was gone, Ambler designed a key of sorts to identify the different kinds of notebooks and journals, partial manuscripts, and correspondence. Among piles of unopened mail, he found four opened royalty statements containing checks amounting to hundreds of dollars, which he gave to Andrea. She was fine with the inventory system and after they ate a quick lunch she helped list the documents and notebooks he was taking to the library.

At one point, Andrea stopped, holding an open spiral notebook in her hands, and looked at Ambler. "I know it's terrible to speak badly of the dead. Yet it's difficult for me to think kindly of Sandi's mother. She did desert Sandi. A child doesn't recover from that . . . and now poor Carolyn. Her mother has deserted her now, too."

Ambler took a moment to tell Andrea about Johnny, deserted by his mother who also died in tragic circumstances and by his father, Ambler's son, who was in prison, a desertion also.

"The poor boy. His father in prison is as much or more punishing him as it is punishing the father."

Ambler liked Andrea Eagan immensely. Sandra Dean was lucky to have had her for a friend and it was fortunate that Carolyn would have Andrea in her life. "When was the last time you saw or spoke to Dr. Dean . . . Sandi?"

Andrea quickly looked away from him, embarrassed for her friend. After a silence during which Ambler left her to her thoughts and continued with the inventory, she asked, "Is it true, what Simon said, that she was with a man who killed her, and she'd been with other men when she went on trips that we all thought were conferences for her work?"

Ambler told her about the man murdered in her hotel room, about her journal, and the other men she'd been with. When he got to McNulty, he told her the truth. "The man she was with, who's accused of murdering her is a friend of mine."

Again, despite her guilelessness, Andrea put things together quickly. "Is that why you're here? To find something in Sandi's life, through her mother's journals, that points to someone else who killed her?"

Ambler started to speak before he knew what he'd say, acting on an impulse to deny. But before he said anything, he caught himself and waited for her to continue her accusation.

No accusation came. "I'm so bewildered . . . and hurt. To be so close to someone and not know an entire part of her life. I feel like a woman whose husband is arrested as a child molester or a serial rapist and she had no idea. Since Sandi died I've wondered if you ever really know anyone."

Ambler put down the journal he was skimming. "I suspect most people have secrets. It may not always be a bad thing."

"And there's Carolyn. Sandi was determined Carolyn would have the mother and father she didn't have." Andrea spoke softly. "Sandi tried so hard to please everyone. How could someone murder her?" Andrea began to cry. Instinctively, he moved toward her, and—he guessed instinctive for her, too—she moved toward him. She bowed and leaned her head against his chest.

After a moment, she lifted her head and stepped back from him. "Thank you. You must be kind. I think I felt that when I first met you."

They continued listing the journals and notebooks, with simple designations for writing journal, diary, financial records, correspondence, and miscellaneous. Ambler had brought file boxes with him from the library; in some of the boxes they put photos, postcards, Christmas cards, and such. Ambler designated one box for Andrea to use for anything she wanted to save for Carolyn.

Holding up one of the journals, Andrea said, "This one's more like a diary than the others that are ideas for books."

"Mrs. Galloway did both, sometimes in the same notebook. She used what happened in her life as raw material for her books."

"You know, Sandi kept diaries, too. She had journals she wrote in by hand, keeping secrets, like little girls do."

When they were nearly finished and the sun was declining over the lagoon and a kind golden amber sunlight filled the room through the large windows over the desk, Andrea asked him why McNulty was accused of murdering Sandi and why Ambler thought he didn't kill her.

He told her McNulty had been with Sandra from the time of Ted Doyle's murder in her hotel room in the city until she was murdered in Stamford. That was so far the evidence against him. "He tried to protect her from herself." Ambler softened his tone. "Sandra whom I knew as Shannon put herself in dangerous situations. I don't know why. She was reckless in the way someone who's self-destructive risks hurting themselves."

"Why? Why was she like that?"

Ambler didn't know. He shook his head and picked up one of the file boxes to carry to his car.

Andrea picked up a box and walked along with him. "My husband's a psychologist. I know what he'd say. Sandi did something—or something was done to her—that she felt she should be punished for. It might have been her mother leaving her. She might have felt that was her fault. It's not actually that simple. But it was something like that."

When they'd finished loading the file boxes, they stood awkwardly between the cars. It was as if a bond had grown between them. Ambler asked about Carolyn.

"She's staying for now with my husband and me. Simon's a wreck, wrapped up in his own misery and not so aware of anyone else's. Carolyn didn't want to go back home yet. She doesn't want to go to school yet either. We play with her and hug her a lot, trying to let her talk when she wants and not talk when she wants to be quiet."

Before Andrea got in her car, she hugged Ambler. Then, as

she opened the door, she turned and said. "I hope you find out your friend didn't kill Sandi."

Ambler nodded. "Does the name Dillard Wainwright mean anything to you?"

Andrea shook her head. "Should it?"

"I don't know." Ambler closed the car door behind her.

Chapter 18

Ambler dropped the file boxes at the library's loading dock on 40th Street and returned the rental car to the garage on 31st Street near Eighth Avenue. He thought about going back to the library to sift through the diaries but went home to see Johnny instead. On the way back from Long Island, he kept thinking about Carolyn and how awful it was for her, which brought him to thinking about Johnny.

Not for the first time, he thought involving himself in homicide investigations put him in danger of becoming a homicide himself. The danger was remote, yet more likely than if he had another avocation, like bowling or bird-watching. It was okay for him to take that chance for himself. He wasn't sure it was okay for him to take the chance that Johnny could lose another person he put his love and trust into. Of course, Johnny would have his grandmother, such as she was, and he'd have Adele, as Carolyn had Andrea. Still . . . Ambler realized he wasn't rushing home so much because the boy needed him—he was fine with Denise—but because he needed the boy.

Denise met him at the door. He stopped short when he saw

her furrowed brow and her pretty green eyes darkened with worry. "Someone called because someone had a heart attack and is in the hospital."

"Who?" Ambler pushed past her.

"I wrote it down and the number." She handed him an envelope on which she'd written Kevin McNulty and a phone number.

The phone number was a cell phone for Brian McNulty's son, the younger Kevin McNulty. His grandfather was in the cardiac care unit at Maimonides Medical Center.

"They admitted him and no one will tell me anything about his condition," the young man said when Ambler called him back. Kevin tried to sound calm and confident but his voice shook. "I'm on my way to the city now. I should be there in a couple of hours."

McNulty had asked Ambler to look after his father and his son. He hadn't expected something like this. "What about your dad?"

Young Kevin hesitated. "Maybe we shouldn't talk on the phone."

"I'll meet you at the hospital." Maimonides was in Borough Park, an Orthodox Jewish neighborhood in the middle of Brooklyn. He asked Denise to stay with Johnny for a few hours and told Johnny he was going to visit McNulty's dad in the hospital. The hospital was near a D train stop, so the subway would be faster than a car service. He arrived before Kevin Jr. and wasn't allowed into the CardioThoracic Intensive Care Unit because he wasn't a relative. He thought about arguing but stopped when he was told Mr. McNulty's sister was with him at the moment. He could speak with her when she finished her visit.

"Sister?" Ambler didn't know the senior McNulty had a sister or McNulty an aunt. It was a surprise when Ambler discovered McNulty had a father and a son. Nothing else he could do, Ambler sat down in an antiseptic hallway to wait for the son in question, who arrived about an hour later.

"They wouldn't let me in," Ambler told the breathless young man. "Your father's aunt is in there now."

Kevin Jr.'s eyes sprang open. "His what?" He recovered quickly, cast a quick look behind him at the nurses' station, and nodded at Ambler. He lowered his voice. "Aunt . . . Fay, right? I guess I can go in." Kevin headed for the nurses' station but before he reached it, a matronly figure pushed through the closed doors marked CTICU and came toward him, grabbing his arm and propelling him back toward Ambler.

"How do you do?" the matronly figure said to Ambler. "I'm Kevin's sister Bridie. My brother is holding his own but would prefer to not have visitors for the time being. Let's go where we can talk. I cased the place when I came in. I didn't see any police. But you never know."

By this time, Ambler caught on. "Your father really did have a heart attack, right?"

McNulty shot a sidelong glance at Ambler. "Do you think I'd take a chance on coming into the city if he hadn't?" He cuffed his son on the shoulder. "Go flag down a livery cab and have it wait around the corner." To Ambler, he said, "We'll walk out together in a couple of minutes, hold my arm like a dutiful nephew or whatever."

"Precautions are good," Ambler said. "My detective friend, Mike Cosgrove's daughter is with Johnny. She knows I went to the hospital to see your father. She knows the name. She might mention it. If she does, Mike will add things up."

They met the livery cab on the corner. McNulty's apartment might still be watched. If Mike suspected Ambler went to meet McNulty, Ambler's apartment would be watched also. On the bright side, it was unlikely they were being followed. "Maybe we should go to Adele's apartment for now, and get you a hotel after that."

"Brooklyn's changed," McNulty said, watching gentrification unfold out the livery cab window.

The three of them felt like a crowd in the living room of Adele's small apartment. She made them coffee and sandwiches and they crowded into her combination living room–dining room. McNulty told them his father had had triple bypass surgery and was recovering.

"It's going to be a long haul," he said. "He's going to need someone to look after him." He stared off into space for a moment. "It should be me. I owe him that." He turned to Ambler. "I don't suppose you found out anything helpful."

Ambler told him about Sandra's mother's death and Sandra's car in her mother's garage.

"We stopped there. Part of Sandi's plan . . . as much of a plan as she had. You think Sandi's mother was murdered? The cops think I did it? Now I murder old ladies?" He glared at each of them in turn, including his son.

"Not so old," Ambler said.

McNulty nodded. "No offense."

"The police don't think she was murdered, so no one's accusing you . . . yet."

"There's a break." McNulty told the ceiling. "What about the names I gave you?"

"Mike Cosgrove's interviewing them. I asked him to."

"Would he tell you if he found something?"

"He'd tell me some things, maybe not other things. If he finds something, he'll follow it up. At the moment, there's a what he'd call person of interest. Did Sandra ever mention a Peter Esposito? He's one of the men in her journal."

"She didn't much talk about that part of her life. Except she'd run into men who'd become obsessed with her and it scared her when men were like that. I told her it was because she was pretty and charming. She said it wasn't that. Men like that wanted to own her. They cared about what they wanted from her, not her." McNulty was quiet for a moment. "At least one of the men scared her. She never said which one. That's why I gave you the names in her journal."

"Did she ever mention Dillard Wainwright?"

McNulty raised an eyebrow, heightened interest. "The guy her mother ran off with? Sandi knew him, all right."

Despite asking the question, Ambler hadn't expected that answer. "His name was in her journal, but she didn't write about him in the section of the journal you gave me."

"They emailed."

"Did she stay in touch with any of the other men she—"

"He's the only one I know of. They weren't love letters they sent each other."

"Did she have her laptop the night she was . . . Did she have the laptop the last time you saw her?"

The silence in Adele's living room was as brittle as ice. "She had it in the hotel room the night she was murdered."

"Do you know what happened to it?"

McNulty's face was expressionless. "The murderer took it or the cops found it." He met Ambler's gaze with sadness in his own. "I don't have it if that's what you're asking."

"If the police found it, they might still have it or they gave it to her husband," Ambler said. "Mike could find out. But how could I ask him without letting on I've seen you?"

"Ask her husband." McNulty said.

"He doesn't get along so well with Raymond," Adele said.

She didn't say why but McNulty understood. "He thinks you have a horse in the race, eh?"

McNulty left with his son soon after that, telling Ambler and Adele they were better off not knowing where he was going. It turned out to not to make much difference. Ambler stayed talking with Adele for a while.

"Why don't you ask your new friend Andrea Eagan to get the laptop for you?" Adele said. "She's made quite a hit with you. And maybe you with her?" Something about Adele's tone wasn't right.

"She helped me get Jayne Galloway's journals and diaries. I like her."

"I can tell. You spent a pleasant afternoon together on Long Island. How nice. I'm sure you're anxious to see her again." Adele rattled together the small plates and cups she picked up from the table and dropped them with a clatter into the sink.

Ambler caught on. His enthusiasm for Andrea came through too strongly when he described the afternoon he spent with her. "Oh my God, no, Adele. It's not like that. She's young. She's married."

"Oh?" She stood with her hand on her hip in the doorway to the kitchen. "Sandra Dean was married, too."

Ambler felt a kind of pleasurable warmth. Adele was jealous.

"What are you smirking about?" Adele went back to rattling the dishes in the kitchen sink.

When Ambler got back to his apartment, he and Johnny walked Denise to Third Avenue and put her in a cab to go home. He kissed her on top of her head and asked how things were going at home. Family stuff hadn't been going well for her for a while.

"Not so good," she said. "Mom and Dad are getting a divorce."

"Oh?"

"That's not so bad. What's bad is Dad moved out and I have to stay with my mother. I'm not sure I can stand it."

"Oh," said Ambler again. He tried not to talk to Denise about her family. His sympathy was certainly with Mike; still, he didn't want to say anything against her mother. There were always two sides to these stories. "Where's your dad staying?"

"He's staying with a couple of friends, two other divorced cops. A real bachelor's pad. Beer cans and dirty dishes. He's trying to get his own apartment so I can stay with him, at least some of the time."

"Poor Denise," Ambler said, and kissed her on the top of her head again. "Things will get better."

She looked at him, her eyes large with bewilderment. "You've said that before and things haven't gotten better." She let that sink in but then cheered up. "Anyway, I'm happy to babysit anytime." She caught Johnny's truculent expression. "I don't mean babysit. You know what I mean. Hang with Johnny if you need to be out somewhere. I can cook, you know. Make dinner. I can stay overnight if you have . . ." she dramatically cleared her throat, ". . . somewhere you want to be. If Adele needs a hand some evening . . . or something." Denise tried to suppress her giggles but couldn't.

Ambler gave her a gentle shove into the cab and closed the door on her giggles and winks.

"What did she mean, if Adele needs a hand some evening?" Johnny asked as they walked back to the apartment.

Ambler was at a loss for an answer. His cheeks burned.

"I can still stay at Adele's anytime I want, right?" Johnny looked up at Ambler, worry crinkling his eyes.

"Of course you can."

"We can both stay there sometime, right?"

Ambler smiled. "Maybe."

Chapter 19

Ambler awoke the next morning to a phone call from Mike Cosgrove. "We locked up your bartender friend," he said by way of greeting.

The world crashed around Ambler. He didn't ask the particulars. "Where is he?"

"They're holding him at the twenty-six."

Twenty-six was the 26th Precinct in Manhattan, nowhere near Maimonides in Brooklyn. Not near Adele's apartment either. It was uptown in Harlem and covered McNulty's neighborhood on the Upper West Side.

Cosgrove wasn't finished. "I got something else. The cops in Nassau found your parrot. There's a group on Long Island that specializes in finding lost parrots." He sighed dramatically. "We got a group for everything in New York."

"That's Long Island, not the city."

"Same thing. Most everyone out there's from the city."

Not only did the group find the parrot, some of the volunteers knew the parrot, Buster, because Jayne Galloway was one of the lost-parrot group volunteers.

"The parrot got loose. That happens." Mike said.

"All the windows and doors were closed."

"It could have gotten out before her death. It could have been missing for days."

"She would have searched for it, told someone, contacted the lost-parrot group."

"You want to say someone let it out? You got that and Dr. Dean's car in the victim's garage. You want me to talk to Nassau County about the suspicion Mrs. Galloway was murdered. If I do, the person of interest is your pal McNulty."

"I think not." Ambler told Mike about receiving Jayne Galloway's phone call after Sandra Dean's death and that she and McNulty were at Jayne Galloway's the night they left the city after Ted Doyle's murder.

"And how do you know this?"

Ambler realized he'd made a mistake.

Mike was a bulldog. If you let something slip, he latched on and didn't let go. "We're not talking about harboring here, are we?"

"McNulty's father had a heart attack. He's in the hospital. That's why McNulty is in the city." Ambler paused and made a half-hearted effort. "I was going to call you . . ."

Mike laughed, not something he did often. "Yeah. I'm hard to reach sometimes. . . . And you get busy, things slip your mind. I know how that is."

"Okay, Mike, you made your point." Neither explanation nor apology would do any good. Mike would forgive or he wouldn't. "There might be something else." Ambler told him about Dillard Wainwright. "Besides the research she did in the library, she was in email contact with him shortly before her death. Now, he's been missing from his job and his home since right around the time of the murders."

Mike had a way of creating a different sort of silence, even on the phone, when he listened intently. "His name is on the list you gave me. You're not saying he was one of her, uh, love interests?"

"I'm saying he might be a suspect in her murder."

Mike grumbled. "Hard to keep up with your expanding list of suspects. But I'll try. Right now, we have the bartender to talk about. He was breaking into his apartment."

"His own apartment?"

"They're holding him for Connecticut. If you're on your good behavior they might let you see him at the precinct. He's already lawyered up, so I'm not going to talk to him. Check with his lawyer."

Ambler called David Levinson, who picked up the phone on the second ring. "Yep, he called me. The asshole. I told him I knew a hundred good criminal defense attorneys and begged him to call one of them." The lawyer paused for effect. He liked to hear himself talk, yet Ambler usually enjoyed his banter. He was also, thanks to McNulty, working on an appeal for Ambler's son, Johnny's dad. "Of course, McNulty wouldn't hear of it. He'd have to pay. . . . I'm on my way uptown."

Ambler said he'd meet him at the 26th Precinct after he dropped Johnny at school. Again, he had to take a cab and Finnegan wasn't available, so it wasn't cheap.

Surprising to Ambler when he got to the precinct, David Levinson was sitting with the cops behind the desk chuckling and trading wisecracks. He'd had arranged to have donuts and coffee delivered from the donut shop on Broadway. It was coffee-break time and Levinson was one of the boys. He'd done pro bono work for the police union, it turned out, so the cops put up with him.

"McNulty's in the query room," Levinson pointed his donut toward a hallway. Ambler followed the hallway to a door marked INTERROGATION. He knocked. Something buzzed so he opened the door. McNulty, wearing jeans and a blue workshirt that was too big for him, sat at a metal table on a metal chair;

two other chairs were around the table, all of them bolted to the floor. A tape recorder on the room's only shelf wasn't running. The walls were gray and bare, except for a large mirror in the middle of one wall that was obviously, even to Ambler, a two-way mirror.

"You okay?" Ambler asked.

McNulty rolled his eyes. "Couldn't be better."

"What happened?"

"I made a mistake." His smile was rueful. "I didn't have my apartment key, so I was picking the lock. A long time ago, I learned from a friend in the business how to pick locks. I'm pretty good at it."

"A locksmith?"

McNulty scowled. "A burglar. . . . The old lady across the hall heard me, so she started screaming like a fucking banshee. Beats me why'd she scream about an old lady. By the time I quieted her down—she freaked out again when she realized it was me and not an old lady—the night doorman had called the cops. He's the spare guy—my luck—and the jerk didn't recognize me either."

"Were you dressed like Mrs. Doubtfire?"

McNulty grimaced. "The regular night guy's a friend of mine. He was off last night. How was I supposed to know?" When McNulty didn't see any police watching the place, he slipped in when the door man was occupied. He wasn't going to turn on the lights or do anything in the apartment except crash for the night.

"More bad luck. A couple of cruisers were in front of the all-night coffee shop on the corner. They were told a robbery was in progress, so they're surprised to find a matronly lady, even more surprised when they found she had balls."

Ambler glanced at the two-way mirror. "Do we need to be circumspect?"

McNulty gave the mirror a hard stare. "What do I have

to hide? My life's an open book. My turncoat lawyer is watching through the window with the cops. Tell me whatever you want."

"Sandra's mother called me not long before her death. I believe she had something to tell me about Ted Doyle's murder, or why Sandra was in hiding, or who killed Sandra, something that had bearing on Sandra's death. Why did you and Sandra go to her mother? Why did Sandra run away after Ted Doyle's murder if she was innocent?"

McNulty spoke softly, despite what he'd said about being overheard. "Sandi headed that way when we left the city. She didn't tell me why. I didn't know we were going to see her mother until we got there. Sandi was wound pretty tight. We didn't talk much. She was afraid; that's why she ran. I took it she was afraid of whoever murdered the guy." He met Ambler's gaze with the familiar flicker of mischief in his eyes. "Why I went with her? I've asked myself that." His expression said the rest.

"Was her mother expecting you?"

McNulty looked into the two-way mirror, maybe he was looking at himself. "She was expecting her. I was a surprise. Sandi wasn't telling me, or her mother either, everything that was going on. When push came to shove, Sandi took her own counsel. She wanted to get her daughter back before her husband found out what happened."

"The murder in her hotel room? She didn't tell him about it?"

McNulty shook his head. "I don't know all of what she told her husband. I only overheard some. But I'd say not that. She spoke to him on the phone a couple of times over a couple of days. She was lying to him. He'd found out something about her. She told him she was sorry and wanted him to say it was okay for her to come home. She wanted her daughter." McNulty stood up and walked around in the small space of the query room. "I'm used to working standing up. I'm not used to sitting so much."

He sat down again. "She may have been lying to me, too. Those days with her are a blur. We talked. She cried a lot and slept on and off." He glanced at the mirror again and spoke softly. "We did other things. I thought I knew what she wanted; now I'm not so sure. I don't know if I believe what she told me. She was in trouble, deep trouble; she was desperate. She'd use me or anyone else to get herself out of it. Was that what she was doing—using her mother, using her husband, using me? I don't know. What I know is she wanted to be with her kid."

Ambler felt a wave of sadness and a rush of sympathy for McNulty, for Sandra Dean. "What was the trouble?"

McNulty met Ambler's gaze with a fathomless gaze of his own. "I thought it would come clear. She'd get to a place where she'd see her way out and she'd tell me. The answer was right around the corner, coming any minute. . . . And it never did come."

"Did she tell you anything about the murdered man?"

"No."

"She never told you who he was, why she was with him, why she was with another man when she was making plans with you?"

"I told you—or maybe I told Adele—she said it wasn't like that."

"Did you believe her?"

"I did then."

"Do you now?"

The expression in his eyes went dark. "I don't know."

They were quiet for a moment. Ambler had more questions but wasn't sure McNulty had the answers. People remember their view of things, and even then they don't remember everything. He tried one more time. "What about her husband?"

"What about him?"

"What did he know? Did she tell him about the murder?"

"I told you, no."

"He must have known something? Did he know she'd been unfaithful? Did he know she was with you?"

McNulty took a deep breath and sat back as well as he could in the uncomfortable metal chair; he made an effort to gather his thoughts. "I didn't know what I was doing. I didn't know what she was doing. Any minute, I expected the cops to come barreling through the door. I was thinking about her and me together, how that was going to happen. At the time—being the idiot I am—I thought she was thinking that, too." He lifted a baleful gaze toward Ambler. "You're asking me to make sense of what was going on when what was going on made no sense. I was in the middle of it, not like you looking at it from the outside saying, 'Well, what have we here?'"

McNulty was frustrated. Ambler didn't want to make it worse, so he spoke carefully. "I'm trying to understand how she came to be speaking with her husband and what she told him." Ambler recalled his first meeting with Simon Dean when he'd told him his wife and McNulty were most likely together. Did he already know that at the time? Or did Ambler reveal that his wife was with another man and could that have led to Sandra Dean's death? Might he be responsible for her murder?

Ambler adjusted himself on his own uncomfortable chair. "Could her husband have killed her?"

McNulty frowned. "The only one I know didn't kill her is me." He looked at Ambler curiously. "Where did that come from?"

Ambler told him what he'd said to Simon Dean.

"I don't think it was like that with him. She felt sorry for him, like she wronged him. If she thought he'd kill her, why would she go home to him? That's what she was trying to do. And who killed the guy in New York?"

"How did her husband know where she was?"

"As far as I know, he didn't. From what I heard of the phone call, she let him think she was in the city. How would he know where she was?"

"That's what I asked you."

McNulty shook his head and looked quizzically at Ambler. "Don't take this the wrong way, Ray. I have great faith in you." He leaned back and spread himself out again as best he could in the chair he sat in. "You're wasting your time. If I knew why Sandi was killed, that would help. I don't. She was scared something or someone would catch up with her. Someone she wrote about in her journal? Someone from her past? I don't know." He leaned toward Ambler. "Are you catching my drift? I don't know what the fuck happened!"

A knock on the door and it opened; David Levinson stuck his head in. "Your turncoat attorney here. You're on your way up the river, McNulty, figuratively speaking." Levinson chuckled, his usual cheerful self. "Don't worry, pal. I'll get you out if it's the last thing I do." He took a moment to glance about the query room. His tone changed then to a kind of resonating baritone, a courtroom voice that caused you to sit up and take notice. "I'm taking my dad to visit your dad tonight. We'll keep an eye on him. I'll see you at the arraignment in Stamford. I'm waiving extradition. The jails are nicer in Connecticut."

Ambler walked out with David Levinson leaving McNulty behind. In front of the precinct house, Levinson hailed a cab and told Ambler he'd drop him at the library. On the way downtown, Levinson said, "My dad and Kevin McNulty went underground together during the red scare witch hunt days in the fifties. Neither Brian nor I saw our fathers for two years. We have a common mistrust of the state. He won't let on—tough guys don't cry. He's scared. He believes he's doomed."

"Is he?"

"We'll try some things, establish an alibi for the time of the murder if we can, poke some holes in the case the police are building, dispute the basis of the charges against him. I don't know what makes for a murder conviction in Connecticut. In the Bronx, he'd most likely walk."

"What would be different?"

"Juries. Community standards. I don't know the cops in Stamford. I don't know the ADAs. To people up there, I'm a slick city lawyer. He'd do better with a local attorney. But a murder trial is expensive, twenty grand or more at the low end. He's stuck with me."

Ambler stared out the cab window at Central Park sliding past. A golden haze hung over the park. The trees had mostly turned, the leaves varying shades of yellow, some brown, a stunning reddish orange here and there. "What kind of evidence do they have?"

"He was with her. She's dead. He ran. Throw in some forensic bullshit. His fingerprints will be in the hotel room, his DNA on her. It's enough to convince some people. We'll see what we get in discovery."

After Levinson dropped him at the library, Ambler moped through the afternoon trying to get some work done. This included a screening interview with a researcher who'd applied to use the collection of a defunct paperback publisher of detective novels and adventure fiction in the 1950s. He did the interview, set her up with boxes of correspondence between the editor and his stable of authors, and then browsed through auction catalogs for the rest of the day.

Mike Cosgrove called right before he left work. "The guys in Nassau want to know what they should do with the parrot."

Ambler had no idea what to do with the parrot. "I guess it belongs to Carolyn. She's the only heir." He paused. "Hold on. I think I can help you out. . . . I'll call you back."

Ambler wanted to see Sandra's email correspondence with Dillard Wainwright, which might be on her laptop. Simon most likely had her laptop and would probably not give it to him. Now he had an idea. He disconnected with Mike and called the cell phone number he had for Andrea Eagan.

"Oh, hello," she said, her tone stilted, almost a whisper, and after a pause, "I didn't expect to hear from you." She lowered her voice even more. "Can I call you back?" He'd started to tell her why he was calling and hesitated. "It won't be long—" Her tone warned him she wanted him to understand what she meant without telling him.

He did have a glimmering. "Sure. My number—"

"I have your number," she said so quietly there was almost no sound.

When she was gone, he didn't know what to do with himself. The questions he wanted to ask her were stuck in his head, blocking any other thoughts. He must have been staring into space for some time. When he looked up, Adele was in the doorway.

"Let's go," she said.

He didn't know what she meant. The day had been crazy and his brain was fried; then, he remembered. It was Friday evening. They were taking Johnny for pizza and a movie. He hemmed and hawed. He'd called Andrea from his desk phone and wanted to wait for her phone call, afraid that if he didn't talk to Andrea now, he might not get the chance. Strangely, he was reluctant to tell Adele for whom he was waiting.

"Well?" Adele's hand was on her hip, an ominous sign.

"I need to wait for a phone call. Can you hang on a few minutes?"

"I can. I don't know if Denise can. It's her Friday night, too, and she can't leave Johnny alone. Who's the call from?"

He knew she'd ask. She had an uncanny way of knowing when he didn't want to tell her something. He gave up and told her. She grumbled but said she'd pick up Johnny, and they'd meet him at the pizza place. He watched her walk away, unhurried, erect, the gentle sway of her hips. She had that way, too, of knowing how to help him when he needed help.

Andrea called a few minutes later. "Sorry," she said. "I didn't want Simon to overhear me. Something about you drives him straight up a wall. He was angry that I let you take Sandi's mother's papers. He went storming out to his lawyer's to try to get a court order to get them back."

Ambler was surprised and not surprised. Simon had turned on him because of McNulty. "We have lawyers, too. I don't think we'll need to give up the papers."

"I think his lawyer told him that. He said he'd get them from you himself. He might. He's like that."

"When I first met Simon, I found him an easygoing guy, if maybe a bit straitlaced and old fashioned." Ambler paused. "Murders have ramifications. I don't blame him for lashing out when he's suffering so much."

"I guess."

He told her about Jayne Galloway's parrot.

"Carolyn would love to have the parrot," she sounded girlish, excited for Carolyn; then she paused. "Simon would have a cow. Let me think about what I can do."

Ambler moved on to the real reason he'd called. "Do you remember I asked you about Dillard Wainwright?" She did, so he told her about the emails between Wainwright and Sandra Dean. "He's disappeared. I'm hoping something on Sandra's laptop will help me find him. I was hoping you'd ask Simon for me. That doesn't seem like much of a plan after what you've told me."

She was apologetic. "I'm sorry Simon's such a jerk. He's sure your friend the bartender killed Sandi and that you're trying to get him off by finding someone else to cast suspicion on."

Ambler had to admit that what Simon thought wasn't so far from the truth. He did want to find someone to cast suspicion on. He didn't tell Andrea this.

A half hour later, he caught up with Adele and Johnny at their Friday night pizza hangout, a family-run Italian restaurant that had been on Third Avenue as long as he could remember, and was soon to be swept into the dustbin of history by voracious developers and greedy landlords. He ate two slices of cold, congealed pizza.

"We saved it for you," Adele said with what he thought was smug satisfaction.

After the movie, he and Johnny walked Adele home through the clear and crisp New York autumn night. Ambler told her about his phone call with Andrea Eagan and that he'd need to ask Simon for the laptop himself. "He'll probably say no."

"I understand he's upset," Adele said after a moment. "I don't like that he won't allow for the possibility McNulty might be innocent."

After Ambler and Johnny left Adele, Ambler started walking toward his apartment. Johnny stopped and asked if they should take a cab. "Are you tired?" Ambler asked. Johnny usually liked to walk. They seldom took cabs. He noticed what might be rebuke in the boy's expression. "Is something wrong?"

"I thought we should get home quicker. We're going to see my dad tomorrow. Did you forget?" There was a twitching around his mouth and his eyes were liquid.

Ambler had forgotten. How could he? The visit was arranged. They didn't need reservations for the train. It wasn't that. He wasn't mentally ready. Usually, the week before a visit to his dad, Johnny was beside himself with anticipation and excitement. And he hadn't been. But of course Ambler had hardly seen the boy the past week. Distracted, he hadn't paid attention to him. That wasn't right.

"It slipped my mind, Johnny. I've been preoccupied. We're fine. There's no problem. We'll get a cab. We'll need to get up early."

Johnny was satisfied. Ambler stared glumly out the window at the city sliding by. It wasn't only Johnny he neglected. He'd not thought about his son either, fulfilling John's prophecy that once you're locked up everyone soon forgets about you. He'd also forgotten to ask David Levinson about John's appeal.

He felt like telling Johnny how awful he felt and how sorry he was, yet this would be self-serving, asking for forgiveness or understanding or pity he didn't deserve. He'd neglected his son when John was a boy because he was so absorbed in his study, writing his dissertation—absorbed in himself really—that he didn't have time for others, even his son, and now he was doing this same thing—which he swore he would never do—to his grandchild.

The visits to John had taken on an entirely new, and vibrant, life since Johnny became part of the visits. Ambler's job now was pretty much to hold father's and son's coats as they went about their visit. He was fine with this. John, having reclaimed his son and with an attorney working on an appeal of his conviction, was hopeful for the first time. He wouldn't be exonerated. He'd killed a man. But Ambler believed without a doubt, as John had told him, that the killing was an accident. He shot a man in a fight as they struggled for the man's—his crazy housemate—gun. David Levinson thought he could win a new trial and get the charge reduced to involuntary manslaughter, instead of the first-degree manslaughter John was convicted of.

The trip the next morning to Shawangunk, the prison where John was housed, required a ninety-minute train ride along the Hudson and a half-hour cab ride from the railroad station plus at least another half hour, more often an hour, to get through the visitor processing at the prison. Almost as soon as Ambler and Johnny sat down with John at a table in the visiting room—not unlike a high school cafeteria—John asked, as Ambler feared he would, about his appeal. Ambler said weakly they were working on it but nothing new.

During their weekly phone call, Johnny had told his father

about Sandra Dean's murder and McNulty's arrest. Even if John didn't know McNulty, he'd heard enough about him over the years to know Ambler would have taken up his cause. John remembered also that Ambler met the attorney who was doing his appeal through McNulty. Fortunately, he was satisfied with Ambler's answer that there wasn't anything new.

Something else Ambler didn't tell John was that he hadn't figured out yet how to pay the attorney. With all of that, the visit with John was so guilt-inducing that Ambler called David Levinson from the railroad station platform as he and Johnny waited for the train back to the city. Levinson said he wanted to hire an investigator to search for the girlfriend of the man John had shot. In looking over the records of the case, he came across something in the DA's files—the name of a second potential witness, a friend of this girlfriend—that wasn't in the files of the legal aid attorney who represented John.

"I have a call in to your son's 18-B attorney; he's still on the job, the poor bastard."

"Did his attorney make a mistake?"

"It's not a mistake. Those panel guys need to take on impossible workloads to make a living. I used to be one. Even the good ones don't have the resources or the time—"

Ambler got the idea. "I should have hired a private attorney like you for John's original trial."

For once, Levinson was slow to respond. "Since it went to trial, it would have cost you at least twenty to thirty grand. If it didn't go to trial, ten grand at least, and he would have still gone to prison . . . maybe not for so long."

Ambler went cold. "How much are we talking about for the appeal?"

Levinson chuckled. "The meter's running. Usually, I get five grand up front. Let's see what I can do. With McNulty's case on the cuff, I'll have to go back to driving a cab part-time to make ends meet, as it is."

Ambler tried to laugh but couldn't. He'd been rocked to his toes by the realization that if he'd come up with the money for a private attorney for John's original trial—though the Lord knows where he would have gotten the money—his son wouldn't be rotting away in prison. And it struck him deep in his heart that John was street smart enough to have known that all along. This time, he was going to come up with the money to pay for the appeal . . . somehow.

McNulty's arraignment was in Stamford Monday morning. David Levinson rented a car to drive up for the appearance, and Ambler took the morning off and went with him. It was something he felt he should do, though he did it with reluctance. The last time he'd been in a courtroom he listened to the sentence imposed on his son and watched him being led away. The fear, bewilderment, and anger in his son's eyes that day seared a hole in his heart. He still saw John's haggard face on nights he lay sleepless staring at his ceiling.

Levinson was on his cell phone the entire trip up to Connecticut, explaining court and arraignment proceedings to the mother of one of his clients. He went over the same thing a half-dozen times with amazing patience. Ambler was glad Levinson was occupied so he didn't have to talk to him.

The courtroom proceedings were sparsely attended. He half expected to see Simon Dean, but he wasn't there. Ambler sat in an aisle seat in the middle row of the gallery. Levinson went to the front where he introduced himself to the judge and shook hands with some attorneys standing around and then sat down at a table. McNulty came in through a side door handcuffed with a guard at his elbow. He was bent at the waist, almost a bow, whether this was caused by the pull of the handcuffs or McNulty's state of mind, Ambler didn't know. Levinson got up from the table and stood beside McNulty. He put his hand on his shoulder and said something into his ear. Ambler couldn't hear what Levinson said or much of what anyone said, except for the judge who had a microphone in front of him.

Levinson made a presentation the judge didn't show much interest in. A young woman in a blue business suit said something to the judge also. The judge asked McNulty a question. McNulty said, "Not guilty." He said this loudly enough to startle the few people sitting in the gallery, including Ambler. Levinson said something else. The judge said something. Even with the microphone, Ambler only recognized the word "remanded." There was a kind of silence, everything in suspended animation, until the guard led McNulty out. He shuffled out, the same way he shuffled in, his head bowed. Ambler wasn't sure if McNulty saw him or not.

For the first part of the ride back to the city, he and Levinson were deep in their own thoughts. Ambler watched the fall foliage alongside the parkway slide by and let his mind wander from McNulty to Ted Doyle to Sandra to Jayne Galloway.

Levinson broke his silence as they settled into a traffic tie-up on the Henry Hudson Parkway. "This isn't my favorite subject," he said.

Ambler waited.

Levinson kept his eyes on the road. "McNulty's case will take a lot of time. That's time with no income. I need billable hours to keep my practice going. I understand you may not be able to come up with a retainer as quickly as you'd like. I have to do it this way. If I'm not getting paid for your son's case, I have to put his case on the back burner to work billable hours."

"I understand." This didn't mean Ambler knew how to get the money. He'd already tapped his pension for legal expenses for Johnny's adoption and a custody battle with Lisa Young; he didn't think he could go to the well again.

He caught Levinson sneaking a glance at him. "Look. I'll keep working on it," the lawyer said. "It won't move as fast. I'd like to hire an investigator. . . ."

"I know. I need to arrange some things."

Chapter 20

The next-to-last man on Cosgrove's list, Alan Hoffman, proved difficult for Mike Cosgrove to find. The last man on the list, Dillard Wainwright, the guy Ray was interested in, was worse. He was in the National Missing and Unidentified Persons System. Disappearing from a job and a life meant something, especially when the guy's name pops up in a homicide investigation.

Cosgrove was running checks on Peter Esposito and planned to interview him again the next time Esposito came to the city. He wanted to check the Commodore Hotel records, but at the moment, he didn't have enough evidence for a warrant, and the hotel had a policy of not releasing its guest records without a warrant. The desk clerk he spoke with knew Esposito as did one of the bartenders and a waitress. None of them remembered if he stayed in the hotel the night of Ted Doyle's murder.

Most of the Dean woman's assignations had been at the Commodore, so he tried the hotel again this time looking for Alan Hoffman, stopping off late in the evening when the night auditor would be on the desk. The head of security for the hotel was an ex-cop, full of himself, protecting the hotel as if he were the palace guard. The night auditor was a regular guy who saw the hotel's promotional bullshit about its "beautiful people" clientele for what it was.

What happened, as sometimes happens, was that Cosgrove was right for the wrong reason. The auditor knew Alan Hoffman and told Cosgrove he never registered at the hotel because he was local and a regular at the hotel bar. The bartender knew him, too. Alan Hoffman was a cop, a detective, who at one time stopped in regularly but hadn't been in for a long time.

"Do you remember him meeting a woman here one night, a pretty blonde, not a kid, not yet middle aged?"

"Al wasn't the kind of guy who was looking for that," the bartender, whose name tag read Moses, said. "He came in by himself, had a couple of pops, maybe talked with someone on the next barstool. A lot of times he talked to me. What he talked about was baseball, coaching kids playing baseball in Riverdale, or taking his boy to Yankee games."

The bartender went to refresh the drinks of a couple at the far end of the bar. When he came back to Cosgrove, he said. "I'm wrong. You mean the blonde woman who got killed? He did meet her." Moses was a big, light-skinned, black guy, athletic looking, still in good shape. Cosgrove thought he might have played football. He was soft spoken when you'd expect him to bluster from his size and how he carried himself.

"A year ago, maybe longer, Al ran into her here at the bar. She'd been drinking. They talked till closing. He took her under his wing and walked her out. I figured he was being a gentleman, making sure she got back to her room with no trouble. I'd done that, too, once, walked her out of here so she got back to her room okay. She invited me in. I didn't take her up on it. Drunk women are trouble." The bartender met Cosgrove's gaze.

"She was proper, well-spoken, until she had a few drinks,

even then she was well-spoken but out of control. She'd blurt things out, be in your face." He chuckled. "But you had to like her. Once in a while, when she'd start an argument, she surprised herself, like a kid does something and the grown-ups laugh and hc looks bewildered because he doesn't know what he's done."

The next afternoon, Cosgrove found Alan Hoffman working in the 90th Precinct community affairs youth division in the Williamsburg section of Brooklyn.

"I work with the kids in the projects, the Williamsburg Houses," Hoffman said after Cosgrove introduced himself.

Cosgrove had decided to drop in at the precinct rather than call ahead. When he told Hoffman why he was there, the color drained from the man's face. His voice shook. "Can we go outside? . . . Take a walk?" It was a supplication spoken in a whisper.

Hoffman led the way though they walked side by side. Cosgrove, not wanting to interrupt the other man's wrestling match with his conscience, kept quiet as they walked to a park a couple of blocks from the precinct where there was a fenced-in baseball diamond. It reminded Cosgrove of what the bartender at the hotel told him. They leaned against the black wire fence, side by side, watching a man hit grounders to a boy about Ray's grandson's age who wore a Mets cap and fielded the ground balls smoothly.

"I transferred out here because of that. One night. One time." Hoffman's voice was strained and he didn't look at Cosgrove. "I've been married fifteen years." When he did glance at Cosgrove, he seemed to ask for help. "I was going to walk her to the elevator. She asked me to walk her to her room. I had my hand under her elbow, kind of steering her. She wore high heel shoes and was kind of wobbly. The whole time she talked. She was afraid in New York, she told me, and didn't like being by herself in the city. A couple of times as we walked, she said

I was sweet. When she said that, she'd stop and turn toward me and look into my eyes. Hers were dark and pretty and sad. When we go to her room, she told me she had a couple of little bottles of scotch from an airplane and invited me for a drink. The next thing I knew we were in her room and she was in my arms.

"When we'd finished, she cried. I held her and she cried and told me she was ashamed of herself. 'I'm not like that,' she said. She had a husband and a daughter. 'The person who did that isn't me.' She turned on me. 'Did you put something in my drink?'

"She scared me. She didn't want to believe she'd seduced me. I was afraid of what she might say, of what she might do. I'd lose my wife. I'd lose my kids. I couldn't stand that. I was mad at myself, too. What was I doing in bed half drunk with a crazy woman screaming I doctored her drink?" He stared at the baseball field.

Cosgrove had been quiet since he'd introduced himself back at the precinct. After a moment, he realized Hoffman was crying. Tears trickled down his face. He put his hand near his eyes to kind of shade them, so Cosgrove walked away from him. There was a dog run next to the ball field near where they'd been standing, so he went and watched the dogs play; the big dogs played with the little dogs, purebred fluffy dogs that looked like powder puffs and scruffy mid-sized mutts and mongrels, growling and play fighting, all of them cheerful and proud of themselves. He watched the dogs until he felt Hoffman beside him.

"I should have stepped up when I saw she'd been murdered. I felt terribly sorry for her." He watched the sky for a couple of minutes. Cosgrove looked up, too, and wondered what the other man saw. "She made trouble for herself. I tried to tell her . . ."

More was coming. Cosgrove had heard enough confessions

to know when one was coming. The guy starts off with what you knew, confirming things you'd found out or figured out. When you were ready to wrap things up, something in a tone of voice or a word or two you weren't expecting, and you knew to keep quiet, leave things alone. If you disappeared and let the guy talk, you might find yourself solving a couple of cases you didn't know you were investigating. He didn't know what was coming from Hoffman but something was.

"She called me. I was surprised she remembered me. She wanted me to buy a handgun for her. I told her I couldn't do that. She didn't tell me why she wanted the gun. I assumed she was afraid. She didn't tell me what she was afraid of. I told her if she wasn't doing anything illegal she could get a permit and buy her own gun."

"When was this?"

"Not so long ago, a month or two."

Hoffman didn't have much more to say. He'd told her having a gun wouldn't protect her. That was movie stuff to think it would. She should call the police if she felt threatened or call a private investigator if she didn't want to go to the police. She said she didn't want to do anything her husband would find out about.

"Did you hear from her again?"

This time, Hoffman hung his head and stared at the ground for some time. "Despite what I told you, and what I told you is true . . . I love my family. Despite that, I was drawn to her. Something about her. I wanted to take care of her. She'd cry when we talked on the phone and I'd fall apart. I'd remember her nestled against me. When she cried, I wanted to hold her. I thought something bad might happen to her if I didn't take care of her. I wanted to see her again. She wouldn't. She said she was working on things with her husband."

"What kind of things?"

"She was trying to make things better with him, she said,

so she shouldn't even be talking to me. Except I was a cop. I could tell her what to do. When I said I wanted to be with her, her tone of voice would change, become sweet, even if she was saying it wouldn't work out. It was like she was in my arms again. Yet she could turn it on and off. I'd call her and the tone would be gone. She'd sound angry and distant; I'd feel like a stranger." He looked up at the sky again. "I was a stranger."

Cosgrove didn't know what to make of Hoffman. He said he hadn't seen or spoken to her since she asked him about the gun. You could take what he said as the truth. Or you could wonder if he left something out. In his own way, he was obsessed with her, like Esposito was in his way. Hoffman did own up about phoning her, about her asking him to get her a gun. You had to wonder, too, why she wanted it: to protect herself, to get rid of someone who was a problem to her—her husband, Esposito, someone else?

Cosgrove needed to be careful with Hoffman. He liked the guy and that made it too easy to sympathize with him, to overlook something, to let something go you wouldn't let go with someone else. It was like Ray with McNulty the bartender. Ray wanted too much for McNulty to be innocent. This made him less reliable than he usually was. Cosgrove would need to be extra careful with Hoffman.

Chapter 21

Adele found Raymond in the crime fiction reading room a few minutes after he returned from McNulty's arraignment. "How'd it go?"

"It was awful." Raymond was as dejected as she'd ever seen him.

Her mood deflated quickly, too. She watched him for a few minutes paging through a notebook Jayne Galloway had used to work out an idea for one of her books. He was fixated on Jayne Galloway's parrot and he continued to believe Galloway was murdered, though not by McNulty and Sandra Dean.

He had too many things on his mind, driving himself crazy trying to find an explanation for the murders that didn't include McNulty. On top of that, he didn't know where he was going to get the money to pay for his son's appeal, something else he was determined to do because he believed it was his fault his son was in prison. Lisa Young, Johnny's grandmother, had plenty of money. Raymond should ask her for help, but as was his way, he dragged his feet, hemming and hawing. Old-fashioned sort of guy that he was, he had a difficult time asking for help.

"Are you going to talk to Lisa Young about paying for your son's attorney?" Adele had asked him this before and knew the question irritated him. The muscles in his face tightened and he stared at the notebook he was holding. Adele didn't know Mrs. Young very well. She'd met her and she'd known her daughter, Johnny's mom. The Young side of Johnny's family was wealthy. On the days Johnny spent with his grandmother— Lisa Young and Raymond had joint custody of Johnny—he was a little rich kid. On the days he spent with Raymond, he was the grandson of a civil servant. Raymond was too proud to take what he saw as charity from rich people. On the few occasions Lisa Young suggested he and Johnny visit the Young's ski-slope chalet in Vail or their summer home in Newport, Raymond turned her down.

This afternoon, Adele waited as she skimmed through a notebook from Jayne Galloway's files while Raymond brooded. After a while, she said. "You're not asking her for you. You're asking her for Johnny, for her to pay legal expenses for her grandson's father. It's not going to put a dent in her savings."

"I know that." Raymond spoke sharply.

Adele didn't mind. He was fighting with himself, not with her. Johnny came into her life at the same time he came into Raymond's life. She'd been the one who'd found him trudging up Ninth Avenue lugging a shoeshine kit at a time of night a boy his age shouldn't have been on the street. It was a night she'd never forget; nor would she forget the tragic events that unfolded after that night. She loved Johnny as much as a mother would, though she'd never say that to anyone, not even Raymond. Johnny knew how much she loved him. That was all she needed, and to be with him often.

Raymond was good about that. She was as much involved in Johnny's life as Raymond was. Raymond and Lisa Young had their battles but things were peaceful now, a formal relationship. Lisa had won some battles—Johnny went to the tony

private school that Lisa Young's family had attended for gen-
erations. But the school was here in Manhattan, not a military
academy upstate she proposed sending him to. Lisa Young was
reasonable enough, and rich enough, that Raymond shouldn't
be so reluctant to ask her for help. As much as Adele respected
and cared about Raymond—and maybe loved him—she wasn't
going to let his pride and his grumpy old-man stubbornness
keep Johnny's father from coming home to his son.

After puttering around the Jayne Galloway collection for
another few minutes, opening a notebook, glancing at it, and
then glancing at him, she said, "Mrs. Young is going to be at a
lunch in the library tomorrow—"

Raymond spoke through clenched teeth. "I'll try to catch
her if I'm not too busy." He buried his head in a file box. It was a
clumsy hint to leave. She muttered something that might have
sounded like "asshole" and stomped out.

Late the next morning, Adele sat at her computer trying to
concentrate. Persuading Raymond to ask Mrs. Young to help
with Johnny's father's legal fees was a losing fight. At this very
moment, Lisa Young was here in the building, and Raymond
was nowhere to be found. It wasn't like he'd be asking her to
fund a prison break. Raymond's son was the victim of an in-
justice. He was entitled to a new trial. A new trial would put
things right. Or it wouldn't. Adele didn't know enough about
law to make any guesses about the outcome. Still, it was worth
a try for Johnny's sake.

A few minutes later, she found herself heading down the
marble stairs from the main reading room to the first floor and
the annual library lunch. The lunch should be over now and the
library friends and the trustees would be milling around the Bar-
tos Forum and the rotunda. If she just happened to run into
Mrs. Young, she could reintroduce herself, tell her what a great
job she and Raymond, the grandparents, were doing raising
Johnny—and casually mention that Raymond planned to speak

to her about some new, very positive developments in Johnny's dad's legal case.

She'd never gone behind Raymond's back like this before—well, hardly ever. He might be seriously angry with her for interfering. She'd never do something like this, except for Johnny. If she stopped to think about it, she'd probably wouldn't do it at all. So she didn't stop to think about it.

And there was Lisa Young across the lobby. The woman really did have an otherworldly elegance, due no doubt to the clothes she wore, the simple floral print dress that would cost a month's pay for Adele. As it happened, she didn't need to agonize over her decision because Lisa Young recognized her.

"Adele, isn't it?" She held out her hand. "Johnny never stops talking about you."

"How nice. . . . I think." Opportunity opened like a door in front of her. Or perhaps a precipice. "He speaks glowingly of you also."

She laughed. "I doubt it. I seem always to be reprimanding him."

"He's a rambunctious kid. He needs to be reined in sometimes." Here goes. Adele took a deep breath. "Has he told you the news about his father?"

Lisa Young's smile dropped. Her eyes went cold. "What about him?"

Adele faltered. The woman's expression was ghastly. She might have turned green, as if the mention of Johnny's dad made her sick to her stomach. "Oh . . . It seems as if he might be eligible for a new trial."

Mrs. Young was at a loss for words. Well, not so much at a loss as a shocked disapproving silence.

Adele watched the transformation with dread. Halfheartedly, she said, "It would be wonderful for Johnny if his father was released sooner than expected. . . ."

Mrs. Young's eyes widened. "How wonderful! To have a

convicted murderer in the family. What great dinner party conversations."

Adele's back went up. She didn't care who she was talking to. "He's not a murderer. What happened was an accident. He loves Johnny. He wants to get out of prison so he can be with him. To raise his son."

"God help us." Lisa Young shook her head as if to clear it; she looked like she might need smelling salts. "I'd put that man out of my mind I hoped for good. He was locked away. The man never had anything to do with his son in the first place. It's as if Johnny didn't have a father. If it hadn't been for Johnny's grandfather, I'd have demanded he relinquish his parental rights." She'd become imperious. Adele saw now what Raymond meant by the rich pulling rank. "I should have put my foot down when Ray took the boy to the prison. What harm could it do, I thought. Hah!"

Adele tried again. "Johnny loves his father—" the expression on Lisa Young's face stopped her. The stone-like face said beyond a doubt that Lisa Young had no interest in anything Adele would say. It was a dismissal. There was no hope at all in asking for help with the legal costs. What would she tell Raymond?

Chapter 22

Ambler met Mike Cosgrove for lunch the day after McNulty's arraignment at the Oyster Bar in Grand Central Terminal, a favorite spot for Mike who considered himself something of a gourmet. Mike had learned French cooking and preferred French restaurants but made an exception for the Oyster Bar.

Ambler had called Mike the night before, and Mike had called back this morning while Ambler was trying to make up his mind about talking to Lisa Young. Meeting Mike meant he didn't have to make a decision.

"I told you about Peter Esposito," Mike said, as he poured a glass of Sancerre for each of them. "I wouldn't say there's enough to make him a suspect. There's enough for me to want to know more about him. Nothing really on the others." Cosgrove waved his notebook at Ambler. "Esposito kept calling her. Obsessed. She might have been afraid of him. She was afraid of someone."

McNulty had told Ambler that; McNulty didn't tell Mike. "How do you know?"

"The cop I spoke with."

"Cop?"

Ambler sensed Mike's discomfort. They disagreed on a good few things, but Mike only got defensive when Ambler criticized the police. He had his problems with his fellow workers in blue, especially some unpleasantness with the NYPD Intelligence Division. Yet he circled the wagons when criticism came from the outside, even from Ambler.

Mike told him about his interview with Al Hoffman.

Ambler spoke carefully but directly. "Maybe he's a devoted family man, made a mistake, got carried away, repented, and moved on. That doesn't work if he won't let her go, even as he's telling you he did let her go."

Mike looked at his chowder instead of Ambler. "I know what he said. I know what it sounds like. If he happened to be sharing a hotel room with her when she was murdered, I woulda pulled him in to talk to him some more." He glanced quickly at Ambler and back at the chowder.

"Okay." Ambler said. "Can I talk to him?"

"He's a cop. I don't think you'd get very much. You asked me to do this. You don't trust me now?" He drilled Ambler with his cop stare.

Ambler accepted the rebuke. "She was afraid of someone. That's what Hoffman said. That's what McNulty said, too. That's why he gave me the names in the journal."

"Maybe she was afraid of the bartender."

"She didn't know him then."

"How do you know?"

Ambler shrugged. "You might ask Officer Hoffman if she mentioned Dillard Wainwright. She might have reason to be afraid of him."

"Why?"

"They were in contact. I don't know why they'd be in contact."

"He's in the missing persons database. In theory, he's being looked for."

"Could she have been afraid of Ted Doyle?"

Something sparked in Cosgrove's eyes. "So she got a gun to protect herself from him? Maybe the bartender got it for her, so she shot Doyle or maybe the bartender shot him." His expression was stern. "That's a serious thought. I don't know anything about Doyle, except his wife didn't suspect him of playing around with other women."

"Probably Hoffman's wife and Esposito's wife didn't suspect them either."

Cosgrove started to go after Ambler. Storm clouds rose in his eyes. But he pulled back. Sadness replaced the anger. "People stand to get hurt in this. Got hurt. Lots of disappointment, folks letting other folks down. You and I don't get anywhere trying to outsmart each other."

The truth of what Mike said struck Ambler in a way he didn't expect. He thought about Sandra's husband Simon. How learning about his wife's undertakings must be especially heartbreaking. He hadn't told Mike about Sandra's call to her husband that McNulty mentioned, so he did now.

"I interviewed the husband with the Stamford cops—" Mike said and stopped. He didn't say anything further, and Ambler didn't ask because an interview like that was the kind of police business Mike didn't talk about. Still, Ambler wondered if something came up that gave Mike pause.

They'd finished lunch and sat at their cleared table over coffee. The lunch rush was over, the Saloon dining room empty, except for one other table, and bussers setting up the red-and-white checked tablecloth-covered tables for the evening rush. "It's your turn to get the check," Mike said.

When Ambler returned to work, he found an embossed envelope on his desk, the kind of elegant stationery that might contain an invitation to a wedding, formal dinner, or some such thing. In the upper left corner was the name Mrs. Lisa Young and her address. The invitation was to a formal dinner, the text of the invitation in silver ink crossed out in black. Beneath the crossed out lines was a handwritten message: "Please contact my secretary and make an appointment to speak with me as soon as possible. I'll come to your office." She'd printed a phone number but not bothered to sign the note.

Ambler read the note as short as it was a few times, sensing it was the harbinger of bad news. After a few moments, he called the number. The secretary was well prepared. "She can see you this afternoon after four."

He didn't like that but saw no reason to put the appointment off, so he said, "Four is fine."

What was left of the afternoon, he spent skimming one of Jayne Galloway's notebooks, with no idea what he was looking for, hoping something might jump out at him, the looming appointment with Lisa Young distracting him. Her note almost certainly had to do with Johnny but he couldn't think of anything that had gone wrong lately. Maybe it would be a friendly visit and a chance to ask her about helping with his son's legal expenses.

Around three he heard a tentative knock on the reading room door. A second later, Adele opened the door and stepped in. She took some time to close the door behind her and then leaned against it as if she were trying to stay as far away from Ambler as possible. She looked stricken.

"What's the matter?" He rose from his seat and moved toward her. She shrank from him, pressing harder against the door. He stopped and moved back until he felt the reading table against him.

"I've got to tell you something."

"Sure," he said stupidly. "Do you want to sit down?"

"I've done something awful," she said in a whisper. "You'll never forgive me."

He wanted to say, "Of course, I'll forgive you." Innate caution made him hesitate. He didn't say anything. Could she have done something so awful he'd never forgive her?

"I saw Mrs. Young—"

"She's on her way here."

"No!" Adele let out a wail and burst into tears.

This time, he did go to her and put his arms around her. "It's okay," he said. "Whatever it is, it will be okay."

"You don't understand," she sputtered through her sobs. Finally, she took a breath and told him about talking to Lisa Young and Lisa Young's reaction. "I ruined everything," she said.

Ambler had his arms around her while she talked. Her face was close to his, and her misery provoked in him a powerful tenderness toward her. He pulled her tighter until her tears pressed against his face. After a moment, he lifted her chin and then kissed her full on the mouth. She opened her mouth and pushed against his, their mouths pressed against each other so hard and for so long it began to hurt, her teeth grated against his teeth, their mouths entwined until they pulled away from each other gasping.

"I'm such a fool," Adele said. "Oh Raymond . . ."

His hand against the back of her head, he pulled her gently to his chest. "You're the most wonderful woman on earth. . . ." He had to catch his breath. "I wanted to kiss you forever."

She laughed, as much a gasp or a choked cry. "If you do it like that, you can kiss me as long as you like."

The moment passed and as their senses returned they were shy around one another again. "It could easily have been me putting her off," Ambler said. "Years ago, my father told me it was very difficult to separate rich people from their money."

Adele chuckled. "I should have approached her more carefully." She looked at him with that guilelessness he found so attractive in her. "I thought she'd know it would be good for Johnny for his father to be with him."

"One would think that." Ambler didn't blame Adele for taking on Lisa Young. He really wouldn't have handled it any better. At least, he didn't have to put off any longer talking about his son's legal expenses. Adele was right. It was for Johnny. Ambler wasn't going to apologize for Adele and he wasn't going to let Johnny's grandmother off the hook. His resolve was building.

He bumped his forehead against Adele's. "You did fine. You softened her up. We aren't done yet."

She leaned her face toward his. They kissed gently and again less gently. She laughed and danced away from him, blowing a kiss from the door.

He didn't brace himself for Lisa Young's visit, yet he was prepared for disagreement, for conflict. Over time, he'd found it worked best to give in to her on most things and make a stand when it was crucial. She was used to getting what she wanted and had resources to unleash when she didn't. She or her husband might well socialize with the judge who sentenced John and attend fund-raising dinners with the DA in charge of the prosecution.

Ambler couldn't match what she and her family could do for Johnny. The school he went to was a pathway to the best colleges. She bought him clothes from stores Ambler read about in the papers. Johnny's bedroom at the Young's Central Park West apartment was bigger than Ambler's apartment and had in it a big screen TV, an Xbox, and video games that boys Johnny's age wanted. Johnny had watched the Yankees from the Young's law firm's corporate box and Rangers games from rinkside seats at the Garden. Now, the boy complained about Ambler's nosebleed seats at Knicks games.

So far, Johnny had navigated his two worlds pretty well, from the rent-stabilized walk-up in Murray Hill to the mansion on Central Park West. Still, Ambler treaded lightly. If he

crossed Grandma Young, she'd come after him with another
custody battle, turn loose her battalion of high-priced lawyers,
and call in favors from whatever elected officials her husband
and his white-shoe law firm had in their pockets.

Lisa Young arrived a few minutes after four, greeting Ambler with a kind of easy charm, friendly and effortless, gracious
but reserved. It was the type of friendly greeting she might use
for the doorman or other subordinate who wasn't involved in
her life in an appreciable way. At least, she came alone. In the
past, when it was just them talking they'd at times found a kind
of sympathetic understanding of one another. Beneath the pol-
ished public persona who hobnobbed with the city's elite and
the crown heads of small European countries lurked a woman
with some sensitivity. Ambler was one of only a few people
who knew she'd once lived a very different life as an avant-
garde poet and semi-notorious bohemian.

"You spoke with Adele," Ambler said as soon as she was
seated across the library table from him. They'd shaken hands
when she arrived, their only salutation when they met. He
knew, from the very few social engagements he'd attended
with her, that she usually favored a brief hug and peck-on-the-
cheek greeting. For some reason, such a greeting never clicked
for them. He brought up her conversation with Adele because if
that was why she was there, he didn't want to pretend she was
there for some other purpose.

"I'm not unsympathetic." She nodded toward the door.
"Perhaps you could leave work a little early and we could get a
drink. I have an engagement at six, so it would need to be now."

He answered quickly. "I probably shouldn't."

She would understand this as a rebuff. He was okay with
Adele taking matters into her own hands; she did it because she
loved Johnny. He wasn't okay with Lisa Young's disparaging his
son. He and Lisa Young had never spoken about her daughter

and his son. The two had never married. Lisa Young never met Ambler's son John. She'd deserted her own daughter when Johnny's mother was about Johnny's age. Nor had Lisa Young known about or taken any responsibility for her grandson until after her daughter's death.

"Just as well." She cleared her throat, a sign of anxiety unusual for her, yet looked steadily at him. "I understand there are extenuating circumstances surrounding your son's incarceration." She paused, expecting him to say something. He didn't so she looked away. "It's difficult for you to see my position. I doubt you will. All the same, I want you to understand what it is. My husband has strong beliefs about family, about heredity. It was difficult for him to accept a grandson who wasn't his by blood."

Ambler wanted to say, "We're not talking about a Thoroughbred." Used to viewing herself and the wealthy around her as superior to everyone else, she wouldn't know she was being insulting. Ambler had no interest in arguing, but his reaction to her arrogance must have shown in his expression because she seemed to reconsider what she'd said.

"Arnold is a kind man. As you know, I have my own youthful indiscretions to be ashamed of. He's done well in adjusting to Johnny. He's quite fond of him and will grow fonder of him as time goes on."

She wasn't saying what he'd expected her to say, so Ambler tried to make sure he heard what she said instead of what he thought she was going to say. What he hadn't understood right away was that his son John coming back into the picture brought with him not only his prison pallor but his presence recalled Johnny's humble beginnings, the wayward life of Lisa's daughter, as well as Lisa's own wayward past. He understood her position, yet what happened in the past did happen and most often wasn't inclined to stay there.

Ambler chose his words carefully. "I more or less understand your problem."

Her tone was firm. "Johnny's father took no interest in the boy until you forced the issue. He's in prison and likely to stay there. No purpose is served by dragging Johnny up there to see an absent father whose only interest is that the boy might help him get out of jail sooner."

Ambler's heart stopped. A chill like cold rain soaked through him. The room darkened around them. He knew what was coming. He saw a battle in front of him and defeat looming over it. He felt like he was falling even though he was seated, so he clutched at the arms of his chair. He knew the expression she saw on his face was one of helplessness, a useless begging for mercy.

She paused to stiffen her resolve. He could see it in the tightening of her face muscles. "I'm asking that you cease Johnny's prison visits, at least for a few years until he's older and less impressionable." She held up her hand to stop what he would say, not sensing how far beyond him speech was. "I've spoken to my attorneys and I'm confident I'm on firm legal ground. I don't want to take that route; litigious battles aren't good for Johnny."

The timbre of her voice changed to something that she might think was sympathetic but to him reeked of condescension. "You and I have worked through disagreements in the past. I'm sure we can with this." She spoke with a kind of "buck-up-old-chap," cheerfulness, the tone a winner uses to a sucker who lost his paycheck in a poker game. "In a few years, with good behavior on your son's part, Arnold and I might help with parole or a new trial."

Anger surged through Ambler, rose in his throat like bile. His thoughts blurred. His hands tightened into fists. He feared if she said another word, he'd smash her across the face and knock her and the chair she sat in into the hallway. "You'd better leave," he said.

Her eyes widened and she thrust herself out of her chair, reaching the door before she'd fully stood up. She straightened to her full height and left without another word.

Chapter 23

"Oh God, Raymond! You're as white as a ghost. Was it as bad as I think?" Adele stood transfixed in the doorway.

He told her about Lisa Young's threat.

She came in and sat down in the chair across from him, the chair Lisa Young had vacated. "She can't do that. It would break Johnny's heart to stop seeing his father."

"I guess it's back to the courts." Ambler's voice wavered.

"It's my fault. I shouldn't have talked to her."

It wasn't Adele's fault. He told her that and she acted like she believed him. Despite that, she'd blame herself. Really, there wasn't anyone to blame. This was how people like Lisa Young were. If they didn't have control of something, they made some calls. She could always find something on him to take to the family court judge. Nothing stuck to her, despite the fact she'd deserted her own daughter.

"We'll figure something out." Adele said before she left to go back to work. "She's not going to do this to Johnny."

Adele was right. They would do something. He had no idea

what, and whatever it was might not work. But if it didn't work, they'd go down in flames together, he, Adele, and Johnny.

As if things weren't bad enough, an hour later as Ambler got ready to leave for the day, Harry knocked on the crime fiction reading room door. This seldom happened and was never good news when it did happen, especially troubling when Harry looked at him sympathetically as he did now.

"What?" Ambler asked.

"I think as your supervisor I should be entitled to hazardous duty pay."

Ambler threw up his hands "How do you think I feel?"

Harry nodded, the nod slight, barely perceptible, yet he kept nodding, the thought of whatever woe he was bringing to Ambler sticking with him that long.

"Yes?"

"Father Jerome, the priest in Connecticut, your emissary to Simon Dean, called." He began his barely perceptible nod again. "Mr. Dean believes you've taken materials belonging to Jayne Galloway that you were not authorized to take."

"That's not true." Ambler told him the deed of gift from Galloway included all of her notebooks, including those she was continuing to work in. Those were to come to the library when she died.

"I'm told you surreptitiously removed them from Mrs. Galloway's house after her death when they'd become part of her estate and properly belonged to Carolyn Dean her heir."

"You were there when we arranged for me to go and get the materials." Ambler told Harry about the trip to Jayne Galloway's house with Simon Dean's sister, Andrea. "Dean was preoccupied. Nothing underhanded, the notebooks and papers were part of the collection Jayne Galloway gave to the library."

"What would be the harm in letting Mr. Dean have the documents with the understanding he'll return them when the estate is probated?"

Ambler knew why he wanted to keep the notebooks. Something Jayne Galloway wrote in her journal might point to Sandra Dean's killer. He didn't know why Simon Dean was making a fuss. Simon Dean had not had anything to do with Jayne Galloway for years. And as far as he knew his wife hadn't had anything to do with her mother either. Except Sandra Dean had gone to her mother's house right before her death. But Simon wouldn't know this. The police hadn't released any information about Jayne Galloway's death. The only reason for Simon to start a fight about the journals was to make things difficult for Ambler and thereby for McNulty.

He tried to explain this to Harry. "Simon Dean is sure McNulty killed his wife and he thinks I'm trying create doubt and confusion about the murder so McNulty gets to go free. There's no reason he'd want the journals except to make things difficult for me."

Harry pursed his lips. "It's not in the library's interest to have a dispute with a grieving man whose wife was murdered."

"The library has a legal right to the papers. He can sue us if he doesn't think so."

Harry's expression was sympathetic. "You're wrong, Ray. The man lost his wife. I thought you'd be more understanding. Think over his request. We can talk in the morning."

That evening, Ambler and Johnny had just finished dinner when Mike Cosgrove called. Johnny was especially quiet this evening, answering questions about school and his day and anything else Ambler asked with mumbling, mostly monosyllabic, answers. It was as if Johnny had a premonition that something was wrong in his life. Ambler normally didn't press him when he didn't want to talk but the boy usually came around. This night, Ambler was hoping he didn't come around, afraid where the conversation might lead.

"Go watch TV in the bedroom," he said after he answered the phone.

"Why can't I listen?" Johnny knew it was Mike on the phone and the call would be about McNulty. He'd been especially worried about his honorary uncle since the arrest.

"I'll tell you later. I'd like some privacy now." This usually worked because Johnny saw it as a request, not a directive. He'd still try to listen through the door.

"There's something I want to ask you," Mike said, "about what we talked about at lunch. You met Simon Dean a couple of times. What can you tell me about him?"

Ambler was intrigued. This was the second time Mike brought up Simon Dean. They were silent for a moment. Ambler ran some thoughts through his mind, realizing as he did that he hadn't formed much of an impression of Dean at all. After their first meeting he thought of Dean as a guy destined from birth to be conventional: a respectable professional job, in his case architect, a house in the suburbs, the house and the suburb for him on the upper end of upper middle class, a wife, a child. Dean probably played golf, drank California Chardonnay and Merlot. Despite this, or maybe because of it, Ambler liked him when they first met, a down-to-earth guy, few pretensions, now a man with trouble and sorrow, a wife he thought he knew but didn't who was now dead leaving him a young daughter to raise.

Ambler had never thought he himself was destined for the suburbs; at one point a long time ago, he, too, had a wife and child and had expected that to last, so much so he paid too little attention to the family he had and it got away from him. His wife was swallowed up by the nightlife; John, his son, left to fend for himself until something happened in a split second that altered his life forever and put him in prison.

It was easy for Ambler to think Dean judged him too quickly and unfairly as he sought to prove McNulty innocent of Dean's wife's murder. But to be fair, Dean's judgment was understandable also. So what he felt about Dean was mostly sympathy tinged with irritation for getting in the way of his investigation. He told Mike most of this. "Strange he should come up now."

"Not so strange for a husband to be questioned about his wife's murder," Cosgrove said. "You told me Sandra Dean talked to him after Ted Doyle was murdered. I take it that comes from the bartender. What did they talk about?"

Ambler told him as best he remembered that the calls were about Sandra asking her husband to let her return home.

"So the husband knew she'd done something he disapproved of or she would have just gone home. Did she tell him about the murder?"

"He knew something about what his wife had been doing. I don't know what. McNulty said she didn't tell him about the murder. What are you looking for?"

"Connecting dots. I want to establish where everyone was at the time of Ted Doyle's murder. When I think about it now, I find a lot of holes. Sandra Dean was murdered before I'd even got my boots on to go after the Ted Doyle case." He paused. "McNulty didn't by any chance tell you where he was at the time of Doyle's murder?"

Ambler had to admit that he hadn't. "I assume he was someplace else."

"Assuming that would get you an F on the homicide investigation final exam."

"I'll ask him. Meanwhile, we have the jealous husband motive. You don't have a suspect in your case. How about him?"

"You're wrong. I have a suspect. A jealous bartender."

Ambler didn't argue. Instead, not sure why he did, he told Mike about his disagreement with Simon Dean over Jayne Galloway's notebooks. "He's not very cooperative."

"Why would he be? No reason for him to think you're on his side."

"If he wants the truth about his wife's death, I'm on his side."

"To be honest, Ray, I'm not sure what side you're on. You're too close to the suspect."

Ignoring the criticism, Ambler told Mike again about Dillard Wainwright and Sandra Dean exchanging email messages. "Simon Dean has Sandra's laptop. The messages are likely on the laptop. I can't get it from him. You could. Don't you guys have ways to get into someone's email even without the laptop?"

"I don't know what the department does with computers and I'm afraid to find out." Ambler knew Mike well enough that he could hear him thinking. He waited until Mike said, "Dillard Wainwright is the one guy on the list I can't find. What would Simon Dean know about him?"

"That's not what I said. I doubt Simon Dean would know anything about him. Sandra was exchanging emails with her mother's ex-husband shortly before she was murdered. I want to know what that was about."

"You make leaps I can't follow. How do you know they were exchanging emails."

"McNulty."

Mike groaned or maybe it was a moan. "There's a reliable source for you."

"Even if you only—"

"Stop. I heard what you said. You're confusing me now. I'll get back to you." He disconnected.

Ambler had a lot to think about himself, so he sat for a while until Johnny interrupted his thoughts.

"Are they going to let Uncle McNulty go?"

"Not yet. We're working on it."

Johnny took a moment to think over his response. "Are you sure you're doing it right?"

Ambler wasn't at all sure he was doing it right. "I won't know until I get an answer or find out there isn't one."

"You'll find an answer. It's Uncle McNulty. You have to. Can I help?"

"At the moment, you help by taking care of the dog when I can't and understanding when you need to go to Adele's or spend an extra day at your grandmother's."

"Are you always going to be tracking down murderers?" Johnny's voice was quieter than usual.

The question surprised Ambler, compounding his worry that the detective work he did scared his grandson. "I don't know. Would you like it if I didn't do this anymore?"

Johnny's tone brightened. "No. Not that. I was thinking when my dad got out of prison he could help. You guys could become partners. And then when I grow up, I could be a partner, too. We could chase all the bad guys. And Adele, too." He wrinkled his nose. "I mean we wouldn't chase Adele. She'd help us chase bad guys."

Ambler laughed in spite of the dread he felt at the mention of Johnny's dad. "That's a good plan."

Later, Ambler stared at the bedroom ceiling long into the night battling the belief that he would never find the money to pay the attorney to appeal his son's conviction. Worse, Lisa Young would sic her lawyers on him, and the family court judge would order him to stop taking Johnny to visit his father. With all this closing in, he was bound to make a mistake, miss something important about the murders, and end up watching McNulty go to prison, too.

When Ambler headed to work the next morning after dropping Johnny at school, he was a wreck, fixated on the thought that everything doesn't always turn out all right in the end. In recent years, he'd had his world-weary, jaded bartender friend as an antidote when he'd lost his way. "Something will turn up," McNulty would say. For both their sakes, would that this be true.

As soon as he opened the door of the crime fiction reading room, he let out an audible groan. He'd forgotten he was supposed to meet with Harry. Thinking he was alone—though he'd been running late and the library was open—a woman's voice from quite near startled him. "Are you all right?" He turned and saw Andrea Eagan behind him.

"I'm fine. . . . What are you doing here? . . ." He shook his head. "Not that. I'm sorry. How are you?"

Her eyes shone. Her expression was that of a young girl who'd made up her mind to cause mischief. "I've brought you Sandi's laptop."

Ambler pushed open the door in front of them. "Come in. Come in." Excited, beside himself, he started to go first, thought better of it, turned around in the doorway, bumping into Andrea and pushing her back out the door. His thoughts were flying.

When he finally got them both inside the reading room, she handed him a laptop carrying case. "I'll need it back by the end of the day. I can't stay."

Ambler was speechless.

She looked art him curiously and said, "I know the password. I played around and after a while figured it out. Her daughter's name and the year she was born."

"Great. How? . . ."

She read his mind. "Simon doesn't know I took it. My husband doesn't know either. They think I'm on a shopping trip to the city, so I need to do some shopping."

"I appreciate your doing this." Boy did that sound lame. He tried again. "I'm sorry. I don't know what to say. I'm overwhelmed."

"I'm not sure why I'm doing this." The expression in her eyes went wild for a moment. "It's for Sandi. The man you asked me if I knew, Wainwright. I found messages from him in her email." She looked behind her. "I've got to go. I'll be back by four thirty. That's the latest I can stay."

When she left, he opened the laptop. While it was booting up, he remembered Harry, so he closed it and hid it at the bottom of a file box in front of one of the bookcases, catching himself looking furtively over his shoulder as he did so.

Harry was in a better mood this morning. Ambler, on the other hand, was keyed up. "Sorry I'm late. A reader in the crime fiction room."

"That's fine." Harry had brought coffee and Danish. "When I left you yesterday, I felt we misunderstood one another. Fortunately, I spoke to Adele. We had a long talk."

Ambler had a moment's panic trying to remember what Adele might know that he didn't want her telling Harry. He certainly didn't want Harry to know he had Sandra Dean's purloined laptop in his office.

"She reminded me of how important your friendship with Mr. McNulty is to you. I was callous in how I spoke about him. Adele doesn't believe he did what he's accused of. This weighs heavily on you both. I understand."

For the second time that morning, Ambler was at a loss for words.

Harry's expression as he munched on his cheese Danish suggested the contentment people feel when they've gotten something weighty off of their chest. At his essence, Harry was a kind man. Fate had done him a disservice by putting him in a position of authority. He'd be much happier, like Ferdinand the Bull, under a tree smelling the flowers.

"There's something you should know," Ambler said, and before he knew he was going to, told Harry about his falling out with Lisa Young.

"I'd expect more compassion from Mrs. Young," Harry said. "You have to wonder if her concern is the child's welfare or her social standing."

"I'm telling you because she could cause trouble. I'm still going to fight her."

"I imagine you would." Harry cleared his throat. "There's still the question of Mr. Dean and the journals. I told him I would discuss the issue with you. He wasn't pleased."

Chapter 24

As soon as he got back to his office, Ambler searched through the emails on the laptop until he found the messages to and from Wainwright. Sandra used the name Sandra Dean not Shannon. "You're a fraud," the first message from her said, "and I'm going to prove it."

Wainwright replied as if he'd expected her message. He called her Dr. Dean. "Everything is not as it seems, Dr. Dean."

"You ruined my mother's life," she wrote. "You ruined my life. You made her leave me."

Wainwright responded. "Your father kept your mother from you. Your mother and I wanted you to be with us. Have you asked her? You weren't told the truth."

Sandra didn't believe him. He responded with a lengthy email that told her how her separation from her mother came about. What struck Ambler was the self-justification and under-tone of panic in Wainwright's message.

In the email, he told Sandra he was still married to his first wife when Jayne Galloway left her husband to come live with him. He was on the faculty of a conservative Catholic college, about to be considered for tenure. His tenure application was not especially strong and would have been denied if he were discovered to be involved in two messy divorces: his own, and Jayne's. Sandra's father threatened a public fight with charges of infidelity, adultery, and desertion. His price for cooperation and a quiet divorce was for Jayne Galloway to relinquish her parental rights. "He forced her to choose between you and me," he wrote. "It was the most unfair choice possible for her."

Sandra's response was simply, "She should have chosen me."

There were other emails. Wainwright knew Jayne Galloway was dying of cancer and encouraged Sandra to forgive her, to visit her. She told him she didn't need his advice about her mother.

"Everyone she loved turned against her," he wrote.

"She did it to herself," Sandra wrote back.

Some emails might have been deleted because a couple of threads of discussion weren't followed up. The most interesting of these was from Wainwright. "You have to wonder about a husband who keeps his wife from her mother." He most likely meant Sandra's father. But he wrote wife not daughter. If what Jayne Galloway said about Simon Dean's dislike of her were true, Wainwright might have meant Simon keeping Sandra from her mother. So how would Wainwright know that and what did it mean? The next message from Wainwright told Sandra he'd be in the city and asked her to meet him for lunch. She responded that she would. There were no emails after that, so no telling if the lunch took place.

He was going through the emails a second time to make sure he hadn't missed anything when Andrea Eagan arrived in the late afternoon to pick up the laptop. He asked if she'd read the emails. She hadn't, so he gave her a summary. "Sandra blamed Wainwright for her mother leaving her. That's what the correspondence is mostly about."

Andrea smiled wanly. "That was hard for Sandi. I don't

think she ever forgave her mother, even though I think she tried to. I'd read a couple of Jayne Galloway's books." Andrea waved her arms at the shelves of books surrounding her. "I'm a mystery reader, you know. I love your reading room. When Sandi found out I'd read them, she wanted me to tell her about the books, as if it might tell her about her mother."

"What did you tell her?"

"I said the books were good, but somber, dark, not a lot of tranquility restored to Cabot Cove."

"Are you aware that Sandra did reunite with her mother?" He told her Sandra and McNulty went to Jayne Galloway's house on Long Island after the murder in New York and exchanged cars. "Previously, she'd hired a private detective to track down Sandra only to be rebuffed by her and her husband."

"I guess I'm not surprised she went to her mother's when she was in trouble." Andrea walked over to the library table Ambler used as a desk and sat down, so he did, too. "I remember when her mother tried to find her. Sandi told me about it at the time. She was excited about seeing her mother. That's when we talked about her mother's books; I think Sandi began reading them. And then she and Simon turned against Mrs. Galloway, and nothing came of the visit."

Ambler turned to Sandra Dean's laptop and found the message from Wainwright he wanted and read it to her: "'You have to wonder about a husband who keeps his wife from her mother.' Could he have meant Simon?"

Andrea's voice had a ghostly quality. "Yes he meant Simon. But how would he know? I truly believe Sandi wanted to see her mother again. Simon wouldn't allow it."

"Wouldn't allow it?"

"I feel like a traitor talking about him like this. He is my brother. And he's not an ogre. He cared about Sandi, in his own way." She shook head. "It's just his way was . . . Oh boy!" She laughed.

"Simon was way too influenced by the Old Testament—or something he read from the Dark Ages. He was lord of the manor. Sandi made him dinner every night after working all day. He never washed a dish, ran a vacuum cleaner, or God help us changed a diaper. When Sandi traveled, she left dinner for him and Carolyn to heat up. Simon ruled over her. That's what made me so mad, that she'd put up with that. Now he thinks he's in charge of her in death, able to decide what people can know about her.

"Simon despised Mrs. Galloway for what she did to Sandi. Sandi didn't tell me he forbade her to see her mother. But I'm sure he did." Andrea turned up her nose and curled her lip, not a sneer, an expression of distaste. "Believe me. Simon was in charge. He missed the humility part of the Lord's teachings when he was in the seminary."

"Simon studied to be a priest?"

Andrea laughed. "When Simon was a teenager, he thought he was mystic. We all thought he'd become a priest. My parents sent him to a Catholic seminary in Pennsylvania for high school. Then, something happened at the seminary. He came home near the end of his senior year and never went back. No one told me why. It wasn't like I was his confidant, anyway. It didn't change him. He was still devout and arrogant about it, and still is.

"When the time came to talk about marriage, he required Sandi become a Catholic. He wouldn't marry her unless she converted. Worse, he's the old 'binding with briars my joys and desires' kind of Catholic, strict, patriarchal. Sandi wore a head covering to Mass. She might as well have walked three steps behind him.

"Truthfully, I never knew what Sandi saw in Simon. Once, before they were married when they were engaged, she and I shared a bottle of wine, two bottles if you must know." She winked. "Too much wine, because I tried to talk her out of marrying him.

"Sandi had a difficult life. And then she married Simon who wasn't right for her. Forgive me for saying she deserved better. Simon is an emotional void, a tyrant. She loved him, getting nothing in return. Who knows why people do what they do? He helped her through medical school. I guess that's something."

Andrea was right, even if she didn't believe she was right. There was risk in judging someone else's relationship from the outside. It wasn't so clear to Ambler who was the wronged person in the marriage of Simon and Sandra Dean. He tried to say this to Andrea, that Sandra might have caused Simon suffering, too.

"Yes. There's that. I didn't know Sandi as well as I thought I did. Yet if either of them were to have a secret life, I would have bet on Simon. He was a sphinx even as a kid. You never knew what he felt, what he thought, what he liked or didn't like. I grew up with a stranger for a brother, an imperious stranger."

Ambler was surprised by Andrea's take on her brother and didn't know how to respond. Not that he didn't believe her. It wasn't uncommon for someone to show a different side to the world at large than to those close to them. He didn't think Andrea was trying to malign her brother. It was as if there was some truth about him she thought Ambler should know and in an oblique way was telling him.

"Your brother and Sandra had an unhappy marriage?"

Andrea shook her head. "I guess I can't say that. One never knows what goes on in private between two people. I do know what I saw, and I know Simon. He was unreasonably demanding of her. He demeaned her in front of others. She was a brilliant doctor and he talked down to her. Other times, he ignored her in front of people. She'd say something to him and he wouldn't respond."

Ambler remembered what Cosgrove and McNulty had said about Sandra's fear of someone. "Was she afraid of him?"

Andrea shook her head. "No. It wasn't like that. He never hit her or threatened her. They didn't have arguments or fights, not that I saw. His was a kind of subtle emotional abuse. I don't think he even knew when he humiliated her. Simon came first, everyone else, including Sandi, a distant second. Maybe it was different when they were alone. She loved him. She bought into his idea that it was her duty to be his handmaid. I think it drove her crazy."

When Andrea made ready to leave, Ambler walked around the library table to stand beside her. She was clumsy getting the laptop into its case. He thought she acted worried now that the time for returning the laptop got closer.

"Are you sure this will be okay?" He touched her shoulder.

She laughed uneasily. "I can handle Simon. He's tried to boss me around since we were kids. I've never put up with his crap." She met Ambler's gaze; there was fear and defiance in her eyes. "I don't know why he's being such a pill. He thinks the bartender killed Sandi, but it might be he's not absolutely sure, so he's afraid you'll prove him wrong." She imitated a stern male tone. "And Simon has to be right."

Ambler was drawn to the genuineness of her expression, the genuineness of her. She reminded him for the moment that goodness existed in the world. They looked at each other for a moment until she opened her arms slightly and leaned into him. He hugged her. "Thank you," he said. "You've taken a big chance to help me."

"Not just you. I'm not sure why but I believe you wouldn't do what you're doing if you believed your friend the bartender killed Sandi. I want to know what really happened to her."

Ambler hugged her again. As he let go of her and turned, he heard a throat being cleared and knew it was Adele. He also knew—or learned for the first time—that the sound of a throat being cleared could convey criticism. "Adele!" he said much louder than he intended, letting go of Andrea's arm and taking a slight hop back from her. "You remember Andrea."

Andrea, still guileless, smiled and held out her hand. Adele held out her hand, smiling also, but shooting a quick glance at Ambler that felt like a hard poke in the eye.

As they watched Andrea walk away, Adele said, "That was cozy." Her glare had not diminished.

"It wasn't cozy," he said—correcting himself to, "She brought me Sandra's laptop."

Adele sat down. "And?"

He told her what he'd learned from the emails.

"So Mr. Wainwright reappears. What was the fraud she accused him of?"

"It's strange. Neither of them said what it was. Yet, you can tell from Wainwright's explanations and justifications that he knew."

"So what does it mean he's a fraud? He's missing and a fraud."

Ambler wasn't really listening to Adele who began talking about a number of different things at once. He was mentally sifting through the emails he'd read and what Andrea had said. Adele liked to think out loud if someone else was present, while Ambler preferred to keep his thoughts to himself. After a short pause, she said, "So much of who we are is determined when we're kids and have no choice about what's happening to us. And her mother, too. I bet the man she left for this Wainwright person drove her to it. I wonder if she writes about him in her journals. . . ."

Ambler shook his head. He didn't know what Adele was talking about but didn't want to admit it.

Adele slapped her hand on the library table. "What were the dates of the emails?"

Ambler was totally lost. "What emails?"

She gave him a pained look. "Do you know what we're talking about?"

After a moment, he caught up with her and looked at his notes. "The first one, from Sandra, is dated September 2."

Adele stood. "That's it. Look at the dates. She was here at the library on September 2 reading about Wainwright in her mother's journals, right before she disappeared and not long before she was murdered. That's when she emailed Wainwright. Whatever made him a fraud, she found in those journals."

Wainwright disappeared from his college campus at the beginning of the college's autumn quarter, the first week in September, around the time of the emails. Ambler had stored the boxes holding the Galloway collection temporarily on open shelves on the mezzanine level of the crime fiction reading room and had kept them there after Sandra Dean's disappearance and then her death.

"Do you know which boxes Sandra was using?" Adele watched the box in front of her as if she expected it to talk.

When Ambler found the right file boxes, Adele began searching the files containing the correspondence between Jayne Galloway and Dillard Wainwright, the correspondence was long enough ago to be handwritten or typed letters. Ambler gave her the journals in which Galloway wrote about her first contact with Dillard Wainwright.

While Adele did that, Ambler dug out the more recent journals he'd retrieved from Jayne Galloway's house on Long Island after her death. He and Adele worked together on either side of the library table in the middle of the crime fiction reading room for a couple of hours.

At 7:30, they met Johnny and his newly titled "after-school companion," former babysitter, Denise Cosgrove, at an Indian restaurant on Lexington Avenue for dinner. Johnny and Denise had been taking Lola to obedience classes and, having successfully completed her training, Lola had been awarded her canine good citizen certificate, so it was something of a celebration, though without Lola.

The next morning on their walk, Johnny showed off Lola's good behavior, which went pretty well until she snatched half of a bagel from a tyke in a stroller. Later that morning, Johnny went to school, Lola went to doggy daycare, and Ambler went to work.

After a mid-morning department staff meeting, Harry called Ambler aside to tell him Simon Dean would be at the library at noon. "We'll meet in my office," Harry said.

"Good luck," Ambler said. "He's—"

"The meeting is with Mr. Dean, me, and you."

"Oh dear," said Ambler.

Simon Dean was sitting in a wooden armchair in front of Harry's desk when Ambler arrived for the meeting. He stood and held out his hand, smiling, not the aggrieved widower Ambler expected to confront, but a different person nonetheless than Ambler would have thought him to be before Andrea's description the day before.

Ambler shook hands and sat down in a matching armchair across from Dean.

Dean's expression was earnest. "I was wrong to say I knew for sure who killed my wife. Normally, I don't jump to conclusions. I'm a methodical person. I was beside myself with grief." He paused and closed his eyes, as if to compose himself. "I wanted to punish her killer . . . to punish someone. I know you have a right to think your friend is innocent."

Ambler didn't know what Dean was up to, or if he was up to anything. Whichever it was, Simon Dean was in charge. It was his show, although he seemed to be waiting for a response from Ambler without having asked a question.

Not getting one, Dean turned his attention to Harry. "I understand Mr. Ambler wants to prove his friend innocent of my wife's murder. It's understandable he'd want to do so, even if I think him misguided." Dean pulled himself up straighter. "Obtaining documents from my wife's mother's house under false pretenses is something different. It was wrong. Everything that

belonged to my wife's mother, my mother-in-law, rightly belongs to my daughter."

He spoke to Harry as if he were the parent and Ambler a
child who'd thrown his baseball through Simon Dean's window or stomped through his petunia bed. "I don't care about
Mrs. Galloway's belongings, papers or otherwise. I didn't like
her. She abandoned Sandra when she was a child. She took no
interest in her granddaughter." He turned to Ambler. "I'm protecting my daughter, doing for her what she'd do for herself if
she could." His tone softened. "I know you mean Carolyn no
harm, that you wouldn't purposefully make her unhappy, least
of all now."

Ambler nodded, a reflex.

"She wants anything connected to her mother, anything
she can hold on to. She asked me to take her to her grandmother's house because that was where her mother was as a
little girl."

Simon was laying it on thick. Ambler assumed it was for
Harry's benefit. Sandra Dean hadn't been a little girl at Jayne
Galloway's house on Long Island. Simon knew that.

Ambler started to say there was nothing in Jayne Galloway's
journals about Sandra as a little girl. But he realized he didn't
know that for sure. And even if he did know, why wouldn't the
little girl want to, deserve to, find out for herself? He wanted
to put his hands around Dean's throat and choke him until he
stopped talking about his daughter.

Harry, by pretty obvious telepathy, let Ambler know he
wasn't going to be any help on this. Ambler didn't want to argue with Dean but he wasn't going to give him the journals
either. Bringing in the little girl wasn't fair, but it was effec-
tive. It was also clear that Dean, despite his agreeable manner,
wasn't going to be reasoned with.

"I couldn't be sorrier for your daughter," Ambler said

quietly. "She's a sweet child. My grandson lost his mother, so I know how deeply that hurts and how slow it is to heal." His eyes were locked onto Dean's as he spoke, so he could see fury gathering behind the man's earnest gaze.

"You're wrong that the journals or any part of Jayne Galloway's papers belong to Carolyn. The collection legally and rightly belongs to the library. Mrs. Galloway made that decision. She donated her papers, specifically including journals in her possession at the time of her death, to the library. I'm not sure I could undo the bequest if I wanted to."

"And of course you don't want to." Dean's tone was measured. He kept his gaze on Ambler but he was talking to Harry, expecting Harry to overrule Ambler, something Harry might do. "Are those journals for your investigation? Do you think something in them will help free your friend the bartender? That's ridiculous. What could they possibly mean to you?"

Ambler was taken aback. Did Dean read his mind, follow his thinking somehow? He did want the journals for his investigation, but he wasn't going to tell Simon that. "The journals are part of the library's collection. They're not mine to give back."

Dean turned from Ambler to Harry. "I guess I should take my request to the library's Board of Trustees. They might have sympathy for a child who's lost her mother."

This struck a nerve with Harry who made no effort to hide his concern, unlike Ambler who—picturing Lisa Young and what she might do when she heard Simon's story—did make an effort to cover his reaction.

"No need to do that," Harry said. "The board would send your request to me and we'd be right back where we started. Ray and I understand your request. I'm not sure how we can resolve our differences. But resolve them we will."

Ambler didn't have much faith differences would be resolved. But he'd hand the reins to Harry for the time being. Everyone stood. Ambler shook hands awkwardly with Simon Dean, meeting the man's gaze with difficulty. Dean showed his own reluctance by looking away almost immediately as their eyes met.

Chapter 25

Adele met Raymond in the crime fiction reading room Tuesday evening, to continue their effort to discover in Jayne Galloway's journals and notebooks why Sandra Dean called Dillard Wainwright a fraud. Raymond told her about his meeting with Simon Dean the previous day.

"I can understand that." It wasn't what Raymond wanted to hear, but she felt badly for Dean and for his daughter Carolyn. "The poor little girl doesn't have her mother anymore." Adele felt tears forming behind her eyes. She'd cry; she couldn't help it, despite her tears unsettling Raymond. He didn't know what to do when she cried, so he sometimes pretended it wasn't happening until she stopped on her own. Other times, he rushed to her like she was a child who needed a hug. And maybe she was.

This was one of the pretend-it-wasn't-happening times, so she wiped her eyes and began reading one of the journals. In this one, Jayne Galloway wrote about the husband she would soon leave. After reading for a while, Adele stuck a marker in the notebook and closed it. "I was right about her first husband, Sandra's father. He was a *prick* . . . if you'll excuse the term."

Adele knew Raymond felt awkward. He was a prude in some ways, not a prude maybe, but old fashioned in an almost endearing way—not totally endearing because his uneasiness with her rough-around-the-edges, Brooklyn-girl manners, while gentlemanly, had remnants of male supremacy, an expectation of female gentility, the price a woman paid for her place on the pedestal.

Sandra's father, Martin Galloway, distinguished attorney that he might have been, was a controlling, dominating son of a bitch. Adele recognized the behavior from her own father, who'd died when she was a teen. The Mr. Galloway described in Jayne Galloway's journals didn't push his wife around or threaten her with abuse. His life away from her was more important than the life lived with her. She was something to him—the mother of his daughter, a homemaker, an element of his conventional respectability. Otherwise, he wasn't interested. Her writing was her little hobby. The child was her responsibility. She ran the house. His life was out in the world, long hours at the office, travel for court cases, testimonials, conferences, dinner at his club. That sort of thing.

"She left him because he wasn't there in the first place," Adele told Raymond but he didn't understand. When you came right down to it, he had some of those lolling-about-in-a-world-of-his-own characteristics himself.

"You would think she'd take her daughter," he said.

"You'd think that, wouldn't you? A lot of mothers wouldn't leave without their child. A lot of mothers stayed in not-so-fulfilling relationships, not to say abusive ones, because they wouldn't leave their kids. How well did that turn out?" Adele went back to the journal.

"You're looking for something about Dillard Wainwright being a fraud, right?" Raymond reminded her.

Truthfully, she had gotten sidetracked, so she got herself back on track, zipping through the entries except when Wainwright's name popped up. When he did pop up, he didn't come across as much of an improvement over the guy Jayne had left. Adele was tempted to slow down by a section that described Jayne's anguish over being separated from her daughter. Adele fought off the urge to keep reading those pages by promising herself she'd go back and read all of it when she found what she was looking for on Wainwright, if she ever did.

The longer she kept at the journals the less sure she was she'd find anything about Wainwright being a fraud. Where Galloway wrote about Wainwright, she wrote glowingly. Nonetheless, he came across as self-absorbed and insecure. The writer's block he suffered became as much a concern for Galloway as it must have been for him. Galloway had never experienced the phenomenon; she'd published four books by that time. She didn't understand his problem but tried to sympathize.

Wainwright's struggle with writer's block was already wearing on Adele. Galloway was more sympathetic. Still, she wrote she didn't know how to tell Wainwright that the voice in a story he showed her was so pompous it became a parody of itself. When she did tell him simply that the story didn't work for her, he became despondent. If he didn't get something published by that fall, he would be turned down for tenure.

By this time, Adele's eyes were getting droopy. As a mystery writer, Jayne Galloway might keep her readers on the edge of their seats, but her journals were as dry as dust, at least the parts of them having do with Wainwright. And then there it was. The word jumped out of the journal and bopped her in the eye—"fraud." She reached across the table and clutched Raymond's arm. His eyes had glazed over, too, from the journals, so he jumped when she grabbed him. "I found it." Her voice was a hoarse whisper.

What Adele found, what Sandra had found—there was a faint pencil mark at the top of the page—was an ethical dilemma for Jayne Galloway: Wainwright wanted to submit a story that Galloway wrote to a literary journal under his name. She'd argued with herself—not with him—deciding in the end that it wasn't a big deal. "It's fraud," she wrote. "But it's not stealing money or fudging an experiment. It's a short story in a small magazine that hardly anyone but the editor will ever read." Dillard would get tenure, which was a big deal. Getting the publishing credit and tenure would free him from his writer's block, so he could go on to be the writer he was destined to be.

"A woman in love can rationalize anything," Adele said to Ambler. "Though it really doesn't seem like a big deal." She watched Ambler's expression crumble and realized the mistake she made. "I forgot," she said.

He looked at her blankly. His Ph.D. dissertation had been rejected by his university because he was falsely accused of plagiarism. Someone—he was sure it was the FBI in retribution for his exposing their dirty tricks—doctored his dissertation. Adele knew that. "It's not the same thing. You were set up." She reached for him and looked into his eyes. "I know you."

He smiled. "So you're not rationalizing."

She wouldn't have cared if she was rationalizing. She let go of his hand and lowered her gaze. "Well, there you have it. Sandra discovered Wainwright got tenure under false pretenses."

"Not to be taken lightly," Ambler said. "The college would revoke his tenure. The dishonesty would throw into question all of his scholarly work. Then there's the scandal and the embarrassment."

Raymond knew the fallout from bitter experience. He never spoke about the plagiarism accusation against him and its consequences—a master's degree, not a Ph.D., a job in the library instead of an academic career—so Adele didn't either. "Sandra was going to tell the world and Wainwright needed to stop her."

"If she was going to expose him, she could have done it. Why tell him about it first?"

"Why?" Adele had a glimmering. "Blackmail?"

Raymond shook his head. "What could she want from him?"

The question didn't ask for an answer. She answered anyway. "To torture him before she exposed his false credentials. He disappeared from his college right after she accused him. Right after he killed her." Another thought caught up with her. "He killed Jayne Galloway, too. Sandra discovered his fraud in her mother's journals, so he went to get the journals from Galloway. When she wouldn't turn them over, he killed her."

"Why did he kill Ted Doyle?"

"Who?"

"The man murdered in Sandra Dean's hotel room."

"Oh." She'd forgotten about that. "So Wainwright isn't the killer after all? He had no reason at all to kill Mr. Doyle."

"We don't know."

Raymond was like that. As soon as it looked like they'd gotten somewhere, he pointed out they hadn't. Now, she wasn't sure what they did know, except that the missing Dillard Wainwright was a fraud and Sandra knew it. And that had to mean something.

After a few moments, Raymond said. "I discovered from Wainwright's emails that he'd been in touch with Jayne Galloway. He knew she was sick and tried to persuade Sandra to visit her."

"So her more recent journals might have something about Wainwright, too."

"Sandra was in touch with her mother at least twice, the first time led to her searching her mother's papers in the library. For some reason, she used the name Shannon Darling and not her own name. She visited her mother again after Ted Doyle was murdered in her hotel room. Jayne Galloway lied when she told me she hadn't seen her daughter and didn't recognize the photo I showed her. She'd seen Sandra a day or so before. She knew her daughter was hiding. She probably knew who killed Ted Doyle and that Sandra and McNulty were fugitives. That's what she knew that I know about. She knew something else that I don't know about and that's why she wanted to talk to me."

"And now?"

"We look through the journals and hope we find that something."

Chapter 26

Mike Cosgrove took another trip to Connecticut, driving the parkways to Greenwich this time. There was so much greenery just a few miles outside the city you might be in the country. Though not so green now in the fall with the leaves on the trees turning. Even the north Bronx, Riverdale, was country-like with its canopies of trees and rock formations. You wondered why people packed themselves together in the city, on top of one another in apartment buildings.

Plenty of trees and bushes when you got off the parkway in Greenwich, too—you probably should call them shrubs in a neighborhood of mansions like this. The houses set back from the road behind stone walls—sometimes tall walls you couldn't see over, sometimes short ones—were straight out of the *House & Garden* magazine his wife used to get a long time ago. The stone walls he turned in between to reach Simon Dean's house were short ones.

A small girl, whom he at first thought was a small boy because she wore a baseball uniform, opened the door. He realized it was Carolyn the victim's daughter, who was as cute as a button.

"Whom should I say is calling?" she asked when he asked to see her father.

He smiled. Denise was mannerly like that when she was that age. He felt a pang of memory. How determined Denise was to do things correctly. A wave of sorrow followed as he thought about this little girl's dead mother, remembering the fear that hit him every so often that if one time he made a wrong move, he'd leave Denise without a father.

Her distracted-looking father was in the hallway, not far behind her, so she didn't have to announce the caller. Dean wore that familiar expression of curiosity and worry folks took on when a police detective waited at the door to see them. Cosgrove had called Dan Green, the Stamford detective, to tell him he was in town to talk to Dean again. Green asked if anything new had come up. Cosgrove told him no and his reason for talking with Dean, or part of the reason anyway, was the Doyle homicide.

"Sorry to bother you again." Cosgrove held out his hand to Dean. Shaking hands was something he didn't usually do, but it seemed the right thing here. "As I might have told you the last time, I'm investigating a murder that took place in a hotel room in New York City a few days before your wife's murder. If you remember, I told you the hotel room was registered to your wife under a different name."

You couldn't blame Dean for taking a minute to catch up with the conversation. He'd expect the visit to be about his wife's murder. "Why would I know anything about that?"

Still in the doorway, Cosgrove glanced over Dean's shoulder. He wasn't looking for anything. The gesture sometimes got the person you were interviewing to invite you in. Standing in the doorway asking your questions suggested a short interview. Cosgrove hadn't driven all the way up from the city to have a short interview.

At first, Dean didn't bite, just stood in front of him looking puzzled.

"This is difficult; I know." Cosgrove held the man's gaze. "You were hoping for news on your wife's murder. And I'm bringing you a different complication to worry about. You're saying to yourself, 'What's this have to do with my wife's murder?'" Sensing Dean's attention to what he was saying, his guard down for a moment, Cosgrove asked, "Do you mind if I come in for a moment?"

Irritation flashed in Dean's eyes, but he invited Cosgrove in. "I don't like my daughter being exposed to this sort of thing."

"Saying I'm sorry doesn't help much; I know. Still, I'm sorry to put you through this. I'll be careful what I say. I'd like to know what your wife told you about the incident in the hotel."

Dean sat stiffly on the arm of an easy chair across from him. "She didn't tell me anything about it."

Cosgrove found he was sitting stiffly himself, so he leaned back into the couch he sat on. "That's strange. You did talk to her? You didn't mention that the first time I saw you."

Dean shook his head. "She was gone a few days. I didn't know where she was. When she called . . ." He paused, withdrawing into his memory. "She was confused when she called. I don't remember when it was, how long before . . ." His voice trailed off. "She said she was sorry. I didn't understand. I didn't know what she was sorry for. I told her to come home. Whatever it was, we'd work it out. I was angry. I wanted her to stop whining, come home, face up to whatever she'd done. I was too hard on her. If I'd known . . ."

Cosgrove kept quiet. You got more from sympathetic listening than from asking questions.

"It would be a long road back for us," Dean said. "I thought with God's help I would forgive her. Looking back, I realize she was hysterical on the phone. The bartender had his clutches into her, holding her against her will or tricking her in some way—the Stockholm syndrome. You know what that is: when the captive becomes dependent on the captor, thinks the captor is protecting them. I knew the bartender was bad news. I should have gone to get her. I was mad so I didn't." He glared at Cosgrove, bitter sorrow in his eyes. "Who wouldn't be mad? Your wife—"

"Excuse me. What do you mean you knew the bartender was bad news?"

Dean hesitated, as if he didn't mean to be talking about this. But now that he started, he came up with something Cosgrove would bet he hadn't planned on bringing up. "Brian McNulty was involved in my wife's life before he killed her. He corrupted her when she was a teenager."

Cosgrove didn't want Dean to know that this was important news to him, at least not yet, so he tried to stay expressionless. He'd wait to ask why Dean didn't say he knew the bartender when the question came up in the first interview. "Your wife had been in touch with him all along?"

"Sandra hadn't seen him for years." Dean sat back in his chair for the first time. "I don't like talking about my wife like this. She knew him when she was growing up. I don't know the entire story. He was a bartender in her neighborhood. When she was a teenager, he served her underage, gave her drugs. She went to his apartment to smoke pot, drink. He was a degenerate who preyed on young girls.

"Sandra was a wild teenager; reckless, self-destructive when she was young. It wasn't her fault. She was all but abandoned by her family. Her mother deserted her. Her father ignored her. The bartender took advantage of her.

"He encouraged her recklessness. Enabled her or whatever you call it. I don't know everything that happened in her life then, only what she wanted to tell me. I tried not to imagine. She was ashamed, so I didn't ask for details. The bartender took advantage of her, I'm sure, in every way possible." Dean fixed his gaze on Cosgrove to make his point. "But something happened. She outgrew him. She got sick and ended up in the hospital. It was serious, an infection. She almost died. A doctor helped her, a woman doctor. It was kind of a miracle that she lived. God was on her side. And Sandra changed. She went to college and then to medical school. We met and married when she was in medical school. She became a mother, a wonderful mother, and a doctor.

"At some point, I don't know why, that depraved side of her came back. The bartender found her and brought her back to the debased life she'd left behind, reawakened the reckless, dangerous side of her. She went on trips. I thought the trips were to medical conferences or meetings. Now I know she went to the city to meet him."

"You had a lot to be angry at her about."

Dean stared at Cosgrove for a moment. "I did have a lot of anger. She betrayed me. She defied me."

"But you were going to let her back into your life. A lot of men finding this out about their wife would send her on her way, wouldn't take her back." Cosgrove watched for a reaction. Dean had motive, a reason he might want to kill his wife. No surprise. That motive had been there all along—the wronged husband killing the unfaithful wife. They used to say a jury would never convict a man for it. Still, lots of husbands betrayed by unfaithful wives and wives betrayed by unfaithful husbands don't murder their errant spouses despite the motive.

"I believe in the sanctity of marriage," Dean said. "I knew it would be difficult to forgive her. But she had been a dutiful wife and she promised she could be again."

On the drive back to the city, Cosgrove went over the interview in his mind. Dean didn't mention the phone calls from his wife the first time Cosgrove interviewed him. This time he did. The first time, he didn't mention his wife had a history with McNulty either, although Cosgrove had asked about McNulty.

In Cosgrove's notes, Dean's answer was, "He's the bartender who killed my wife."

Often, you get a different answer in a second interview; that's why you do them. The new information wasn't so good for the case Ray was trying to make for the bartender. Cosgrove didn't take any pleasure in proving Ray wrong about McNulty; the guy was Ray's friend. Ray hadn't told him McNulty had a past with the victim. If Ray knew, he should have told him. Cosgrove suspected Ray didn't know. Not surprising McNulty would want to keep that to himself, not something to put on an employee-of-the-month application even for a bartender.

He'd asked Dean if he knew Dillard Wainwright. Dean said he'd never heard of him. Dean didn't want to hand over the laptop Ray was interested in either. He said it was an invasion of his wife's privacy. Cosgrove could've pressed the issue, but he didn't, and he didn't tell Dean why he wanted the laptop. Ray wanted it to follow up on emails between Sandra Dean and Dillard Wainwright. Cosgrove had his own interest he didn't tell Ray about. He wanted to see if there was any correspondence between her and Peter Esposito.

Cosgrove felt sorry for Simon Dean who was yet to learn about the half dozen or so men his wife had been with in the months or years before she died. Yet something about the man bothered him. Dean wasn't evasive; he'd opened up about more than you'd expect him to. Yet what he opened up about fit together almost too well. And "dutiful wife," what the hell was that?

Dean said his wife had a reckless side. You'd think that of the bartender, too. A nice enough guy, not mean, no nasty side to speak of. That wild streak was there though. You'd see it in his attitude. A guy who marched to his own tune.

He called Ray and told him to meet him for a drink at this place on Third Avenue near Ray's apartment. What he had to tell him wasn't something he wanted to say over the phone. It wasn't something he wanted to tell him face-to-face either. Yet it had to be done and Cosgrove, who wasn't much of a drinker, figured it would go down better for both of them with a drink.

Ray ordered a scotch and Cosgrove a beer. They faced each other in a booth across from the bar in the fading light of late afternoon. It wouldn't be right to pussyfoot around, so Cosgrove didn't.

Ray took it like a man. You could see the surprise light up his eyes.

Cosgrove asked anyway. "Did he tell you he had a past with Sandra Dean?"

"No." Ray threw back the scotch he'd been sipping. "Where's this leave us?"

Cosgrove lowered his voice. "I wouldn't want to be the bartender."

"You're going to forget the other suspects?"

"I didn't say that."

"What if one of them turns up in her phone records right before she was killed?" Ray was a bulldog on things like this.

"I didn't say I was done. The Stamford investigators have her phone. I'd like to know the last time she spoke with Peter Esposito, or Hoffman for that matter. I'm giving you a heads-up. I thought you should know your friend wasn't as pure as the driven snow."

"Did you ask Simon Dean about the laptop?"

"He didn't want to let it go just yet."

"Wainwright?"

"He never heard of him."

Cosgrove took a deep breath. In the past, if they were talking about a suspect and something like this—holding back important information—came up, Ray would know you confront the suspect with the information he's withheld that he doesn't know you know. Seeing his story fall apart in front of his eyes often pushed the suspect to tell the real story, to come out with the truth. Yet Ray didn't propose doing that. "Do you want to ask McNulty about the lapses in his story or do you want me to?" Cosgrove waited.

"I'd like to hear his side of the story," Ray said after a long moment. He folded his arms across his chest. "I don't think you can call this inquiry over until one of us has spoken with Dillard Wainwright."

Cosgrove hadn't forgotten about Wainwright or Esposito. But Ray was barreling on about emails and something he found in one of the collections in his library. "Plagiarism is a big deal," Ray said. "It would cost Wainwright his career, his reputation."

Cosgrove nodded. He wasn't sure about plagiarism but a ruined reputation was something. It was a motive, and motive was in short supply in this case. This gnawed at him. All along, he hadn't felt great about how the case unfolded. Sometimes in the past, he'd started off on the wrong foot, begun with a faulty assumption. You can do everything right in an investigation, but if you start off wrong you won't get to the right conclusion. Getting it right was finding the connections. When you knew how people connected to one another and what someone got out of the murder—money, revenge, safety, freedom—you could narrow in on who.

"I don't have the faith in the bartender that you do," Cosgrove said. "I'd be okay if I found the solid piece of evidence that nails McNulty. I could take a couple of days off and find an apartment. Everything points to him. Except I don't have that one piece—a gun, a motive, a witness, but most of all a clear motive. The problem was I barely got started on the first murder before the second one happened, so I let that one tell me about the first one." He stood, feeling a new determination. "I put the horse before the cart so now I'm going back to the beginning."

Ray stood also. "It's 'the cart before the horse.' The horse is supposed to go before the cart. 'You put the cart before the horse.'"

Cosgrove scowled. "Why would you put a cart before a horse?"

They left the bar together and stood on the sidewalk in front of the bar watching the traffic, mostly yellow cabs and trucks, jostling for position as they swarmed uptown. "I'm going to stop at the precinct and take a look at the murder book for the Doyle killing. Maybe I'll find something I missed. What's up with you?"

Ray wasn't a smiley faced guy at the best of times. Today he was more hangdog than usual. "Everything I need to do—my son's appeal, McNulty's bail—requires money. I think I'll rob a bank."

"That's where the money is." Cosgrove chuckled.

Chapter 27

Not long after Ambler got home after talking with Mike, Denise Cosgrove dropped Johnny off. She didn't want to stay and practically shoved Johnny through the door. "Here. You can have him."

"What's wrong?" Ambler caught the door before she could close it.

"Ask him. He's been a shithead to me all the way home." She paused and cast a sympathetic, sisterly glance at Johnny. "He got in trouble at school today. You have to call the head-master."

Johnny hurried back to the bedroom and attempted to bury himself in his schoolwork.

Ambler followed him. "What's up?" The dog had jumped up and nestled in beside him on his bed.

Johnny groused and mumbled, repeating the word 'nothing' after each of Ambler's questions. Eventually, with fits and starts and long silences, the story came out. He'd been in a fight at school. This was a first.

"It wasn't nothin' just pushing and shoving, me and Jeff, not even a fight. Everyone freaked out, even though we were over it afterward. It didn't mean anything. . . . I sort of started it. I pushed him but I didn't really mean it. We're friends."

The tony Upper East Side liberal private school wasn't the place for schoolyard fights. That one of the combatants was black set off alarms among the administration of a looming race war. But Ambler wasn't especially worried. The kid Johnny fought with was a sweet, quiet boy who never stopped smiling. He and Johnny were almost exactly the same size and inseparable at school, both good soccer players who could run like hares. Ambler wasn't prone to lecturing, so he didn't. Something else was behind what happened, and he was afraid he knew what it was. Johnny had been his usual upbeat self when Ambler dropped him off at school the previous morning. He hadn't seen him since then because he'd spent last night at his grandmother's.

"If that's everything, I think we're okay. I'll call the headmaster. Should I call Jeff's mother?"

"She'll probably call you. She has to call the headmaster, too. She really doesn't like it when Jeff gets in trouble."

Jeff's mom, an attorney and a single mother, ran a tight ship. He liked her and she liked Johnny as a friend for Jeff, despite Johnny's somewhat shady background, which brought Ambler to where he thought the problem lay. "How did things go at your grandmother's this week?"

Johnny stiffened. "Okay, I guess." He stuck his nose in his history book.

Ambler waited, fighting off the urge to prod the boy. He sat down on the side of the bed.

Johnny's tears started before his words came. Ambler wanted to reach for him, to hug him, but held back. "She said I couldn't visit Dad anymore. . . . She wasn't going to let me." He looked up with tear-stained cheeks. "What's the matter with her? . . . I hate her. I'm not going there anymore."

Ambler's chest tightened. His own eyes teared. He was the grown-up; he was supposed to have the answers. This time he didn't. He didn't know what to do and he didn't know what to say, as much at a loss as Johnny was. "I don't know what's wrong with her." It was the truth, even if it wasn't any help. He wished Adele was there. She comforted Johnny in ways he wished he could. Johnny knew she was on his side no matter what. More often than Ambler would have expected, he found himself lined up against the two of them.

He left Johnny to his tears and went into the other room to call her. When he told her what happened, something she'd been expecting, too, she said she'd pick up dinner and come over. He told himself Johnny's father wouldn't be taken away from him no matter what Lisa Young did. He'd take Johnny to see his father, Lisa Young and court orders be damned. What could they do to him? They could take Johnny away from him is what they could do. His chest tightened, this time with anxiety.

He went back into the room. Johnny lay on the bed next to the dog stroking his coat. "Adele's coming over and bringing dinner. Wanna take a walk with Lola while we wait?"

Lola was a great city dog. She was fine with going for walks. She quite enjoyed them and took an interest in her surroundings, mostly the scents. Yet she didn't insist on walking; she was willing to wait for someone to get around to taking her. Once underway, she'd head whatever way the person at the other end of the leash wanted to go. She didn't yank the leash, and when she did stop to sniff either end of the dogs she came across in her travels, she did so without getting especially excited about it and didn't yap at them. The only times she sprang into action and had to be wrestled back was when she saw a cat. This didn't happen often. Both Ambler and Johnny had learned to spot the cat before she did and take evasive action.

The walk was usually around the block, sometimes an extra block or two up or down Lexington or Third before turning. Once in a while, the walk was over to the river. More often, it was in the other direction to Madison Square Park and the dog run. This was Lola's favorite. She came to life in an entirely new way. Back among her own folks, she could be herself, running and jumping and wrestling and racing, hanging with the pack. That is where they went this evening. Leaning against the fence watching Lola cavort, Ambler relaxed. He and Johnny hadn't spoken on the way over. Johnny held Lola on the leash and Ambler walked beside him. Now, here, leaning on the fence, he put his arm around his grandson's shoulder, and the boy leaned against him.

"Your grandmother isn't doing this to be mean. In her own way, she's trying to do what's best for you. She doesn't understand—"

"I don't care. She's a old asshole!"

Ambler stepped back, his voice rising. "You can't talk like that. She's—"

Johnny stepped back from him, too. "I can, too. I'm not going back there. I don't care what you say either." His voice broke and the tears came.

This was no time to try to discipline him. For one of the few times since Johnny came into his life, Ambler felt he couldn't control his grandson, and it scared him; despite his utter dependence in most things, Johnny really was an independent entity.

"I'm on your side, Johnny." Ambler said simply. "Your dad's my son. Fathers care for sons like sons care for fathers. I'm going to be honest with you. I don't know what to do. But we'll figure it out."

Johnny brightened slightly. From wherever he got it, the kid had an invincible optimism. "Adele will know what to do." He called Lola, whose ears went up as she cocked her head and turned to him. "C'mon, girl." She trotted over. Ambler raised his eyebrows. She didn't come when he called her.

Adele was waiting in the doorway with a bag of Chinese

food when they got back. Upstairs, he and Adele dished the food onto plates while Johnny fed Lola. He told her what Johnny said in the park. Adele stopped scooping and turned on him. "She's trying to take his father away from him, the father he's given his heart and soul to." She glared at Ambler like Johnny had done in the park. "She is an old asshole."

They ate Szechuan noodles, moo shu pork, and bok choy and talked about Johnny's dad's appeal, McNulty's murder charge, and the lawyer handling both cases. Johnny was pleased to be part of the conversation and finally ready to talk about his grandmother. Ambler told him he had to keep going to his grandparents no matter how angry he was at her because that was the way the law and the family court worked. Adele told him they'd get things figured out somehow and, after a lot of grumbling, he agreed he'd go but he wasn't going to pretend he wasn't mad at her.

"Mr. Young is supposed to take me to a Yankee playoff game this weekend. He has box seats."

"Great," Adele said. "That should be fun."

"I've never gone anywhere with him by myself before." He looked at Ambler. "I wish you could go."

"I wish I could, too." Ambler said. He and Johnny went to a few games at the Stadium each year. But the closest he ever got to the playing field was the second deck. With a rush of sadness, he remembered he'd talked to Johnny about the Yankees the first time he'd ever met him, before he knew he was his grandson. He remembered taking his own son to Yankee Stadium, one of the few decent things he did as a father.

"I won't know what to say to him," Johnny said.

"Don't worry," Adele said. "I'll tell you a secret. Adults believe it's their responsibility to find something to talk to kids about. No adult expects a kid to know what to talk about."

"Is that true?" Johnny looked at Ambler.

"Actually, I think it is true." He glanced at Adele, who was quite at ease.

Back at the library the next morning, he was met by what was for him a rush of researchers to get settled in. One was a women's studies professor from CUNY, researching academic mysteries written by women, reminding him, as if he needed reminding, of introducing Sandra Dean to the crime fiction collection. This reader he was familiar with. She'd been doing work in the crime fiction collection off and on for years. Like many of the library's readers, she was the standoffish sort, so their interactions had been limited to a smile and a nod and a comment on the weather now and again.

Ambler had spoken to her more recently about Jayne Galloway. She knew the writer's work and was interested when he told her the library had acquired Galloway's papers because some of Galloway's mysteries had an academic setting. Ambler hadn't read any of Galloway's academic mysteries, which he thought about now, remembering that Galloway often used happenings in her own life as fodder for the fictional worlds she created. He wondered if one of her books with an academic setting might have a character based on Wainwright. It was a long shot and he wasn't sure even if there was such a character this would tell him anything. But it was worth a try.

When the reader came back from lunch, he asked her. She consulted an annotated bibliography of women's academic mysteries she'd put together and found a stand-alone suspense novel by Jayne Galloway with an exclusive women's college as the setting. The story was the investigation of the campus murder of a young woman. The sleuth, a young English professor, took on the role of amateur detective when it was discovered that the man she was in love with, a distinguished scholar, had been having an affair with the young murder victim. It was a well-worn plot. The professor was a suspect but too obvious a suspect to be the actual killer. What sparked Ambler's interest, something that would strike a chord only with him, was that the distinguished professor was a Poe scholar.

Ambler didn't know enough about Wainwright's characteristics, mannerisms, or affectations to know if the character in the novel was based on him. What Ambler did know was that Wainwright was a Poe scholar. Most intriguing was that the professor in the story had a hideaway cabin in the woods outside of a small town a few miles from the college.

Ambler trotted down to the map division on the first floor, found the Massachusetts map, and located a dozen or more small towns around Pine Grove College. He wasn't sure how you found out if someone owned property in a particular place, so he asked one of the librarians in the map division. She set him up with an online link to the Registry of Deeds in Hampshire County, Massachusetts, and the counties surrounding it. In something less than twenty minutes, he discovered Dillard Wainwright owned a house in Amherst where the college was located and another dwelling in the town of Greenfield, twenty miles outside of Amherst in Franklin County.

Ambler stared at the screen in front of him, reading the details of the listing over and over as if it might tell him if Wainwright was in his cabin.

"There's no reason to think he'd be there," Adele said when he caught up with her and told her what he'd found.

"We don't have any place else to look." Ambler was already planning his trip.

"You're not going to go there?" Adele's eyes opened wider. "Suppose he is there. And suppose he is the killer." Her voice dropped to a whisper. "He'll kill you."

Ambler was excited. For now, all he wanted was to know if Wainwright was in his cabin. He'd decide what to do about it once he knew that. "He's a college professor not a gunslinger," he told Adele as he headed out the door.

Ambler had considered the possible danger, but it wasn't enough to dissuade him. He'd wondered about Wainwright since he first came across the man's name in Sandra Dean's journal. Ambler's plan was he would concoct a story—he was gathering biographical information on Jayne Galloway—that had nothing to do with Sandra Dean or murder.

Chapter 28

It didn't take long for Mike Cosgrove to go through the murder book on Ted Doyle. Crime scene and forensics stuff, interviews with hotel staff, longer interviews with the hotel security director and Moses, the bartender in the lobby lounge who knew McNulty, and the interview he did with Doyle's widow when she came into the city to identify the body. When he read over the interview with the hotel bartender, something about the bartender's answers bothered him. Moses said he remembered Sandra Dean, whom he knew as Shannon, talking to a man, maybe the victim. That was about all. Other times she'd been in the bar, she'd caused something of a commotion, talking too loud, butting into conversations, toying with men she came across. This time she wasn't doing any of that, maybe not a big deal, yet it was something he didn't pick up on the first time through.

Cosgrove pulled down a photo of Peter Esposito from the website of the company Esposito worked for, and he had a photo of Simon Dean, that, too, from a company website. Dean was actually a vice president of the architectural company he worked for. No one so far had asked if either of these men was in the hotel the night of Ted Doyle's murder. Maybe nothing would come of any of this. If nothing else, Ray would know he did a thorough job despite his suspicions about McNulty's guilt.

Ted Doyle's widow had told him her husband was in the city on business. The security company said he wasn't on a job. Not a big deal but another discrepancy to check out. Cosgrove met Mrs. Doyle, this time at her home, a modest ranch house on a quiet street of similar modest homes and well-kept yards, in Massapequa, a small town in Nassau County that had grown into a colony where working and retired cops from the city and Long Island lived.

Cosgrove knew a few guys who lived there himself. The murder victim, Ted Doyle, retired from the NYPD after his twenty-two years had been working for Continental Security Consultants for about half as long. He was in his early sixties when he was killed. The widow was small and gray—thin gray hair and a grayish hue to her complexion; her eyes were a kind of blue faded to gray. He thought she looked sad, though depressed was more likely.

"I appreciate your speaking with me again. I know it's difficult," Cosgrove said.

"Ted would have wanted me to." She stood in the doorway, holding the door. "Come in."

The worst part of this was talking about "the other woman." He didn't know an easy way to do it, so he tried a roundabout approach and asked about her husband's time on the force.

What she told him was about what he expected. As with most cops, nothing about his time on the job was remarkable. He stood on corners, drove a patrol car. When he made detective, he worked grand larceny. He looked into a lot of burglaries, wrote a ton of paper, and kept his nose clean. Because he'd been a detective, when he was hired at the security company after his retirement, they assigned him to investigations—domestic cases, missing persons, surveillance in a divorce case, and such. He also did some work for attorneys who hired the agency for investigations in criminal cases.

"He was old school," the widow said. "The company let him stay that way. He didn't want to learn about all that computer stuff they do." Her face began to crumble, her lip tremble. "Then, when he died they turned nasty. He was on a job when he went into the city and was killed. I should have gotten a special compensation package because he was killed on the job, in the line of duty. But they're not giving it to me. They say he was off-duty when he was killed."

"I don't suppose you know anything about the case he was on." For some reason, she'd led him into the kitchen, rather than the living room, and he now sat somewhat uncomfortably on a wooden chair at the kitchen table.

"He never told me anything specific about his work, never anyone's name. You're not supposed to. If something was confidential, he kept it confidential. He was loyal to the security company; he never criticized or complained. Now look. They're stealing his compensation package." Her eyes reddened. Cosgrove had already upset her and he hadn't even gotten to the "other woman" questions. Still, that's why he was there, so he asked.

"It might have happened," she said. "Nothing's impossible." She'd thought about this, he could tell, wrestled with it, laid awake at night reliving it. "Men are men. I know cops. My father was a cop and my brother. Too much drinking, too many badge bunnies. Ted wasn't like that. We raised three boys. He coached them in baseball and basketball when they were young. When they were older, in high school, if he wasn't working he went to their games. We had a good life. He liked being home. If you look in the garage, you'll see his woodworking shop. We took vacations together. We liked each other's company."

Still, Ted Doyle may have lived a life on the wild side when his wife wasn't looking. Some guys got away with it, pulled the wool over their wives' eyes, brought them flowers and told them lies. Mrs. Doyle knew of no bars Ted frequented. As far as she knew, he'd drink a beer or two but didn't go to bars as a regular thing. He was a stick-in-the-mud.

When Cosgrove got back to the city, he checked around, made a few calls, and spoke to a couple of guys who knew Ted Doyle. The cops he spoke with said the same thing: easygoing, straight as an arrow, by the book. The clichés told him they didn't know Doyle very well, which was how it was with some cops. They did their job, kept to themselves, went home after work.

Continental Security Consultants in Glen Cove, Long Island, was less than forthcoming, as he'd expected they might be. None of the first three people he spoke to on the phone would own up to the fact that Ted Doyle had worked there, much less talk about him. Cosgrove finally got to a director of something or other, also retired from NYPD. The guy knew of Cosgrove from a case Cosgrove worked that left a sour taste in the mouth of NYPD Intelligence, which didn't help any.

"Our client list is confidential," the director of something or other told him. "I don't see how talking to someone here about one of our consultants would help you."

In the old days, they were private eyes, shamuses, gumshoes; now they were consultants. He hoped the pay was better. "Suppose you let me decide that." Cosgrove said.

The guy was condescending, his tone formal. You'd think you were talking to a guy who'd found out you used to sleep with his wife. "There really isn't anything I can help you with. I don't want to waste your time."

"Was he in the city working on a job?"

"He wasn't on the job when he was murdered."

"How do you know?"

"Answering that question would be a breach of confidentiality. Our consultants write reports. Ted kept his up-to-date."

Cosgrove didn't know if he could subpoena the reports. He didn't know if the guy was bullshitting him about breaching confidentiality. He didn't think a security agency had any special protections. "Let me tell you what I'm thinking and you can tell me if I'm close." He didn't wait for an answer. "Doyle might have been working on a case that involved dangerous people, the kind of case that might get an investigator killed."

"Almost any case can turn dangerous. Our consultants are licensed to carry a concealed weapon. He wasn't armed. I can tell you this because you know it already. He could have been carrying if he thought he was in danger. As I said, he wasn't on the job when he was killed. If he had been, we'd treat this differently."

The guy had more to say about what men did on their own time and how easy it was to get mixed up with the wrong woman. Cosgrove wasn't interested. "You say he wasn't on the job the night he was killed. Was he on a job, doing surveillance, doing anything in the city that day?"

"No."

"Can you tell me where he was working without violating your principles?"

After a pause, the director of something or other said, "He had a couple of cases on the island. Nothing in the city."

"A case on Long Island might have taken him into the city."

"It might have. We have no reason to believe it did."

Cosgrove had no reason not to believe what the Continental Security guy told him. He had no reason to disbelieve Mrs. Doyle either, except her husband might have lied to her so he could pick up a loose woman. He may have been doing things like that for years without her knowledge, yet nothing pointed to that. That the security agency denied Ted Doyle's compensation package rankled Cosgrove. He wouldn't put it past this smooth corporate entity to lie about an employee being on the clock to protect itself from a big payout. But he wasn't about to ask the company shill on the phone about it. He wasn't going to call Mrs. Doyle or her late husband liars either. He'd find the answer before letting go.

His next stop that evening was at the hotel to talk to Moses, the bartender who'd been behind the bar the night Ted Doyle was murdered. This was the guy who pointed him toward the cop Al Hoffman, who'd had a fling with the woman he knew as Shannon Darling and who sometime later asked him to get her a gun.

Moses remembered Cosgrove. "Did you find Al Hoffman?" he asked when Cosgrove sidled up to the bar.

Cosgrove told him he had and asked if he remembered the night of Ted Doyle's murder.

"I went through that with another detective right after it happened. I told him everything I remembered. He took notes. Don't you guys talk to one another?"

"I read his notes." Everybody and his brother watched cop shows on TV and think they know police procedure better than you do. "Sometimes we get new information that brings up new questions. Sometimes a witness like you remembers something you didn't think of last time." He'd made this speech as often as he'd given someone Miranda rights. "I won't take much of your time." He glanced along the empty bar to make a point.

The bartender went back to cutting limes. "Shoot."

Cosgrove rolled his eyes. Were all New York bartenders smart-asses? "You'd seen this woman, the victim, a number of times, meeting different men here. Was anything different about the night she met the man who was murdered?"

Moses stopped cutting and placed the knife he was using on the cutting board. He met Cosgrove's gaze. "She'd been with McNulty earlier. Next thing, she was talking to this other guy."

"Had you ever seen this other guy before, the man who was murdered?"

"I might have. If I saw him, I don't remember. I don't remember everybody. Your question about different," he picked up his paring knife and waved it at Cosgrove before attacking the lime again. "It was." He concentrated on cutting the lime for the moment. "She hadn't been at the bar long, nursing a scotch and water. He came in, took the stool beside her, ordered a beer. They talked for a couple of minutes, not long enough for a second beer, and then they left together."

This gave Cosgrove something to think about. He ordered a beer himself and sat down on the barstool he'd been standing behind. The bartender continued prepping the fruit for the evening. "That's how the hookers do it so they're not soliciting in the bar. The meet-up's been arranged. That's how it works with those matchmaking computer dates, too. It's been arranged."

"What did you think of her?"

Moses adjusted his stance, standing slightly taller, suggesting to Cosgrove that he appreciated being asked for his judgment. "Sometimes, she was trouble. I told you the last time you were here I walked her to her room one night she'd had too much. I didn't take her up on her offer. After that, for all she cared, I could have been a vending machine. A woman goes from man to man at the bar, she's trouble.

"When she came with McNulty, she was different, relaxed like they were old friends. Other times, by herself, she was nervous, looking over her shoulder like she might get caught. Wrapped up in something going on in her head. I see lots of people lost in their thoughts, deep in a funk. Sad, maybe. Depressed. I leave them alone. Bartenders have a saying: Beware the solitary drinker."

Cosgrove took out the photo of Simon Dean and showed it to him. Moses shook his head. He didn't recognize Dean. The barman's reaction to the next photo was different.

"Sure. That's Mr. Esposito." Moses kept hold of the photo and looked at again. "What do you want to know about him?"

"He's a regular?"

"Whenever he's in town. He's been coming in for years."

Something about Moses's expression told Cosgrove he had something to say about Esposito, something he wasn't sure he should say, or wasn't sure he wanted to say, so Cosgrove moved cautiously. "Did you ever see him with Sandra Dean, the woman you knew as Shannon?"

Moses nodded. "As soon as I saw this picture, I wondered why you hadn't asked me about him before."

Cosgrove's attention spiked. "Why's that?"

It turned out Moses had been working the bar the evening of Peter Esposito's confrontation with Sandra Dean and the man she was talking with. He told Cosgrove essentially the same story Esposito had told him about the confrontation that ended with Sandra Dean and Esposito being asked to leave the bar. "I saw that coming, too."

"You saw there'd be a confrontation?"

"Mr. Esposito met the lady sometime before. I don't know about that. I don't remember if I witnessed them meeting. Mr. Esposito thought I did witness it and he knew I knew the lady in question. Every time for maybe a year—a half-dozen times—he came in, he'd ask if I'd seen her. Maybe I had once but I didn't remember much about it. He'd ask me and then he'd tell me about her." Moses glanced around the room—the bar was a kind of sectioned off part of the lobby—as if he were hoping a customer or two might come along to rescue him. He turned a pained look toward Cosgrove. "I don't like to talk about folks who tell me things at the bar. Folks expect us bartenders to be discreet. I'm telling you this because you're a cop and we're talking about a lady who got killed."

"I understand. I appreciate it. Everything you saw, everything you tell me, is important."

"The liquor talks, you know. Mostly what folks tell me goes in one ear and out the other. I don't hold them to it." Moses fixed his gaze on Cosgrove. "Men talk about woman trouble."

He laughed good-naturedly. "I don't understand women any better than they do. None of us do, right?"

Cosgrove agreed.

"He told me he and Shannon had fallen in love when they met here. That was okay. She's a pretty woman. Any man could get taken with her. The thing with Mr. Esposito was he told me she was in love with him." Moses opened his eyes wide in mock surprise. "She was married, he told me. He said it was complicated. She denied it to herself, he said. Yet he knew she was in love with him. They talked on the phone a lot, he said. And everything was going to work out. I'd nod my head and let him talk.

"And then that night he saw her with this other man, I knew there'd be trouble. I felt like I should have told him before he should let her go, forget about her. His ideas about her being in love with him didn't make no sense. This night, it was too late. Nothing was going to keep him away from her."

"Did he come back after that? Has he been in the bar since then?"

"He's been back. He didn't talk about her no more, though." Moses chuckled. "We had a what do you call it? A kind of silent understanding that none of that ever happened."

Cosgrove looked at his notebook. "Do you know when he was here last?" Cosgrove was looking for the date of Ted Doyle's murder. "Is there a way to find out if he was here on or around September 7?"

Moses didn't remember and told Cosgrove he'd need to ask the manager for the hotel records.

"Credit card dupes?" Cosgrove asked.

"I'm pretty sure he'd charge everything to his room."

Once more, Cosgrove needed the hotel records. This time, he might have enough to persuade the manager to let him take a look. Failing that, he might have enough to get a warrant.

Chapter 29

Ambler took a United Airlines flight out of Newark Airport at 8:15 the morning after he discovered Wainwright's cabin in the woods and arrived at Bradley International Airport north of Hartford, Connecticut, an hour later. He drove another hour north to Amherst, Massachusetts, and took a seat in the office of Amelia Hamilton, the chair of the Pine Grove College English Department.

He had what he thought was a plausible scenario for seeking out Wainwright and thought he'd try it out on the person who first told him Wainwright was missing. Perhaps he'd also find out what folks at the college thought of Wainwright, though it was unlikely anyone thought of him as a murderer on the loose.

Professor Hamilton was friendly, yet formal and cautious, measuring each word and keeping a shrewd eye on him.

"I'm not familiar with the author . . . Jayne Gardner, is it?"

"Jayne Galloway. She's a mystery writer."

Something went on behind Professor Hamilton's eyes. "And you say you're a curator at the New York Public Library?

I love the library. We go to New York a few times a year for the theater . . . but always to the library."

"I curate the crime fiction collection."

She seemed to sniff when he said this. "Crime fiction? I didn't know there was such a thing." She raised her head and sniffed again. "Not crime. Not crime fiction. I meant that the library would hold such a collection."

Ambler tried to keep the irritation out of his voice. "It's a minor collection."

"I'm sure." She flipped back her hair.

He told her about Jayne Galloway's connection to Wainwright. "There might be correspondence; perhaps Professor Wainwright held onto an unfinished manuscript or drafts of her manuscripts."

When Professor Hamilton talked about Wainwright, she used a lot of words without saying much. "What reputation he has would be for his scholarly work on the dark romantics rather than his literary work. I'd forgotten he wrote fiction. . . . Early in his career, I remember, he published in some literary journals. His fiction was part of his portfolio for his tenure review if I remember correctly—"

Ambler didn't mention the fraud accusation. "Was that important to his gaining tenure?"

She took a moment to answer. "I'm certain it would have been. His scholarly publications came later. Those were impressive, monographs on Poe. Because of those, at one point he was a sought after scholar. Pine Grove made a handsome offer to retain him—reduced teaching time, research support, an early sabbatical—as a university was wooing him." She paused. "He's not lived up to his promise." She said this wistfully, reflecting perhaps her wish the college had let him go when they had the chance.

"At the time he disappeared had he been under pressure of any sort at the college? Anything on campus or in his personal life that he might want to escape from?"

She made a face like swallowing bitter medicine. "I'm not sure what you mean."

Ambler softened his interrogator's tone. "Were there any complaints against him . . . criticism, questions about his teaching or scholarly work, his relationships with students?"

Her expression softened as she took a moment to consider this. "Dillard was idiosyncratic, not to say an oddball. He thought a lot of himself, as if having accepted a position here at Pine Grove when he might have been at a university entitled him to more approbation than he received. His colleagues took notice of his disdain. . . . He wasn't well liked. We're a small collegial faculty and pride ourselves on that collegiality. We act courteously toward everyone. With him, it required effort.

"Dillard had always been aloof. The past year or two, he'd been even more remote. If he hadn't been a no-show for his class, we might not have discovered he was missing."

"What happens when he comes back?"

She raised her eyebrows. "If he comes back . . ."

"You don't expect him to?"

She folded her hands on the desk in front of her. "Nothing like this has ever happened at Pine Grove College. I don't want to judge before the facts. His disappearance might have been beyond his control. Something might have happened to his mind."

"To his mind?"

She shook her head. "As I said, he was odd, and lately more erratic."

"Do you suspect foul play?"

"Foul play?" She recoiled from the question. "What a remarkable term to encounter in the day-to-day life of the college. It's a concept out of your world, Mr. Ambler, not ours." Her gaze, out of nowhere, was piercing. "Do you suspect *foul play?*"

For a moment he was tempted to tell her what he did suspect but decided not to. It wouldn't help him. And it wouldn't help her to think of her colleague as a murder suspect, especially if Wainwright was innocent. He asked if Wainwright had a second home or a family vacation place he might visit. She didn't know of any. He asked if Wainwright had been with or talked with anyone on campus in the days before he disappeared. She said no.

This was probably all he was going to get. Professor Hamilton didn't question his reason for searching out Wainwright; though once she'd thought it through she might wonder why a curator would search for a missing person on the off-chance he might have a manuscript or some letters to add to his collection. Leaving her to her soon-to-come misgivings, he headed out into the country with directions to a cabin owned by the missing Dillard Wainwright.

Forty-five minutes later, not far outside a small town, he found the turnoff to Wainwright's cabin, a worn one-lane macadam roadway. The tightness that had been building in his chest became an iron grip as he closed in on the cabin. Excitement more than fear caused the tightness, though he wasn't aware of the cause. He thought of himself as a calm man. If he was afraid, it was measured. He knew there was some danger in front of him. Wainwright might see through his charade, might freak out at being found, might have a gun.

The undertaking had risks but it wasn't foolhardy. He didn't know what he'd do if Wainwright wasn't there, and he didn't have much of a plan if he was there. He wouldn't try to apprehend him and had no plan to bring up Sandra Dean's murder or even mention her name—any of her names. Finding Wainwright would be enough . . . for now. He'd ask a few questions about Jayne Galloway, inquire about letters and drafts of manuscripts, and see where that took him.

The man who opened the warped wooden door and stood tentatively in the doorway of the weathered, shingled, one-story structure, something between a shack and a cabin, blinked at Ambler with the dazed amazement of someone coming into daylight after a long time in the dark. His hair was long, stringy, and unwashed, his facial hair more scruff than beard; only a couple of the buttons on his flannel shirt were buttoned and those were in the wrong buttonholes, leaving the tail of the shirt a couple of inches longer on one side than the other.

Ambler's heart sank; he almost sank with it as the adrenaline and excitement he'd built up gushed out. "Sorry to bother you," he said after they had stared at each other for a long moment. "I'm looking for Dillard Wainwright."

"Who?" The man's expression became even more puzzled.

Ambler kept calm. "I understand Dillard Wainwright owns this property. I thought he might be here. You—"

"He does?"

Something was off with this man, Ambler saw now. His movements, slight as they were, were awkward, disjointed. Something was missing in his expression; what should have been interest or inquiry was at once vacant and too curious. "Do you know Dillard Wainwright?"

"No. . . . No. I don't think so."

Ambler wasn't going to let this go. He stuck out his hand and introduced himself. The man stared at the hand for a long moment before he grasped it, or more precisely, placed his hand gently in Ambler's, as if he were making a present of it.

"I wonder if I might talk with you for a moment?"

The man nodded but didn't move.

Ambler scrutinized the face in front of him. In the only photo he'd ever seen of Wainwright on the book jacket, he was much younger with no beard. The resemblance might be slight but he had a sense this was who stood in front of him, a disheveled and deranged version of Wainwright. He didn't want to let go. "Have you been here long?"

The man turned to look at the bare-bones room behind him. "Here? I guess so."

"Where were you before?"

He withdrew into himself, seeking answers somewhere in his memory. "I'm confused," he said. "Who are you, again?"

Ambler told him.

The man shook his head. "I've had some problems, memory failure; I might as well tell you. I don't know how I got to this house. I'm pretty sure I belong here, but I don't know the name you mentioned."

"You have amnesia?"

"That's what they tell me." He scrutinized Ambler's face. "I do recall bits and pieces."

They had, without either mentioning it, moved to the interior of the cabin and seated themselves across from one another on the only two chairs at a plain rectangular wooden table. "You've lost your identity? You don't know who you are?"

"I'm told it's temporary." The man's gaze searched Ambler's, an engagement with him that wasn't there before. "Dissociative fugue."

"I don't know what that is."

"Neither do I. They told me but I don't get it."

"Are you alone here? Do you have anyone to help you?"

"Folks around and in Greenfield help me out. I've been seen by doctors there."

"Did they try to find out who you are?"

He waited to answer, perhaps deciding how much to tell. Ambler got the sense that this coyness was a practiced art. "I didn't want them to."

"Didn't they trace you through the cabin, find its owner?"

"No one knows I live here. I don't want them to." He watched Ambler for his reaction. "It might be I thought they could trace me through the cabin and that's why I didn't tell them. . . . I didn't think of that at the time. To them, I'm a homeless eccentric who lives in the woods and through the generosity of strangers is given food and sustenance; I go to a soup kitchen. Folks give me handouts. I stand in front the hardware store in Greenfield.

Someone picks me up now and then to do laboring work. I'll do lawn work or painting or filling nail holes for drywallers." He looked at his hands and then turned his palms toward Ambler. There were dried blisters on their way to becoming callouses.

The cabin was rustic, rudimentary, yet with most of the essentials, an indoor toilet, a galley kitchen with a propane stove, electricity for a small ancient refrigerator and lights. The walls and floors of the main room were wood, probably pine. A door opened to what was most likely a small bedroom. A good-sized bookcase leaned against one wall. No television, no computer in sight.

"Do you read?" Ambler gestured toward the books.

The man looked toward the bookcase also. "I pick up books at a thrift store in Greenfield; some days I read in the library."

Ambler felt his way carefully. The man appeared to enjoy their chat, making no effort to end it. You wouldn't know anything was wrong with him when he talked about the present. "When you read a book, do you ever remember you've read it before?"

The question energized Wainwright. He leaned forward eagerly. "Yes. Yes. . . ." He went to the bookcase, took out a book, and handed it to Ambler. "Short stories by Edgar Allan Poe. The first time I picked up the book I remembered the stories as I read them."

This made more sense to Ambler than it did to the man telling him. Wainwright said he was told there was a good chance his memory would return on its own. It was curious that he wanted to wait for that, rather than be told his identity. You'd think he'd be anxious to find out who he was, unless he was afraid of what he might find out about himself.

Ambler scrutinized the man. Could this be an act? Dillard Wainwright, sound of mind, hiding in plain sight so to speak by playing the role of a hermit? "You do have some memories, I think you said."

He met Ambler's gaze. "I remember a childhood I assume is mine. Bits and pieces of other places and situations. No family or a job. I remember being in college. . . . I dream about a college. I need to complete a course, in math I think, in order to graduate; in the dream I realize it's the end of the year and I've forgotten to attend the class. In another dream, I'm teaching the class. Again, I've forgotten to attend. The students come to class anyway and are there when I arrive finally, again too late in the semester."

"Do you have any dreams that are violent?" Ambler thought of asking about memories of violence, but dreams were safer.

A dark cloud passed behind Wainwright's eyes. He took a long time to answer. "I don't think so. Why do you ask?" He was perceptive for someone without all his marbles.

"It's hard to explain."

The man fidgeted. He'd look at Ambler and then look away, at his bookshelf, at the table. After a moment, he said. "I'm torn between asking you to tell me about the man you think I am and asking you not to, to leave me in peace and let my memories return of their own accord."

Ambler didn't want to tell him about Dillard Wainwright yet; he certainly didn't want to tell this man he was a suspect— at least in Ambler's eyes—in a murder case. Even a rough outline of what Ambler knew might kick-start other memories that would remind him, if he was Wainwright, of what he did and cause him to disappear for real and purposefully this time. "I don't think I should tell you," Ambler said. "I'm not qualified to help you work through whatever's going on with you."

"I think that's best also." The man's expression was friendly and more open than at any other time since they'd begun talking. "The down side of that approach is—I guess—my memory might not come back."

Ambler's new friend told him a believable story of what happened to him. He'd found himself one afternoon in the cabin they were now in, not knowing how he got there and with memories only of a long-ago past. He remembered going to college and he remembered his childhood; he had disassociated memories of people and places that weren't linked to each other or to him. He'd been diagnosed and was told there was no medical treatment for his disorder, except talk therapy with a psychiatrist or psychologist, which he chose not to do, preferring to wait for his memory to come back.

He had everything he needed for day-to-day life in the cabin. He didn't know if he'd brought supplies with him or the supplies were in the cabin when he got there. "I'm okay here and content to see what happens." He said this matter-of-factly. "If my memory comes back, I'll return to the life I had. If I die before it comes back, so be it; I'll die anonymously. I have enough bits and pieces of memory to suspect I don't have a family and that no one will miss me."

He chuckled, a strange sound, out of place, incongruous. "Perhaps I'll leave a great fortune unattended." Something twinkled in his eyes. You almost thought him kindly. "If the person you have in mind has a great fortune, we might explore that. Otherwise, I'd prefer you leave me to my odd life here for the time being."

"Your diagnosis, dissociative fugue. Do you know when it started or do you know the date you were first diagnosed?"

"I don't know when it started." He stood and went to his bookshelf. "I have an appointment card here, so I might know when I was diagnosed." He rustled through some papers. "September 14." He examined the appointment card a couple of times before putting it back on the shelf.

"Do you have a car? I didn't see one."

"I do. It's around back. I must have driven it here." He spoke ruefully. "It's not running now. I haven't gotten it fixed."

Ambler felt uneasy leaving. He judged that Wainwright, if it was Wainwright, was playing straight with him and hoped he'd stay where he was because there was a strong likelihood Ambler would be coming back. But there was a chance Wainwright might become unnerved by their encounter and hightail it out of there as soon as Ambler left. One of Ambler's fictional private eyes could call the agency and have an operative sent out to keep an eye on the cabin. If he had proof that Wainwright was a legitimate murder suspect, he might persuade the local police to put a tail on him. He had neither of these resources, so he needed to do some checking in a hurry.

He returned to Amherst. His plan was to search Wainwright's house but he wanted to do it under the cover of darkness. So he had a sandwich at a pleasant restaurant on North Pleasant Street, walked around the pretty town, visited the library, sat for a time in the town common facing the Lord Jeffery Inn, and stopped by the Emily Dickinson Museum, which he learned from a plaque in front was the house where she lived pretty much as a recluse.

In the late afternoon, he walked through the small tree-lined streets of large wooden-frame houses behind the main street of the town until he found the one belonging to Dillard Wainwright, which like the others was set back from the street by a large front yard. It wasn't the largest house on the street and it wasn't ornate.

Someone had kept the lawn under control. A large hedge along the sidewalk in front had grown fairly high, six feet, maybe more. The street was quiet. He would be taking a chance. But today was his chance-taking day. If he were discovered, he was prepared to say he'd been sent to pick up some things by Dillard Wainwright. As he checked out the house, he realized his plan to wait for darkness would be a mistake. It made more sense to go in now when he wouldn't need to turn on any lights—and even if he did, they'd not be noticeable.

He walked from the front to the back of the house. This wasn't a neighborhood that expected burglaries which might incline folks to be careless about locks and not worry about alarms. The back door of Wainwright's house had small glass windows in the top half. If push came to shove, he could break a window and reach inside to open the door. Since Wainwright left in a hurry and in all likelihood no one else had been in the house, he hoped a door or window might have been left unlocked. The hedge provided cover and shrubs and bushes walled off the back and both sides of the yard. He tried a couple of the downstairs windows, which were locked.

In the back of the house, he tried the metal cover of a stairway leading down to a basement door. The metal door—like the cover of a storm cellar—was unlocked. The stairway was damp and filled with cobwebs. It was dark and the only flashlight he had was the one on his cell phone. This worked well enough for him to see that the small windowpane next to the doorknob on the door to the basement had been knocked out. He reached through, felt his way to the sliding bolt above the doorknob, slid that open, and turned the doorknob from the inside.

Once inside, he found his ways upstairs, did a quick survey— two bedrooms, one used as an office or library. The makeshift office had two solid walls of books, a neat desk, a few baskets half the size of a laundry basket holding papers and documents. A computer sat on the desk. It was unlikely he could open it without a password, so he was better off searching the baskets of papers and documents. He didn't know what he was looking for: something to prove the man in the cabin was Wainwright? an elaborate murder plan written out in detail? a confession?

What he did find in one of the baskets, which might have been what he was looking for, was a file of printed emails. Wainwright had printed out his email exchange with Sandra Dean. He'd also printed out an exchange of emails with Jayne Galloway, all were from around the same time, early September. The first email from Jayne Galloway was an answer to an email Wainwright must have sent to her complaining about her daughter's threat to expose him as a fraud.

Galloway's answer was short but friendlier than Ambler would have expected, as though she and Wainwright were old friends catching up after enough time had passed to let bygones be bygones. She told him gently she had no influence over her daughter. She also wrote: "Sandra's been reading through the journals and diaries I donated to the 42nd Street Library—I'm as surprised as you are—and she found the entry you wrote me about where I revealed that I gave you a short story to submit to a literary journal under your name. She's going to send it to your dean and there's nothing I can do to stop her." Galloway didn't remember writing that she'd given him a story of hers to submit under his name, but it would be silly for her to try to deny something she'd written in her own journal. "I don't think the consequences will be as dire as you believe, Dillard."

In another email she told him she had cancer and was dying and was trying to make amends with her daughter before it was too late. The message was sad, filled with regret; a lot of sorrow and guilt, not the best way to feel about yourself at the end of your life. Wainwright's effort at sympathy was perfunctory. He was too worried about his own situation to be concerned about Jayne Galloway's so much more tragic circumstances.

The final email in the folder made Ambler's hair stand on end. The date was September 3, four days before Ted Doyle was murdered and nine or ten days before Sandra Dean's murder. The email from Jayne Galloway read:

> Don't threaten me! And don't you dare threaten Sandra! I can't stop her from turning over what she found to your dean. You're being hysterical. Your life isn't ruined. If worst comes to worst, offer to retire. They'll let you slip away quietly to

avoid a scandal. You should have retired years ago anyway.
Don't go off the deep end over this.

Ambler's hands holding the letter shook. Wainwright could
have easily gotten to the city and found Sandra Dean. But why
would he have murdered Ted Doyle? One answer was it could
have been a botched attempt to kill Sandra. Doyle got in the
way trying to protect Sandra and took the bullet. And Sandra
escaped. But why was Ted Doyle there? How did Wainwright
find her again in Connecticut? Through Jayne Galloway? The
Nassau police dusted Galloway's house for fingerprints. His
prints might turn up. There was no sign of Wainwright's memory disorder in the emails and a lot of questions that needed
answering. Ambler's mind raced.

He felt the familiar rush of excitement that came when
the facts to support his thinking began to fall into place. At the
same time and in a strange way, he felt a small wave of disappointment. This muddled reaction lasted for a few more
minutes while he sifted through the rest of the papers and documents in the basket.

Then, he froze when he picked up a brochure announcing a
symposium of the Poe Studies Association in San Francisco with
Dillard Wainwright as keynote speaker. The scholar at the podium
in the photo was a dead ringer—minus the scruffy beard—for the
man Ambler spoke with that afternoon in a cabin in the woods
outside Greenfield, Massachusetts. What stopped Ambler's heart
was not the photo that proved he'd found Dillard Wainwright. It
was the dates of the conference. The date of Wainwright's talk
was too familiar. He looked at the calendar on his iPhone and ran
Sandra Dean's name through Google to make sure.

Dillard Wainwright spoke at a conference on the other
side of the country on September 12, the night Sandra Dean
was murdered. There was one remaining possibility. Ambler

called the Poe Association office at San Diego State University
and was told that Professor Wainwright did indeed give the address. They were puzzled, however, that they hadn't been able
to reach him since then, and he hadn't returned the form for his
honorarium.

Ambler didn't go back to Wainwright's cabin. He thought
he might but decided not to, partly because he'd miss his plane.
But also because Wainwright had no idea he was a murder
suspect so it wouldn't mean much to him that he was no longer a suspect and whatever shock or anxiety set off the man's
amnesia—possibly Sandra Dean's threat to expose him as a
fraud and ruin his academic career—might still be hanging
over his head. Ambler didn't tell the college the whereabouts
of their missing professor either since he'd told Wainwright he
wouldn't. He'd done enough meddling in Wainwright's life. He
could leave the guy alone, at least for a while.

"I was wrong," he told Adele on the phone before his
plane took off. He said simply that he'd found Wainwright
and that Wainwright couldn't have committed the murders.
He'd tell her the rest of the story when he saw her. She said it
wouldn't be too late for him to pick up Johnny and she'd wait
dinner for him if he wanted to come over when he got back
to the city.

He switched his phone to airplane mode and put it away
for the flight. Usually, when something like this happened—
his number one suspect exonerated by circumstances of time
and place—he crawled off by himself like an old dog to lick his
wounds. This time was different. He looked forward to being
with Johnny and Adele. He wouldn't think yet about where he
went wrong or what he missed or where he'd start over from.
All of that could rest for a while in the back of his mind. He began reading from the book of poems he picked up at the Emily
Dickinson Museum store.

I shall know why, when time is over,
And I have ceased to wonder why;

He fell asleep shortly after the plane left the runway and woke up when the captain announced their descent into Newark airport.

Chapter 30

Shortly after Mike Cosgrove got to work, he got a phone call.

"What I thought I had blew up in my face," Ray told him.

"Happens to me all the time." Cosgrove took a guess at what had happened. "You found that missing professor?"

"Wainwright. For one thing, he has a weird form of amnesia. The kicker is he was in California at the time of Sandra Dean's murder."

"He could have hired someone."

"You can look into that if you want. I don't see any reason to."

Ray sounded discouraged. But he was right. Not much reason to think murder for hire. Nothing professional about the hits. "Maybe you saved me some time," Cosgrove said. This wasn't true, and Ray knew it.

"I didn't know I was going to find him." This was Ray trying for an apology for following a lead without letting Cosgrove in on it. "I wasn't sure I'd found him even when I found him." He told him about Wainwright and the cabin in the woods.

"He wasn't my suspect anyway," Cosgrove said. It was a

cheap shot and he was sorry he took it. "Look, Ray. Let's see what happens in Connecticut and with this other thing I'm looking into." He told him what he could about Peter Esposito. "I'm going to meet with an ADA this afternoon to see if I can get a search warrant for the hotel records."

"Do you have something that points to Esposito that you haven't told me?"

"Nothing concrete. I'm following my hunches." He paused not sure if he should keep going, but he did, "As a favor to you."

"A favor to me? You've seen enough to hang this on McNulty, but you'll do me a favor by following a hunch. Thanks a lot. Do you have any other other hunches? What about Simon Dean? Do you have any hunches about him?"

"That's enough, Ray." Cosgrove kept his tone even. "You had Wainwright figured for it. That fell through. Now, you don't have anyone, so you get pissed off at me." His voice rose despite his effort to keep it level. "Tell me something that raises doubt the bartender isn't our guy. You got nothing. Zilch. Nada." He'd had enough of this. "I'll talk to you later." He hung up.

Cosgrove stared out into the squad room. Dozens of cops and criminals, victims and witnesses milled around the cluttered desks or sat in straight-backed chairs alongside one of the detective's desks, twenty people talking at the same time, none of it registered.

The worst thing when you arrested someone, got them convicted, watched them get led away to their sentence, the worst thing was not being sure. They said they didn't do it. A lot of them said that; you knew they were guilty as sin. Sometimes, the guy said, "No, man. You're wrong. It wasn't me." You looked him in the eye. He looked you in the eye. You saw something. For a moment you thought maybe you're wrong. Maybe he didn't do it. That was the worst.

He called David Levinson, McNulty's lawyer, and told him he wanted to talk to McNulty. "I know it's unusual."

The lawyer wasn't enthusiastic. "Suppose you ask me what you want to ask him."

"You wouldn't know the answers."

"Try me."

Cosgrove thought about that. What he was doing wasn't right. By rights, the Stamford cops should be in on any interview he did with the bartender, as well as McNulty's lawyer, and probably someone from the DA's office. How the hell were you supposed to get anything done with forty-five people looking over your shoulder? He was going out on a limb for Ray and the jerk didn't get it. "What if Ray talks to him and I listen in?"

"What are you after?"

"I don't want to go into that now."

Cosgrove called Ray and told him what he wanted to do.

"I know you're trying to help," Ray said. "Sorry about before."

"You talk to the lawyer. It's better if we can do it without him. Otherwise, he's got to keep his mouth shut."

Cosgrove took comp time. If he wasn't on the clock, it wasn't official so maybe he didn't need to follow protocol. He rode up to Stamford with Ray and the lawyer. The lawyer yacked for pretty much the entire trip, laying out the reasons no decent attorney would let his client talk to a cop without the attorney present. Levinson followed this with stories of clients who'd done stupid things, like talking to the cops without him, and gotten themselves in trouble. From there, he went on about how he helped out the cop union, but they didn't listen to him either. Levinson was one of those guys who talked whether anyone listened or not. By the time he'd gotten to all he'd done for the PBA, Cosgrove had stopped listening. Either Levinson didn't notice or didn't care. As far as Cosgrove could tell, Ray stopped listening long before he did.

McNulty approached them cautiously. They had a private interview room because it was an attorney visit. McNulty looked from the attorney to Ray and then his gaze settled on Cosgrove who saw a hint of fear. "What's this?" McNulty asked. "The hanging party? Where's the priest?"

Cosgrove began to think this wasn't going to work out. Mc-Nulty would clam up and the trip would be wasted. Ray should take the lead. He was the guy's friend. "No one's out to get you," Cosgrove said. "We got something we need you to clear up, something I came across and asked Ray. He didn't know so we're asking you."

McNulty turned to Levinson, the lawyer. "Am I supposed to answer?"

"I don't know what they're going to ask." Levinson was calm, light on his feet, ready to bob and weave.

Ray cleared his throat and everyone turned to face him, as if he were about to read their rich uncle's will. "Simon Dean told Mike you knew Sandra when she was a teenager. I didn't know if you did or not. You never mentioned it."

"Lots of things I didn't mention about Sandi." McNulty closed his eyes. When he opened them, he looked at the ceiling.

Cosgrove watched for the lie. In the fluorescent light, Mc-Nulty's skin was a ghastly yellow, bags under his eyes.

"I knew her. That was years ago. I knew lots of people." He met Cosgrove's gaze, even though he might have been talking to Ray. "I was young, too." He nodded a couple of times, like a bow. "Not as young as her."

Levinson waved his hand. "Let's hold up here. I don't like where this is going. You asked a question. He answered it." Levinson turned to McNulty. "That's enough, Brian. Nothing you say is going to help you. There's a time and a place for questions. That's the courtroom."

"Explaining himself, if that's what he wants to do, might help him." Cosgrove watched McNulty. "I came here as a favor to Ray. By rights, I should have the state's attorney with me, not just you with him." He nodded toward Levinson. Cosgrove wasn't sure where he was going with this. Ray bailed him out.

"Mike's not here officially." Ray was talking to Levinson. "He's here on his own time because he wants to get it right. We need something. We don't have anything."

"That guy Sandi was emailing, her mother's friend?" It was McNulty.

Ray answered. "Nothing. He was in California. No question about it."

"The list of men I gave you?"

"Mike found and questioned everyone she wrote about in the journal."

"And?" McNulty's expression was doleful.

"I'm not finished." Cosgrove met McNulty's gaze, the bartender's eyes pools of despair. "Nothing to hang your hat on, a couple of unanswered questions from one guy." He caught a glimpse of Levinson out of the corner of his eye. The lawyer didn't look ready to jump in. "It would be good if you could tell us more about Sandi—Sandra Dean." Cosgrove kept an eye on the lawyer. "I'm not trying to catch you on anything." He raised the flat of his hand toward the lawyer, as if he were back in the old days directing traffic, though he spoke to McNulty. "Whatever you want to tell us."

Levinson threw up his hands theatrically. "Who cares about legal advice? We'll just chat. Who cares about procedure? Who cares about rules of evidence? Why don't you whack him around a couple of times and get a confession? Or maybe he could go back and hang himself in his cell?"

"Jesus, David," McNulty said. "Get a grip." He spoke to Ray. "I'm trusting you on this." He turned Cosgrove. "City girls. Too young. Too pretty. They want too much, too early. What they wanted was cocaine. Blow jobs for cocaine. High school girls, groupies." Cosgrove thought McNulty looked sheepish.

"I don't want to be crude about this. They wanted coke and they wanted to be cool. It was cool for them to fuck an older guy. Get him in bed, take him for a ride, watch his face when she told him she was fifteen. You wouldn't know they were that young from looking at them. They thought they knew what they were doing. They were temptresses—gorgeous, wanton, lewd and lascivious, and in over their heads. They were getting taken for a ride; they thought they were driving. I'd find girls kneeling under the table in the back booths. Drunk, high, too young to be out by themselves, much less in a bar, much less . . .

"That's how it was when I met Sandi. She was more innocent than most of them, more sensitive, too smart for her own good. Shy and embarrassed the first time I carded her, she had an ID a blind guy could see was fake. I made her something with lots of fruit juice and hardly any rum. At closing time, she was still at the bar; too shy and too nervous to hook up with anyone. She'd come in late with a couple of girls older than her—or more experienced anyway. They had a whispering and giggling confab and her two friends took off with guys.

"In those days, someone looking like Sandi with a skimpy skirt and a low-cut tank top wouldn't last long on the street by herself at three in the morning. I told her to wait for me. When I came out from behind the bar, she latched onto me, put her arm through mine. She thought she'd picked me up.

"She leaned against me—the girl with faraway eyes. I'm not a saint now and I wasn't then. As young as she was, she'd grown into her body. As we walked, she'd turn and brush her breast across my arm, look into my eyes, giggle and pout. I asked her where she lived. She wouldn't tell me. She wanted to go to my apartment. As tempting as she was, I didn't want to take her home with me so we sat on a bench in the middle of Broadway and talked."

Sadness gathered in the bartender's eyes. Cosgrove thought about his own daughter, around the age Sandra Dean was at the time McNulty was describing, and considered the possibility of Denise picking up a bartender. The city was tough on young girls in a hurry to grow up.

"After that, she came to me with her troubles, which were many. Something went bad with a boyfriend, she'd find me in the bar. When she wanted, she'd come sleep on my couch. I told her she was too good for the barflies with nothing going for them but open-collar shirts, cologne, gold chains around their necks, and a line of bullshit. She was smart, so she couldn't help but see before long how phony the bar scene was.

"She went for a while with a guy who hit her. You wouldn't know he was like that from looking at him, handsome, suit-and-tie slick, razor-cut hair, Wall Street–type. You wouldn't know it from talking to him either. He could talk Yankees, Knicks, movies, music. A good tipper, charming guy, always smiling. Women went for him. He didn't have to go after them.

"She'd come to my apartment crying with a bruised cheek, puffed lip. She said he didn't mean it. He was good to her. He was sorry." McNulty met each of the three men's gaze. "'One time he does that; you're gone.' That's what I told her. She didn't like being told. Some women are that way; whatever their men do to them is their business. I told her if she didn't drop him, I'd take care of him. She didn't, so I had a couple of guys talk to him. He dropped her." McNulty fixed his gaze on Cosgrove. "She went with men who were hard on her. Some women are like that. Don't ask me why.

"She wrote songs and poems. I told her she should become a writer. Her mother was a writer, she told me, and she didn't want to be like her mother. Then, before she got too deep into the nightlife, something happened. Someone—her grandmother, I think—yanked her off the streets and sent her to boarding school. That was it. She was gone.

"I missed her. I knew it was better for her what happened, that she got away. Around that time, I got tangled up with a crazy actress. She kept me occupied. That made it easier. After a while, I didn't look for Sandi every time the barroom door opened.

"I didn't see her for years. And one night she shows up at the Library Tavern." McNulty's face twisted into a pained smile. "I never slept with her back in those days, even though in a way I might have been in love with her. Or that's what I thought when I saw her that night perched on a barstool in the Library Tavern, smiling at me like she used to, like no time had passed."

"How did she know where to find you?" Ray asked before Cosgrove could get to it.

McNulty spoke to the ceiling. "'Of all the gin joints in all the towns in all the world, she walks into mine.'" He chuckled. "Maybe she knew where to find me. Maybe it was an accident, fate. She didn't say. We went back to how we'd been when she was a kid. This time, it was her husband she talked about."

"Hitting her?" Ray jumped in.

"No. Messing with her head, making her think she deserved to be treated like a piece of shit. Sandi was too sensitive; she was fragile; she couldn't handle unpleasantness. I don't know how to say it. Something was missing for her still. Whatever she was missing in those days when she was a kid, whatever she was looking for then, she hadn't found it. The demons that had her then had her again."

It was a nice story. Cosgrove wasn't sure he believed it. Bartenders were good storytellers. "So we're back to the first question. Why didn't you tell anyone she was an old friend?"

The bartender's eyes burned into Cosgrove's. "No one asked."

The lawyer intervened. "Perhaps Brian's learned something from me after all. One doesn't volunteer information to the police, nor answer questions that aren't asked."

Cosgrove's back went up. Lawyers did that to him. He didn't get how they did what they did. Gum up the works. Get everything tangled up so you don't know who knows what. Ray put an oar in this time.

"We're trying to help, David."

"Speak for yourself," said Cosgrove. "How do you get anywhere pussyfooting around like this. 'I object.' 'The question isn't relevant.' Who needs this lawyer crap? It's like bringing your mother on a date." He turned his glare from the lawyer to McNulty. "What else didn't you tell us?"

"How's he supposed to answer that?" Levinson asked.

It was a reasonable objection. Cosgrove was too steamed to acknowledge that it was, so he ignored it. "Why did you bring up her husband?" Cosgrove wasn't sure where he was going with this either.

McNulty registered surprise. "She talked about him. She didn't know why he did what he did, why he treated her the way he did. It made me mad. Sandi was too easy to hurt. It wasn't right to pick on her. It was like smacking a kid, hitting someone smaller than you."

"Did she talk to you about the men she met in bars?"

Sadness in McNulty's eyes again when he looked at Cosgrove to answer. "Not much. She set out to do one thing, talking to someone. Something she didn't intend would happen. She didn't understand herself that way. She didn't know why she'd pick up some guy. That's a lot of why she felt bad about herself. Like I said, demons."

Cosgrove told McNulty she'd asked someone to get her a gun. "Was she afraid of any of those men?"

"She didn't tell me she was. But I thought she was afraid of someone."

"Her husband?" Ray went off on another track. Cosgrove was going to object but let it go. You'd understand why Ray would land on Dean, not many suspects left. Cosgrove was willing to see where he was going with this.

"Not so she needed a gun, I don't think."

It occurred to Cosgrove that she might have wanted to shoot her husband. After some of what he'd heard from the guy, he wouldn't blame her. It was also possible she was afraid of McNulty, which was something the bartender wouldn't bring up.

"I'm interested in the murder of the man in the hotel room in the city," Cosgrove said.

"I don't know anything about it. It happened after I left."

"Why'd you leave? Was she expecting someone else?"

McNulty blinked a couple of times and looked at Levinson. "We had a falling out. Actually, she did the falling out. I got thrown out."

"She asked you to leave?" Cosgrove let his voice soften.

McNulty grimaced. "She was like that. Something would set her off. You'd say something. Something would click in her head. She'd disappear into the foggy ruins of time. A couple of minutes later she'd come back, having decided while she was gone you were her worst enemy. Nothing you could do to change her mind. I knew enough by then to take a hike."

"Why'd you go with her after the murder then?"

"First, I didn't know until later it was after a murder. She came and got me. She had a car in the hotel parking garage and picked me up at my apartment. I get in the car, she said, 'Don't ask, just help me.'"

"Can anyone verify where you were at the time Ted Doyle, the man in the hotel, was murdered?"

"Can you teach the cat to talk?"

"The cat?" Cosgrove cast a confused glance at Ambler before he remembered. "Right. Cat. You were home. No one saw you?"

"The cat."

"You took off with her. Later you learned she was running from a murder. Did she tell you about it?"

"She told me she couldn't tell me about it, except that it wasn't what I thought."

"Where were you when she was killed?"

"We'd decided—she'd decided—she was going home. Whatever truce she was trying to work out with her husband, she'd worked it out. My understanding was she would be there long enough to get things like money, some clothes and such, get her office straightened out, and round up the kid. We hadn't firmed up what would happen after that.

"I went to the city to talk to Ray and Adele. I was worried about the guy killed in her hotel room, that they'd try to hang it on her . . . or me. By then, I thought one of her former—one of the men in that journal had come back into her life and she was scared."

Cosgrove gave Ray a look that might have turned him to dust. "What did you do after you spoke to Ray here?"

"I spent the night at my father's in Brooklyn."

Cosgrove digested this. "That's your alibi? I imagine your father would back you up."

"Of course he would. He's my father."

"He wouldn't lie to back you up, would he?"

McNulty laughed. "Pop? If I lied, he'd swear to it."

The lawyer and Ray laughed, too. Cosgrove felt the veins in his neck popping. "Anyone else see you?"

"The cat. He's crashing at Pop's. And a cab driver friend of mine."

"Not someone who'd lie for you?"

McNulty gave him a look. "I don't have friends who wouldn't lie for me."

"The envelope—" Ray started to say, and stopped. McNulty smiled when he did.

Cosgrove was ready to turn Ray to dust again. It was as if Ray and McNulty spoke in a foreign language to get around him. He tried McNulty again. "You said there were phone

calls—more than one—Sandra Dean made the night before she
was murdered. She called her husband and told him she wanted
to come home. Who else did she call?"

"I don't know. She told me about the calls to her husband. I
overheard a couple. She didn't tell me about any others."

"Could she have called anyone else?"

"Sure. She didn't check in with me on who she was calling."

"You were okay she was leaving you to return to her husband?"

"She went home for her kid. She didn't love her husband.
He didn't love her. He controlled her. She wasn't going to let
him do that anymore. That started before all this happened.
He'd lost control of her and he knew it."

Something was coming to Cosgrove. He'd worried ever
since the first body fell because a murderer was on the loose.
Someone who'd killed once was someone who could kill again.
You had to believe it was easier—and often necessary—after
the first one. The danger escalated when you were closing in,
when you were all but certain you knew the killer. The killer
became more dangerous, like a cornered animal, because he
knew before you did that you'd figured him out.

Cosgrove realized the other three men in the interview
room were staring at him. How long had this been going on?
He brought himself back to the present and McNulty. "Simon
Dean was who told me you knew Sandra Dean when she was
young. How did he know you knew her?"

"I don't know."

"He knew you were with her in the hotel where she was
murdered. Did she tell him on the phone call you overheard?"

"She told him where she was. She didn't say she was with
me. Not that I heard."

"She told him where she was exactly?"

"Did I say that?"

"Did she or didn't she tell him precisely where she was? She had a car. She didn't need him to pick her up."

"I'm not sure if she told him the name of the hotel if that's what you mean."

"How did he know you were with her?" Cosgrove didn't mean to ask McNulty. He was asking himself.

"I don't know. Ask him."

"I told Dean that Sandra and McNulty might be together," Ray said.

Cosgrove turned to his friend. "What else haven't you told me?"

Ray nodded toward McNulty. "You better tell him about you and Sandra stopping off to visit her mother."

McNulty jerked himself up straight. "And have him accuse me of killing an old lady? No way."

Levinson jumped to his feet. "What old lady?"

Ray calmed everyone down and explained the time sequence that made it unlikely, if not impossible, for McNulty and Sandra to have murdered Jayne Galloway. Soon afterward, Ray, the lawyer, and Cosgrove left for the city and McNulty returned to his jail cell.

Chapter 31

Back at the library after the visit to McNulty, Ambler felt a sense of relief. For the first time, McNulty offered an alibi for the night Sandra Dean was murdered. It wasn't airtight since it relied on his father and a cab driver friend as witnesses. Still it was something, and Ambler and Adele could vouch for him being in the city on the evening of Sandra Dean's murder, again not perfect because it was quite a bit earlier than the time of the murder. Still every little bit helped, especially if the police didn't have strong evidence to put McNulty at the scene of the murder.

The alibi was one thing that came up. Something McNulty said about Simon Dean struck a chord with Mike was another. Ambler didn't know what it was, and Mike wasn't going to tell him about a vague suspicion he might have; he'd check it out first.

Ambler had doubts about Dean also; the doubts had been growing since Andrea described him as controlling and domineering. The same way McNulty said Sandra described him. Neither of them said he was threatening, yet a man who needed to dominate his wife or child wanted something different than love. So it was worth passing on to Mike what Andrea said about her brother. If nothing else, it reinforced what McNulty said about him. So Ambler called Mike and gave him Andrea's assessment of her brother. Mike listened without interrupting and said, "He's a queer duck."

Ambler suspected he wouldn't get an answer but asked anyway. "When we were talking to McNulty, you asked him some pointed questions about Simon Dean, what were you getting at?"

Mike took his time but he did answer. "Some inconsistencies in what he told me about the phone calls with his wife between the time of the Doyle murder and his wife's murder. When I talked to him with the Stamford police right after her murder, he didn't tell us about any calls with his wife or that he knew McNulty or knew McNulty and Sandra Dean were together. The next time I interviewed him, he mentioned all of those things. I didn't know how he could know McNulty was with his wife. You answered that for me."

"Right. I told him. But he might have already known. It's pretty clear he was concealing things. Why would he do that?"

Mike laughed. "You have brass balls criticizing someone for concealing information. We'll see what happens when we turn the screws on Mr. Dean."

"Have you been hiding?" Adele asked from the crime fiction room doorway as he hung up his phone. She held two containers of coffee. "I hope you broke McNulty out of jail."

Ambler told her about the visit to the jail and that McNulty had known Sandra years before she turned up at the Library Tavern. He also told her that the shadow of suspicion had now fallen on Simon Dean.

"McNulty knowing Sandra explains some things," she said. "A couple of times, he spoke of her like she was someone he

knew, rather than someone he recently met. He was so protective of her." Adele was also interested in Simon Dean as a suspect. "I wish McNulty had given us Sandra's entire journal. I'm
sure she would have written about her husband."

"There might have been something he didn't want us to see."

"Or there were things he thought we didn't need to see and
he wanted to protect her privacy. He had her journal the first
time he asked you to investigate the men she'd been seeing. I
wonder—"

"The police might have found it," Ambler said. "Wait. If he's
telling the truth, McNulty didn't go back to Stamford after he
saw us until after Sandra was dead. The night she was murdered
he stayed at his father's apartment. Or he says he did. Let's believe him. It looks like I'm headed to Brooklyn. Wanna come?"

Adele raised her eyebrows, somehow an accusation. "I'm
going to read Jayne Galloway's journals. You were rushing me
last time. . . . She wrote about her awful first husband. Maybe
she wrote about Sandra's awful husband, too."

Kevin McNulty was a frailer man than the
last time Ambler visited his apartment. That time, the senior
McNulty had the stature and vitality of his younger self. Not a
big man, he had broad shoulders, thick workingman's hands,
a bright penetrating gaze, and energy, spirit. His brush with
death knocked some of that out of him. While his gaze was still
bright, it had sunken into his face and held a depth of sadness
that wasn't there before. The shirt and sweater he wore hung
loosely from his shoulders.

"I haven't gotten up to see Brian yet," he said after they'd
shaken hands in the apartment doorway. "How's he holding up?"

"He's good. I just saw him. Things might be looking up."
They walked to the small living room and sat across from each
other. "He wouldn't want you to visit now. You need to rest.
Visiting the jail is stressful for anyone."

The senior McNulty had a home health care aide. "Compliments of the city," he said. "Finally getting something out of sixty years of paying taxes." He did physical therapy every other day and took a lot of pills. That was all he had to say about that.

Ambler told him about Sandra Dean's journal and why he wanted it. "Brian led me to believe he might have left it here."

"Oh?" Kevin's expression was shrewd. He might have been a poker player. Or he might have been an old trade union leader negotiating with the boss. You weren't going to get something for nothing. He asked Ambler what his thinking was about the murders and the journal.

Amber told him about the men in the journal. "I want to know what else she might have written about." He didn't want to bring up Simon Dean.

"Diaries are private," Kevin McNulty said. "People who write them often don't want anyone to read what's in them. Often they ask that they be destroyed when they die. There's a privacy question here, isn't there? Perhaps she asked Brian to destroy them."

Ambler didn't understand what the older man was saying, or he didn't understand why he said what he said.

Kevin McNulty spoke slowly, perhaps reluctantly. "My wife left her diaries behind when she died. She was too ill to tend to them herself at the end. She asked me to destroy them, to not read them and to destroy them." His eyes were liquid when his gaze met Ambler's. "I wanted very much not to do that. The diaries were her words, something of her still in my life. I agonized. In the end, I destroyed them without reading them. I still wish I could have read them. But they were her thoughts, her words. She had a right to keep them to herself even after her death."

They sat in silence. Twice church bells rang in the distance. The other sound was an old-fashioned clock ticking. He'd given the frail old man a moral dilemma to wrestle with. For some—maybe for him before this old Communist reminded him—expediency would trump morality. What were the rights of the murdered? Should their privacy trump catching their killer? Do the living have a right to reveal the secrets of the dead—even to exonerate one's son?

"I understand this is difficult," Ambler said. "If Brian destroyed the journals because she asked him to, so be it. If they exist and there's a moral wrong to be done, I'll pay the price. I've asked myself if Sandra would reveal her secrets to protect a person who gave up a lot to protect her. Knowing what I've learned of her, I'd say yes."

Kevin McNulty thought that over. He stood. "At the very top of the bookcase is a flat package. You'll need to stand on a chair and feel for it."

Ambler did and took down a thick manila envelope containing two hardcover notebooks.

"Brian said to hang onto it until he told me what to do. I should ask him." His gaze met Ambler's. "I'm old and tired and want my son out of prison."

Ambler began reading the journals on the train back to Manhattan, thinking he'd skim through them until he found something that helped make sense of Sandra Dean's murder. But he stopped skimming almost as soon as he started. The first journal entry was from soon after Sandra's daughter Carolyn was born. In neat, precise handwriting, she noted what the baby wore on a given day and what she ate and if she burped and the first time she smiled. The words sparkled. She wrote that she couldn't find the words to describe her happiness but she did find them.

And then another few pages in she began questioning the happiness she felt. Here, Simon appeared. He came across as his sister, Andrea, portrayed him, although Sandra didn't seem aware that she described an ogre. "I get so tired," Sandra wrote. "I'm cranky and anxious when Carolyn cries and I can't comfort her. Simon looks at me like I'm an idiot who doesn't know how to be a mother. His look says any other mother would know what to do. And he's right. I don't know what to do. I don't know how to help her. I didn't have a mother." The entries went on like that, about what was wrong with her, what Simon found wrong with her. She shouldn't have had a baby if she didn't know how to take care of one. What was she thinking?

The journal entries went back and forth, good days and bad days. The baby got a cold. She cried a lot. She was up all night, her nose stuffed up and caked with glop. Sandra was exhausted. She couldn't stay awake. Simon was furious with her. After that, the journal entries about Carolyn became sporadic. The tone changed. The sense of wonder was gone. The writing was matter-of-fact, straightforward. Carolyn smiled. Carolyn had a cold. Carolyn sat up for the first time.

When Sandra wrote about herself, it was criticism. She should do this. She shouldn't do that. She began smoking again. She drank too much. She had a blackout. She had an argument with a stranger at a party. Simon said she embarrassed him. She didn't remember doing that. Simon embarrassed her. She remembered that.

Ambler kept reading after he got home on into the night. He felt voyeuristic doing it but couldn't tear himself away. Sandra's criticism of herself was so sad. She was never good enough for Simon. She didn't, even in the privacy of her journal, criticize him; yet she seemed to record every criticism he made of her and believe them all.

And then near the end, there came one long entry where everything changed. "I hope someone delivers this diary to Simon after I'm dead, which I'm terrified will be soon. He's so sure he's in control, so sure I would not, could not, oppose him, betray him, he'd keel over dead from the shock, spontaneously combust. Ha!

"I've been damaged," she wrote. "But I'm getting better. I have Carolyn. And Brian will help me. He knows me. He knows me better than anyone. He knows everything and he loves me."

There was one entry after that Ambler didn't understand; it ended too soon; it needed to tell him more. He went back and pored through the sections he'd skimmed hoping he'd missed something, searching for even a hint of when and why Sandra began trying to get her and her daughter out of her tormented marriage. When he didn't find anything, he called Adele to help him figure it out. It was near midnight when he called, not realizing how late it was, not knowing he would wake her, until she answered in a panic. "Raymond, what's wrong? Are you okay? Why are you calling? Did—"

"No. No. Everything's all right. I didn't look at the time. I've been reading Sandra's journal."

"You found it?" Her voice rose. "Why didn't you tell me?"

He had no idea why he didn't tell her, why he didn't call earlier. "I got engrossed in reading it and forgot about everything. I didn't know what time it was. I forgot to eat dinner. I didn't even call Johnny at his grandmother's to say goodnight."

A strange pause at the other end of the line told him something was up. "What?" he barked.

"Johnny's here." Her voice was small.

"No." Ambler groaned, partly a groan, partly a wail.

"It's okay. I called Lisa Young. She understands . . . sort of. She apologized to him over the phone for whatever it was she said about his father. That was why he left. She said he could stay here tonight."

"And why didn't you call me? He's my grandson. . . ." He was sorry before the words left his mouth, before he heard the gasp at the other end of the line. He never pulled rank like that, never meant to, didn't mean to now. "I'm sorry. I didn't mean that," he said.

Adele was as close to Johnny as any mother would be. In Ambler's secret dream there was an idyllic world where he, Johnny, and Adele were together. But on too many days, life, and with it too many obstacles, came between them, between him and Adele. The threads that held them together—he and Johnny and Adele—were delicate, too easily snapped, which is what he'd done now, snapped them.

"It's okay." Adele's tone was strained.

"It's not okay. It's not right or true. I'm sorry I said it."

"Johnny thought you'd make him go back. You probably would have." Her voice cracked. "I overstepped—"

"You didn't." He tried again. There was no undoing what he'd done. His attempt to put her in her place was pure meanness. No one loved Johnny more than Adele.

Speaking stiffly, she said she'd take Johnny to school in the morning and see Ambler at the library.

The next morning, when she stopped by the crime fiction room to tell him Johnny was off to school, she was more formal than ever, distant, like the hired help reporting, not how he wanted her to be with him. Despite that, during her lunch break she came back to read more of Jayne Galloway's journals.

Ambler paced the small space of the reading room in front of the library table she sat at and told her about Sandra Dean's diary. "She was in love with McNulty. She was pulling herself out of the doldrums." He stopped pacing. "The reason I called last night, in her last entry—Wait. I have it here." He took the diary off a bookshelf and read from it. "Now that I know about Simon, now with proof, no court in the world would give him custody. What a fool I've been not to see what he's been doing."

"What?" Adele whispered.

"I don't know. I hoped this might make sense to you, that I missed something you'd picked up on."

Adele closed her eyes and shook her head.

"I'm meeting Mike after work. Maybe with what he thinks he has on Simon, he'll figure out what she means." He lowered his voice. "Do you want to come? I'm meeting him at the Canopy Bar."

"Why would I come?" Adele sounded angry, still hurt from what he'd said last night.

"I just thought you would."

Ambler met Mike at the Canopy Bar, across from the main door of the Oyster Bar. The small bar was always busy at rush hour; the patrons stopped for a drink and left for their trains so there was constant turnover. As Mike's pal Marcelo the bartender told the drinkers, "If you miss your train, you're in someone else's seat."

They ordered martinis and oysters and Ambler told Mike about Sandra Dean's journal. She planned to leave her husband and take their daughter. She was in love with McNulty. She'd found out something incriminating about Simon Dean. Ambler read Mike the last cryptic passage from her journal.

"What does that mean?" Mike asked. The oyster tray arrived and they each prepared an oyster.

"I hoped you might know. Why do you suspect Dean?"

Mike didn't like someone telling him what he thought. "You don't know as much as you think you do. You said he was a suspect. I didn't."

"You don't want to tell me. I'm okay with that."

Mike tended to his oyster.

"She wrote in her journal that she loved McNulty. She wrote that she was pulling herself out of her morass. Why as soon as McNulty left that evening, did she pick up another man? And how would Simon know where she was and what she was doing?"

"Whoa." Mike pointed an oyster shell at Ambler. "Who said he knew where she was?"

Ambler reached into his book bag for the journal. At the same time, he saw movement out of the corner of his eye, something familiar, and realized Adele was coming toward him.

Her face was frozen into a fearful expression. "I found something you need to see." Her hands shook as she placed one of Jayne Galloway's journals in front of Ambler.

"You took this from the library—"

"Never mind that." One finger marked a page in the closed journal. She opened to that page. She hadn't spoken to Mike or even looked at him, focused almost desperately on Ambler. She pointed to a paragraph with the finger that had marked the page.

Ambler read: "Sandra is deadly serious that Simon would harm Carolyn if the police come for him." Adele pulled back the journal. "Jayne Galloway hired a private detective to investigate Simon Dean. He found something terrible."

"A private detective?" It was Mike. "When?"

"Not long before Sandra was murdered. She told Sandra about the report and Sandra didn't believe her . . . or she did believe her and wouldn't let her tell anyone. I'm not sure what she meant."

Mike listened impatiently. "Did she mention the detective's name?"

"I don't think so."

"I need to know the name," Mike said.

Ambler was puzzled. Mike looked like he was about to explode. "What?"

"Ted Doyle was a security consultant, a private detective."

Ambler felt as shocked as Mike looked. "When I first visited Jayne Galloway, she told me she used a private detective to find Sandra. He found her. That report might be among Galloway's papers at the library."

"If you'd check on that," Mike pushed himself back from the table and waved for the server. "I'm gonna lean on some closed-mouthed smart-asses on Long Island."

"What about Carolyn?" Adele's tone stopped both of them. "What about Simon Dean's daughter? Did he kill her mother?"

Cosgrove gave Adele a measured look. "We're about to find out."

Adele grabbed Cosgrove's arm. "You can't! He'll hurt that child. Sandra was sure of it, and I believe her."

"We won't let that happen." Mike put his free hand on Adele's shoulder. "We know how to do this. I won't let her get hurt."

"How do you know?"

"Because we'll stay calm and do it right. Let's get the story straight first. We don't know what Simon Dean did or didn't do." Adele loosened her hold on Mike's arm. "If we could find that private investigator's report, it would help."

Chapter 32

It didn't take Ambler long to find the report from Continental Security Consultants once they got back to the crime fiction room. The letter with the report was signed Theodore Doyle, Licensed Investigator.

Mike wasn't triumphant when Ambler showed him the name. His rugged face reflected a kind of grim satisfaction. "I've got to confirm what we think we know. You two sit tight." His gaze darted from one to the other. "This is police business now." He glared at Adele. "You care about that kid, you gotta trust me."

Mike was right. Matching wits with a professional homicide detective like Mike over examining data and making inferences was one thing. When lives were at stake, what Mike brought to the battle outweighed anything he and Adele could do. There was one thing.

"We could ask Simon's sister Andrea to gather up Carolyn and take her someplace safe."

Mike shook his head. "His sister? I don't think so, Ray. Blood runs thick. She could feel she had to protect her brother."

"Sandra was her friend. If she knew he killed her—"

"We can't tell her that." Mike spoke sharply. Tension was high for all of them. "We don't know for sure ourselves. Like I said, let's get the story straight and go from there. What we know is that Ted Doyle, on assignment from Jayne Galloway, found her daughter.

"We *surmise* Doyle was the private eye who discovered something incriminating about Simon Dean. We *surmise* Doyle was on that case when he came to the Commodore Hotel to meet Sandra Dean to tell her about the report on her husband. And we *surmise* Simon Dean followed him there or waited for him there and killed him. For one thing, we need the second report, the one that incriminates Simon Dean. If there is one, it's on file at Continental Security. I'll get it if I have to throw the bastards running the place in the slammer.

"We also need proof Simon Dean knew about the report and knew where his wife was on the night Ted Doyle was murdered."

"And on the night his wife was murdered," Ambler said.

"We need to move carefully."

When Mike left to deal with the "smart-asses on Long Island," Ambler and Adele went back to work. Ambler read through the initial report from Ted Doyle. Doyle found Sandra Dean apparently without much difficulty, as Adele had found her. Doyle noted in his report there were some question marks—blank spaces—in Simon Dean's background. Because of this he couldn't vouch for the authenticity of Mr. Dean's background report and recommended a follow-up investigation if Mrs. Galloway wanted to know about Dean's life before he met Sandra. Doyle was satisfied that his report on Sandra Dean, nee Galloway, was accurate.

When Ambler finished reading the report, he began searching through boxes of unorganized papers and documents taken from Jayne Galloway's house. When he didn't find the second report, he worried it might have been hidden somewhere in her house, and kicked himself for not looking more thoroughly when he had the chance. It was also possible Sandra Dean had hidden it somewhere or Simon Dean had gotten his hands on it, which meant they'd never find it. For now, he'd hope Mike came up with something. He went back to Sandra's journals.

Because of the unfolding crisis, Ambler called Denise and asked her to stay at his apartment with Johnny. He spoke to Johnny, who'd made up with Denise and agreed to return to his grandmother's the next day. He gave Denise his credit card number and told her to order whatever she and Johnny wanted for dinner. It was a treat for Denise. She didn't have to put up with her mother complaining about her father, got paid for doing her homework, and could eat something special for dinner on Ambler's dime.

"I should take up babysitting," Adele said.

"You're basically Johnny's mother," Ambler said.

"Oh?" She looked at him like she didn't remember who he was. "How interesting."

Ambler, as was often the case, didn't know what her look meant.

He'd already noticed Sandra Dean had an appealing voice in her journal entries, and here it was again, bright, lively, a fresh use of language and sparkling images. She'd inherited her mother's talent. McNulty was right, she could have been a writer. One side of her was tragic, sad, depressed, doomed. Now he saw another side where she was smart, interesting, fun. She saw more deeply into situations or people than you'd expect, and made observations that surprised you.

When Adele called his name, jarred out of his thoughts, he felt like he was coming in out of a storm.

"I called you three times. I thought you fell asleep. Were you in a trance?"

He shook his head to clear it. "I guess so."

"I found something. It's confusing and you need to read

between the lines. I think Jayne Galloway saw Sandra recently. Whatever happened when they met, she learned Simon had forbidden Sandra to see or talk to her. Galloway asks herself, or maybe she asks Sandra, why a husband would want to keep his wife from her mother. I'm guessing that's when she hired the private detective again to investigate Simon's blurry past." She handed him the journal she'd been reading in. "Can I look at that one while you look at this?"

Ambler hesitated, as if he felt embarrassed to have been so touched by what he'd read and didn't want Adele to know. The feeling was unexpected. His reaction surprised Adele also.

"Is there something there you don't want me to see? I'm a big girl. I can take it."

"It's not that." He handed the journal to her. "I found Sandra's writing charming." He said this he realized as a kind of inoculation against Adele judging it differently.

"I guess she was charming." Adele began reading.

Ambler picked up Jayne Galloway's journal and turned to the section Adele had pointed out. It began: "Why would a husband keep his wife from her mother? Why does a husband keep his wife from having friends? Simon doesn't think he's met his match. But he has. I know why a man keeps a woman behind blank walls."

A frustrated Mike called him that night. Johnny was watching TV and Ambler was cleaning up the kitchen after he ate Denise's and Johnny's leftover Chinese food for his dinner.

"I finally got some information from those assholes at Continental Security. Doyle was hired in late August by Jayne Galloway to do a background check on Simon Dean. Doyle, as you know, had done work for Galloway before, finding her daughter. What he found this time is Simon Dean, when he was in his late teens, was in a seminary in Pennsylvania studying to be a priest. During that time he impregnated a sixteen-year-old girl who then committed suicide."

Ambler started to ask a question.

Cosgrove headed him off. "I know what you're thinking. Doyle's report referenced a police report on the death."

"Murders can look like suicides," Ambler said.

"Really?" Talk about dripping with sarcasm. "Even in the burg where this happened, unattended deaths are suspicious until proven otherwise."

"Everyone makes mistakes."

"This death happened almost twenty years ago in a small city where they don't have many unattended deaths suspicious or otherwise. I spoke to a captain, who, it turned out, was involved in the investigation. And there was an investigation.

"The parents of the victim didn't believe their daughter committed suicide. They swore Simon Dean killed her. The investigation was thorough and the cops there did everything pretty much right. The captain I spoke with knows what he's talking about. He said she killed herself. He also said Dean was psychologically abusive to her and drove her to suicide. He basically handed her the gun.

"The girl was innocent. She ran away from home to be with him. He got her a furnished room in the town near the seminary, and then he drove her friends away, turned her against her parents. When she was a complete wreck—though God knows why still in love with him—he left her. He was nice enough to leave a gun behind in her room, so she put a bullet in her head.

"Because it was ruled a suicide, the file was sealed. Simon Dean has no record as an abuser or anything else. The age of consent in Pennsylvania is sixteen. He was never charged with anything related to her death, though a lot of people hated him. When the priests found out what he'd been up to, they eased him out of the seminary. He came back to Connecticut, more or less erased from the seminary history books. I'm not sure even his parents knew what happened there."

"The private eye verified all this?" Ambler's thoughts raced ahead.

"He spoke to the suicide victim's parents, people who knew her. He spoke to Captain Robinson who investigated the case. He didn't see the file that was sealed. Robinson can unseal it if we ever bring a charge against Simon Dean—"

"What do you mean 'if we ever?'"

"We don't have enough to charge him."

"Sandra Dean didn't commit suicide. She was murdered." Ambler paused to line up his thoughts. "We thought she picked up Ted Doyle in the hotel bar as she'd done before with other men. What happened was she met him at the hotel because he was bringing her a report that told her that her psychologically abusive husband had driven a young girl to suicide."

"How did Simon Dean know, Ray? How did he know about Ted Doyle and his investigation? How did he know Ted Doyle was meeting his wife in the city? How did he know where his wife was in the city? No one's put him in the city at the time of the murder. I showed his photo to the hotel bartender. He couldn't identify him."

"Someone might have seen Simon at the hotel that night. Has anyone asked about that? Dean could have found out about the private eye from Jayne Galloway. That's why he killed her. He knew she'd tell me about the private eye's report and his background."

"Where's your evidence, Ray? I can—"

"Wait a minute. What about Sandra's murder?" He stopped for a moment and ran back through his memory. "What do you have on him for that?"

Mike's voice was weary. "What I told you. Some things he told me maybe don't add up. Maybe if I question him again, he'll slip up. Lies are tough to keep straight. Otherwise, I don't have enough evidence."

"If you—"

"If nothing."

"You don't—"

Mike's tone was sharp. "You're good at a lot of things, Ray. Number one, you don't twist what you know to make it fit what you want it to mean." Mike coughed into the phone. Ambler knew to keep quiet. "Another thing is you don't get in my way. That's unusual for an amateur. And you are an amateur; as good as you are, you're an amateur. For some reason, this time you're not helping."

Ambler absorbed what he heard. Mike handled himself as he always did, not forgetting he was a cop. He, Ambler, wasn't himself this time; he was too eager to close the case before he had the evidence—the data—that proved Simon Dean the killer. This made him careless, and untrustworthy.

Chapter 33

The next day was Saturday. It was a day off for Ambler and Adele, both of whom had used up vacation days already since McNulty disappeared. He dropped Johnny at his grandmother's, avoiding any discussion with her or Johnny about the recent difficulties. The boy had enough on his mind. On Sunday, he was going to Yankee Stadium with his imperious Wall Street–lawyer grandfather to sit in the law firm's box seats alongside the Yankee dugout for Game 2 of the Division Series against the Tigers.

Once Johnny was under the protection of the doorman at his grandmother's Central Park West apartment building, Ambler headed to the library despite his day off. When he arrived, the first thing he did was dig through boxes of loose papers from the Galloway papers a second time until this time he did find the second report on Simon Dean from Ted Doyle of Continental Security Consultants. It was pretty much what Mike had told him. He also found a letter from Doyle that was more helpful than the report. The letter must have been in response to a question from Jayne Galloway; that letter wasn't included. Ted Doyle wrote that he would be willing to deliver the report to

Sandra Dean himself. Jayne, it appeared, worried her daughter might not believe what happened with Simon if the report came from her. Ambler made a copy of the report and the letter.

He then dug into Jayne Galloway's more recent journals, where he hoped to discover how Simon Dean learned of Ted Doyle's investigation. Poking around at the edge of his consciousness was this idea that he should talk to Andrea. She might be able to get Sandra's laptop again and look through her emails for anything Simon might have discovered that would have told him about Ted Doyle's report. The problem was Mike wanted him to stay away from her. Mike could be right, too, that at some point—a murder charge, for instance—family loyalty might outweigh Andrea's anger over her brother's treatment of Sandra.

Shortly before noon, Adele bounded into the reading room. She was antsy and thought they needed to do something. "He threatened to harm his daughter if the police came for him. What kind of man is that? Shouldn't that be enough to go arrest him?"

Ambler knew it would be difficult to calm her down. "Mike can't go to Connecticut and arrest someone even if he wanted to. He'd have to get a warrant and have the local police make the arrest. They might not understand about Carolyn."

"We could go there."

"And do what?"

"Get Carolyn away from him."

"Kidnap her?"

"I didn't say that."

"What would you call it?"

"We'd rescue her."

"What we need to do is find something in these journals that gives Mike enough evidence to get a warrant for Simon."

Adele scrunched up her face into a scowl. "And what would that be . . . a note perhaps: To Whom It May Concern, Simon

Dean is a murderer. If you look in his backyard you'll find buried bodies and in the garage a pile of guns and some video tapes of him committing the crimes?"

"No bricks without clay."

"Easy for you . . ." Her nostrils flared. "How can you be so uncaring? Aren't you angry? Aren't you scared for Carolyn?" Her voice quavered. Her eyes reddened.

Adele's fury unnerved him but didn't stop him. "You can't pretend you know something that you don't know. I want to do the same thing. We can't."

"We know that man killed Sandra!" The expression in Adele's eyes was wild.

Ambler spoke softly. "We don't know that for sure. I wish we did."

"We should hang him up by his thumbs and beat a confession out of him."

"You don't mean that."

"I do mean it."

Adele snatched one of Sandra's journals off the table and began going through it. It was a while before she spoke; when she did he could barely hear her. "I'm frustrated, Raymond. I know we need to be sure before accusing someone. Yet I am sure. Can't you believe your heart when it tells you something is true even if you don't have all the . . . data?"

"If you believe Poirot, intuition comes from some kind of facts buried in your subconscious. Some piece of information, something we absorbed without realizing it, might tell us why you're so sure Simon Dean is the killer."

Adele stared over the top of the notebook she held in front of her. "When I think back, I didn't trust from the beginning Simon Dean insisting McNulty was the murderer. How could he be so sure?" Her gaze met Ambler's. "He wouldn't be. The killer could have been any of the men she'd been with. Why did he insist it was McNulty? I bet it was because he already knew

they'd run off together. He killed her and planned to have Mc-
Nulty blamed for it. That was his revenge."

Ambler tried to recall his state of mind when Simon Dean
confronted him and Adele. He'd taught himself to be hyperalert,
aware of everything down to the smallest detail, the most insig-
nificant nuance when he thought about a murder. He should
have been suspicious at that time also, at least questioned what
he was hearing. Yet he didn't do that. Dean had come to the
library a day after identifying his wife's body. Ambler should
have questioned why? Was there a possible reason beyond the
one stated? He should have considered Dean a suspect then,
however remote the possibility. Dean was the cuckolded husband. Of course, he was a suspect.

"He was distraught." Adele said. Once more, she knew what
he was thinking. Ambler might as well have his thoughts flashing on his forehead. "And so were you. It's unnerving that a
man whose wife has been murdered accuses you of hiding information about the murderer." She chuckled, a little chirp. "In
your Ross Macdonald books, people come and ask Lew Archer
to investigate. They come to tell you *not to*."

"Funny." Ambler was impatient. He realized it was with
himself not with Adele. That was the second blunder he'd made.
"Then, there was the wild-goose chase with Dillard Wainwright.
Concentrating on Wainwright, I ignored too many things I'd
observed. Making an observation doesn't mean anything if you
don't connect it to other observations that add up to something.
I observed things about Simon Dean but didn't connect them.
Dean was enraged that Andrea let me take Jayne Galloway's
journals. He wouldn't let me see Sandra's laptop. He came to the
library determined to get back Jayne Galloway's journals."

Adele interrupted him. "Also how smug and arrogant he
was. Guys that handsome think they can do anything. They
get away with murder—" Her eyes opened wider and her hand
flew to her mouth.

Ambler didn't react. "Suppose you're Simon Dean. Of course, you're going to be the first suspect. So you make sure someone else becomes the chief suspect. And you make sure no one can find any evidence against you."

"Like the private detective's report." Adele walked to the door of the reading room. "Dean knows it's here in her papers or she wrote something about it in her journals, so he has to keep all that away from you. He wasn't able to do that, so he knows we'll find it. That means he knows we'll find him out. And that means the police will come for him. And that means we have to go get that little girl."

Ambler knew what she was going to say.

"You have to show the report to Andrea. You think highly of her, right? She's devoted to her niece. She's helped you before. How could she not protect the girl?"

Ambler could think of a lot of reasons. "She might not believe us. She thought her brother was being stubborn and stupid, so she helped me. That's a far cry from believing her brother is a murderer and would kill his own daughter."

"We have to convince her, that's all. You can tell her the truth or make something up. Tell her you won a trip to Disney-land and want to take Carolyn." Adele held up her hand to stop him before he could speak again. "Wait. We don't have to convince her. The report from the private detective will convince her. Show it to her and tell her what it means."

Ambler was weakening. "Mike said we had to stay away from her. We could screw up everything he's doing."

"We could. But we're not going to. We're going to get that little girl out of the way and leave everything else to him."

He knew he wasn't going to change Adele's mind. "We have to talk to Mike before we do anything." Ambler was ada-mant; he'd go to the mat on this one. "Too many things could go wrong. We can't cross him up. One of us not knowing what the other one is doing is a disaster waiting to happen."

"He'll stop us."

Ambler knew he was right about this. "The fact is he can't stop us. If I want to call Andrea, I can. There's nothing illegal about it."

Adele came around slowly. She was impulsive but not reckless. Still, she had an independent streak. She trusted her own judgment. If she made up her mind to do something, you might as well get out of her way. Here, she relented.

Ambler called Mike and told him what they wanted to do and why. As he expected, Mike wasn't pleased. He was as stubborn as Adele. Ambler was in the middle—like the guy breaking up a fight—getting pummeled from both sides. When Adele sensed Mike was resisting, she performed a choreography of her eyes and mouth, with an occasional sigh, and a now-and-again huff that told Ambler he better not give in.

Finally, Mike had enough. "I can't stop you." He used the tone mothers use when they tell you, "Go ahead, ruin your life." Mike cleared his throat. "Don't get me wrong. I'd rather the kid is out of there when I talk to Simon Dean tomorrow. Everything's calm now. No one's overreacting. That doesn't mean things will be calm five minutes from now."

Mike was going to Greenwich in the morning to reinterview Simon Dean and had made an appointment to talk with a lieutenant in the detective division of the Greenwich Police Department.

"It's a courtesy, to let him know I'm there," he said. " I like to let interested parties know what's going on. No Lone Ranger stuff for me." Mike paused significantly. "Didn't used to be for you either. Sometimes, going in is easy. Not so for getting out. I hope you have a plan if this goes wrong. I think they call it an exit strategy." He lowered his voice. "Miss Morgan isn't behind this, by any chance?"

Ambler didn't answer. Miss Morgan was tapping her foot and glowering at him.

When he finished with Mike, Ambler made the call to Andrea. He told her he couldn't explain now but needed to talk to
her and would like to come out to Connecticut this evening.

"It must be very important." A chilly edge to her voice
caught Ambler by surprise.

"It is important." She waited for him to say more, height-
ening his concern. He didn't want to tell her over the phone.
"Something has come to light about your brother."

"I see." Her tone grew frostier.

"This is something from his past you may or may not know
about."

"I'm not sure I want to speak with you about my brother."

Ambler waited, with a sinking feeling, for her to say more.
When she didn't, he said, "May I ask why?"

"Simon said you were trying to prove he killed Sandi. You
never told me that. He said your bartender friend raped Sandi
and held her against her will. He said you were an experienced
crime investigator and you weren't telling me the truth."

"And you believed him?"

"I don't know who to believe, so I'm being careful around
both of you." Her voice shook.

Ambler had no choice. He told her he had a private investigator's report on Simon that she needed to see.

"Does it say my brother killed Sandi?" It was an accusation
not a question.

"It doesn't." Ambler was losing her. He'd underestimated
Simon again. "The private investigator was the man mur-
dered in Sandra's hotel room in New York. His name was Ted
Doyle."

Andrea silence lasted a long time. "God. I don't know what
to think. How do I know you're telling me the truth?"

"I'll come there and show you the report and something
Jayne Galloway wrote in her journal." He paused not sure if he
should go on. But he did. "I'm afraid for Carolyn."

"So am I," Andrea said in a small voice after a long pause. "I guess I'm afraid for Simon, too . . . what I might find out about him."

Ambler fought back the urge to press her.

"Can you bring me those things tonight? Carolyn's with Simon at my mother's farm in Kent. They'll be back tomorrow morning. My husband is traveling. He'll be back tomorrow also. I'd like to do this as soon as possible."

Ambler gave his spare apartment key to Adele so she could wait for Johnny and was on the next train to Greenwich.

Chapter 34

Mike Cosgrove was making another drive to the suburbs. He felt like a commuter and wondered what his life would have been like if he'd gotten a normal job, raised a family, and really did commute to the city each morning from the suburbs. His digestion would be better for one thing, and his blood pressure.

What he didn't like was the chance he was taking. A third interview with a suspect, under the guise of clearing up something, would put the suspect on guard. On the one hand, sometimes it was good to let a suspect know you were on to him. It increased his panic and the likelihood of making a mistake. Other times, it blew up in your face. That raising suspicions this time might put a child at risk gave Cosgrove pause. He could let Dean know he'd rip his heart out with his bare hands if he did anything to the kid. For a moment, he let himself think that Dean wouldn't follow through on the threat, yet he'd seen too much incomprehensible evil in his years on the job to buy that.

For a few more miles, he thought about hunches. He didn't like them unless something substantial led to the hunch. Simon

Dean hated McNulty the bartender, saw him as the ruination of his wife. What slipped out the last time was that Dean hated his wife, too, hated her and the bartender separately and jointly.

Cosgrove hadn't taken notes at the last interview; the observation came to him when he wrote his notes later and from something McNulty said later on. He wasn't sure Dean recognized he'd given away that he hated her. Dean might not even know he hated his wife. Most times when Cosgrove caught a suspect's slipup, it was while questioning him. Usually, the suspect caught it, too, either from Cosgrove's reaction or from hearing what he said out loud.

Simon Dean was a calculating guy. Some people are like that, careful thinkers, pick their words, say as little as possible. Someone with something to hide is always careful, aware when talking to a cop that they could give something away. The last time he questioned Dean, Dean's anger got the best of his caution when he talked about McNulty and his wife Sandra having a past together. It was more than anger. Simon Dean's long-simmering anger had festered into hatred. It snuck up on him when Dean pictured his wife and McNulty together.

Dean's other slip, if it was a slip, was that he didn't mention the phone calls with his wife shortly before she was murdered until Cosgrove brought them up. He said he'd forgotten. Questionable that he wouldn't remember the last time he spoke with his wife before she was murdered. A possibility Cosgrove kept in mind was that Dean's lies—if they were lies—were calculated to implicate the bartender. He wanted the murder rap hung on McNulty and would manufacture evidence to make sure the bartender didn't walk. This could be because Dean had convinced himself McNulty was guilty. It would also be the case if Dean knew McNulty didn't kill his wife and wanted to set him up for the rap.

The lieutenant Cosgrove met with when he got to Greenwich whose name was Murphy, had followed Sandra Dean's

murder. He knew of Simon Dean because they attended the
same church, where Dean was a lector. Cosgrove, a Catholic
himself, didn't remember what a lector was. He might if he went
to Mass more than once or twice a year. He didn't want to show
his ignorance, so he sort of lowered his brow to look knowl-
edgeable. The lieutenant remembered the murder in the hotel
room in the city also, Cosgrove's case.

"When his wife was murdered, we got notice from Stamford. I went to notify Simon myself. That's about it. I saw him at
Mass the following Sunday with his daughter. I told him I was
sorry for his loss. I don't think he knew who I was."

Cosgrove told Murphy about Ted Doyle's murder and that
he'd come back to clear up some things with Dean. The lieutenant didn't press him but his expression changed enough—
furrowed brow, a hardness in his eyes that wasn't there
before—to suggest he understood that Cosgrove considered
Dean a suspect. Cosgrove would have told him more if he'd
asked but didn't want to throw accusations around if he didn't
have to. He also told Murphy about the private detective's report, and that Ted Doyle had done the investigation and written the report. The lieutenant wasn't aware of any allegations
against Simon Dean.

"Anything bother you about Dean's reactions when you
told him of his wife's death?" Cosgrove asked. Good cops paid
attention to how people, especially spouses, reacted to news of
a murder.

Murphy took a moment to answer. "I was thinking about
that, well, not directly thinking it. You know how you let ideas
run through your head sometimes without making a judgment
about them? We don't have a lot of homicides here. Some years
none. My last one was four years ago. The year before that I had
two."

Cosgrove didn't know where he was going with this but
could wait to find out.

"Dr. Dean called the police on her husband once a couple of years ago." Murphy glanced behind him and behind Cosgrove. "This is off the record. We're a small town, a small police force. Everybody knows everybody's business, even if officially we don't know it. She and Mr. Dean had disagreed about disciplining their daughter. She inquired about a law, CGS 53-21, felony risk of injury to a minor.

"It was pretty smart of her to know about the law. It has to do with physical or mental abuse of a child, including spanking, if it's excessive, by a parent. The officer explained the law, and she passed the explanation along to her husband while she was still on the phone with the officer, and then hung up.

"I knew Simon Dean from seeing him at church. I was raised to go to Mass on Sunday. My folks live in town and go to church every Sunday. It's old fashioned; still, I go most Sundays with my wife and kids. After the phone call, I'd watch him. He was old fashioned, too, in a different way, that hellfire and brimstone way you see in the movies, the stern preacher who keeps his wife in sackcloth and ashes. Stiff. Suit and tie. No emotion in his readings. No emotion with his wife and daughter. A cold and joyless family. I didn't like him.

"When I notified him of his wife's death, he took the news the same way, cold, no emotion. He might be a stiff upper lip guy. He might not show emotion to a stranger. But when I told him about his wife, I'd swear he didn't care.

"So something bothered me about him at the time, too. . . . In fact, every time I saw him, he bothered me. He thought he was better than everyone else, disapproved of everyone. When I worked juvenile, I saw too many kids with that kind of superior-acting, holier-than-thou, super-strict father get themselves into terrible messes. That doesn't prove anything. If you want me in on the interview, I'd do it. You want me to question neighbors, her friends, his friends, people around town, see what I come up with, I can do that, too."

Cosgrove met Murphy's gaze. He believed he saw an honest man and not for the first time in his life was glad he'd found an ally when he needed one. He told Murphy the rest of the story, including his hunch about the things that didn't add up and Dean's threat against his daughter.

"If there's going to be an arrest," Cosgrove said, "I'll get a warrant and you can do it. I'm hoping we're not dealing with a homicidal maniac. I also might be wrong. He may be a brokenhearted, widowed guy with a daughter to raise, and I'm adding to his misery.

"One more thing," Cosgrove said as he was getting ready to leave. They'd decided Cosgrove would do the interview alone so as not to spook Dean. Murphy would follow Cosgrove into the Greenwich backcountry and arrange for backup if needed. The final thing Cosgrove told him was Ambler and Adele's plan for Andrea Eagan to take Carolyn for the afternoon.

Murphy didn't understand the role Ambler and Adele played in the operation. He asked a second time after Cosgrove's half-hearted attempt to explain. After the second failed explanation, Murphy let it go.

"I'm hoping they don't show up here in town, that they call Andrea and make up some reason she needs to take Carolyn," Cosgrove said. "But you never know."

"Friends of the suspect?" Murphy tried again.

"It's more than that. They're tangled up with the family. The mother donated her papers to the library." He paused. "She might have been murdered, too. . . . Believe me, you don't want me to try to explain all that to you now. At least the bartender's in jail or he'd be here mucking up the works, too."

"The accused?"

"They became part of my life a while back. I can't get rid of them. It's a curse." Cosgrove sighed heavily.

His cell phone rang.

"Andrea called me this morning." It was Ambler and his

voice was ragged. "Simon got home and discovered Sandra's laptop was missing—"

"Slow down," Cosgrove cut him off. "I don't know what you're talking about."

Ray explained he'd gone to Greenwich last night after all to show Ted Doyle's report on Dean to Andrea. She'd finally believed Ray and the private eye report and Ray persuaded her to get Sandra Dean's laptop from her brother's house while he was away—one questionable move compounded with another questionable move Cosgrove could have told them.

"Andrea told him she borrowed the laptop to get some photos. He didn't believe her. He knows he's being investigated. He asked her to bring the laptop back. Now, she's at his house. Before he found out about the laptop, she'd arranged to pick up Carolyn for the day. When she got there, she told him she forgot the laptop. He wouldn't let Carolyn leave with her. Andrea's afraid to leave without the child. She said she knows Simon has guns in the house."

"Where are you?"

"Adele and I are on a train leaving Grand Central. We're bringing the laptop to Dean to try to trade it to get Andrea and Carolyn out of there."

Cosgrove suppressed a groan. "You can't—"

"Wait," Ray said. "There's more. Adele and I found an email exchange between Sandra and her mother about Ted Doyle. They arranged for Doyle to meet Sandra in the city. Sandra told her mother she would be registered at the Commodore as Shannon Darling." Ray's voice rose for emphasis. "Simon could have seen those emails. That's why he wants the laptop—"

Cosgrove interrupted again. "If he knew the emails were there, he would have erased them."

Ray was silent a long moment.

"This is important." Cosgrove held the floor. "When you get to Greenwich, go to a coffee shop or someplace and wait for me to call you. If it makes sense to string Dean along with the laptop, I'll call you. Don't go to Dean's house. I'm with the Greenwich police. I'll have them stop you if you try."

"Okay. Okay. What do I tell Andrea? Should she and Carolyn try to get out?"

"I understand. It's hard on you. It's hard on her." He softened his voice. "She needs to sit tight. We have a couple of things to try, and we have people who handle hostage situations. They know what to do better than I do . . . and better than you do."

"A hostage situation?" Ray's voice shook.

When Cosgrove ended the call with Ray, he briefed Lieutenant Murphy and then called his homicide chief. He told him where he was and what had happened and asked him to send a team to the hotel where Ted Doyle was murdered with a photo of Simon Dean. He also asked that someone check the crime scene report from the Doyle murder for unmatched fingerprints and DNA samples. He asked Murphy to ask the Stamford police to do the same thing on their end for the crime scene report from Sandra Dean's murder.

Murphy activated the department's special response unit and called in the hostage negotiating team.

"If we can place Simon Dean at either of the murder locations, we'll get a warrant," Cosgrove said.

"Do we take over now or wait for the warrant?" Murphy was ready to go.

Cosgrove said he wanted to follow the plan they'd talked about. "It's remotely possible he's not a murderer." Cosgrove planned to visit Dean and tell him he had some things he wanted to clear up. Simon might believe him. He was arrogant enough to think he could outsmart a dumb cop.

"Then there'd be a good guy with a gun inside the house, not just the daughter and her aunt."

"Suppose he doesn't let you in?"

"We'd be where we are now."

"Should I go with you?"

Cosgrove shook his head. "I'd like that. Believe me I would. But it wouldn't look like I was clearing something up. It would look like something else."

Murphy held out his hand. "You're not serving a warrant, not making an arrest. You're entitled to visit one of our citizens even if you are a New York City cop. Nice of you to let me know."

Cosgrove shook his hand. "I wish it was easier sometimes."

Chapter 35

A half hour later, Cosgrove approached Simon Dean's stately home with dread. He'd spoken confidently to Murphy and to Ray and Adele when he told them what he was going to do. It was a confidence he didn't feel. He'd done this kind of thing before. Sometimes it didn't work out. The suspect went bonkers. All hell broke loose. Someone died. His hope was Simon would continue to act the part of the solid citizen, crime victim that Cosgrove would treat him as until he dropped the report from Ted Doyle on him. Despite what Ray said, Simon had no reason to think of himself as a suspect; except perhaps the tiny voice inside his head, guilt, whispering to him.

No little girl opened the door this time. He tried not to think about the kid. Over Simon's shoulder when he opened the door, Cosgrove caught a quick glimpse of the woman who must be Simon's sister in a room that might be a den at the back of the house. She met his gaze and closed the door to the room. The expression in her eyes was fright but not entreaty. He didn't know what she saw in his eyes. He tried to suggest reassurance, let her know he was there to help. Probably his eyes didn't suggest anything. He could be the Fuller Brush man for all she knew.

The Greenwich cops set up a perimeter and a command post, brought in the department's special response unit and a hostage negotiator. As always, you hoped for a peaceful end to a confrontation. Hope for the best. Prepare for the worst.

Dean might have thought he'd put on a calm facade. To Cosgrove, Dean looked like he was barely under control. Cosgrove waited a moment appraising him. A small softball bat leaned against the wall leading to the living room, reminding Cosgrove of his last visit when Carolyn in her baseball uniform opened the door.

"I'm really busy," Dean said. "You should have told me you were coming." He tried to keep his tone pleasant, but there was an edge to it. "I don't have a moment to spare right now." He glanced over his shoulder and back at Cosgrove. "We'll have to reschedule."

The response threw Cosgrove off course for a moment. You think you know what to expect but you seldom do. "I should have called. I know, and I'm sorry for not doing that." He shook his head as a rebuke to himself. "To tell the truth"— didn't he always say that when he was about to twist the truth—"I didn't plan to talk to you today at all. I was here to talk to the Greenwich police." He'd let Dean wonder about that for a moment.

Dean's response was immediate and blunt. "Was it about me?"

Cosgrove nodded. "Yes and no. I wanted to know if you'd reported your wife missing."

Dean's face tightened. The words were clipped. "I didn't know she was missing. I thought she was at a medical conference." He paused one beat. "I said I don't have time for this." He swung the door he was holding back and forth, as if he might close it.

Cosgrove spoke sternly. "You're going to have to talk to me. New information has come up that differs with what you told me the last time we spoke." He relaxed his stance. "I'm sure you can explain and get everything straight." He regarded Dean the way a kindly uncle might. "So let's get this taken care of now before someone else gets involved and things get worse."

Dean responded like a child to the voice of authority. He calmed down. He wasn't shocked. No outrage. He was prepared. He'd expected an accusation. What you might think would be an incredulous: "Are you accusing me?" "Do you doubt my word?" "Can I call my lawyer?" was instead an acknowledgment. "I'm sure it's something the bartender told you. Or perhaps that slimy librarian has manufactured some new evidence. He can't prove his friend innocent, so he's trying to make me guilty." Dean spoke quietly. "They're both slick. The bartender comes off as a clumsy fool. In reality, he's a master manipulator. He turned my wife against me."

Cosgrove rubbed his chin and tried to act surprised. "I wondered about their relationship."

You could see a glimmer of confidence in Dean's eyes, the lapse of a not-so-good poker player with a handful of aces. "He deceived her. I'd think that was obvious. As he deceives the librarian, and it looks like you, too."

"Well," Cosgrove tried to sound confused. "The truth is"— here it was again—"what I want to ask you about is something that came up with the bartender . . . and with you."

Dean glanced away quickly and back at Cosgrove. He attempted a contemptuous laugh. "What did he say?"

"Did your wife tell you where she was and who she was with when she called you the night before her murder?"

Dean's face was too expressive for him to be a good liar. Or he had more lies than he could keep track of. For a moment, his gaze went everywhere except toward Cosgrove. When he did look Cosgrove in the eye, he couldn't hold his gaze steady.

Beads of sweat broke out on his forehead. "I don't remember the phone call well. I don't remember what she told me. You can't expect—"

"Do you remember what you told me about the call?"

His gaze darted around everywhere but at Cosgrove again. "She was sorry. . . . She said she was sorry. She wanted to come home." His voice took on a higher pitch. "I don't remember what else. We talked about things. She was my wife. We had things we said to one another. I was angry."

"If she was sorry and wanted to come home, why didn't she?"

"Why didn't she what?"

"Come home. What kept her from coming home if that's what she wanted to do?"

Something went on behind Dean's eyes that made his facial expression almost evil. "The bartender. I told you he manipulated her."

"Did you argue about that?"

"That and other things. We had—" he glanced around him, searching for help. "Why are you browbeating me?" His uncertain gaze finally landed on Cosgrove. "What are you getting at?"

Cosgrove didn't get why Simon Dean was reacting as if he'd been found out, when Cosgrove hadn't found out anything. "I'm asking about the phone conversation with your wife, why you didn't demand she come home right away. Why didn't she leave right away?"

"The bartender—"

"She was having fun with the bartender?"

"He manipulated her."

"She wronged you. Why would you forgive her? She and McNulty were playing you, weren't they?"

Cosgrove could see in Dean's eyes that his rage was returning. "He killed her so she couldn't leave. She wanted to leave. She couldn't."

"She wouldn't tell you where she was because she didn't want you to come get her just yet—"

"She'd tell me. I didn't want to know where she was."

"Why?"

You could see in Dean's face that he didn't have an answer; he'd made a false step and he knew it. For a moment, his expression was peaceful, as if he were relieved and ready now to surrender. He was close to tears.

Cosgrove dared to hope he might have a confession coming. "There's one more thing coming down the pike you ought to know about. We've got a private investigator's report." Cosgrove kept his eyes on Dean's face so he saw the recognition. "I don't have to tell you what's in it—"

Something beyond Cosgrove caught Dean's eye. His expression twisted into a sneer. He watched something in the distance. "Are there other police out there?" The sound of his voice was ghostly.

"It's okay," Cosgrove said. "No one's out to get you. You've been wronged. Let's talk man-to-man. I understand. A lot of people will. There'll be a lot of sympathy for you."

"What are you talking about?" Dean's voice was strained. The evil expression that had crept into his face earlier blossomed and took over. Cosgrove stared into rage and hatred.

"Don't," Cosgrove shouted, reaching for his gun in a holster on his chest under his arm. Before he could get to it, Dean pushed the front door violently into his face and sprang away from the doorway. In the time it took Cosgrove to open the door again, Dean had dashed across the foyer and the living room into the den with his sister and Carolyn and closed the door.

"Fuck," Cosgrove said. He called the number he had for Lieutenant Murphy and told him what happened. In a flash, the driveway and road in front of Dean's house filled with police cars and flashing red lights. Cosgrove kept the front door open and stood in the foyer watching the den with the closed door, his gun in his hand. It was better to keep Dean localized rather than let him have the entire house.

"I blew it," he said when Murphy came up the walk to the front door. "You got a good sniper? I saw windows in the room they're in."

Murphy gestured with his head toward the door to the den. "Do you want to try your luck again before the hostage negotiator?"

Cosgrove said he did.

"Phones?" Murphy asked. "The hostage negotiators will need phone numbers for Dean or the aunt. I can have someone look them up."

Cosgrove looked at his own phone. "I know someone who has at least one of those numbers."

Chapter 36

When Ambler's cell phone rang, he knew it would be Mike. No preliminaries. "Do you have a phone number for Simon Dean?"

From Mike's tone, he knew there was trouble and not to get in Mike's way with questions. "I don't. I have Andrea's number." He gave it to Cosgrove.

"Dean is holed up with the kid and the aunt." Mike gave a quick recap.

"I'm sure he isn't going to be persuaded by talk," Ambler said. "What can I do?"

"I don't suppose you pray," Mike said.

"I'll ask Adele."

When Mike hung up, Ambler told Adele about the call and asked about praying.

"I am," she said. "What else do we do?"

"Nothing but wait."

They'd found a lunch counter on Greenwich Avenue, a relic of days past, and sat across from one another in a booth over stale coffee.

"We can't just sit here," she said.

Ambler was rethinking everything he'd done trying to find where he went wrong, so he didn't say anything.

"We have the laptop. We can still try to trade it for Dean letting Carolyn and Andrea go. Why's that not a good idea?"

"It's too late. Nothing's going to change Dean's mind now. He's hate-filled enough to have murdered his wife and taken his daughter hostage. What can you say to him?"

Adele stared at him before she spoke. "Someone might talk to him. What about Harry? Priests are supposed to counsel people."

"Not Harry." Ambler remembered Simon's spiritual adviser, the priest who'd been with Simon at Sandra's funeral. He looked up the phone number for the Catholic church in a phone book attached to the world's last remaining phone booth at the back of the lunch counter. When he called, he was told by the person answering the phone that the priest was away from the rectory on a police emergency.

"That's got to be Simon Dean," Adele said when Ambler told her. "Let's go."

He thought about arguing but what else would they do? They could stay where they were and feel anxious and useless or they could stand around outside the Dean residence feeling anxious and useless. The counterperson at the lunch counter called a taxi for them and the taxi took them out along a country road until they reached a cordoned-off section on a narrow part of the road lined with stonewalls and acres of fields behind the walls, blocked now by a fleet of police vehicles with flashing lights.

"What's going to happen?" Adele put her arm through Ambler's arm and pulled herself closer to him. "This feels ominous."

They'd gotten out of the taxi and were standing next to a couple of uniformed cops behind a barrier of yellow crime-scene tape that looked tragically out of place in the bucolic setting. "My guess is Simon will ask for safe passage for him and his daughter."

"Will the police let him do that, let him get away with Carolyn?" Adele spoke out of a sense of wonder, as if they'd come upon a strange new world.

Ambler watched the activity unfold in front of them. A dozen or more police, many of them in riot gear, others in their regular uniforms, stood together in small groups, while others moved quickly from vehicle to vehicle with urgency and a sense of purpose. At the farthest point of the gathering an ambulance was parked and in front of it for some reason a fire truck. Ambler slipped his arm loose from Adele's arm and put it around her shoulder. "They have him now," he said. "I think it will end here."

Adele stepped back from him. "What do you mean?"

"They'll try to get him to surrender. If he doesn't, they'll take him out."

"Take him out?" Adele's eyes were wide.

Reporters and TV cameras had arrived. With the police cars, ambulances, and TV trucks, the bucolic, suburban road resembled a grotesque amusement park. No one was going to update them on anything; they'd have to watch and wait. After a few minutes, they listened in as a uniformed police officer spoke to the assembled reporters, telling them mostly what Ambler and Adele already knew. A hostage negotiating team was on the scene. A man with a gun was inside the house with hostages. The next report would be in two hours unless something changed.

After what seemed hours, the priest, Fr. Jerome, came out and spoke to the TV cameras. He was a young man with the aura of a fawn, who looked nervous, if not terrified, stumbling over his words. He said "Mr. Dean is distraught," a number of times—not a term you want bandied about in this sort of situation—and mentioned praying at least as often as he said "distraught."

Chapter 37

Cosgrove caught the last couple of minutes of Fr. Jerome's counseling of Simon Dean. It didn't go well, and ended with what sounded like a denunciation of God by Dean for the misery He'd sent Simon's way. The priest was ashen as he approached Cosgrove.

"I'm afraid Simon has lost his mind," he said when they met in the foyer. "All we can do is pray God gives him the grace to restore his faith, and gives you the grace to get through to him."

Cosgrove searched the priest's face. How earnest and humble he was. It reminded Cosgrove that he once believed. At the moment, he could sure use some divine inspiration. He patted the priest on the shoulder. "Maybe what you said to him will sink in. If we can keep him talking, we have a chance."

Cosgrove took a deep breath and knocked on the door to the den housing Dean, Carolyn, and Andrea. He didn't get a response. "Hey, Mr. Dean. Mike Cosgrove here," he shouted. "I said before we should have a chat. You have a lot coming at you, a lot to think about. Things maybe look bleak. I'm not gonna say you're not in a bad spot. You are. I'm a man who's had woman trouble, trouble with his wife. I'm divorced now. I know the pain a woman can bring a man. I'm a father, too, of a beautiful girl, like you are."

He heard movement behind the door. Simon spoke, "You're wasting your time. I told the first cop what I wanted. A car and an open road and then I want a private plane. Free passage for my daughter and me to a country with no extradition."

"They're looking into that. It might not be possible—"

"That's the only way anyone leaves here."

Cosgrove found himself nodding for no reason since no one could see him. "I understand. We're working on it. There's a lot of pieces involved besides the police to get something like than done: the governor, the State Department. There's security issues. Even if we can do it, it takes time. Days most likely."

Cosgrove kept up his patter. He offered to send out for food. He offered to let Dean move his captives to the master bedroom suite, where there was a bathroom. He offered to hand him a bottle of scotch when he noticed a home bar against a wall in the living room. Dean didn't fall for the scotch offer. He did move to the master bedroom, keeping Carolyn close to him, making sure he couldn't become a target. Cosgrove followed and stood outside another door.

He began again. "I'm gonna tell you something." It was weird talking to a blank door. "I know you'll want to reject this out of hand. The thing is it might be different than you think, so I'd ask you to listen." He listened himself to silence. "Let's say you plead to something. You have us over a barrel. I can't speak for the prosecutor, but I could take a deal to him. Anything you want to propose. Instead of murder one, you plead to manslaughter. You get—"

Dean's voice was weary. "I'm tired of listening to you."

Cosgrove was tired of listening to himself, yet he wasn't giving up. When the food arrived from the Chinese restaurant,

he took a break. Murphy asked if he wanted the hostage negotiator. Cosgrove said he wanted to try one more time.

He went back to the door. "Think of something yourself.
Anything at all. Who knows? You might get acquitted. Like I
said, you'd have a sympathetic audience. A lot of folks, jurors,
would understand why you did what you did. You tell the
prosecutor about the bartender. What he did to your wife. He
turned her against you, lied to her. Manipulated her, you said. If
you told the whole story, people would get it. Extenuating circumstances. Who knows what the bartender might have done
to her anyway? And then we don't know the whole story from
your point of view. If we did, we'd see things differently, understand what happened differently."

"Goddamn McNulty!" Dean's voice shook with anger.
Cosgrove had gotten through to him, hit a nerve. "Damn him
to hell! It's his fault. He's the murderer. He made it happen."
Dean's tone softened. "I didn't want to kill Sandra. I don't want
to do this. I don't want anything to happen to Carolyn. If you
want to help, get us out of here. Carolyn and I will be okay if
you get us out of here."

Cosgrove didn't know if he should approach the angry
Dean or the softening Dean. He spoke carefully. "I know you
don't want to harm your daughter. That's the last thing you
want. We—"

Dean roared. His voice blasted through the bedroom door.
"Shut up! Goddamn it. Shut up! Get away from here. I'll shoot
through the door."

Instinctively, Cosgrove stepped to the side of the door. He'd
gotten under Simon's skin. Now, he had to keep him from falling apart. Cool him down, and keep him talking. "I'm gonna
tell you the truth," Cosgrove said. At least this time, he would
tell the truth. "You're not going to get a car and a plane and
safe passage. We might set it up to look like we're doing it. It

would be an ambush." Cosgrove took a deep breath. "I'm giving it to you like a man. You're trapped. Let your daughter and
her aunt go. You can have me as a hostage. Make a run for it like
a man, not hiding behind a kid. You and me."

There was a long pause. Cosgrove thought of another hundred things to say but bit his tongue. If he got the hostages out
of there, with a bit of luck he could keep himself out of the way
and the sniper would have a shot at Dean. The master bedroom
had windows on three walls. If Murphy could borrow a couple
of snipers from surrounding towns, the chances were good one
of them would get a bead on Dean.

"Not you."

"What?" Cosgrove wasn't sure what he heard. He thought
to argue and realized he didn't know what he'd argue against.
Before he found the words, Dean spoke again.

"I want the bartender. I want McNulty. Bring him as a hostage. I'll let Carolyn and Andrea leave and take my chances."

Chapter 38

"He'll kill him," Adele said.

Mike had finished telling them what Simon Dean proposed. Ambler had the same thought himself and was sure the thought had occurred to Mike.

"I'd rather do it myself," Mike said. "He wouldn't buy it."

"What about me?" Ambler said. "I could bring him the laptop."

"I thought of that. Someone we send in would know what was going to happen and know to stay out of the sniper's line of fire. The kid and her aunt don't know what's going on, don't know what to do. It's risky with them in the room. Our best bet is to get them out. The thing is, he wants McNulty. It's too late for the laptop. We're too far in for Dean to care about the emails anymore."

"Raymond and I could both go."

Cosgrove rolled his eyes. "And leave Ray's grandson an orphan?"

They went back and forth until Ambler had enough. "We have to leave it up to McNulty. Can you get him here?"

"Can you get him out of jail?" Adele asked.

"Give me his lawyer's phone number." Mike called his captain in New York. After that, he called David Levinson and spoke to him at length. When he hung up, he said "My boss will call the Stamford DA. Levinson can have McNulty out in an hour or so. I talked to Murphy and he's okay with it. If McNulty wants to do it, we can have him here in a couple of hours."

An hour later Ambler got a call from David Levinson "You want McNulty to go from prison to being a killer's hostage? I can't think of a reason on earth for him to do that. But he says he will."

"He wants to be a saint," Ambler said.

Two hours later, Ambler and Adele watched McNulty arrive. Before they could talk to him, a team from Greenwich's special response unit took him under their wing. They outfitted him, despite his protests, with a Kevlar vest and a sweatshirt, and taught him how to move in it. They also tried to teach him evasive movements.

"I know how to duck already," McNulty told them. "I'm a bartender." He asked for a cigarette.

"I didn't know he smoked," Adele said.

"He doesn't."

McNulty wouldn't show it, but Ambler knew the bartender wasn't any more ready to die than he was. When McNulty was outfitted and stood back from the cops who'd been outfitting him, Adele and Ambler walked over.

McNulty looked at the cigarette in his hand. "I stopped smoking twenty years ago. I liked smoking. I stopped because I had a kid. So I told myself then if I was ever sentenced to the electric chair, I'd start smoking again." He looked at the fashionable house in front of him. "This is close enough."

"Whatever you need," Ambler said.

"I need a drink." He smile sheepishly and nodded toward the response team. "Those guys know what they're doing. All

I got to do is get this jerk near a window before he shoots me and stay out of the way when they shoot him." He glanced from Ambler to Adele and smiled. "What could go wrong?"

Adele burst into tears and lunged for McNulty. She threw her arms around his neck and buried her face in his chest. Or tried to until she clunked against the vest. Snipers took up positions near windows on three sides of the house. Another sniper was on the roof of a house across the street from the front door. Now that Cosgrove was out of the house, Dean could move about freely and had become a moving target. A hostage negotiator worked out the details of the release of Andrea and Carolyn with him over the phone. The negotiator told him a car was waiting and that he and McNulty had safe passage.

Everyone bought into the charade, though everyone knew, and Ambler figured Dean knew, too, he wasn't coming out of the house alive. The question was whether McNulty would.

The late afternoon sun was low in the sky behind the houses on the far side of the street—a good thing. It was behind the police as they faced the front door, with Dean looking into it, not the police or McNulty looking into it. Two officers from the response unit, one on either side of McNulty, walked with him to the front door. They were there to make sure he made it through the door and the hostages made it out. The sniper on the roof across the street watched for an opening. If he could get a bead on Dean without endangering the hostages or McNulty, it would end there.

Ambler and Adele watched from the street clutching each other like storybook children lost in the woods. Ambler didn't breathe. He'd never wanted to watch someone get shot. But he did this time. He blamed himself. He'd been too slow putting everything together. There should be no hostage and Simon Dean should be in a jail cell.

The door opened. Andrea and Carolyn appeared in the doorway and then on the walk. Hunched over, they ran with the two officers from the response unit who covered Andrea and Carolyn with their bodies and backed toward the street, their powerful rifles trained on the door. McNulty went in. The door closed.

Others from the response unit ran toward Carolyn and Andrea. Ambler's eyes were glued to the door. Adele's fingers dug into his arm. Ambler pictured himself running to the door. Bursting in. The element of surprise. Two of them, he and McNulty, could take Dean. He listened for the report of the sniper's rifle. He listened. He waited. There was a report, a gunshot but from inside.

The air was electric.

The door opened. McNulty walked out. Ambler's heart sank as he saw in his mind's eye his friend taking a few steps and falling, clutching his chest. But McNulty kept walking. The response team rushed, some to him, the rest into the house. Hordes of them. Adele and Ambler rushed toward McNulty until the police stopped them. The response team guys embraced McNulty. They laughed, pounded him on the back, whooped and cheered like he just scored the Super Bowl winning touchdown.

After a couple of moments, McNulty worked his way through the cops and over to Ambler and Adele. Adele reached for him with her arms and clutched him. He'd taken another cigarette from the response team and held it up away from her over her head while he looked at Ambler and then at the cigarette. "My last one."

"What happened?"

"Let's go somewhere and get a drink."

Chapter 39

McNulty couldn't get a drink for hours, tied up in debriefings with the police. By the time he did get the drink, with Ambler and Adele, at an upscale steakhouse, which he insisted was the only place in Greenwich that would know how to make a martini, he'd told his story a half-dozen times. "You need a bartender born before 1960 for a decent martini," he told them.

"I was supposed to get him near a window and duck. I didn't see any windows in that doorway and I was looking down the barrel of a gun as big around as a manhole. Dean closed the door and ducked away from it. I expect he thought, correctly, someone would shoot him if he didn't. I was sorry someone didn't.

"For a moment, while he did that, he took his eyes off me. I saw a baseball bat leaning against the wall." McNulty gazed at the ceiling. "God must have put it there. I bent, grabbed it with two hands, and swung with one motion. Dean had turned toward me with the gun pointed at me. But he hadn't planned to pull the trigger yet. He wasn't ready to shoot because he was trying to say something to me. I didn't think we had anything to talk about. I caught him under the right ear.

"The gun went off and he dropped it. I was going to whack him again . . . and again after that. For what he did. For Sandi . . . and then I didn't. She wouldn't want me to, so it wouldn't be right to splatter him."

"You saved Sandra's daughter," Adele said. "That's what she'd have wanted you to do."

McNulty looked at her. His eyes were liquid. "Sandi was too sensitive, too gentle. You couldn't do something brutal in her memory. She wouldn't want that."

The next evening, Ambler, Adele, and Mike Cosgrove had dinner at a French bistro back in the city on Madison Avenue not far from Ambler's apartment, a favorite of Mike's. McNulty was visiting his pop and retrieving his cat. He'd taken Johnny with him.

"We're getting old," Mike said. "Both of us got this one wrong."

"Because Simon Dean was so convincing," Adele said. "And McNulty was such a good suspect. And Simon convinced everyone Sandra was a wanton woman."

"A damaged woman," Ambler said.

"Men are ready to believe a woman who betrays a man is depraved, not the other way around," Adele said. "That's why you thought of that murdered man—"

"Ted Doyle."

"—as someone Sandra seduced. If you paid attention to his being a private detective, you'd have found out what he was investigating much sooner."

Cosgrove listened attentively. "All of the men she wrote about, except that one asshole, spent just one night with her. Still, they were half in love with her. They didn't want to let her go. And her husband . . ." Cosgrove shook his head.

"Simon had twisted ideas about sex. Who knows what went on in his head? He convinced Sandra she was a slut. She was ashamed of herself. Telling her that was cruel. A woman's sexuality can be fragile." Adele looked at Cosgrove and then Ambler. "Does a man ever wonder if he's a slut?"

Neither man answered. Adele slid closer to Ambler along the banquette until her thigh pressed against his. "And then Sandra started to see what Simon was doing and realized she wasn't so bad. Simon needed her to feel ashamed. It was how he controlled her. Simon was evil.

"When I talked with Andrea after the standoff was over, she told me Simon tried to explain what went wrong while they were cooped up in that house. He told her he was sorry about Sandra. He didn't mean for this to happen. When he discovered her unfaithfulness, he started monitoring her emails. He thought since she was a wanton woman, she couldn't help herself, so he said he forgave her. But he didn't forgive her. He hated her for being that wanton woman. He found out from the emails about the private investigator her mother hired that Sandi had a hotel room in New York under a fake name. He knew about McNulty, too.

"He knew they wouldn't be far away," Adele said. "I think Sandra might have told him where they were anyway. Andrea said what happened in the hotel in New York—at least what Simon said happened—was he went there to confront the private investigator. He brought his gun to scare the investigator and to scare Sandra. He snuck up on the man. When they got in the hotel room, he put the gun to the guy's head. The man did something and the gun went off."

"A bullet through Ted Doyle's head." Mike said.

"Dean ran. Sandra ran. When Sandra called him the next day, he didn't believe she'd forgiven him and wanted to come home. He knew what she was up to. He knew she wanted Carolyn and

once she had her daughter, she would leave him and go with Mc-
Nulty. He played along with her and made a plan to kill her and
blame both murders on McNulty."

Mike held out his arms expansively. He was halfway
through a Manhattan, a cocktail before dinner unusual for
him. "She thought her lies convinced her husband she was coming home. His lies convinced her he wanted her to come home.
She didn't know he was lying. He knew she was lying. In a way,
that was her fatal flaw. Getting men to want her was too easy
for her. So when he said he wanted her, she believed him when
she shouldn't have."

"That's one way of looking at it," Adele shot him a wither-
ing glance.

Cosgrove looked puzzled for a moment and then turned to
the menu. "I suggest either the crab and avocado napoleon or
the escargot appetizer."

That night, Ambler called Andrea Eagan.
He didn't know if she'd want to talk to him and wasn't sure
why he called. Her husband answered her phone. Ambler told
him who he was. The man wasn't unfriendly or impolite. He
told Ambler he was screening Andrea's calls because the press
kept calling and she didn't want to talk to them anymore. Ambler said he'd call back another time. Bob, her husband, told
him to wait.

The next thing he heard was Andrea's voice.

"I don't know where to start," Ambler said. "I'm sorry about
everything. Your friend, your brother, putting you in danger. I
also want to thank you. Without you—"

"I'm exhausted," she said. "I'm not even sure I realize what
happened. I'm numb. Yet, I'm safe. Carolyn is safe. We're here
with a man who loves both of us. Terrible things happened.
Now they've stopped happening. So I'm okay. We're okay." She
laughed. He hoped it wasn't hysteria.

"Time will sort most of it out," Ambler said. "It all goes somewhere. It's still there in your head, but less of a presence." He didn't know if he was being comforting or alarming.

"I hope your friend is all right. After everyone thought he was so evil, he did such a brave thing."

"McNulty and Sandra had a foolish romantic idea about living happily ever after. He did what he did to get Carolyn safe."

"And brained Simon in the process." She laughed softly. "I wish I'd seen it. Simon is alive. I wouldn't say he's well. He's under police guard in intensive care. My husband Bob talked to a lawyer friend of his who said we have a really good chance to get custody of Carolyn since Simon would be in prison for a long time and because he threatened to harm her and took her hostage. He said the lawyers might get Simon to give up his parental rights as part of a plea deal since the court would probably terminate his parental rights anyway."

"I hope so," Ambler said.

"After spending that crazy day with him," Andrea said. "I think it should be an insanity plea, though I don't think that's what they meant."

"By the way," Ambler said. "Whenever Carolyn wants to come to the library to see her grandmother's papers, you're more than—"

Andrea started to laugh and stopped abruptly. "She never asked about her grandmother's papers. Simon made that up. She's happy with the parrot. He's great; he talks."

"The parrot," Ambler said. Too bad the parrot couldn't tell them how he got out of Jayne Galloway's house. It wouldn't make any difference now anyway unless the Nassau police charged McNulty.

Andrea laughed softly. "We'll definitely be coming to the library, even if not to see the collection. We'll want to see you again. And Adele told me the Winnie-the-Pooh stuffed animals are part of the library's collection."

Ambler was bone weary but had one more call. Cosgrove told him Nassau had closed the case on Jayne Galloway. She died a natural death.

"I don't think so," Ambler said. "How did the parrot get out?"

"An unsolved mystery," Mike said.

One would think after solving the case and freeing Mc-Nulty, Ambler would feel triumphant. But he didn't. He thought about Ted Doyle and Jayne Galloway and Sandra Dean in their graves, Simon Dean in the hospital, Dillard Wainwright blissfully oblivious in his cabin in the woods, his son John in prison. At least McNulty might be back. The bartenders union was trying to get him reinstated at the Library Tavern.

It was time to walk the dog. He called Lola and Johnny. He'd hardly spoken to his grandson since he returned from Connecticut, except to tell him what happened, as little of it as he could get away with. Johnny was just glad McNulty was out of jail.

The real autumn was underway in the city and the smell of winter rode on the chilly wind that met them at the corner. Lola jerked up her head and sniffed the air; she liked the cold. Maybe she was part husky.

"You never told me about the Yankee game you went to with Mr. Young."

Johnny was animated. "It was cool. The Yanks beat the Tigers. Mr. Young is different when he's at the stadium. He drank beer and cheered a lot. He really likes Mariano Rivera." Johnny paused. "Maybe he's happier when his wife's not around."

Ambler smiled.

"He bought hot dogs and said I knew a lot about baseball for someone my age. I told him you and my dad were Yankee fans." They stopped and Lola sat down on the sidewalk and looked up. She seemed concerned. "I told him about my dad, how I visited him in the prison and he taught me about baseball and lots of other stuff."

"Oh?" Ambler said.

"He said for me to ask you if you wanted to go to a ball game with us sometime."

"That would be interesting," Ambler said.